PASSION MARKS

MARKS

A NOVEL

PASSION MARKS

A NOVEL

LEE HAYES

STREBOR BOOKS
NEW YORK LONDON TORONTO SYDNEY

Published by

SBI

Strebor Books
P.O. Box 6505
Largo, MD 20792
http://www.streborbooks.com

ISBN-13 978-1-59309-149-1
ISBN-10   1-59309-149-4
LCCN 2003105030

First Strebor Books mass market paperback edition April 2007

10 9 8 7 6 5 4 3 2 1

Manufactured in the United States of America

For information regarding special discounts for bulk purchases,
please contact Simon & Schuster Special Sales at 1-800-456-6798
or business@simonandschuster.com

DEDICATED TO

the survivors, the wishers,
the hopers, the dreamers
and the lovers of the world...
I salute you.

ACKNOWLEDGMENTS

There are so many people that have contributed something meaningful to my life that a few kind words in the beginning of a book cannot possibly express my love and gratitude. One day, I'd like to shout it from the highest mountain. Until that day, this will have to do...

First and foremost, I would like to thank **GOD** for his mercy, comfort and blessings. In this crazy, lopsided world where lies often become the truth and pain shatters faith, we often lose our way. Experience has taught me that the very essence of faith requires us to believe *especially* in the toughest of times. Faith requires us to *STAND* for it is in that darkest hour that we are measured and defined. If you do nothing else...*just stand*.

There is nothing I can say or do that will adequately thank my parents, John and Patsy, for the love they have always given. From the depths of my soul I thank you both. Just know that without your love and support, none of this would be possible. I love you both more than you will know.

To my sister and brother, Regina and Michael, thank you for love and acceptance.

To my nieces and nephews, know that this world is yours and you become more than you ever thought possible. Learn to live and to dream...

Craig, you are more than amazing. Your infectious spirit and warm smile mean the world to me. Part of me *will always* be you and I know part of you *will always* belong to me. There is no denying who we are to each other. Thank you for being irreplaceable, wondrous and for sharing this love. I'll be right here waiting...with open arms.

To S.A.M.: You are simply the best. Undoubtedly, you are one of the best men I have ever known and I am humbled by your presence. Thank you, just for sharing a piece of your life with me...you deserve the best because that is what you are and what you give.

Thank you, J.D., for being more than a friend for the past five years. Thank you for naming the book (you don't know it, but one day we were on the phone having a conversation and you used the phrase *"passion marks"* and it became clear.) After changing the title many times, all it took was a word from more than a friend.

To Tremayne, your help and faith in me has uplifted me. Thank you for loving me unconditionally and completely and thank you for giving unselfishly of your talents to *Passion Marks*.

I have to thank the often imitated, never duplicated, Vanderbilts: LaTrina Jenkins aka Calvin N., Allman A., Derrick B., Demarcus H., David H. (aka Hoffa), for eternal friendship and eternal memories. You have my love and eternal friendship.

Wow! Douglass P., my *BSF*, you are loved and appreciated more than you'll ever know…I truly thank you for who you are, all you do and all you have done… may you continue to be blessed with happiness and joy…

Jason B., Chris S., John F., Marlon H., Michael G., and Big Mike…mad love to all. You all have inspired me more than you'll ever know. You have been my brothers, counselors, supporters and friends. I sing this song to you all in the way that only I can ('cause you know my next project is a CD): "…*thank you for being a friend*…" You are valued in so *many ways*… I love you all.

To Robert…you are a friend and a brother indeed… I am eternally grateful for the love you have given…

Aaron S. in Hotlanta…your words and friendship are invaluable. May success and love always shine upon you. I am honored and blessed to call you friend.

Eric T…man, you are more than my brother… you are indeed special…and thanks for being the first contributor to the book! I send so much love to you as you have embarked upon a new life…you are the bravest man I know.

To my girl, Ronda Brown…you are *still* da baddest bitch I know…and that is a compliment! You are a true diva…smart, sexy, intelligent, and funny. You are simply marvelous. Thank you for coming into my life and bringing your energy and vibe. You are the best thing to leave UT…and Spring '94 (with the exception of me, LOL).

Timothy Lee…you are as wild and crazy today as you were when you first came into my life two years ago. When you finish the novel that is your life, I will be the first to buy it 'cause I know it will be filled with scandal. Just remember…Just remember those immortal words. "I don't give a fuck…"

John (Harpo)…thanks for being a true friend here in D.C. (District of Chaos).

To Michele Roland…I haven't seen you in a while, but you are still a *phenomenal woman*…thanks for being my first editor…

Erica Kennedy "E-boogie"…you are as talented as you are beautiful…stay strong, crazy and keep the X-factor going…thank you for your help and friendship.

Demond F. (Buttercup)…thank you so much for your friendship and your support. You keep me smiling every day and I have nothing but love for you.

And finally, thanks to B.J. Armstrong. Words cannot do justice to what you have meant to me and who you are—my first kiss, my first lover and my first love.

Thank you. Thank you. "The night we met, I often remember, two strangers meeting for the very first time…" December 9, 1994. Seeing you unexpectedly in D.C. on the eighth anniversary of our meeting was more than a coincidence…it was meant to be. The universe has a plan.

If I have forgotten anyone, it was not intentional…J

PART I

CHAPTER 1

The black cordless phone slammed against the right side of my face with such force that it sent my entire body reeling over the white sofa. I rolled over it and onto the coffee table, shattering the glass top. Instantly, my face went numb. I lay on the floor in a daze, trying to ascertain the extent of the damage: the pain was intense. I rubbed my face with my hands while I tried to ignore the warm feel of blood as it oozed out of my back and soaked my shirt. When I found the strength, I looked above me and saw him looming like a volcano suddenly compelled to erupt. His savagely contorted face burned with the fire of his words and the anger that dripped from his thick breath. When I attempted to sit up, I felt his shoe in my chest, kicking me back to the carpet. His words failed to convey any meaning through the depth of my pain, but the anger on his face spoke volumes. I closed my eyes, praying this nightmare would end; instead of ending, his body suddenly pressed down on my chest, and unrelenting fists pounded my face. I tried to shield my face from his blows with my arms, even while his frame weighed heavily upon me.

By this time, my lungs were on the verge of collapse and I gasped desperately for air. I was far too weak to force him off me, and when I struck him in the eye with my fist, it only made him pound harder. Through his anger, and between the unbroken chains of profanity, he yelled something about blood on the carpet, *as if it was my fault*, and then pulled me up from where I lay like a rag doll. He stood me up so I could look directly in his brown eyes, and then he slapped me so hard across the face that I crashed into the wall, narrowly escaping the flames of the fireplace. Just as he raced toward me, I stood up, and with all the force I could muster, I slammed my fist into his face. He stumbled. I threw my body into him with the force of a linebacker. He tried to withstand the force, but he lost his balance, and we both tumbled onto the floor. His head hit the side of the entertainment center, and blood began to run down his face from the open wound. I pounded his face with my fist, and then slammed his head onto the floor repeatedly like a man possessed. He looked worn out. It was over.

I rolled off him and onto my back, taking a moment to breathe as I looked up at the ceiling. Slowly, I moved away from him. That's when I felt his fist connect with the back of my head. He plowed into me like a truck from behind, and I flew into the fifty-gallon aquarium, shattering the glass and sending the helpless fish to the floor. They flipped and flopped, gasping for air; within moments they'd be dead. He grabbed my left leg and pulled me with ease across the carpet, unmoved by my struggle for freedom. My attempt at liberation from his massive hands proved futile, and he continued dragging me across the white carpet, leaving behind a trail the color red.

When we reached the staircase, he gave my body a tremendous yank to assert his control. With sudden prowess, he moved behind me, pushed my body down, and forced my stomach into the stairs. I could feel his gigantic hands on the back of my neck as he pressed my face into the carpet. I was pinned down, unable to move. He ripped off my bloodstained shirt and tossed it aside. As he whispered something in my ear, his hands grabbed my ass. The heat of his breath scalding my neck was far worse than the words he spoke. He grabbed me by the waist and raised my body up just enough for him to undo my belt. As he pulled down my pants and underwear in one swift motion, I braced myself. His accelerated breathing became louder and louder in anticipation. I tried to prepare myself for the violation. I knew that he would do everything in his power to make it hurt—to make me scream for mercy. He had a special affinity for delivering pain. This time I would deny him the perverse pleasure of hearing me scream.

Behind me, I heard him unzip his pants; that was the catalyst that brought tears to my eyes. I would not let them fall. My tears would only add to his callous joy, so I withheld them. My legs were then forced apart, and I knew there was no turning back. With his arm still pressed against the back of my neck, and my face forcibly held against the floor, I felt his thick flesh force its way into me, connecting in a vile union. The pain of that first thrust when it broke through my barrier almost caused me to let out a loud scream, but I held it in. His bursts rocked my body, and the pain increased the longer he stayed in me. I reached my hands behind my back and tried to push him off me, but my effort proved pointless. He pushed harder and harder, while his inhuman grunts filled the room, like the howl of a wolf in the darkness of night. The force of his thrusts rolled my body back and forth, back and forth, back and forth, for what seemed like an endless moment in time. My face dug deeper into the stair, and the burn from the carpet on my face was becoming painful. His panting was vicious, much like an animal that suddenly realized the extent of its power and its victory. All the while, his voice shouted despicable words, and with each debilitating push from his body into mine, his voice became louder. *This had to end.* All of the hurt my body suffered now went to my head, and I could feel myself losing consciousness. He turned my head toward him, forcing me to look into his hollow eyes. Blood stained his face. His muscles inside of me began to contract, and I knew it would be over soon. He pushed harder, faster, harder, and still faster, until I felt the release of his hot fluids. He pulled out of my body while still enjoying his eruption. His juices spilled on my back, and then rolled down my side. It was over. From behind, he wrapped his hands around my waist and pulled me into his powerful chest. He held me there for a few seconds, gently kissed the back of my neck, and released me. *"Clean up this mess,"* he said as he motioned toward the war-torn room. He climbed over me, and made his way up the staircase. When I looked up, I saw the back of his naked body reach the top of the stairs and disappear into darkness.

There were no words with enough power to capture the way I felt. I remained laying face down in the carpet, naked except for one sock dangling off my foot, unwilling—perhaps unable—to move. I felt stinging sensations pulsating on my back from the glass still buried beneath my skin. I tried to check my back to see if it had stopped bleeding, but I really wasn't concerned about those cuts; my attention was singularly focused on bigger issues. My entire body, wrapped in a throbbing blanket of pain, felt limp. After a few deep breaths, I managed to regain some control of my tattered frame, and forced myself to slide slowly to the bottom of the staircase, where I pulled my knees into my chest, and rested in the corner like a small child hiding from monsters under the bed. The sweet smell of jasmine still clung in the air, much like a damp mist over a lake in the early morning. With my right hand, I caressed my face— the swelling had already begun. I needed to crawl into the kitchen to get some ice, but that distance seemed unconquerable. The dimly lit house, once full of noise, now sat quiet as if the weakened sky had nothing left to give after its storm. The only audible sounds came from the rain lightly pounding against the windows, and the murmur of the rolling thunder. The lightning flashes offered a brief illumination, but I longed for the darkness to bury my shame.

The entire evening replayed in my head like a big-screen horror movie. I paid close attention to the details to see if I could figure out where it went wrong. Alluring candles, sweet incense, and a basket full of fabulous seafood in front of the fireplace. Sexy love ballads from the stereo, expensive wine, and vases full of freshly cut colorful roses all over the house. It all seemed so perfect. James and I had held each other closely while staring seductively in each other's eyes;

this was the man that I adored. The evening conversation had been full of love and comforting smiles. His soothing caresses brought me to the ultimate state of relaxation. I thought the dark days were long behind us, forever sealed by the hands of time. For the first time in months, it seemed that we could be the happy couple I envisioned.

This wasn't the first time I had felt his fists and been burned by his quick temper. Throughout the course of our relationship, violence was not uncommon, especially during his times of stress related to his firm, Lancaster Computer Systems. A year ago LCS made an acquisition of a smaller computer firm in Austin; this transaction brought out the worst in James. Some nights when he came home, I feared for my safety, and at times, for my life, not knowing what to expect when he walked through the door. It was like rolling the dice.

Partly, it was my fault. I knew this. Sometimes, maybe out of boredom, I would intentionally antagonize him just to get a reaction. I wanted to see how far I could push him. I wanted to know whether or not I had the power to make him lose control. During stressful times, instead of being supportive and appreciative, I managed to say or do the wrong thing. But this attack was by far one of the most vicious outbursts I'd suffered at his hands.

Over and over again, I replayed the evening. The

phone rang and he picked up. While he was on the phone, I decided to go into the kitchen for more wine, and when I returned something in him had changed. He seemed irritable and ended the phone call by slamming the phone on its base. As I approached him, the phone rang again. I answered it without thinking. By the time I heard his commands to let it ring, it was too late. I should have noticed the look on his face. I should have heard his words. I should not have let anything interrupt the mood. He stood up and held his hand out for the phone, and I innocently gave it to him. That's when everything changed. *It was my fault.* If only I hadn't answered that call. If only I had listened to him. I would have to start paying more attention to his needs. The phone call could have waited.

As I dragged myself up from the corner with considerable effort, I wondered how many men and women were in situations similar to mine. The lyrics to that old song "How Could You Hurt the One You Love?" came to mind. I managed to limp slowly to the restroom without losing my balance. I held a firm grip on the black sink for support, and when I flipped the light switch on, I let out a shriek as I looked at the broken and tattered image that stood before me in the mirror. *Surely, this wasn't me.* The mirror played a cruel joke. My eyes were beginning to close from the swelling, and bloodstains covered my face. My swollen lips pulsated with a heavy pain. Numerous purple and black bruises covered my chest, and the gentlest touch of my passion marks caused a horrible sensation. Still holding onto the sink, I turned to examine my back in the mirror, but when I turned, a sudden explosion of pain enveloped my body. The room started to spin, and before I even realized what was happening, I collapsed to the floor in a fit of pain. The plush mauve rug did little to break my fall. I heard the sound and felt the thump as my head hit the porcelain tub, and everything went black.

✖✖✖

"Sometimes, Kevin, you reap what you sow." I was star-tled by the familiar voice and when I opened my eyes the apparition stood before me, part flesh and part fantasy, and then vanished into the darkness.

"Keevan? Where are you?" I asked in fright. My heart palpitated with the rapid speed of hummingbird wings, and it felt as if it would beat through my chest.

"I came back." I followed the voice into the den. Keevan stood there, dressed in the same clothing he wore when I found him dead. I walked slowly toward him, with care-fully chosen steps. "I'm your brother. I came back." His words haunted me and his expressions taunted me while his eyes mocked, offering no absolution. He vanished in the same mystery that allowed him to come forth.

CHAPTER 2

A fter what seemed like only moments, I opened my eyes. I looked around and realized that I was upstairs in our bedroom. The green silk sheets were damp and sticky from my sweat. Slowly, I sat up in the bed and wiped some of the moisture from my forehead. James stood in front of the mirror, adding a few last-minute touches to his appearance. His blue Armani suit fit his frame perfectly, and the shiny, metallic silver tie provided the perfect contrast with the dark background. He wore success casually like a pair of expensive shoes with a polished shine. His persona projected an image of confidence and coolness, but that was a mask he wore for others. Only I knew the real James, full of paranoia, pain, suspicion, rage, love, hate, mystery, magic, confusion, all deeply rooted in an overwhelming fear of failure; that's why he pushed himself so hard. He needed to prove that he could successfully overcome his humble beginnings from the projects of the 5th Ward of Houston, and the dire predictions of those who doomed him to fail.

As soon as he realized that I was awake he rushed

over to the bed, and my body contracted as I braced for sudden impact. He took a seat on the bed next to me, his brown eyes filled with sorrow, and stroked my forehead lovingly and with compassion.

"Baby, lie back down and put this on your face. It'll keep the swelling down." He placed an ice pack on my forehead. "I found you last night on the bathroom floor downstairs, so I cleaned you up and put you to bed. What were you dreaming about? You kept mumbling something about Keevan. I haven't seen you sweat this much in awhile." I watched his lips move with quiet grace. I loved him, loathed him, hurt for him, cried for him, despised him, wanted to kill him, wanted to hold him, wanted to be held by him, wanted to see him succeed, longed for his failure, but ultimately, I needed him. I needed his attention. I needed his love. I needed his support. He was the only consistent thing in my life since my brother died. He grabbed my hand and held it as he spoke. "I'm sorry. I know that doesn't make up for what happened. I don't know what to say. Maybe it was the wine that made me snap. I promise you this will never happen again, and I'll never drink again. I never want to hurt you again. You are my world. I will never raise my hand to hit you. I'll make it up to you," he said as tears replaced the usual sparkle in his eyes, and then a small stream of tears ran down his face. I released his grip, and tried to wipe the tears from his face.

"You've made that promise before, but it keeps happening," I said in a low, almost inaudible child-like voice.

"I know I have, but this time I promise it's different," he said with the sincerest expression on his face. Through his eyes, I searched his soul for honesty and sorrow. I knew he wanted to do right, to be better, but I wasn't sure he was capable of such remarkable change.

"I'm sorry I made you act like that," I muttered, trying to find the strength to force a small smile, and trying to find words to absolve his guilt.

"Baby, it's not your fault. Don't apologize for me." He wiped the moisture from his face with his left hand, and caressed my arm with the right. "I have to go to work now. I wish I could stay and take care of you, but I have a meeting that can't be missed. If you need anything, just call me and leave a message with Deborah, okay?" I smiled as best as I could as he walked out of the room. I heard his heavy footsteps bounce down the stairs in their usual rhythmic pattern. Part of me was glad to see him go, but the other part longed for the gentleness of the man who just left the room. Sometimes, I felt there were no limits to what I would do for his love; in spite of his obvious faults, he loved me, and that's what I needed.

✖✖✖

I lay back in the bed, lost in space and time, hearing chaotic voices crying out from the dark corners in my mind. I heard my brother's voice. I needed to find relief from his razor-like words. No one could haunt me like that. Even James' blows failed to hurt as much as my brother's words. The images of him I often saw were more than mere dreams, more concrete than fantasies. He started appearing to me right after his death. Initially, his words served to comfort me and urge me to continue living, even without him. More recently, his words took a sinister twist and became more and more accusatory. I used to want to go to sleep so that I could be reunited with my other half, but the last few weeks' sleep became more and more disturbing. Born eight minutes and fourteen seconds before me, Keevan was technically the oldest twin, and felt a need to protect me. But I let him down when he needed me the most. For that, I would never forgive myself.

I turned my head to the right, and on top of the marble fireplace, in a neat silver frame, was a picture that I would treasure always. A picture of Keevan and me, dressed in white T-shirts and blue jeans, flashing our fraternity hand sign. I thought about the four weeks, four days, eight hours, and nineteen minutes we spent pledging with our other line brothers. I didn't think anything could be much worse than pledging, but his strength carried me through. He picked me up when I fell and when I couldn't stand, he stood for us both. There were times when he weathered my storms without hesitation. He was there for me when I needed him; he was my strength and my rock. I could not have done it without him, but when he needed to be carried, I was nowhere to be seen.

The day we found him he was supposed to pick Tony and me up from the airport in Houston after spending New Year's 2000 in D.C. When our flight landed, Tony and I waited at the gate for him, but Keevan was not there. He was fanatical in his promptness, so when he didn't show up within the first few minutes, I began to worry; I knew something out of the ordinary had happened. After an hour of waiting and calling the apartment, I knew something was wrong. We took a cab from the airport to his apartment, and his car was parked on the back row. We raced frantically to his apartment and I tried to use my spare key to enter, but the keyless deadbolt was locked from the inside. Tony and I banged on the door, but still no movement from the inside could be detected. No television, no radio, no sound emanated from the interior of the apartment at all. We rushed to the other side of the apartment and Tony kicked in the window, slowly removing the jagged glass so that he could enter without harming himself. I watched him bend over and step inside the apartment through the window. He told me to go to the front door and as soon as he got inside, he'd let me in.

The smell. A suffocating odor escaped from the apartment in a nauseating whirlwind. Within seconds, the thick vapors permeated every inch of our clothing with an incomprehensible stench. When I inhaled, the indigestible stench took a defensive position in my throat, making it difficult to breathe, and forcing me to cough. I ran to the back of the apartment toward the bedroom. My heart pounded. Sweat dripped from the palms of my hands in foreboding. Without hesitation, I threw open the door. There he lay, on his stomach, in the middle of his bedroom floor, a few inches from the phone. With outstretched hands, it appeared he was reaching for help. His body, already decomposing, was hardly recognizable. Around his mouth, a thick white foamy matter had begun to grow. A deep rumbling grew in my stomach, and my legs suddenly weakened. I tried to steady myself to exit the room, but I stumbled into the wall. Finally, I managed a small measure of control and made my way out of the crypt.

Once outside the apartment, a stream of tears

flowed from my eyes, almost blinding me to the crowd now gathered outside. Tony tried to comfort me, but his words provided no consolation. While I was off partying in D.C., my brother lay dying— alone. How could I have been so careless as to let him die alone? I should have been there to protect him, to help him, but I wasn't. The whole right half of my body went limp, like a physical part of me died. A vast emptiness swallowed my soul and my descent into darkness began.

CHAPTER 3

I tried to push those images of the past out of my head, but they often overwhelmed me. I thought about how loving and caring James was during this time. I met him four days after Keevan died, and moved in with him within a month. He became my rock and my support, showering me with love and attention, not allowing me to sink into depression. He insisted that I move in with him because he couldn't stand the thought of me living alone in my apartment. He was wonderful at making the decisions for me that I was unable to consider. He moved me into his house, paid off the rest of my lease from my apartment, and made arrangements for me to take a semester off from school. At night, he comforted me when the bad dreams came. Even though I only had six semester hours left before I would receive my master's in business administration, I knew I would not be able to handle school. Keevan and I were both to attain our degrees in the spring of 2000. Shortly after Keevan's death—I think it must have been March—the fights began. When it started, it only added to the stress that I felt from learning to live without my brother. On some unconscious level, I felt I deserved the beatings as punishment. Soon enough, the abuse was something I expected, and something that somehow comforted me, as strange as that may seem.

If what Keevan said about reaping what you sow is true, I guess I'm paying the price for my sins now. Even though we were identical twins, the similarities were only skin deep at times. Keevan was more responsible. I lived life in a flash of color, bedazzled by adventure. He was quiet; I was outspoken. He took time to consider the feelings of others, and tried not to hurt anyone. Me? I just wanted to have my fun. Even as children, our differences were apparent.

When we were five years old, we lived in an old, wooden house with paint chipping on almost every board. When it rained, we'd sometimes have to take some pots from the kitchen and put them in the middle of the floor to catch the water as it fell from the roof. Behind the house was an empty field full of weeds and dry grass with an occasional burst of yellow or blue from a blooming flower. Anytime I wanted to get away from my family I'd sneak to the back and crawl through the old rusty metal fence. I'd pretend I was a construction worker, like my dad, and that I had to rebuild the house. There was a hole I discovered I could fit through, and when my mother saw me sneaking back there once, she forbade me from doing it again because it was dangerous. Of course, that only made me more determined. One day, I was playing with some matches and I heard her calling my name. I got scared and dropped the matches on the ground and hid down low in the weeds so she couldn't see me. As soon as she left, I ran out and raced around to the other side of the house, climbed in the kitchen window and made it to my room. I pretended I was asleep when she had called me.

In the middle of dinner—meatloaf, mashed potatoes, corn, and some peach cobbler for dessert—there was a banging and a scream at the door. Who could be interrupting this meal? Our neighbor, Mrs. Giles, burst into the house even before Mamma made it to the door. Mrs. Giles was the nosiest woman in the world, forever peeping out her window at all hours of the day or night, just so that she would be the first to find out the latest gossip, which she would then spread through the proverbial grapevine. She came into the room screaming something about a fire in the field, and we needed to get out of the house. I overheard her telling Mamma that the twin in the purple T-shirt was in the back right before the fire started. *She never could tell us apart.* Keevan looked at his orange shirt, then looked at my purple shirt, and shook his head. Mamma ran to the back of the house, looked out the kitchen window and saw the fire just a few feet from the window. In a panic, she rushed us all out of the house. The strong March winds blew the fire closer. The smoke had already set in over the neighborhood, and people exited their homes just to see what was going on. When no one was looking, Keevan took off his shirt and gave it to me. He told me to hurry up and take off my shirt, which I did. Luckily, the fire department was able to put out the flames before any real damage was done. Then, I remember Keevan getting the beating of a lifetime, a beating that I was supposed to receive. I guess Mamma didn't take the time out to really examine us before she started swinging. The beating must have lasted for hours, and I went to my room, closed the door, and pretended not to hear his cries. My brother had taken the punishment for me because he loved me.

I've done some pretty bad things to people in my lifetime. So has everyone. People say that what you put out there comes back to you times three. It's called Karma. I never believed in that old law, so I didn't pay it any attention. But I've learned to respect its universal truth. Never did I expect the harshness of the reality I now live. Life without Keevan is sometimes unbearable. Those childhood sins didn't compare to the biggest mistake I'd ever made in my life. I had lived life with a philosophy of no regrets. Now, I had regrets.

Over a year later, I remained with James, deeply

entrenched in this lifestyle, still dealing with death and violence, with my spirit suffering. Mamma used to say when you lose your spirit, you've lost life. I felt like I was sleepwalking. When he returned home this evening, I knew what to expect—some marvelously expensive gift to make up for what he did. This predictable cycle began a long time ago. After the first beating, he bought me an expensive Gucci watch that was fit for a king. He bought rings, and nice trips around the world, all to say he was sorry. I had so many rings that they overflowed in the jewelry box he bought. I never wore any of them.

The Mercedes I drove was a gift after he broke my left arm by repeatedly kicking it as I lay on the concrete near the pool. None of the material things he provided meant anything to me. I didn't stay with him because I loved the house or the car. I stayed with him because I couldn't take care of myself, and after what happened to Keevan, I refused to live alone. Many times I know I should have left, but who would've taken care of me? I had no money, no job, and no place to live. James didn't *allow* me to work. He denied me a lot of the things that were important to any man. People often choose the path of least resistance simply because of the familiarity of the known. Leaving terrified me. So I stayed, out of fear of being alone. I stayed out of shame and guilt. The world is full of contradictions.

CHAPTER 4

A few Friday evenings later, time's remarkable ability to heal all wounds repaired my body, but my spirit was another story. The weeks after that last episode of violence passed without significance, or further explanations. The mind's power to forget astounded even myself. The sun had begun its slow descent in the sky, leaving behind a fantastic medley of bright oranges and shimmering purples. I stood on the balcony of our bedroom and looked at the colors as they reflected off the rippling water of the pool. In one hand, I held a tall, half-empty glass of 151 and Coke, and a burning cigarette dangled between the fingers of my other one. I didn't smoke often, but something about having a drink and a cigarette on a night like this felt right. My mind danced over a spectrum of complicated issues. I thought about Keevan. I missed him. I thought about James. He'd been out of town since Tuesday trying to wrap up a deal on an emerging firm in Austin. He had been working on this for a long time, but the deal had yet to be finalized.

The phone had rung twice during the course of

the evening, and I was relieved that neither call was from James. The first was the caterers from the Cajun Kitchen confirming our order for the party Saturday night. We were having a circuit party and I still had not finished my to-do list. A group of down-low professional gay black men in Houston had formed an organization called "The Circuit," which was essentially a way for them to get together without having to risk exposure at a gay club. It was our turn to host the event, which rotated every month.

The second call was from Danea, who would be pulling into my driveway at any minute. We had plans to head to the Galleria to do some shopping, but still I had not moved, much less gotten dressed. Instead, I stared blankly into the evening sky, sipping rum and Coke, and allowing a dark cloud of memories to hover over me and drench my spirits. If Keevan were here, I knew I would not be in this situation. None of this would be real.

Just as I took the last sip of my drink, the doorbell rang. It could only be Danea. It rang again. And again. Finally, I made a move toward the stairs. When I reached the middle of the staircase, I heard familiar voices. Danea. And Tony. And Daryl. *Shit*. I looked a mess. Just as I turned to head back up the stairs I heard Danea call out to me. Her voice carried a bit of worry, like an overprotective mother. That was just her nature.

"Kevin," she called out as she walked to the stereo and hit the power button, bringing an abrupt end to the harmony of Patti LaBelle, singing "Don't Block Your Blessings." "The door was unlocked, so we came in, and why aren't you ready? It's already late." They looked at me as if my next words would somehow justify my lateness. Instead, I stared at them without saying a word. I can only imagine the way I must have looked to them. "Did you hear me? Put some clothes on so we can get to this mall." I turned back and moved down the stairs right past the three of them. I heard Danea sigh in her *ain't-this-some-shit* voice. I moved over to the bar where I proceeded to pour myself another drink. Something told me I needed it.

"What are you drinking?" Daryl asked as he headed in my direction.

"Rum and Coke. Would you like one?"

"No, he wouldn't," Danea interjected in her mothering tone. "And you shouldn't be drinking either. We should be leaving."

"Just calm down a bit, Danea. It's Friday. Have a drink," I said with a full smile.

"All you do lately is drink," she snapped.

"There's nothing like a stiff cocktail on a Friday evening," I said with a little edge when I looked at Daryl. "I just felt like having a drink, is that all right?"

"No, it's not all right. Every time I see you, there's

27

a drink in your hand. That's not like you. And something tells me this is not your first drink tonight." Her thinly braided hair dangled just above her shoulders as she spoke.

"No, it's not, if you must know," I said with an impish grin. "I'm going upstairs to put on some clothes so we can go. Give me fifteen minutes." Danea continued to talk, but it was going in one ear and out the other.

"Kevin…Kevin, did you hear me? Are you listening? See, this is what I'm talking about. Something with you is not right. Are you on drugs?" she inserted quickly.

"Danea…" Daryl said.

"No, Daryl, we need to talk about this. It's not like we haven't all discussed it before." Danea stood before me and assumed control of the room. Her presence was formidable, the confidence gained from years of courtroom experience as an attorney. In spite of her passion and her concern, I remained unfettered by her words. "Look at you, you look awful."

"Well, thank you. I do try." My words dripped with a heavy dose of sarcasm as I brought the glass closer to my lips and took a long sip.

"I'm serious. Your eyes are bloodshot almost every time I see you—which hasn't been often lately. You're off in a world of your own, not letting anyone near you." Danea approached me at the bar and placed her well-manicured hand on the countertop. "And what's the deal with this house?" she asked, looking around curiously. " Every time I come over here you have new furniture. Y'all buy new furniture more than I buy shoes." I didn't bother to respond. What could I say? *We buy new shit to hide all the bloodstains?*

"Kevin," she began again, "the only reason I'm saying this is cause I—*we*—love you, and as friends we have a responsibility to each other. If you're in trouble, we are here to help, but you've got to let us. We don't know what's wrong unless you tell us." I looked into her eyes and saw genuine concern coming from the woman who I have called a best friend for years. Her hand rubbed mine gently while I looked at the same expressions of concern on Tony's and Daryl's faces. They were reaching out to me, but I was on my own little island. The words I needed to share with them were on the way out, but got caught in my throat. I wanted to shout out and break down, but my life is *my* business. I had gotten myself in this situation, and I'd have to get myself out. I couldn't bear the thought of having them take care of me. Depending on James was bad enough in and of itself. I didn't want to be seen as a victim, or as if I couldn't control my own life. The thought of being seen as weak, even if I was, bothered me tremendously. My manhood would be questioned. I couldn't have that. In spite of the circumstances and how I lived now, I am a man; I will always be a man.

"Danea, listen, everything is fine. I am not on drugs.

I ain't no crackhead. I'm just chillin', you know what I mean? Really. Trust me, if there was anything wrong, you'd be the first to know. You're my best friends." I forced a smile and tried to sound reassuring, but this was not an Academy Award-winning performance. "Now, are we going to the mall or not? I just have to run upstairs and get ready. I'll be right back." Before any more objections could be noted I was gone. By the time I navigated my way out of the den and up the staircase, I was slightly out of breath. I walked into the bedroom-sized closet searching for something simple to put on. I grabbed a pair of black Kenneth Cole slacks and a red form-fitting sweater. After I found my shoes, I grabbed the gold card from the table, and went downstairs. I intentionally took the back staircase so they wouldn't hear me approach. As I neared the den, I could hear Danea's voice, so I slowed down my pace just enough to catch wind of their conversation, which I knew was about me.

"I'm worried about him. Something is seriously wrong."

"I don't think there's anything wrong with him," Daryl said casually.

"Of course you don't, you can't see past his smile," she said with a sharp tone.

"What does that mean?"

"Daryl, *puh-leeze*. Don't play crazy with me. You know what I'm talking about."

"Whatever Danea, Kevin and I are just friends. Good friends. Don't you think you're being too hard on him? He has been through a lot over the last year."

"That's *exactly* what I'm talking about. He has been through a lot, but how many times has he called any of us for support? How many conversations have any of us had with him about Keevan? I think he's holding it all in, and if he doesn't release his feelings, they'll kill him."

"You're being way too dramatic," Tony interrupted as if he could no longer remain silent. Besides, he's got James. I'm sure he talks to him."

"Well, that does little to ease my mind. There's something about James I just don't like. You two can keep lying to yourselves and acting as if everything with him is okay, but if you're really his friends you'll help me find out what's wrong. I don't think I can do it on my own. Have either of you noticed anything strange?"

After a few seconds of quiet contemplation Tony responded, "He has been distant lately, but that's only to be expected."

"I just think he needs time to find himself again. Losing your brother—your identical twin brother at that—would take a lot of getting used to for anyone. It changes everything." I liked the way Daryl came to my defense, and he was right; I just needed some time and space.

"I know, but his changes aren't healthy."

Their conversation had already gone too far, and I wanted to break it up before it went any further. I let them know that I was approaching by intentionally dropping my wallet on the wooden floor, and shuffling my feet. Instantly, the voices ceased.

"Okay, are we ready?" I emerged triumphantly into the room. They looked at me like I'd been resurrected. I grabbed my keys from the table and headed toward the door. "Are you all coming or not?" I said while holding the door wide open. I was feeling a little intoxicated, but I don't think any of them noticed. The four of us climbed into Danea's BMW and headed away from the house. The eyes of the two lion statues guarding the gates to the manor followed us. Out of the mirror, the huge red brick structure loomed behind us. My penitentiary. That house was the source of so much shame and misery. From the outside, it looked like the perfect world: exclusive Houston neighborhood, fancy cars, and wealth. If only they knew.

For the first few minutes, we rode in virtual silence. The low murmur of the voice on the radio provided the only conversation. Danea seemed singularly focused on the road ahead, and Tony and Daryl were as quiet as church mice in the back. I felt as if the car was closing in on me and all eyes were focused in my direction. What were they thinking? Did they know more than they let on? Were they planning on doing further investigations? How soon would they find out the truth? Part of me wanted them to find out, but I didn't know how to prepare myself for their reactions.

I could visualize the looks of shock and disgust on their faces if the truth was ever discovered. I had been through hell with James, and the list of shameless acts could fill a book. My friends couldn't handle the truth, or at least I couldn't handle them knowing it; there were definitely things I never would reveal to them, things I never wanted to relive that went far beyond the immense physical abuse.

We pulled into the parking lot of the mall and drove around to Saks Fifth Avenue. The valet parking attendant rushed to the car, and Danea politely handed him the keys as we exited the vehicle. She was a remarkable woman—a diva. Professionally, I knew of no sharper attorney. She had graduated from Howard Law at the top of her class and passed the Texas bar exam her first time. The sheer strength of her presence usually elicited the truth in the courtroom, yet I managed to keep my little, dark secrets neatly packed away from her scope.

When we entered Saks, I was on a mission to find something new and exciting. I didn't know what I was looking for, but I'd know it when I saw it. Since I was here, I felt obligated to buy James something, even though he didn't deserve it. I guess I hoped that it would somehow pacify him when he got home. We stopped at a rack and I picked up a thin, gray sweater.

"Have you looked at the price of that?" Tony said in a half-whisper.

"It's cool, it ain't my money," I said jokingly. I picked up the sweater and casually glanced at it.

"See, I need a man like James so I can shop my ass off all day. Where can I pick one up?" Tony said with a smile. "Hook a brotha up!"

"Money ain't everything, Tony. Don't believe the hype," I said flatly.

"I learned a long time ago that bad *financin'* fucks up the *romancin'*," he shot back at me.

"I have to agree with him on that one," Danea chimed in. "I can't stand a broke man."

"If I meet any of his friends that are your type, I'll let you know." I lied. The last thing Tony needed was to meet some of James' friends. He'd be eaten alive.

"Keep in mind that *rich* is my type."

We continued our stroll through the store looking at everything from shoes to suits, but still I didn't see what I was looking for. On the way to the register, I stopped at a display to look at the dress shirt the mannequin was wearing. As we stood there, my attention was drawn to an attractive woman standing to my left, looking casually at ties. I tried to appear as if I was unaware of her alluring smile, but I caught myself smiling back. Then she made a move in my direction.

"Excuse me," she said, "but I know you. Kevin, right? You went to college in Austin?" It was hard not to notice her full lips, colored a light red, as they moved smoothly over her pearly white teeth. She was very beautiful, standing about five feet eight inches, with a perfect hourglass figure. The pink silk blouse she wore blended well with her mahogany skin, and the tight black Guess jeans she wore didn't leave much room for guessing.

"As a matter of fact I did. I did my undergraduate work there. I hated it," I added in jest. My mind raced through all of the faces that I remembered from the University of Texas at Austin. She looked vaguely familiar.

"I know what you mean. When I graduated, I practically ran across the stage trying to hurry up and get out of that city." She let out a cool laugh as she grabbed my arm. "I'm RaChelle Roland. It's nice to see you," she said as she extended her hand. "You look even better now than you did at UT." I smiled and put out my hand to shake hers, and felt her index finger scrape the palm of my hand as I pulled away. I'm sure it wasn't deliberate.

"That's a great shirt. It would look good on you," she pointed out with a wink of the eye. " So, how long you been in Houston?"

"About two years. I just finished my MBA this past December."

"Congratulations. I just moved here from Dallas. I only know a few people here, though. It's hard meeting people. Especially with work."

"What do you do?"

"I'm vice president of human resources for Inertia Mutual Funds."

"Sounds like a great job."

"It is. It can be a headache at times, but I can handle myself," she said slyly. "Listen, I'm gonna give you my business card because I have to get going. Give me a call sometime and maybe we can do lunch...or something."

"Okay, RaChelle. It was nice seeing you. I will definitely give you a call."

RaChelle strutted away like a true ebony queen. When she walked, her hips confidently shifted from side to side. Some women work overtime trying to be attractive, but her beauty was natural. The only thing she gave a lot of was glamour.

"Okay, what was that all about?" Daryl asked.

"That was nothing. She and I used to go to school together in Austin. I really don't remember her, though. She gave me her business card."

"That's not all she wanted to give you," Danea said with a smile.

"What are you talking about now?"

"Kevin, don't act like you didn't see the way she was all over you. She looked like she was ready to sop you up with a biscuit," Daryl said.

"Really? I didn't notice." I lied again.

"You should tell that girl that you are *strictly dickly*," Tony added with his special blend of colorful humor. "You are the man. Still plucking fish out of the sea with your bare hands," he said with laughter. I smirked, turned on my heels, and headed to the register.

At the counter, I pulled out the Gold MasterCard to pay for the shirt. As the clerk handed me the receipt, my pager went off. It was a "911" call from James. *Damn.* I knew he'd be pissed off because he got home and I wasn't there. I had forgotten what time his plane was scheduled to arrive.

"Okay, I really have to get home. *Now*." And before either of them could respond I headed quickly toward the exit, leaving them standing there puzzled. I knew they'd be right behind me.

After they dropped me off, I slowly crept into the house, hoping to avoid him. Just as I turned to lock the door I heard the room come alive with movement. My heart skipped a beat. I wasn't sure how to prepare myself for what might lie ahead. It could be Another Love TKO.

"Hey, baby," he said as he gave me a kiss on the forehead. "What's in the bag?"

"Umm, a sweater…for you. I didn't have time to get it wrapped." *What? No yelling, no anger, no fists?* Although I was confused, I thought the moment seemed like a great opportunity to talk with James about something that had been on my mind. I didn't know how to broach the subject, because we'd talked about it before, and it had turned into a heated debate. James was fiercely opposed to me getting a job, and I hoped that I would be able to eventually wear him down and get him to agree.

"Thanks for the gift," he said. "I have wonderful news. You know that Austin deal that has kept me so busy lately? Well, it worked out! Everything has been taken care of. The acquisition is complete!" A huge smile adorned his face and he looked like a child who had just scored his first touchdown. He grabbed me tightly by the waist and held me close. He was really excited. I hoped this didn't mean he'd be around here more often. I had learned to appreciate his business trips and his times away.

"Congratulations!" I said as I feigned excitement. "I knew everything would work out for you." He pulled me even closer, and gave me a passionate kiss. Before I knew it I blurted out the words, "James, I want to talk to you." I wasn't sure if this was the right time to bring it up, but with James, there never was a right time. I didn't mean to rush into the conversation, but since he was in a good mood I decided to take my best shot. I grabbed his hand and led him to the sofa, hoping that he would be reasonable at least.

"You know it's been a few months since I've graduated. I'm ready to get a job." Silence. He pushed away from me, and his face showed a mosaic of disapproval.

"What?" he asked.

"I think—I mean—I want a job. I could get a job that doesn't interfere with our lives," I explained.

"Why do you do this to me? It never fails. Every time I'm in a good mood you fuck it up. It's like you intentionally say shit that you know will piss me off."

He shook his head disapprovingly and walked away. *Like I needed his permission.* I wasn't letting this issue go, so I followed him upstairs to continue my pitch in the bedroom. I had to sell my idea to him. *I guess those marketing classes will come in use.* "We've had this conversation before. The answer was no then, and it's no now. Did you think I'd change my mind?"

"James, come on, be reasonable. I am a young educated professional man who should be embarking upon a career. Instead, what do I do? Nothing. I sit around the house. I need a challenge. I want to use my MBA. You have LCS; you're living your dream. I want that same opportunity."

"A degree you got through my good graces, I might add. Don't press your luck. You don't think taking care of me and this house and our lives is a challenge?"

"It's not that," I pleaded, "I just want to earn my own money." *Shit. I didn't mean to say that.*

"Oh, now we get to the heart of the issue. Is there something wrong with my money? You've never had a problem spending it. Or driving that fancy Mercedes. Or wearing those expensive clothes." He went into the closet and started throwing my clothing on the floor to add weight to his point. Armani suits, leather jackets, Gucci shoes all hit the floor. I didn't budge. I just looked at him. "My money bought all of these things that you're so fond of!"

"James..."

"Do you really think I'm stupid? What's wrong with you? The last couple of months you've been making a lot of demands. First, you complain about how lonely you are since I hadn't let you associate with your friends. So what did I do? I gave in to you and let their triflin' asses come over, and you know how I feel about that bitch, Danea. I give an inch and you take a fuckin' mile." He moved closer to me with his lips clenched tightly together. "Listen carefully 'cause I'm saying this just once more. I don't want to have this discussion again. You will *not* get a job. This is not up for negotiation. Your full-time job is to take care of us. Make sure we're happy. There is a lot of shit that needs to be done around this house before this party tomorrow that you could have been doing, but instead you went to the fuckin' mall. This place is a mess. And look at you. You look like hell, and you're getting fat. You don't have time for a job."

"I run five miles every day. I weigh myself every day. I am the same size I was when I used to run track," I said in defense of myself. My teeth gritted together in my tightly closed mouth. His well-chosen words felt like daggers stabbing at my heart. I hated him for having that power over me. I hated myself even more for giving him that power.

"Maybe you need to run six miles," he said in the coldest tone.

"Go to hell," I mumbled as I turned to leave the room.

"If I did, I'm sure I'd see your dead brother." I felt as if he had knocked the wind out of my stomach and tears burned the back of my eyes. My pain was exposed. I continued walking toward the door, refusing to let him see the fruits of his hateful labor.

CHAPTER 5

It was a gray February evening and the cool air caused the hair on the back of my neck to stand on end. I had gone to great lengths to ensure that the party would be a success, and finally the night had arrived. I loved parties, but I admit that I had not been in a festive mood the entire year. I decorated the house; well, I hired the decorators and the caterers, at any rate. The red and white decorations throughout the house added a touch of life to the usually empty home. The music of the DJ pumping throughout the house reminded me of the fun times I used to have when Keevan and I partied together. Once, when we were in Dallas, we went out to a club called the Metro. It was packed to the nines. People were pressed against each other—some by choice; most by circumstance—and the music was thumping. Keevan drank so much and danced so long that I had to practically carry him out of the club. Those were the days.

By 11 p.m. our house—James' house—was packed with some of Houston's finest black men of all shades and colors. There were mocha men, coffee brown men, and dark chocolate men. We had bald men and dreaded men, short men, tall men, men with terrific bodies, men with not so terrific bodies, but all had nice smiles. There were older men and younger men; we had the spectrum covered.

When Tony arrived, I knew the party would be jumpin'. He wouldn't miss this party for anything in the world, and I was really excited about seeing him and the rest of my friends. He was always the life of the party. As I stood in the front of the crowd, greeting each guest as they entered, I heard Tony's high-pitched laughter creep up behind me.

"Kevin, this party is off da hook! Where did all these men come from? I ain't never seen them at the club," Tony said, showing his pearly white teeth. He never had any problems meeting men. He had this slick way of charming his way into the hearts of unsuspecting people. His thick lips accentuated his smile, and his wavy hair was always perfectly cut. Standing next to him was Daryl, in a tight-fitted black shirt that hugged his muscular frame. He was shorter than Tony, but his aura was more distinguished. His presence made the difference. Daryl's intense sensuality oozed from his pores, and dripped from his tongue like sweet honey when he spoke. It was a kind of natural charisma that required no extra effort on his part. He was charming, intelligent, and as TLC would say, "crazysexycool." His caramel-colored skin always glowed. Even the braces on his teeth were sexy.

Daryl and I had been friends for what seemed like forever, but there always was some sexual tension between us. For years, neither of us acknowledged it, but one day we talked about it. We were afraid that dating or becoming sexually involved would erode our friendship and affect our group of friends as a whole. There were many times I wanted to tell him that I thought we'd made a mistake by not exploring a relationship, but the words never came out right. Then I met James. The rest is history, or as it often seemed, his story.

"Okay, where's Danea? I thought she was dropping by?" I asked. It's hard to quantify friendships, but Danea was the friend who I could always turn to for advice. Once, in a moment of weakness, I jokingly mentioned something about a fight I had with James, but something in my voice must have told more. She interrogated me like I was on the witness stand until I finally broke down and told her it was a physical fight. I told her it only happened once. I knew she didn't believe me, but she couldn't prove anything else, so she had to let it go. I knew how her mind worked, and I knew that from that day on, she would wonder incessantly about me and James' relationship, but I opted to plead the fifth from that day forth.

"You know she loves us, but this isn't exactly her scene. She wanted to go somewhere she could actually meet some men she can date, instead of being around all these punks," Tony said in between gulps of his Hennessy and Coke. "You see that guy over there in the corner?"

"Yeah? Who is he?" I asked, leaning a little to the right to get a better look.

"He's waiting for me. Fine, ain't he?"

"He's pretty good-looking," Daryl added. "What's his name?"

"Let's see, that one I'll call…*rent*. I've already met *insurance* and *phone bill* earlier tonight." We all laughed. Tony was such a clown, and I don't know what he did to get guys to pay his bills, but whatever it was, it worked—time and time again. He was always the crazy one in the group. "I think that guy works for FedEx. He's like a district manager or something. I don't know who does their hiring, but they sure know how to recruit some boys. Hell, they can overnight me a package anytime."

"Shut up, Tony," we both said, trying not to laugh. "It doesn't take much to deliver you," I added.

"Don't start no mess. I'm having a good time," he replied.

"What happened to LaMont? I thought you two were getting back together—for the tenth time," Daryl said.

"LaMont has issues. He has this jealousy thing he needs to work on. I told him if he ain't *feedin'*, *fuckin'*, *or financin'* me, then he ain't got shit to say about where I go. He didn't really understand that, so he had to go." Tony took a long gulp from his glass as if there wasn't any more alcohol in the house. He moved his straw around his drink, trying to stab the cherry buried beneath the ice cubes.

"You need to slow down with that drink," Daryl interjected. "You know how you get when you drink."

"And how do I get?" he snapped back.

"Do I have to spell it out for you?

"Why don't you?"

"Okay, you get *ho-ish*. I'm not baby-sitting you tonight. You ain't messing up my groove. I mean it," Daryl stated.

Whenever Tony drank too much, his alter ego would emerge, and the first thing he'd lose was his clothing, especially while on the dance floor. It was truly not uncommon to see him out there on the floor, shirtless, moving his little ass to some hypnotic beat. The next thing he'd lose was his mind.

"I'm not asking you to baby-sit me. I'm a grown man. And that's my song," he said as he started grooving to the beat of the music. "I'm hitting the dance floor, so I'll holla at you later." We watched as he danced his way through the crowded room. The sea of bodies collectively parted as he made his way through the crowd to take his place in the center of the room.

"Tony," Daryl yelled, "keep your clothes on!" We both laughed as Tony waved away Daryl's comments.

"Your friend is a fool," I said to Daryl.

"Oh no, that's your friend. I love him, but that boy can work a nerve," Daryl said with a smile.

"He worries me sometimes," I added.

"How so?" Daryl inquired.

"This wild streak he has. You know how he has to be at every party and ain't satisfied unless he leaves with a handful of phone numbers. I know he's relatively new to this gay thing, but I think he's confusing his *life* with this *lifestyle*. Being gay ain't about parties, clubs, and an endless line of men. If he ain't careful, he's gonna get hurt, or hurt somebody."

"That's why we're his friends. We gotta have his back. I have your back, too, you know," he said with a change in tone.

"You know he's trouble," I said playfully.

"Yeah, but that's what makes him who he is. And don't act as if you are so innocent. I can think of some stories about you, like the time…"

"Please, don't remind me," I interjected.

"Speaking of friends, where's yours?" he asked, referring to James.

"I don't know. I'm sure he's around here somewhere."

"Wait a minute. That didn't sound right. What's going on?" I looked away from him to avoid his eye contact, knowing that he had read through my thinly veiled sarcasm. I get so tired of pretending. I felt like I was wearing a mask that hid my true face from the rest of the world. No one knew the real me.

"Everything in Camelot is wonderful. Couldn't be better," I said in the same derisive tone. At times, I wanted more than anything to confide in someone, but I just couldn't let it all out. I just wasn't ready.

"I'm not asking about Camelot, I'm asking about you," Daryl said. He looked at me in a curious manner, studying every inch of my face, like I was a specimen in some laboratory Petri dish.

"Why are you looking at me like that?"

"I was trying to read your thoughts."

"You don't want to do that."

"Are you happy, Kevin? I mean truly happy?"

"What does that mean?"

"You know what I mean. Are you happy with your life? Are you happy with James?"

"What's not to be happy about? I live in this big-ass house with James, who gives me everything that I could possibly ask for. Everything is fine," I lied. "Besides, I learned a long time ago that happiness is simply a decision. Enough about me," I said, trying to change the subject. "What about you and your love life? You still seeing that model, what's his name, Tyrek?"

"His name is Terrell, and no, I ain't seeing him. He was starting to get on my nerves. Way too much attitude. Just once I'd like to date someone who is complete, you know what I mean?"

"I remember those days of being single and looking for quality people," I said.

"I'm not looking for perfection, just someone I can vibe with on a lot of different levels. He doesn't have to be rich, or look like a model. He can't be a dog either; I need him to be complete. I'm just sick and tired of being sick and tired with these tired ass Negroes. What you lack in one area, make up for in another area, that's all I say. Just be balanced. Is that too much too ask?" Daryl asked as if I, of all people, could honestly answer.

"It seems like a simple request to me, but it is hard to find. But you know they say good things come to those who wait," I said, trying to convince myself as well as Daryl.

"Hell, how long do I have to wait? I want mine now."

"Maybe I'm the wrong person to ask that. I don't have the answer."

"I think you might be the right person to ask," he said in his seductive tone.

"Okay, so Terrell is out," I said, refocusing our conversation on the subject at hand. "Who's your next *conquest?*"

"I don't know about a conquest, but I do have my eye on someone very special."

"Anyone I know?"

"Yes," he said, staring deeply into my eyes. "You know him very well." I smiled a bit in approval. At that moment, Tony made his way through the crowd looking like he'd just seen a resurrected Tupac Shakur.

"You guys will never believe who I just saw on the dance floor! Daryl, you remember that crazy nigga I told you I met on AOL? He's here, over by the table, loading his plate like it's his last meal!"

"You mean *crying* guy?"

"Yes! He's here! You have got to see this fool!"

"Who are you two talking about?" I asked.

"Let's walk through the kitchen to the other side. I don't want him to see me.

Come on." We followed him into the kitchen and looked out of the door into the dining room. When we opened the door, I saw a rather large man hovering over the table, piling his plate high with shrimp, crawfish, crab cakes, and jambalaya. I hoped there'd be something left for the other guests after he moved on. I knew the food was good, but damn! We closed the door and went back into the kitchen. After about five minutes of laughter, we regained our composure and Tony began to tell us the story.

"Okay, here's what happened. You know I talk to

people on the Net sometimes. Well, I'd seen this guy on there just about every time I logged on, so of course, we began to chat. He said he'd just moved here from Dallas and was looking to meet some friends in the Houston area. So I'm thinking, he seems cool, let me meet the brother." Tony paused to shove a shrimp in his mouth from the extra platter that sat on the kitchen counter. "Anyway, he told me that his birthday was coming up and he didn't know anyone in the area to hang with. It just so happened that Alex was having a party that weekend. So of course, being the kind soul that I am, I invited him to the party. So I told the brotha that I'd pick him up at 7 o'clock that evening 'cause I had to be in his area around that time. I told him I'd call him at 5 o'clock to confirm."

"Why do I feel like this story is about to get crazy? I interrupted.

"Wait, I haven't even gotten started yet. So Saturday comes. It's 5 o'clock. I call. No answer. I called again at 5:30; no answer. So I start getting ready. I took my shower and got my clothes together. At 6:45, I'm on my way out the door when the phone rings. Something told me not to answer it, but I did. It was him. I told him that I couldn't come and get him now since it was so late and I had a few errands to run before the party and his house is way out of the way. Then the brotha started *crying*."

"What do you mean crying?"

"I mean *boo-hoo-tears-running-down-his-face-ruin-ing-his-makeup* kind of crying. He was talkin' 'bout it's his birthday and he had just lost track of time. I was so mad, but he was making me feel guilty so I told him he needed to be ready 'cause I was on my way. I get to his house and this nigga came to the door looking like Aunt Esther from *Sanford and Son*, talking about he needed fifteen more minutes to pack a bag."

"To pack a bag? Pack a bag for what?" I asked in disbelief.

"My point exactly. Why the hell did he need an overnight bag? Who the hell did he think he was staying with? Anyway, we get to the party and at some point he locks himself into Alex's bedroom with a bottle of Jack Daniel's talking about nobody bought him any gifts for his birthday. When he finally came out, I had to take his triflin' ass home and he cried all the way back to his house like a bitch."

"Did he think this was a birthday party for him?" Daryl asked.

"I don't know what he thought or expected. All I know is he is crazy. Basically, he is certifiable; an absolute nut." Tony turned quickly toward me and asked, "So, why is he at your party?"

"That's a good question. He must have come here with someone," I replied. "We do our best to make it an A-list affair, but there's only so much you can do. Sometimes, even the crazies slip through the cracks." *The last thing we needed in this house was another crazy person.*

"I want to dance, but I don't want him to see me," Tony said. He stood there for a few seconds looking toward the dance floor, a drink in his hand, and a scowl on his face. "Fuck that, he ain't ruining my evening. I'm 'bout to get back out on the dance floor and shake my butt to Lil' Kim."

A tight beat bounced out of the stereo speakers and Tony was gone. The song sounded good and I, too, felt like following Tony to the floor, but I stayed put. Everyone else jumped to their feet and raced to the floor like it was the last song of the night.

Just as Tony moved toward the dance floor, I saw James making his way through the crowd, with his friend Carl in tow. Carl was creepy and always seemed to have an ulterior motive for everything he did, even something simple as saying hello.

I took another gulp of my Long Island Iced Tea, closed my eyes for a brief second, and hoped they'd disappear. If only I could click my heels together and send them both to Kansas. James walked over to me and planted a soft kiss on my lips.

"I hope we're not interrupting," he said.

"No, we were just sitting here talking about you,"

Daryl said snidely, and let out a little laugh. It was interesting to watch James and Daryl interact with each other. They didn't like each other at all, and they revealed little bits of truth in humor. I knew James thought there was something going on between Daryl and me, but he was wrong, for the most part.

"I'm sure it was all good," he said with a smirk. He positioned himself directly in front of Daryl so that Daryl could only see his back.

"I'm going to the bar; anybody need a drink?" Daryl asked.

Before anyone could respond, Daryl walked away, shaking his head.

"James tells me that you have your MBA," Carl said. "Well, when you want a job, I could use someone with your talent," he added with a sleazy sort of smile. Every time I talked with him I felt the need to take a bath. The colored contacts that he wore clashed violently with his skin tone. From across the room you could see that his eyes didn't blend. He was wearing a gray snakeskin suit with big cowboy boots. Someone should have told him this ain't the wild, wild West, and he clearly was no Will Smith. He looked liked a total mess. Even pimps have better taste.

As the evening wore on, the crowd thinned out until only a few people remained. I was careful not to devote too much time to Daryl, but I already knew James would have something to say about it. As much as I hated to admit it, I was glad when Daryl had to take Tony home after Tony began his usual striptease. The sooner they left, the less drama there would be. In my heart, I knew there was more to my feelings for Daryl than just friendship.

Several times throughout the evening, I even noticed Carl looking at me provocatively; his not-so-subtle gazes made me want to ask him if his wife and two sons knew he was here hanging out with a bunch of gay men. I wondered what excuse he used this time to get away from her. I despised married men who crept out on their women with other men. They weren't gay, so they said, but only messed around with men. Whatever name they chose to call themselves, the effect was the same; a rose by any other name smells just as sweet. Well, almost any rose. Carl had a stench that was all his own.

CHAPTER 6

As the last couple of guys left the party, I let out a sigh of relief; it was finally over, and I was exhausted. The place was a wreck. A big heart-shaped purple stain on the carpet took up space near the piano, and many empty glasses littered the room. This was new carpet; I had to get the old carpet replaced after my blood stained it, and now we'd have to have this cleaned or replaced, too. If James saw the stain, he'd probably have a fit. I took a quick tour of the downstairs area just to figure out exactly how much cleaning would have to be done. I hadn't seen this kind of mess since the parties my fraternity used to have. If this party wasn't da bomb, then it looked like it had been.

As I walked through the house, I turned off all the lights, with the exception of a lamp in the corner, letting darkness encompass the room. I wasn't sure where James and Carl had gone, but I was glad that I was alone in the house. I felt exhausted and I really wanted to rest. I walked upstairs slowly and when I got to the bedroom door, I heard a few deep moans coming from inside the room. Slowly, I opened the door, and

saw Carl, naked and on his knees, in front of James'
nude body. When they heard the door open, they both
looked at me, smiled, and continued their business as
if my presence didn't matter. Disgustedly, I began to
pull the door closed when I heard James' voice.

"I was wondering when you were gonna get up
here," James said. "Take your clothes off," he commanded casually. His stare bore through me, like he
was trying to communicate only with his mind. I
stood there for a second, wanting to leave the room—
needing to leave the room—but unable to move. Carl
got up and stood next to James, and they both faced
me like drill sergeants, with their naked parts at full
salute.

"Come here," James ordered. Before I could move,
he came toward me, grabbed me by the hand, and
pulled my body gently into his. He moved his face
close to my ear, and I could feel his wet tongue caressing my lobe. "I need you to do this for me, baby. I'll
take care of you; everything will be okay. Just do
what I tell you and everything will be great. Take
your clothes off." He whispered in my ear so that
Carl could not hear him. I felt his teeth bite down on
my earlobe just enough to cause a hint of pain, and I
moved away from him slowly.

"I'm not doing this again. You said we'd never do
this again," I said in a whisper while thinking of an

escape. James pretended not to hear me, and he took my arm and led me into the bathroom. As soon as the door closed, he pinned me against the wall with his body. His breath dripped with the nauseating smell of alcohol, among other things.

"Why do you have to fight me about everything I ask you to do? You know how hard my week has been. I'm asking you to do this one thing for me to help me relax. Is that too much to ask?"

"Get out of my face, James."

"Make me."

"I'm tired, and I don't feel like this shit tonight. Move out of the way."

"Take your clothes off."

"Fuck you." He gave me a small slap across the face. It didn't hurt, but it was just enough to get his point across.

"Hit me again, nigga, and we're gonna tear up this bathroom. Do you really want Carl to hear us fighting in here?" He thought about it for a moment and then stepped back a little bit.

"I don't understand why you have to give me shit about this. It's not like we haven't done it before. I do everything for you. I haven't even said anything about you being all up in Daryl's face tonight."

"What the hell are you talking about?"

"Don't try to act innocent. You two were so close I

thought you were gonna fuck. Everyone saw it. All of my friends. You embarrassed me."

"That's your jealous mind playing tricks on you. Daryl is just a friend. Nothing more."

"I want you to come into the bedroom with us. I need you to do this for me. I will never ask you again. I promise."

"That's what you said last time."

"Fine." He moved away and turned as if he was leaving the room. "One more thing, while I'm out here, why don't I call Danea and the rest of your friends and fill them in on the details about Keevan's death that they're missing? You remember those little details that you forgot to tell them about Darius? Or maybe I'll fill them in on your little episode after his death. How 'bout that?" He looked at me briefly and then turned to leave the room; he was already turning the doorknob. He had the upper hand, and he knew it. There were some things in my past that I just wasn't ready to face. He'd won again.

"James, wait. Don't do that."

"Why shouldn't I? You don't do anything for me." With my head bowed, I slowly began to unbutton my shirt. He had me in a corner.

"I'll be in the room in a few minutes." He looked at me and smiled in victory.

"You have five minutes." I shook my head from

side to side, not wanting to face up to this reality. James closed the door behind him. I couldn't look at myself in the mirror. *The things we do for love.* The sound of the cool running water drowned the voices seeping in from the bedroom. I splashed my face with water several times before getting up the nerve to leave. I knew I didn't have a choice because either I would come out willingly, or James would force his way back in and drag me out.

I walked into the bedroom, trying to cling to what little dignity I could, and went immediately to the right side of the bed. On the nightstand were several small joints and a couple of nicely rolled blunts. I walked over, picked up a thick one, lit it and inhaled deeply several times until I started choking. A sudden rush went to my head, and for a second I got dizzy. James walked over to the other side of the room and took a seat next to Carl on the small love seat near the fireplace. They started kissing and caressing each other, holding and massaging each other's parts, all while the walls of the room closed in on me, trapping me like an animal in a cage. I had nowhere to go.

"Get the rest of your clothes off and get your pretty ass over here," I heard James say between moans of pleasure. Before I could stop it, a tear poured out of my eye and rolled swiftly down my cheek. Quickly, I wiped it away. No tears. Not for or because of that bastard. I stood up, head held high, trying to seem proud, and methodically began removing my clothing, one piece at a time, hiding my emotions, until I stood there naked. I wanted to crawl under a rock to hide my humiliation. James called again, this time with less patience. I walked over to the pair, and Carl immediately got up, and started rubbing my body as James sat back. He smiled as he stroked himself. Carl started kissing my ear, and my neck, and slowly I felt his wet mouth leaving a trail down my entire body. I quivered.

"I've waited so long to taste you," he whispered. I waited for the effects of the alcohol and the drugs so that the pain would go away. Carl took my hand and led me to the bed. He pushed me onto it before climbing on top of me. His body covered my frame, and as he rolled over onto his back, he took my head and tried to force my face down toward his middle section. I refused to comply. Instead, he reversed the motion and went down on me. I lay on my back on the bed, this bed of lies, and James joined us. He took his place on my left side, Carl on my right, and I could feel their bodies rubbing against mine. The friction caused a sensation to flow through me. In a choreographed moment, they each—one on each side—slithered up toward my chest, with their forked tongues leaving a slimy trail along the sides of my body. I felt them tease and play with my nipples. As much as I hated them, this act, this house, their smells, their bodies, the pleasure caused by their gyrating tongues could not be denied. I began to throb. Then, the moaning began. I hated them. They slid their way back down my body and I felt two distinct tongues on my heated erection. One of them, I didn't look to see which one, inserted me into the warmth of his mouth. As much as I loathed them, I couldn't help but respect the power of their tongues on my flesh.

James gave me a curt look and we both stood up. Carl, smiling like a kid in a candy store, slowly fell to his knees in front of us. I looked down just as he wrapped his hands around our throbbing dicks. His hands moved up and down our shafts, and his tongue caressed the heads, first slowly, then much rougher and faster. His hands elicited deep moans from the both of us. James leaned his face close to mine and started tongue kissing me as Carl inserted the heads of both of our dicks into his mouth at once. He had some special skills. Inside his mouth, I could feel the head of my dick rub against the head of James' dick as Carl's tongue grazed and tickled my hole, and then he did the same thing to James, I presumed. James' hands on my nipples sent jolts through my body and made my knees weak.

Carl laid me down on the bed, reached over onto

the night table, grabbed a condom, and put it on me. I could see him fingering himself and enjoying the pleasures of self-touch. He slowly sat his ass down onto my dick, and began to work his body in an erotic rhythm. James now circled the bed with a camcorder, calling out orders as he if was the director of some movie, telling me to smile and look happy as Carl's body connected with mine. He rode me like a champion jockey. James put the camcorder down, moved his body in front of Carl and above my face and inserted his dick into Carl's eager mouth.

We moved from the bed to the chair diagonally positioned against the wall opposite the fireplace. Carl laid back, spread his legs high in the air like a church steeple, and inserted his fingers into his hole. He started with one, then two, then three, until he had four in his spot. He moaned and groaned in a state of ecstasy. "Fuck me," he commanded. James moved behind him and held up his legs. Carl, just like the other married bisexual or gay men I had encountered in my life, wanted to be fucked, and hard. I knew I had to comply. I moved over to him, forced my dick into his dark hole and pounded him with so much force that he howled. Sweat dripped from my forehead and raced down my face as I plowed into his ass like a man possessed. "Fuck me, nigga!" He kept begging for it, so I gave it to him. I fucked him harder and dug deeper. I wasn't sure if his expressions and gasps were pleasure or pain. I wanted to destroy him. James looked at me. I looked back at him. I wanted to hurt Carl, so each thrust of my body was harder than the one prior to it. Even as I continued my assault James and I maintained eye contact. Carl moaned and yelled and let out gasps, but I didn't stop. I couldn't stop. I could feel deep vibrations running through my body. I knew I was close. I was about to come. I withdrew from him, yanked off the condom, and watched as a milky substance shot out across his body, his face, his hair, and onto James' stomach. They cheered as I exhaled. And then they came.

When it was over, I collapsed on the floor feeling absolutely nothing. This, too, would be added to a long list of other perversions that marked our relationship. So many things I'd done for him; so many times I'd indulged his sexual fantasies, but the price was my soul.

I listened to James and Carl reflect on the evening. "Next time," I heard Carl say, "maybe I'll bring my wife." They laughed. *Next time?* There would be no *next time.* I sat up on the floor and moved toward the night table, lit a joint, and took two deep inhales before I locked myself in the bathroom. I turned on the water in the shower, not knowing if it was hot or cold. Before I stepped into the shower, I went to the sink and rubbed my face with my hands and looked myself over in the mirror. Who had I become?

After I got out of the shower, I climbed into bed and pulled the covers over my head like a child. After a few moments, James entered the room with a smile and kissed me on the cheek. "I love you, Kevin. You know exactly what to do to make me happy," he wryly said. "Before I leave tomorrow, I'll put one of my platinum cards on the table. I want you to treat yourself to anything you want."

CHAPTER 7

I sat around the house in my underwear flipping aimlessly through the endless array of cable stations. The music blared so loudly that I could barely hear the television, even though it was in stereo sound. James caught a Sunday afternoon flight back to Austin, but called several times to see if I was okay, and to see if I had received the flowers that he sent. I remained unfazed by his attempts to win me over with flowers and gifts.

The doorbell had rung several times in the morning with deliveries of different kinds of multicolored flowers and roses. Each one had a card with the words *I love you* printed on them. I guess he thought that the flowers would make me forget. The only thing that was making me feel better was all the Hennessy flowing through my system. At times, I couldn't believe the things that were going on in my life. I'd been in relationships before, but not like this one. Nothing compared to the hardship this love brought with it. I was often so confused that I didn't know if I was coming or going. One minute I felt strong, the next I was weak. I lay there, trying hard to fight sleep, but it was too hard to keep my eyelids from falling shut. Before I knew it, I was out.

✖✖✖

"This humidity is unbearable," James said as he began to undress. "Where are my swimming trunks?"

"They're in the middle drawer," I said. James looked at me sternly and I put my book down and walked over to the dresser and pulled out a pair of black Speedos.

"I want you to go swimming with me. Put your trunks on," he said.

"You know I can't swim. Besides, I need to finish reading for class."

James came over to me and started kissing my neck, sending erotic chills throughout my body.

"Don't worry about it, I'll teach you. Come on, I really want you to go."

"Baby, I don't have time. I still have over fifty pages to read and then write a paper. You know how tough summer school can be."

James backed away from me in anger and started grinding his teeth like an animal. The cold look in his eyes and the intense expression on his face made me nervous. Before I knew it, he pounced. He moved toward me with such speed that I barely saw him coming, and the next thing I knew I felt a pair of massive hands gripped tightly *around my neck as my body was pushed into and then pinned against the wall. I tried to free myself, but he'd gotten the best of me already. He looked me directly in my eyes as he squeezed harder and harder. My struggles did little to remove me from his hands, and I could feel myself getting light-headed and dizzy. I wanted desperately to cough, but there was no air in my throat.*

"Why do you always have to be so difficult!" he said between clenched teeth. "I don't care what you have to do for school. You can stay up all night if you have to, but you are going swimming with me now!" He released his grip around my neck and I collapsed onto the floor in front of the fireplace.

"Go to hell, James!" I said between coughs and gasps. He grabbed at me and I tried to force a punch, but I missed.

"Get up!" he screamed, but I was too busy gasping for air to react. I felt a sudden pain in my rib as he kicked me with considerable force. He grabbed me from the floor and led me out of the bedroom into the hallway. As he forced me to walk, I lost my balance and rolled halfway down the staircase and landed in the middle of the foyer on the hardwood floor. I hit my head so hard that I saw stars. I could still hear him screaming for me to get up. When I failed to comply, he grabbed me by the arm and dragged me through the house until we reached the patio. He released me for a brief time just long enough to unlock and open the sliding door. I could hear the sound of the waves

slapping against the walls of the pool on this windy evening. I thought about trying to run, but before thought could become action, he grabbed me again and dragged me across the rough concrete floor, tearing skin from my flesh.

At the pool, he stood me up, and I began to beg. He threw me into the deepest end of the pool anyway, with full knowledge that I couldn't swim. Scared that I might drown, I moved my arms frantically back and forth in the water in an uncontrolled motion. For a few seconds, I managed to stay afloat, but my lack of skills soon became evident. Water filled my mouth and I began to choke. I tried to scream for James to help me, but the water wouldn't let my voice come through. As I began to sink, I saw James standing on the edge of the pool, looking down at me. I knew I was going to die. Right before I lost consciousness, I heard a splash enter the water and felt a pair of hands around my waist. When we reached the surface, I coughed wildly and started to spit up water. He led me to the steel ladder attached to the side of the pool. I immediately grabbed the bars and pulled myself slowly out of the water.

"You are so pathetic," he said as he turned his back and began to swim the length of the pool as if all was right with the world.

I woke up in a cold sweat. The memories were so real. This was no dream; this was a flashback from my life.

CHAPTER 8

had to get out of that house. I was surrounded by memories, and I thought I heard Keevan's voice. I wasn't sure where I was going. I just got in the car, and decided to see where the road would lead. I ended up at one of Keevan's old hangouts. It took me some time to find a place to park at the Triangle. This was where Houston's young, black, professional crowd would gather after a long day at work to relax, unwind, and take advantage of the drink specials. It had been over a year since I had been here.

As I entered the room, I heard robust laughter and heavy voices. The place was packed. Quickly, I scanned the room to find a place to sit, but all of the tables were taken. I saw an empty stool on the right side of the wooden bar and stepped to it with authority. In the back behind the bar, I couldn't help but notice a very attractive woman in the corner by herself. From what I could gather, she was waiting on someone. Probably her man. And she was running out of patience. The forced smile on her lovely face soon gave way to a slight frown. She kept looking at her watch, then back at herself in the make-up mirror, back at her watch and so forth. All the time, she was fending off hungry eyes from the gentlemen across the room. One man, dressed in a lavender suit, finally stepped up to her, but was quickly dismissed. *Too much soul.* I laughed to myself. Nothing much had changed about the place in my absence.

"Can I help you?" a voice bellowed my direction. Slightly startled, I answered the bartender.

"Yeah, gimme a glass of gin with just a splash of juice."

"What kind of juice?"

"Orange. And let me open a tab." I pulled out a pack of Newports and proceeded to light one. Moments later, he pushed the drink down in front of me and turned to help the next customer. I picked up my glass and took a huge gulp of the drink. It was strong—just what I needed.

It was interesting to watch the dynamics of the room and the games of flirtations played by men and women. A simple glance, then you look away. They look at you and then look away until your eyes just lock together. Then, one of the two had to approach the other one. It was all a game of chance.

"Rough day?"

"What?" I said between a puff on my cigarette and a drink.

"You look like you've had a rough day, that's all."

"A rough couple of years, more like it."

"Let me guess, trouble at the office and with the wife?"

"I'm not married."

"You've got that married look. I've been married four years," he said as he leaned over and waved his ring finger to show off the wedding band. When I turned and really looked at him, I was surprised that I didn't notice how attractive he was sooner. He had a nice set of full red lips and a head full of curly black hair. I didn't know exactly what his ancestry was, but the combination created a beautiful specimen. I could see the African traits, but the rest remained a mystery. His eyes were mesmerizing, deep and dark, and they added character to his masculine face.

"What does that mean, *that married look?*"

"The same look I have. That look of happy to be off work, but not ready to go home to the bullshit."

"Okay, I'm feeling what you're saying now. There's a lot of bullshit in my house. So maybe I do have that married look." I tried not to look too closely into his eyes, but his friendliness made it difficult not to be caught in his web. "What are you drinking?" I asked.

"Long Island Iced Tea."

"Bartender," I called out, "let me get another Long Island for my friend here and another gin for me."

"You didn't have to do that."

"I know."

"Well, thanks, friend," he said slowly as he put out his hand. "I'm Croix. Croix Evans."

"I'm Kevin Davis. Nice to meet you." His thick hands were smooth and sexy and I wanted to hold on, but I knew that would not be wise. "What kind of name is Croix?"

"My parents are from the islands." Without so much as a pause, he spoke again. "So, what's your story?"

"My story? Ummm, I don't know if we have enough time to hear my story. There's so many problems."

"Problems at work?"

"I don't work."

"Okay, no wife, no job, so what's the problem? Hell, if I was in your shoes I'd be a happy muthafucka," he said with a big laugh, but I just shrugged off his comment. "So, what's up then? Why the sad look?"

"You wouldn't understand."

"Can I guess?"

"You can do whatever you like. It's a free country." I was beginning to feel the effects of the drinks on my system, and wanted to order another one.

"Problems with your *lover?*" I turned in his direction to make sure that I'd heard his words correctly. In my mind, the word "lover" could mean a lot of different things, even though I was sure what he meant. I stared into his eyes and found the confirmation that I needed.

"Something like that."

"Why don't we finish this conversation at that table over in the corner. There are too many ears up here," he said, looking at the bartender. He pointed to the table that the young lady had been sitting at earlier. She was gone; I wondered if her man ever showed up.

"That's cool." We walked over and I pulled up a chair in the corner so that my back would not face the open room. Most black men I know hate to sit with their backs toward the room. We had to see who was coming and going. It must be some trait left over from slavery and Jim Crow. He sat in front of me, smiling, carrying two more drinks, apparently not bothered by his position at the table.

"Did you notice that bartender was all up in our conversation?"

"Nah, I wasn't paying attention to him."

"What were you paying attention to, then?" he asked with a flirtatious smile.

"You don't want me to answer that question."

"I wouldn't have asked if I didn't want an answer." I looked at him and was forced to smile. I was getting butterflies in my stomach like I was some nervous schoolboy.

"Anyway, Croix, what's your story?"

"Well, I'm married. With children. Two. Let's see, my oldest is Brianna and she is 4. My son is 2 1/2 and his name is Marcus." He took out his wallet and showed me pictures of his kids like a proud father.

"I must say your kids are beautiful."

"Well, thank you."

"Okay. You're married with children, but you're here flirting with me. What's up with that?"

"Is that what I'm doing? I hadn't noticed." He gave me a little push and then laughed like it was the funniest thing in the world. I just looked at him 'cause I knew there was much more to him than what he was telling me. "Maybe I just enjoy your company."

"Be real. What's going on with you? Are you gay, bisexual…what?" Silence hovered over the table like a dark cloud. He nervously took several sips from his drink and looked around the room like he was a wanted man.

"Something tells me that I can trust you."

"You can, but don't tell me anything you don't want me to know. I'm not gonna pry. Tell me only what you want to share."

"Sounds cool," he said. He took another sip of his drink and tried to look shy. "You're partly right. I am flirting with you. It's not often I meet an attractive down-low brotha." We both smiled. "As far as my sexuality is concerned, honestly, I don't know what I am. No, that's not true, I know what I am; I just don't want to admit it. I was hoping that marriage and children would get rid of these feelings, but these last four years have been hell. Don't get me wrong. I love my wife. I don't always *like* her, but I love her. Not in love, just love. We don't really have anything to talk about except the bills and the kids. I love my kids more than life itself. There's nothing I wouldn't do for them. But trying to live and be someone that I'm not is killing me. I don't have much experience with men. When I was in college, I dated this guy for a year and a half. We lived together and everything was great, or so I thought. One day I caught him in our bed with some other nigga and I swore I'd never give a man, or anyone for that matter, the opportunity to hurt me like that again. He's the only man I've been with. So I started dating women. I knew there was no way I'd fall in love and therefore I'd be safe. One thing led to another, I met Keisha, we dated and finally got married. And so, here I am."

"What made you think I was gay?"

"At first, I didn't. I was just talking. Then I noticed the way you looked at me when we shook hands. I wasn't sure, but I just had this feeling. You obviously ain't no sissy, so it was hard to tell."

"How do you live like that from day to day?"

"You just do it. I ignore my urges and I bury myself

in work, although it's getting hard to resist. I know I would never cheat on my wife, but these feelings are getting strong."

"You just make sure you keep it in your pants. Don't cheat on her. It wouldn't be right. I've seen what shit like this can do to a woman. I knew a woman who almost killed herself when she found out that her boyfriend had sex with one of her brothers. It was a lot of unnecessary drama."

"What's your 'friend's' name?"

"James."

"What does he look like?"

"Why does that matter?"

"Well, when I see something I like, I gotta know my competition," he said with a half-smile. "I'm just kidding."

"I bet you are."

"Why aren't you happy?"

"What?"

"You heard me. Why aren't you happy?"

"Who said I wasn't happy?"

"If either of us were happy at home, we wouldn't be here alone, now would we? So answer the question, Kevin."

"Honestly, I don't know if I ever planned on being happy with James. I've known for a long time that we wouldn't work. But I have to deal with one problem at a time. I have so many. So I stay. What's your excuse?"

"I stay because I love my kids. Besides, where would I go?"

"Anywhere you want to. The world is a big place."

"Yeah, but being alone in a big place is not a great thing."

"I understand completely."

"Why do you stay?"

"I don't really know why I stay. Maybe convenience. Maybe I don't want to be alone. But I can tell you that I'm at this point in my life because of the choices I've made in the past. I'm here and this is where I need to be. There is a lesson to be learned; I just don't know if I'm open to it right now."

The more time we spent talking, the more comfortable I felt with him. It's funny how sometimes we can tell total strangers things we wouldn't tell our best friends. I guess with strangers we don't have to worry about their judgments or opinions. "I do think sometimes being alone is a lot better than settling for what comes your way. I don't know. We have a lot of problems."

"Like what?"

"For one, we fight a lot. I mean physically fight." I did not hesitate when I spoke.

"Are you serious? What do you fight about?"

"What *don't* we fight about is the more appropriate question."

"Damn, man. I'm sorry."

"Don't apologize. It ain't your fault. It's sad because I can see the good in him, but he has this temper and this jealousy. It's hard to deal with."

"So, what do you want?"

I looked down at my watch and noticed it was getting late. I didn't want to go home because I was enjoying his company. "I want to be happy. Just like everyone else. Just like you. But right now, I need to go home. And so do you."

We paid our tab, and left the bar. On the way out, I couldn't help but notice a sadness was overcoming me. I wanted to continue our conversation because we both had a lot that needed to be said. We stopped at his car, a wine-colored Lexus SC400.

"Take a ride with me," he said as he opened his car door.

"What? A ride?"

"That's right, a ride. Houston has a lot of roadway. We could drive forever. Just you and me and the open road. We could leave everyone behind." I knew he was just kidding, but part of me longed to get away from it all.

"Wouldn't that be nice, but I don't think so. I need to get home. Besides, just 'cause we've had a conversation in a bar doesn't mean I know you. You could be an ax-murderer or something," I said, with a slight hint of humor.

"Is this the face of a maniac? Come on, it's just a simple ride. We don't have to go far." He gave me his trusting puppy-dog eyes and finally I submitted. He was hard to resist.

"Okay, I'll go, but keep in mind I have a gun, and I'm not afraid to use it," I said with a smile. I got in the car and he closed the door behind me. As soon as the door closed, I smelled the sweetness of jasmine in the air. It sent a strong vibe through my body.

"You okay?" he asked.

"It's your air freshener. I don't like jasmine."

"We can roll down the windows," he said as the windows lowered and the moon roof slid back to reveal the sky. "If you get cold, just let me know."

"Where are we going?"

"Just sit back and relax."

✖✖✖

We walked along the Galveston beach as the sun made its final dip below the horizon. We laughed and enjoyed this moment. It had been a long time since I'd taken an evening stroll along the Texas coastline. The mystic sounds of the waves told many stories. It told my story. It told Croix's.

"Sometimes I think there has to be more to life," Croix said. "I mean, is anyone truly happy?"

"I have to believe there is love and happiness somewhere in this world. If love didn't exist it would be such a waste."

"If everyone wants to be loved, why are there so many lonely people? If we're all looking for the same thing, why can't we find each other?"

"We don't know how to love, or we're afraid to love. It leaves us vulnerable. It forces us to open our lives to someone. All of the defenses that we spend a lifetime creating around our hearts would have to come down. Once we build them, it's hard to take them down."

"You're a deep brotha," he said with a huge grin. "How many people do you think are having this exact conversation at this exact moment?"

"Hundreds. Thousands. Probably millions."

"If you're right that means there are a lot of lonely people in the world." We walked a little farther and took a seat on the damp wooden bench overlooking the shore. "What brought you out this evening? I go to the Triangle just about every day after work and I've never seen you."

"Keevan." I picked up a handful of small pebbles and began tossing them one by one toward the water. My mind drifted. "I was at home thinking about Keevan, my twin brother. We used to go to the Triangle all the time, before he died."

"I'm sorry."

"Keevan is only a part of the reason. My brother died a year ago. A few weeks after his death, I tried to kill myself." Then, I told my story.

✖✖✖

I wanted to die. I remember thinking that over and over again until it became my most frequent thought. The vast emptiness without Keevan consumed me and I felt like the walking dead. I know people say they want to die as a way of getting attention, but I really meant it. I had it planned out. It would be so serene. I reserved a luxury suite at the Prescott with a spectacular view of downtown. I had the room for the entire weekend. The room was done in all white, which brought a sort of peace to me. I carefully and methodically decorated the room with what seemed like a hundred candles to create the perfect illumination. A picture of Keevan in a silver frame would lie on the bed next to me when I drifted into eternity. Fresh-cut flowers of every variety caused a sweet smell in the air. I would put on a CD and listen to the sound of a gentle storm and raindrops. Those were the last sounds I wanted to hear.

A few months prior to his death, I had gotten a prescription for some sleeping pills and I still had most of them left. I didn't think they'd be strong enough alone, so I decided to go to the store and buy some sleeping pills and some champagne. *I didn't really know how to do it. I mean, how do you kill yourself?*

As calm as I was about planning my suicide, when I got to the store I couldn't help but feel as if all eyes were on me. I spent a nervous twenty minutes in the store pacing back and forth, looking through magazines, and at products of which I had no intention of buying. Out of frustration, I put everything down and walked to the aisle of the store to get my pills. As soon as I turned the corner, I noticed a striking man with defined features staring at me. I walked past him and looked at the variety of over-the-counter medications that were available. I could feel the weight of his stare bearing down upon the back of my head, but when I turned he was gone. I felt relieved. I picked up three boxes of sleeping pills and walked to the counter and paid for them. I hurried out of the store.

In the parking lot, I saw the same man walking toward his car. I stopped for a second just to watch him. He unlocked a Jaguar and opened the door. As I stood there, partially mesmerized by his presence, he turned and looked at me. Our eyes locked. Quickly, I looked down and immediately walked to my car. I could hear a voice calling out to me across the sea of black asphalt, but I ignored it. He called again. This time I could hear distinct footsteps speeding toward me. By the time I got the courage to look up, he was upon me. My heart raced. Something indescribable was in the air. In anxiety, I dropped my keys to the ground and he picked them up and handed them to me.

"*You dropped these,*" *he said with warmth. I took the keys without saying a word. "I know this is going to sound absolutely crazy, but I wouldn't feel right if I let you go.*" *He paused momentarily as if he had to collect his thoughts. "Before you turned down the aisle where I was standing, I knew you were coming. I had this image of you in my head. No, that's not right. It wasn't a picture, but more like a feeling. Like a gut reaction.*"

"*What the hell are you talking about?*"

"*I know how this sounds. You must think I'm crazy, but when you passed, you left an impression upon my heart. Whatever you're feeling hit me hard. I know that sounds strange, but it's true.*" Nigga, puh-leeze, *I thought to myself.*

"*This may in fact be the most creative pickup line I've heard, but it's not gonna work. I don't have time for this,*" *I said as I turned and put my key in the lock.*

"*Don't run away. Don't run away from whatever is chasing you.*" *I stood fixed in place, my back to him. "You're about to do something that is wrong. Look under your heart. Whatever you need is there.*" *At that point, I couldn't hold back my tears. Keevan used to tell me to always look under my heart, and I never thought about what it meant. "Like I said, I just had to tell you that. I don't know what it means.*" *I heard the stranger's footsteps move away from me.*

"*Wait!*" *I screamed. He turned around. I walked over to him. His name was James.*

I reflected on the story I had just told Croix. No

one knew what I had just told; not even my closest friends.

"You see, James and I have this connection. He saved my life that night."

"How did he know what you were about to do? I don't understand."

"I don't understand how he knew either, but I have learned that there are some things in this world that defy explanation. I guess this is one of those things."

"Is that why you stay with him? Because of this connection?" Croix asked.

"More than anything, I think so."

"That's a powerful story."

"I have never told that story to anyone until now." Somehow, I was at ease with my confession and felt calm. "Croix, I hope you don't think I'm out of my mind, but I want to spend some more time with you. I feel a closeness to you."

"What did you have in mind?" he asked with a nervous smile. Whatever I was feeling for him made me want to know him more, made me want to be intimate with this man, this stranger. I didn't know him, nor did he know me, but I opened a part of my life, my history, to him that I had never shared with anyone. We continued to walk in the sand for a few minutes before he answered, "Okay."

We ended up in a nice hotel suite with a huge Jacuzzi

in the bathroom. Since this whole thing was mainly my idea, I chose the hotel. I gave a quick thought about James, and realizing, he was out of town, I pushed the thought away. I didn't need his specter haunting this moment. The view from the balcony overlooked the beach. We both sat on the bed, without words, trying to figure out the next move. I opened the bottle of wine we had picked up before we got to the hotel. After a few sips, we began to loosen up. He looked at me and I could see a deep tenderness in his eyes. I didn't know this man, but I knew we both needed the same thing right now, and it wasn't sex. I wasn't sure what we were doing in the hotel room, but part of me just wanted to extend this time with him into forever.

"Are you okay?" I asked.

"Yeah, I'm fine. I think."

"You're thinking about your wife?"

"No, I'm just thinking about the possibility of what could happen right now." He clutched his glass of wine and I watched his look of contentment change to concern. I shared that same concern. We lay back in the bed, surrounded by quiet darkness, and listened to each other breathe. Slowly, we moved closer to each other. I felt his lips touch mine. It wasn't a sexual kiss, but a kiss of understanding and tenderness. I don't know why it happened. Maybe it was the alcohol. Maybe it was a deep need for affection. Whatever the reason, I'm glad it happened. I'm glad we shared that time that nightt.

As we drove back to the Triangle, we talked about any and everything under the sun. It was rare to meet someone with a genuine spirit. When we got back, I pointed out my car and he pulled next to it. He reached into his wallet and pulled out his business card. He wrote his cell phone number on the back.

"I hope you'll call. I'd like to do this again." We wanted to kiss, but instead I took the number and stared at the paper for a few seconds before responding.

"Of course I'll call. Just remember me when I do," I said with a smile.

"I couldn't forget you." He reached out to shake my hand and we held the grip for a while. I wanted to pull him closer, pull him into me, but I let him go.

"It was nice meeting you, Croix."

"The pleasure was all mine."

CHAPTER 9

This was the Thursday night I had been waiting for. It was the premiere of Danea's musical. I hadn't really seen or heard from her over the last few weeks because rehearsals had gotten really tough. I don't know how she did it. *Attorney by day, star by night.* It had been a while since I really heard her sing and I couldn't wait. I had so much nervous energy building up in me that when I went for my usual run, I jogged an extra mile and a half. When I got home, the sun was hanging low in the sky. I was surprised to find James in the kitchen cooking dinner. The entire house smelled of spices, and from the sweat on his brow I could see that he really meant business. He was a great cook and learned the secrets of Cajun cooking from his grandmother in Baton Rouge. He always told me stories of how when he used to go home she'd always have some great dish smoldering on the stove and some flavorful sauce simmering in a pan. I walked into the kitchen, he smiled, and gave me a big kiss on the lips as if it was the first time we'd seen each other in a month. His lips tasted of sweet spices and wine. He walked over to the refrigerator and poured me a glass.

"Instead of going out to eat, before Danea's play, I decided to cook. I ran some bath water for you, and it should be warm enough for you to relax. I put in some of the bath oil that you like so much." I moved closer to the stove and tried to take a lid off the pan so I could see what he was making.

"No, no, no," he said as he tapped my hand. "You mustn't disturb the chef. You better hurry upstairs before your water gets cold."

Without saying a word, I left the kitchen and went upstairs. Candles adorned almost every inch of the room and the comforting glow almost made it all feel real. We'd been through this before. He would go through this romantic phase and turn on the charm. I don't know if he did it to win my love and trust, or if he did it simply to be cruel by showing me how wonderful he could be. As I entered the warm, fragrant bath, I wondered how long it would last this time. He had the ability to change, but I'm not sure if he had the desire. I hoped for the best. When he was good, he was oh, so good, but when he was bad it was equally intense. This emotional roller coaster that he kept me on was wearing me down. There were days when I had to tiptoe on eggshells just because I didn't know what would set him off.

I wasn't sure how much longer I could live like this. Somehow, that one evening with Croix opened me up to the possibility of being happy. He showed me that there is still some beauty left in people and in the world. I wanted to grab at my chance for happiness, but I felt unworthy. Why should I be happy when Keevan is dead? I deserved James and all the misery he brought. All the games. The lies. I deserved a lot of the misery I felt, but all of the pretending was wearing me down. It was all getting to me. Those walls I had carefully constructed to hold in the truth were falling, brick by brick. I was beginning not to care. I wanted them to fall.

As I lay back in the black marble tub, the water covering my chest, I sipped slowly on the wine. The beautiful sounds of Faith Evans filled the air. I was excited about seeing Danea's show because that was all that she had been talking about for months. A '70s musical revue. She had one of the most beautiful voices I'd ever heard and when she sang she could bring down the house, any house. It was opening night. I knew she'd be nervous, but she could handle it. She was great under pressure. That is one of her many qualities that I admired. She could handle almost anything. I knew James didn't like Danea, but he knew how important this was to me, and part of me was happy that he was going with me. It was hard at times trying to tear him away from his work.

A few minutes later James came into the bathroom. He picked up the cloth and started washing my body. His warm hands felt great as they moved over my tingling skin. He still had that magic touch. He knew exactly how to touch my body to make me shiver. In an erotic circular motion he slowly rubbed soap on my chest and stomach. I stood up, turned around and he methodically caressed my backside with gentle power as he cleaned me with baby strokes. *This is the man that I could love.* He dried me off and pulled me into the bedroom, telling me to lie on the bed on my stomach. He went back into the bathroom and came back moments later with various kinds of oils. He climbed in the bed and straddled me, making sure that he didn't put his weight on my body. The smell of the oil aroused me, and when he poured it on my back, I jumped a little from its coolness. The combination of his hands and the oil quickly began to generate heat. He continued rubbing my back and nibbling on my ear. The coarse stubble on his face scraping against my neck and ears sent powerful volts through my body. He knew my neck was extremely sensitive and he used the hair on his face to make me quiver. He turned me over and massaged my chest with equal thoroughness. He rubbed my chest and licked my love muscle before putting it in his mouth and working me over like a champ. This was one of the few times he'd done that to me, and with skills like that I wished he'd do it more often. My whole body twisted and popped from the warmth of his mouth and the movement of his tongue. He knew exactly what he was doing, and I hadn't felt this great in a long time. Deeper and deeper, slow, then fast, side-to-side, he worked his magic. I couldn't contain myself and I finally reached climax with a big explosion. As the juices sprayed out, he continued jacking me off, and the pure thrills from the combined action were almost too much to take. It was like an erotic torture. He then planted a wild kiss on my lips before getting a towel to clean me up. He went into the closet and handed me my black robe.

Dinner is waiting, he said. It wasn't often that I had dessert before the meal, but this was one time that I appreciated his touch. It took a few minutes for me to finally move.

Downstairs, the table was set in orderly perfection. He poured another glass of wine for me and then went into the kitchen to get the food. The dinner consisted of shrimp with Creole seasoning and dirty rice along with some green beans. The plate looked as if a professional chef had prepared it. James sat across from me and talked a lot about how well LCS was doing and how he was about to do an interview for *Today's Business*, a local magazine with considerable influence within certain segments of the city. The gleam in his eyes was a refreshing change.

"Congratulations. I knew you could do it. I'm so happy for you."

"For us," he inserted.

"By the way, the food is fantastic." We smiled at each other and seemed to enjoy each other's company. Then, the phone rang. James put a bit of food in his mouth before heading into the kitchen to answer the call. I could hear his voice from the kitchen, his tone rising and falling. I assumed that it must've been a business call. He came back into the room and took his seat. He ate the next few bites in silence. *Tension.*

"I can't go with you tonight," he said plainly.

"What? We've been planning this for weeks. We have to go."

"You've been planning this for weeks."

"James, you know how important this evening is to me. I've been looking forward to it for a long time. I really want you to go."

He continued to eat as if my words had no meaning. The veins in his head began to protrude. I slammed my fork down on the plate. "Let me guess, another crisis at LCS?"

"Something came up that I have to handle."

"Surely there's someone that can handle this for you tonight. Isn't that why you pay them? I mean the office isn't even open. Can't you handle this in the morning?" I tried to remove the irritation from my voice before the words left my mouth.

"What do you want me to do? Let my business fall apart just so I can go see your friend try to sing? I have to take care of this. It's important, and I can't go. Period."

"I guess everything is more important than me."

"You know that's not true."

"Do I? I can't believe this shit. Everything was so perfect tonight. Well, I'm going, with or without you."

"Why can't we see it tomorrow?"

"For one thing, we have tickets for tonight. The show is completely sold out for weeks. Secondly, this is opening night and she needs my support. I'm going."

"Will Daryl be there?"

"What? I'm sure he will. This isn't about me and Daryl. This is about you never spending any quality time with me. If you were so concerned about Daryl, you'd go with me," I said. I stood up and threw my napkin down onto the table before turning to leave. James jumped up and blocked my path.

"Don't talk to me like that."

"Whatever." I blew him off.

"Don't start no shit tonight. This is not my fault. If you respected my business and work, then you'd be more sympathetic. I just can't go, and I don't want you to go, either."

"I have to go because my friend needs my support tonight. There is no way that I'm changing my mind." I felt like pushing his buttons. How much prodding would it take for him to lose his cool?

"If you think you're going without me, you'd better think again."

"That's exactly what I'm gonna do. If you wanna come, you know where it is." He stood in my path, and looked at me as if I had wished some evil curse upon him. "What now?"

"I really don't feel like arguing with you, Kevin."

"Then don't. Get out of my way—please." I pushed by him so that I could go upstairs to change. He stood there and watched me walk away. I was expecting a blow to the back of the head, or something, but nothing. He just stood there. I knew he had to meet someone about whatever was going on at LCS and he was not in the mood to fight. This time, I'd won.

Upstairs every piece of clothing I would wear tonight, from my Polo underwear, to my Rolex watch was laid in perfect order on the bed. I looked at the clock and quickly jumped into my clothing, and raced downstairs. I was hoping to avoid any more confrontations with James. I could hear him on the phone in his office gathering papers, slamming drawers, and sounding as if there was some major crisis. With one last mirror check, I darted out of the house without so much as a goodbye.

✖✖✖

I walked into the recently restored theater and its magnificence took my breath away. It was designed with an old Victorian flair, and everything from the lighting to the furniture reflected this style. I was impressed. It had closed about two years earlier due to a fire, and this play that night marked the grand re-opening of the theater. I walked over to the bar and ordered an apple martini. I looked at my watch again. It was surprisingly early. Then, a pair of delicate hands from behind covered my eyes and a voice whispered, "Guess who?" Before I could guess, the lady removed her hands from my face. It was RaChelle.

"Hello, stranger," she said with a flirtatious smile. "How have you been?"

"RaChelle, it's nice seeing you. You look gorgeous." She nodded her head in acknowledgment.

"You know I'm mad at you," she said. "Why haven't you returned any of my phone calls?"

"You haven't called me."

"Kevin, I have left at least three messages at your house. With your roommate, I think." I thought a moment about whether James had told me that she called, but I knew he wouldn't. He hated people calling me. It didn't matter who they were, or even why they called.

"My roommate is not the most dependable person in the world. I apologize."

"You still have my number?"

"Actually, I left it in the pocket of my pants when I sent them to the cleaners. So the answer to your question is no. Once again, I apologize," I said playfully.

"I'm gonna give you my number once more. Be sure not to lose it this time. Keep it close to your heart." She reached into her purse and pulled out the card, which smelled of her sweet perfume. She handed it to me between her left index and middle finger, and when I reached for it, she pulled it back ever so slightly. "Who are you here with?"

"I was coming with my roommate, but he couldn't make it. I have some other friends who are here, but I haven't seen them yet. My friend Danea is starring in the musical."

"Your friend, or your *friend?*" I gave her a look that told her that she'd have to work a little harder than that to find out the details of my life. "I'm just kidding. I'm here with a couple of my sorors." She gazed into my eyes in an attempt to read my thoughts, so I thought I'd play along with her game.

"You mean some lucky gentleman hasn't snatched you off your feet yet? I mean look at you. There aren't too many women who can touch you."

"I know," she said with a sudden air of intriguing confidence. Her enchanting glances were intoxicating. She knew how to work magic. I felt as if I was being pulled into her. As she watched me, my eyes ran up and down the length of her figure. "Call me," she said as she walked away seductively. *If only I was straight*, I said to myself jokingly.

I walked toward the auditorium and looked across a huge room full of excited people. The level of intensity was growing in anticipation of what was sure to be a superb performance. I stood in the doorway, casually looking in the direction of my seat when an usher came and escorted me down the aisle to my section. As we approached, I could hear Tony's boisterous laughter rise above the crowd. He and Daryl seemed to be enjoying the moment. I looked at Daryl, trying not to be captivated by his impressive appearance. He had a way of looking me directly in the eyes when speaking, even as we exchanged simple hellos. I squeezed through Tony and took my seat on the other side of him, next to a woman who didn't seem at all pleased that I was next to her. I smiled. She turned her head.

"Glad you could join us," Daryl said with a pat to my leg.

"You know I wouldn't miss it for the world."

"We haven't seen much of you lately. Where have you been? Wait, let me guess, you and James have been hiding away in his palace? Speaking of which, I thought he was coming with you," Daryl said.

"He was, but of course something came up at LCS."

"I don't want to talk about James. Kevin, I have got to tell you about the new guy I met. He is so fine," Tony interjected.

"What happened to the guy that you met at our party? What was his name? Levi?"

"That's old news," Daryl said. "You know how quickly he goes through men."

"Don't hate, Daryl. It's not a pretty thing. Anyway, Levi and I just didn't work. He was lousy in bed and boring as hell." With a devilish grin, Tony held up the pinky finger on his right hand and wiggled it back and forth. "You know what I mean?" he said, laughing.

"Lower your voice," I said. I looked around and the woman next to me shook her head. She let out an audible sigh as we continued to talk.

"Anyway, I went out to the club last Thursday and met this fine brotha from Philly. He's down here doing some kind of internship at NASA. He is da bomb! I want you to meet him. You always tell me how naïve I am, and I really like him. I want you to tell me what you think of him."

"What's his name?"

"Dexter."

"Dexter?" I repeated.

"It just rolls off the tongue, doesn't it?"

"I bet it does more than just roll off your tongue," Daryl said comically.

Tony looked at him and gave him a slight push in the arm. The theater lights dimmed and a heavy voice announced the beginning of the show. Slowly, the curtain began to open. Danea's powerful voice started with the words to "Proud Mary." Suddenly, she and three other girls dressed in long flowing wigs and small shimmering red dresses burst onto stage.

Danea sang. I mean she really blew, and for the opening act, the crowd rose to its feet and clapped in rhythm to the song. Danea electrified the room. Tony lost control and started singing loudly along with her. The show lasted about two and a half hours, with a brief intermission. It was spectacular. At the end, Danea received a standing ovation.

At the end of the show, we all met in the lobby of the theater so that the actors and performers would have an opportunity to meet and greet their fans. People swarmed around Danea like bees to honey. Still, she managed to make time for us and we got a few good photographs. She had changed her wardrobe several times throughout the course of the show, and she still wore the last dress, a strapless royal blue gown in which she sang Aretha's "Bridge Over Troubled Waters."

We stood there, laughing and enjoying the moment,

when Tony decided we needed one more picture with Danea next to her life-sized cardboard cutout used as advertisement for the show. Daryl moved close to me and we put our arms around each other for a group picture. One of her cast mates took the photo. Daryl and I held our embrace for a few minutes after the picture. His grasp was warm and protective. Just as Daryl and I released our embrace, Tony nodded his head and told me to look behind me. I turned. There was James, standing silently. He needed no words. His feelings were all over his face. He moved toward us.

"What is this? Don't you all look so happy?" he said between clenched lips. I was so embarrassed. All of my friends had gotten quiet, waiting for my reaction.

"Well, hello, James. I hope you enjoyed the performance," Danea said dryly. I wasn't sure how long he'd been there, or even if he'd seen the show.

"I thought you were busy, baby. I guess everything worked itself out?" I said.

"No, I worked it out just like I always do. I got finished a little early and I thought I'd surprise you. I guess the surprise is on me."

"What does that mean?"

"That means I think you should come home...now."

"He can't come home right now. We're all going out to eat," Danea said. Her defense mechanisms were beginning to activate and at any moment this minor confrontation with James could turn into a major brawl.

"Are you going out to eat, Kevin, or are you coming home with me?" he asked calmly, like the air before a storm. The pressure was on me to make a decision. I didn't want to let my friends down, but I didn't want to have to go home and endure another knockdown, drag-out fight. The way he presented me the options left little room for negotiation. My friends were all looking at me to speak. I knew what I wanted to say, but when the words came out, they were all wrong. I tried to pretend as if I wanted to go home with James like we were the happy couple.

"Sorry guys, but let me spend some time with my man tonight. Danea, you know you were fantastic! I want a copy of the performance." I was trying to slink out of the room with some dignity, but it wasn't working.

"Kevin, I thought we were going out to celebrate," Danea said. "You can't leave now." I raised my eyebrows as if to say *sorry*, and I followed James out of the building, tail between my legs. I could feel their stares, but I didn't turn around to acknowledge them.

CHAPTER 10

James tailgated me all the way home. As soon as we walked in, it started. First, the yelling. I tried to ignore it. It got louder, and when he realized that I wasn't listening to his jealous tirade, he picked up a rather expensive crystal vase and hurled it against the wall near me. Had I not seen it coming, I was convinced that it would have hit me. He demanded my attention, and damn it, he'd have it. I picked up the nearest item I could find, which happened to be a brass candlestick, and threw it at him. He managed to dodge the flying object.

"Don't you get tired of this shit!?" I screamed.

"I'm tired of yo' bitch ass disrespecting me! I get to the fuckin' theater and what do I see? I see you all hugged up on the nigga Daryl. What the fuck am I suppose to think?"

"We were taking a fuckin' picture. That's it. Did you see me do anything else?"

"I saw enough."

"This is such a waste of time." I turned and moved toward the stairs. All I wanted was a nice warm bath.

"Don't walk out on me!"

"This conversation is over." I didn't even look back as I made my way up the stairs. I expected him to grab me, and to pull me from the stairs, but he didn't. When I reached the bedroom, I exhaled. I was so tired of being afraid. I immediately went into the restroom and started the water for my bath. I lit a couple of candles, and poured some bath oil into the tub and watched the water flow as I undressed. Slowly, I lowered myself into the tub, and sat back. I closed my eyes and listened to the water and tried to relax. The warm water and the sweet smell helped to ease my embarrassment. I couldn't imagine what they must have been thinking as I slid out of the theater. I knew Danea would be calling me at some point that night or early in the morning. That was her style, but I didn't know what to say to her.

As I took a deep breath, I felt a hand around my throat that pushed me down into the tub. The water covered my face and entered my mouth and nose. James was upon me so quickly that I didn't have a chance to respond. He pinned me to the bottom of the tub, and I struggled to break free. My legs flapped and flopped and water splashed all over the room. I tried to break free, but he continued to hold me down. He jerked me up suddenly, just long enough for me to spit up water and to gasp a couple of deep breaths, and then he forced me back down. I reached at his arms, trying to tear flesh from his bones, but he did not move, nor did he lessen his grip. I managed to grab one marble candleholder and I swung wildly, landing a blow on his forehead. He fell backwards. I jumped up out of the tub and fell to the floor, gasping for air and coughing the water out of my lungs. Naked, and wet, I lay on the floor and looked at James, who was bleeding from his eye. I moved toward him and we fought again. I hit him in the eye with my fist, knowing that in my weakened state he'd beat the shit out of me. We rolled on the floor like a couple of wrestlers. He pounded on me. I pounded on him, and in the meantime, we tore the bathroom apart. He pulled me to my feet, and I felt a slap across my cheek that knocked me onto the sink. When my body hit the floor, he climbed on top of me. His eyes turned black. He opened his mouth and spit in my face. I wanted to kill him. He looked at me and we saw exhaustion in each other's eyes. He climbed off me and made his way over to the medicine cabinet. He applied something to his eye and moved into the bedroom.

I stayed in the bathroom for a while and finally gained enough strength to put on a robe to go downstairs to have a drink. As I passed him in the bedroom, he held a bloodstained washcloth to his eye, and we did not speak in passing. I shook my head at the lunacy of my life. It was almost comedic. Finally, I went upstairs and found James in the bathroom cleaning his wound. The expression on his face begged for my help, but I knew he would never speak those words. I took the towel from him and finished dressing his cut. I climbed into bed first, and he turned off the lights and cuddled with me. I didn't understand how at one moment we could be fighting like cats and dogs, and the next moment we lay in each other's arms.

✖✖✖

After tossing and turning all night, I looked at the clock, and lay my head back down on the pillow at 3:10 a.m. I had spent the past couple of hours trying to find a way to convince myself that it was time to leave this relationship. When I couldn't find a compelling reason, I got up out of bed and walked downstairs, hoping that a glass of warm milk would help me get some rest. As I got to the kitchen, I decided I needed something stronger than milk, so I opted for a glass of straight whiskey. I poured the drink in a tall glass, walked into the den, and turned on the television. Between the early morning infomercials, the old black-and-white comedies, and the network news shows, nothing caught my attention until I ran into an episode of *Jerry Springer*. I put the remote control down and started watching the show titled "I've got a secret to reveal." I watched with casual curiosity as the guest revealed to her boyfriend that *she* was really a *he*. Chaos like only an episode of *Jerry* could bring took control and a fight ensued between the two. People ran from backstage to join in the fight. Fists flew. Kicks were thrown. The drag queen took off her high-heeled shoe and threw it like a missile at her former boyfriend. Between the beeps, it was hard to figure out the exact obscenities that were being used. The crew attempted to get them under control. The crowd rose to their feet and shouted "Jerry, Jerry, Jerry…" I guess there are people worse off than me, or at least just as bad, I thought. The madness of this episode made me laugh because there is no way you couldn't tell that *she* was a *he*; there's no way a man can have sex with a man and not know it's a man. I finished my drink and went back upstairs to bed. When I entered the room, I gasped as I saw my brother, my dead twin brother, standing near the bathroom.

"*I came back*," he said slowly. His appearance was gruesome, his face and body badly swollen and decomposed just like when I found him dead. I stood there, with wide eyes, and watched him for a second. I wanted to reach out to him, to touch him, but when

I moved closer, he disappeared, and I woke up in the bed, the sheets soaked with my sweat. I reached out for James, but he wasn't there. I looked at the clock: 5:28 a.m. I looked closer through the dark and saw the outline of a figure sitting alone in a corner. Keevan? No, it wasn't Keevan.

"James, what are you doing?" There was no answer. Maybe he didn't hear me. Maybe he had fallen asleep in the chair. I got out of bed and walked toward him. I could see the whites of his eyes. I called his name again. When I got closer I could see he was in another place, far away; his face was sullen and his eyes hung low. It looked as if he had been crying. Surely, that wasn't the case. Was he capable of tears?

"What's wrong, James?" He shook his head as if to shake off his trance, realizing that I was next to him.

"What? Hey, baby."

"Why are you sitting in the dark?"

"I couldn't sleep. Why are you awake?"

"I couldn't sleep either. I reached out for you and you weren't there." He stared into the darkness blankly, his eyes unfocused. I'd never seen him so distracted. "You want to tell me what's wrong?"

"Everything's okay. I just had some thinking to do. I needed to clear my head." He grabbed my hand and drew me closer into him. "I was watching you sleep for awhile. You looked so peaceful."

"You were watching me sleep?" I wondered how I could have possibly looked peaceful with that dream about Keevan.

"I love you, Kevin. I really do. I know it's hard for you to see it, but I love you more than anything in the world. You believe me, don't you?"

I was at a loss for words. "Of course I believe you." In his own distorted view of things, maybe this was love for him.

"I can't lose you, Kevin. You are all that I have left."

"What does that mean?"

"It just means you're my world. Do you love me?"

I wasn't sure where all of this emotion was coming from, and I didn't know what he was looking for me to say. "James..."

"I know. Don't say it. Just tell me what I need to do to make you love me like you used to. What do you need? I'll do anything. I'll buy you everything."

"Love is not something you can put a price on, James. Money can't make anyone love you."

"Then tell me what you need. I feel as if I'm losing you. I can't let that happen. Do you hear me? I won't lose you." At least he had taken notice of the vast distance between us. At least he realized that we were in very different places.

"James, what do you want from me?" I asked. He slowly lowered his head as if it suddenly became too heavy to be held up by his neck. He looked at me several times, his eyes unsure of where to look next. "Tell me. What do you really want?"

"I don't know."

"You don't know? I've given up so much to make you happy." He leaned deeper into the chair. "What do you want?" I asked.

"I want to take care of you the way no one ever did for me. I don't know how, though. I want you to *need* me. I want you to *love* me. I feel as if I don't matter to you. No matter what I do for you, it's as if it doesn't matter."

"Instead of loving me, you try to buy and possess me. And when you don't get your way exactly, well, we both know how it usually ends up." He took a deep breath and continued to stare. This was the first real moment we'd shared probably in our entire relationship. I felt as if now was the time to save myself, to free my mind from his grasp, and to let him know that things would change. Right now, he was vulnerable. He opened up to me and for the first time I could see his spirit, or at least a part of it.

Before I could answer, he began to speak again. "I had another impression. Like the one I had when I met you."

"What did you see?"

"I saw empty space and darkness. It was all around

me. I felt as if I was being suffocated. It was everywhere. Do you know how that feels?"

"More than you realize. What does it mean?"

"It means that you'll leave me." He got up and moved toward the bed, leaving me in the corner to ponder his cryptic vision. I watched him climb in and pull the covers over his head. Whatever demons haunted him made him curl up in the fetal position. I thought about him and what struggles he must go through. Then, I thought about the hell he put me through. My sympathies for him were running low.

CHAPTER 11

'd been secretly meeting Croix over the course of the past few weeks. We spent most of our time talking, and working out at Bally's at Fondren and Bellfort. He had a wonderful spirit. When we were together, I felt so free. He was one of the few people who knew the person that I had become since my brother's death. He knew my secrets, and he understood my pain and what I was going through. He had lost his brother when they were children and he said that not a day went by that he didn't think about him. I didn't have a problem sharing the intimate details of my personal life—either. He shared with me many secrets about his relationship with his wife. We found in each other the strength to press on and to improve our lives. It felt as if we connected on a deep and spiritual plane; we had a deep friendship. Nothing sexual had ever occurred between us, not even in the hotel in Galveston. We did share a few kisses back then, but that was it. In our hearts and minds we were probably having an affair, but I guess people are free to think what they want as long as they don't act on it. I only knew that each time we saw each other, we

grew closer. For me, there was power in his friendship.

His struggles to remain faithful to his wife in spite
of his feelings were tearing him apart. He told me
that about a year ago they started having serious
problems and he found out she was having an affair.
He wanted to divorce her then, but he stayed for the
sake of the children. He was raised with the idea that
marriage was permanent. His parents stayed together
for twenty-seven years, for better or for worse, in
sickness and in health. He and his siblings sensed
trouble, but never really said anything. It was only
after the kids were grown that his parents split. But
Croix was realizing that he and his wife were not his
parents.

It was about noon on Saturday, and I was expecting
his phone call. James was out of town, again; something was going wrong in Austin. I had overheard a
brief conversation he had with his attorney, and it
sounded like trouble since they were working on the
weekend.

Croix and I were trying to figure out what we
could do or where we would go in the afternoon, so
we decided to meet in Memorial Park to go jogging.
When I got there, he was standing near the jogging
trail, in a pair of black shorts that showed off his muscular legs. The sunlight was shining off his smooth

skin; he seemed to be glowing. When he saw me, he waved and continued his warm-up.

"Are you ready for this?" he asked as I approached.

"I don't know if I'm awake yet. I couldn't sleep last night."

"More bad dreams?"

"Not really, I just had an uneasy feeling."

"Well, don't think that I'm letting you get out of this. We have five miles to run, so you'd better get ready."

"Don't worry about me. I can still take you."

"Oh, is that a challenge?"

"You a betting man?"

"What's the bet?"

"The loser has to buy lunch…and dinner."

"You're on." I dropped to the ground so that I could warm up. My competitive edge was starting to take over, and I could feel the adrenaline starting to pump. After about ten minutes of stretching, the race began. For a while, we were running neck and neck, often talking and laughing. Toward the last mile, I could see him beginning to slow, but he wouldn't let me get too far ahead of him. As we approached the finish line, I had clearly won the race. I threw up my hands in victory as he bent down to catch his breath.

"Did I mention I used to run track in college?" I asked.

"You are such a cheater."

"How is that cheating?"

"You had an unfair edge," he said between pants.

"You never asked. It wasn't unfair. For all I knew, you could have run a couple of marathons. I think you're trying to get out of buying lunch."

"No, I'm a man of my word, and I'm a fair loser. I'll buy you lunch, but one day we'll have to do this again." I smiled and we started laughing. That was one of the best runs I'd had in a while. He took off his shirt and I watched the sweat glisten on his solid frame. My mind raced over a multitude of explicit images and I smiled. He caught me looking at him and smiled back. He looked like a firm Georgia peach just ready for the plucking. *I'd like to pluck him*, I thought to myself. We both acknowledged our mutual thoughts with a simple glance. I knew he was thinking the same thing about me. *I guess I'll see you next lifetime.* I didn't know what I wanted from him beyond friendship. Maybe just an ear to listen...maybe more.

After lunch and a very stimulating conversation about life, love, and laughter, I returned home and checked the messages. Danea called to tell me about how well all of her shows had gone and she said she had caught "the bug," whatever that meant. She also went on to tell me that she'd be there for me if I needed her, and that I could talk to her about anything. I was touched by her concern. The next message was from

Tony telling me about the new love of his life, but knowing Tony, his new love would last only two weeks.

I stood in the middle of the den and became suddenly overwhelmed with the house. Looking out across the room and through the walls, I felt out of place. Why was I here? Nothing in this house was mine. Everything, from the furniture to wallpaper to the carpet on the floor was James.' Sometimes I felt like an ornament—James' crown jewel. All of the things in this house belonged to him the same way he thought I belonged to him. I heard a comedian once say that if you're living with someone and your name is not on any of the bills, then you're homeless. *Homeless. What a strange word.* At any moment he could walk into this house and tell me that I had to leave. Where would I go? It's time I started thinking about my future. I needed a job. Croix urged me several times to start the process so I soon could be in a position to take care of myself. He gave me the kind of straightforward advice that I needed. He wasn't judgmental, but he offered a lot of support and advice. Not that he said anything that I didn't already know, but hearing it from someone else sometimes validates things. Secretly, I'd been sending out a few resumes here and there using Danea's phone number as my contact number. I couldn't have people calling James' house trying to set up interviews. All I could do now was wait. The thought of working and having that challenge in my life gave me the chance to think about my future for the first time in what seemed like many years. I did have a future, and it could be as bright as I allowed it to be.

When the phone rang, I moved over to pick it up. "Hello?"

"Kevin, it's RaChelle. How are you?"

"What's going on, RaChelle?"

"I was calling to see if you would be interested in going with me to a party this evening. I know it's short notice, but I don't want to go by myself. What do you say?"

"If you had called earlier, I probably would have gone, but now I have plans."

"Can't you break them for me? Come on. It'll be fun. I'll make it worth your while." I didn't have any plans, but I just didn't feel like being bothered with her. I have learned that I have to be in the right mood to deal with her. She seemed to always have one thing on her mind—*me*. By now, I thought she would have gotten the hint that I didn't want her. I think she saw me as a challenge. A woman as fine as she could have any man she wanted, so I was sure she must have been wondering why she didn't have me yet. Maybe I was her personal challenge. She could be really sweet, and sometimes I did enjoy our conversations. That day, I just wasn't feelin' her.

"No, I'm sorry. I can't, but maybe we could do something later on in the week."

"I guess I'll have to take no this time, but I *will* take you up on your offer. Don't forget."

CHAPTER 12

I went downstairs and saw James slumped over his desk as if he was in a football huddle. He was a man driven by ambition and consumed by passion. I just wanted to check on him to make sure everything was okay. I went over to him and placed my hands on his tense shoulders and began to massage his neck. He moaned slightly and allowed himself to feel the magic of my fingers. After a few moments, he told me that he really had a lot of work to do. That was my hint to leave him alone. It was a Sunday afternoon, and usually he'd be busy with work. I don't even know why I felt compelled to check on him—maybe because I began to feel lonely sitting upstairs by myself.

When I got back upstairs, the machine was recording a message. I hadn't even heard the phone, but I listened to the last few sentences from the woman's voice. It was Danea. At the end of the call, I rewound the message and played it in its entirety. Just wanted me to give her a call. I called her right back and she told me that someone had called about a job offer. Quickly, I scribbled down the information on a notepad. I wasn't sure how to react. This is what I wanted, that much I knew. How would I tell James? I thought about it for a few seconds, and realized that James was not going to stop me from working. Finally, I had gotten a job!

I had secretly been on a couple of interviews at Croix's urging, and in the end all it took was a simple phone call. I'd interned during college and in graduate school at Hammond Diversified Services in the accounting department. I called my old manager who had been promoted to human resources director. It just so happened there was a position they had been trying to fill for the last few weeks. I went in for a couple of short and simple interviews, and she told me that everything looked good. She left the message on Danea's machine and offered me the position as new accounts manager and gave me the number to call her at home. I was surprised it had happened so soon. I dialed her number on the bedroom phone, and when she answered, her enthusiastic response made me miss the good times I had working with her. The salary she offered me was more than I had expected, in the mid-60s. I was so excited I let out a big laugh in the house and did the butterfly right where I stood. She wanted me to start on Monday, but I begged her to let me start the following Monday. I had to have time to prepare for this. Now, it was my time to shine.

Before I had time to really process the information, the phone rang. It was RaChelle. She heard the joy in my voice and I finally told her about my job offer. I was careful to whisper so that James would not hear me, but the spark in my voice amplified my words. RaChelle insisted on taking me to lunch to celebrate. I've never been one to turn down a free meal, even if the company was not exactly what I had in mind. Besides, I'd been promising her that we'd do something together for so long that at this point I didn't feel like trying to get out of it. I got dressed and told James that I was leaving. He quickly waved me away, and didn't look up.

✳✳✳

We met in a cozy little French café in downtown Houston at 3:30 p.m. When I got there, she was at the corner table, sipping on a glass of Chardonnay. As soon as I walked in her face gave way to a nice smile as she waved to get my attention. I sat down and gave her a little peck on the cheek. Her mouth reflected a bigger smile. After a few minutes of sitting, our waitress, who was a thin woman with big eyes and a small face, greeted us. Her hair was wrapped in a colorful scarf that matched the tight orange apron around her waist. When she took our order, she spoke with a petite accent that made me think of the islands.

"You've been smiling since the moment you walked in," RaChelle said. "I hope that has something to do with me."

"It has everything to do with you." I must admit I lied, or at least I told her what she wanted to hear. I wasn't sure whether or not flirtatious comments were considered lies. The waitress returned with two glasses of Chardonnay and RaChelle quickly raised her new glass for a toast.

"Here's to a promising future."

"I agree." I wondered whose future she was toasting. Mine, or ours? We ate a light lunch and mostly talked about her, but I didn't mind. Less pressure that way.

I pretended not to notice her veiled looks at the waiter who walked up to help the two women at the table to my right. I must admit, he was *fine*. Did she see my hidden looks as well? At one point, I thought she was going to ask for his number, but instead she stopped him and asked him to get our waitress. For a second, a brief second, a flash of attraction for her raced across my spirit. Just for a second, I thought I was attracted to her like a man is usually attracted to a gorgeous woman. An image of her naked body passed through my mind, but it wasn't a lasting impression.

CHAPTER 13

The phone rang. In the middle of the night, the last thing that I wanted to hear was the sound of the phone. It rang at least two more times before I forced my eyes to open. I looked at the clock: 2:18 a.m. James rolled over, reached out his arm and picked it up. He passed me the phone reluctantly, and then rolled over onto his side so that he was facing me.

"Hello?"

"Kevin?"

"Who is this?"

"It's me. Tony," he said in a whispered tone. "I need help. I need you to come and get me. Please, I don't know who else to call."

"What's wrong?"

"I'll tell you when you get here. Please hurry. I don't know what to do." I sat up in the bed.

"Where are you?"

"I don't know exactly. I'm in 3rd Ward somewhere. On the corner of...I don't know."

"What are you near?" I heard him put the phone down for a second. When he came back he told me he was at a gas station at Elgin and Sampson—which was not in a good neighborhood. "Okay, stay put and I'll be right there."

"Please hurry," he said with all due urgency and then I heard a dial tone. I jumped out of bed and grabbed a pair of sweats and an old sweatshirt.

"Where the hell do you think you are going?" James moaned.

"I have to go get Tony. He's stranded. I don't know what happened."

"Oh, you're playing hero now, huh?" I ignored his comment and continued pulling the blue sweatshirt over my head. I looked in the closet for a pair of shoes, and I ended up with my new pair of Jordans. "Get back in the bed."

"Don't give me a hard time about this. *I have to go*. Tony is stranded in 3rd ward. I can't leave him in the middle of nowhere. If you want to go with me, that's fine, but I won't just leave him by himself."

"Why can't he call someone else? I'm sure Danea is at home. She ain't got no life."

"James..."

"Are you meeting some nigga?" That was the last thing on my mind.

"I don't have time for this. If you want to come with me, then come on."

"You know I have that important meeting in the morning. I don't have time for Tony and his problems."

"Then don't give me a hard time about this."

"You can go, but if I find out that you…"

Before he could finish his sentence, I said, "I'll be back as soon as I can. Bye."

I was out the door, and driving down the highway like a bat out of hell. I blazed through every flashing red light, and every stop sign. I just knew I was going to be pulled over and hauled off to jail. As fast as I drove, it didn't seem like I could get there fast enough. A million thoughts raced through my head, none of them pleasant. As I got deeper into the ward, houses looked more deteriorated, the conditions of the roads worsened, and the buildings looked crumbled. Frantically, I pulled into the gas station, which was closed, and Tony emerged from the shadows. Quickly, he jumped into the car and locked the door.

"Let's get out of here." I pulled into the street and drove away from the station, looking in the rearview mirror to see if anyone was behind us. He sank low into the seat, making it hard to distinguish flesh from leather.

"What's going on?" At first, he didn't speak. I could see him struggling to find words. He sat there and rubbed his face with his hands. I thought I saw a tear forming in the corner of his eye.

"It has been a long night. I can't believe this happened. I can't believe that nigga."

"What happened?"

"I don't know where to begin."

"How about the beginning?" He took a deep breath and a few seconds to gather his thoughts. I anxiously awaited his explanation. Tony was always involved in some situation, but I could tell this was far more serious than even he was used to.

"You remember that guy I was telling you about, Dexter? He picked me up and we went to the club. First we went to Rascal's and then to Nick's. When we got to Rascal's, there weren't a whole lot of people, but it got crowded later. Daryl was there, and when I saw him, he and I talked for a while, and then Dexter and I started dancing. After a few drinks, he wanted to leave. He seemed like he needed to talk. He wanted to take a drive so I said okay. I told Daryl I'd be back in a minute. We ended up stopping and parking in this parking lot at Texas Southern. I thought he wanted to talk, but he had something else on his mind. He wanted a piece of ass. Right there in the parking lot. He and I have not even come close to having sex before, and even if I wanted to have sex at that point, he didn't have a condom. He finally backed off after I insisted and we started talking again. Then something strange happened. He started kissing my neck and then I felt his hand rubbing my thighs. It wasn't a caress, but more of a squeezing. I thought I felt his hands trying to go into my pocket, but I wasn't sure. Can you believe this nigga wanted me to give him money? No, he wanted to *take* my money, not that I had any. He got pissed off and told me to get out. I said no. We started fighting and he pushed me out of the truck. Then the muthafucka drove off. Just like that. He left me here, in the middle of nowhere, with no money, and no place to go. That's when I called you. You don't know how mad I am. I could kill him."

"That's some shit."

"I thought he was such a cool brotha."

"You just never know someone."

"Why can't I find love? All I want is what you and James have. You two are so perfect." His words brought forth the realization that my entire existence was based on a lie. I became angry. Not toward Tony, and not even at James, but at me.

"You *really* don't want what we have."

"Yes, I do. You guys have been together for a long time. You have to admit that sometimes it's hard for gay relationships to last more than a night. You've been with him for over a year."

"I know it's hard to find love, but you can't see love through someone else's eyes, or define it by someone else's standards. You don't know what goes on behind the scenes. Just be patient, and your time will come."

"What do you mean, behind the scenes?"

"Just 'cause we've been together doesn't mean either one of us is happy. You have no idea of the shit I go through with him." I looked at Tony, who stared at me in disbelief. His eyes were wide and his mouth hung low. "You don't understand what a son of a bitch he can be. Sometimes he makes me wish he was dead. Sometimes, I could kill him."

"What? What are you talking about? I thought you were happy. I thought you were the perfect couple. Don't tell me this. I don't want to hear anymore. You're destroying my ideals." He put his hands over his ears as if that would shield him from the truth of my world.

"You know there is no such thing as a perfect couple."

"You were my hope, my incentive to keep trying and looking. I think all of the hope I had of a meaningful relationship just died." Granted, he was being a bit melodramatic, but after what he'd been through that night, I thought I'd give him some latitude.

"Please don't base your dreams on me and James. What about LaMont? How is he doing?"

"Don't bring him up. He is a walking contradiction. I had to let him go."

"Sometimes you gotta do what you gotta do."

He looked at me with sullen eyes, the light of hope clearly dimming. "Kevin, I didn't know."

"Didn't know what? That I hate James at times? That we're not, nor have we been, the perfect couple? It's all bullshit. Our relationship is bullshit."

"If you hate him so much, then why don't you leave?"

"It's not that simple."

"Why isn't it?"

"Because."

"Because what?"

"Just because." I got quiet and focused my energy on the road that lay ahead. I knew Tony wanted to know more, but I'd said too much already. "I really don't want to talk about it." I reached down and turned up the volume on the radio. The sultry sounds of Erykah Badu singing "Tyrone" filled the space in the car. "I'm getting tired of yo shit…" *She didn't know the half of it*, I thought. Tony reached down and turned the radio off.

"I think you really need to talk about what is going on. You have been really distant and closed since…" He paused.

"Since what? Since Keevan died? Is that what you were gonna say?"

"As a matter of fact, yes. Over the last year you've really changed. Holding all this shit in can't be good for you."

"What do you want me to say? What could possibly change by me sitting here and whining like a baby? Talking ain't about shit."

"You don't even sound like you used to. I know you miss Keevan, but…"

"Can you please give it a rest? This conversation is not about me. This night is not about me. This is about you chasing every nigga you see. All this comes from some need you have to feel good about yourself, only you can't feel good about who you are unless you hear it from some nigga, who in the end just wants to *fuck* you. Don't sit there and analyze me. I'm not the one who left the club with some muthafucka I barely knew and ended up stranded by the road." *Wow!* The venom of my words scared me. Words can be the most powerful and underestimated weapons. Funny thing about words: Once they're out, you can't take 'em back.

"I guess you think you're doing much better? Look at you. We all see through your fuckin' shit. Walking around like you own the world and that you have the world at your fingers. You're really too much of a punk to face the world. The world ain't in that big house with the pool and the fancy cars that you *didn't* buy. The world is what goes on while you're shopping at Neiman Marcus. The world is what we go through every day, but you don't remember that world. Don't tell me how to live."

"Fuck you!"

"Fuck you!" My foot pressed harder and harder on the accelerator. I was blinded by anger and all I could see was red. Keevan flashed before my eyes. *The body on the floor. The smell. It was all coming back to me. James. The fights. The humiliation.* I felt dizzy and before I knew it Tony jerked the wheel to keep me from rear-ending the car in front of us. My mind had been so distracted in that instant that I didn't see the red lights ahead of me. We spun across the highway and ended up on the shoulder of the road.

"What the fuck is your problem? Get out of the goddamned car!" He threw open his door and marched across to the driver's side. Without another word, he got behind the wheel of the car and drove to his apartment.

Once inside, he poured two tall glasses of gin, which we drank quickly and without conversation. When he poured the second round, I felt it was time for an explanation.

"I'm sorry, for what I said in the car about you. I was way out of line," I said. I rested my head on the back of the sofa.

"You damned right that you were out of line. But that doesn't mean you were wrong. Shit, I don't know why I act like this. Why do I feel as if I always have to have a man? What the hell is my problem? Sometimes when I'm alone in this apartment at night, the TV's on, or the radio is playing, I really feel as if I'm the only person in the world. I feel so alone. I don't like being alone. It's like the walls are closing in on me. Hell, I must be crazy."

"Nah, you're not crazy. The world is crazy and we all have to be a little bit crazy to survive in it."

"I've always been like this. Always needing to be

the center of attention. Always needing to feel love from some man. Maybe it's some childhood sickness that I never got over."

"Don't go blaming your childhood for something you can control now. Now is now. And how we deal with now is up to us. Some of us do well, and others, like me, don't."

"Dexter really scared me tonight. I didn't know if he was gonna rape me or just rob me. I didn't know what he would do to me. Look at my shirt, it's all ripped up." The jaded look in his eyes revealed a deeper fear than I'd ever seen. *Right now, this moment, is real. No pretense. No judgments. Just emotion.* "Thank you for coming to get me," he said.

"Don't worry about the shirt. I'll buy you another one," I said with a wink. "You wanna know the truth about me and James? We've never been happy or even in love. He doesn't know what love is and he doesn't have time to figure it out. Between his business and our fights, there's not much room for anything else. The fights started early in the relationship, when I was too weak to fight back. Now, I'm too weak to leave. It started with a slap that I dismissed as an impulse. Then it was a kick. Then a punch, and a combination of them. Next thing I was fighting for my life. We fight like street thugs. I'm not small or weak. I'm pretty strong, but he's much bigger and stronger. Sometimes we'd fight all day and make love all night. Sometimes, when I didn't feel like making love, he'd force it."

"What are you saying? You were raped?" Somehow that word didn't seem entirely accurate, but it seemed to be the most appropriate word he could find. His voice was agitated.

"I'm saying that if James wanted sex, we'd have sex. Period."

"Why? Why live like that? You don't have to. You're educated, and have a strong support group of friends who could help you. Why put up with it? You don't have to live like that."

"Yes…I do."

"What does that mean?"

"It just means life has a way of changing on you right when you're looking at it."

"Stop talking in riddles. What's really going on with you? You tried to kill us tonight."

"When I was driving, I just started thinking about Keevan and James and my life. I wasn't trying to kill us. I got distracted."

"Your distraction could have been the end of us."

I looked down at my watch. It was almost 6 a.m. James would be leaving for the office soon.

"I need to go home before James goes to work."

"What? I'm not letting you go back to that place. Not with him. You can stay here with me."

"This is not my home."

"Neither is that house on the hill. I won't let you go back."

"Tony, it's not your choice."

"Think about it. You have no reason to go back to him. Haven't you read about domestic abuse?"

"I'm not some helpless female getting her ass kicked by her man. I know what I'm doing, and right now I need to go home. I know one day I will leave him, but now is not the right time. I'm not ready."

"Not ready? Aren't you tired of getting your ass kicked? What, you need another black eye? How about a broken nose?" His words stung. "I have your keys. I'm not letting you go."

"You can't keep me here."

"I'm not letting you go back there so you can end up dead."

"Don't be so fucking dramatic. I'm not dying anytime soon. Now give me my keys." I held out my hand.

"Don't be stupid, Kevin. Use your head."

I raised my eyebrow and took a step back; I had never seen him so resolute. He was not budging, nor was he giving me my keys. I sat down. I didn't feel like fighting or arguing. This night had taken a lot out of me. I laid my head back on the sofa, kicked off my shoes, and fell asleep.

CHAPTER 14

When I finally woke up, it was well into the morning. Startled, I sprang up from the couch and went to look for Tony in his bedroom. The door was cracked open a bit, and I could hear the sound of water running in the shower. Underneath the sounds of the water, I could hear Tony singing a tune that I couldn't recognize. Then, the phone rang. I pushed open the door to the room and went over to his night table.

"Hello?"

"Kevin?"

"Daryl? 'Sup, man?"

"I was trying to figure out what happened to Tony last night. He disappeared and I've been paging and calling him all night. What's going on?"

"Nothing, everything is fine."

"What are you doing over there?"

"Oh, I just dropped by. I didn't have anything else to do." Without going into details, I convinced Daryl that everything was okay. He said that I sounded as if something was wrong. *After all of the lies I had told since I'd been with James, I thought I was better at story-*

telling. We decided that we'd get together that evening for dinner. He said he'd call Danea to see if she could come, but I knew she'd probably be busy with the show or on a date.

When I got home, the house was empty. James was at work and I had the place to myself. He had left a note by the phone demanding that I call him at work, writing the word *urgent* at the bottom of the page as if that would make me more inclined to call. I walked into the kitchen to check the Caller ID to see if anyone had called. I then walked upstairs and took off all my clothing and got into the Jacuzzi in the master bathroom. The heat of the water relaxed me.

While lounging in the water, the phone rang. I debated on whether or not I should answer it. It kept ringing. Finally, I reached over and picked it up, thinking it might be Tony or Daryl calling.

"Hello?"

"James, please."

"He's not here."

"Is this Kevin?"

"Yes, who is this?"

"This is Carl. How are you?"

"I'm fine, as always. James is at work if you need him." He knew that I knew that he knew that James would be at work at this hour. There was no reason at all for him to call the house.

"Oh really? I thought he may have come home for

a few minutes for lunch. I guess I'll just have to call him later. But since you're on the phone, why don't we talk?"

"We don't have anything to talk about."

"I've been thinking about you. I know that you and James are having problems. I could see it in your eyes. You need a man you can depend on, someone who will treat you right."

"Let me guess, that person is you, right?"

"You know I can make you feel like you're the only man in the world. Just like that night. I loved being with you."

"Is that the same shit you tell your wife after you fuck her? Or does she strap one on and do you?"

"I'm going to pretend like you didn't just say that to me."

"I'm sure James would love to know we had this conversation."

"You going to tell him? I'll just deny it."

"Why don't you give my best to the wife and kids? Or maybe I should call her and tell her myself. How does that sound to you?" There was a heavy silence on the other end of the phone. I could hear him trembling.

"I can't believe you would say some shit like that to me. I thought we were better than that. How about we just forget this entire conversation?"

"Better still, I'll just forget you." I hung up the phone

and hoped the sound of the dial tone rang loudly in his ear. I lay back in the Jacuzzi and laughed. I'd been waiting for the moment when I could tell him off. It was a wonderful experience.

My victory was interrupted by the sound of the doorbell ringing. I got out of the water, threw on a robe, and went downstairs to answer the door. It was Tony.

"What are you doing here?"

"After thinking about last night, I just didn't feel like being alone. I figured you could use some company, too." He walked into the house before I had a chance to respond, and made himself at home. "I guess James is at work?"

"Yeah, he's not here. Is that why you came over? To check on me?"

"That's part of it. You didn't come home last night so I thought he might be upset. I was hoping to prevent a fight between you two."

"I appreciate your concern, but I can take care of myself." I walked over to the bar and started making a drink. "You want a drink?" Before he could answer, I grabbed two glasses and filled them with ice. I grabbed the flask of rum, a can of Coke, and mixed the drinks.

"How are you feeling about what we talked about? About leaving James?" he asked.

"I don't know. I guess I don't care either way."

"What do you mean, you don't care? Do you hear yourself? Stop talking like that. We've lost Keevan. We ain't losing you." I always knew he loved me, but we never really told each other that. "What the hell is the problem? For once, tell me the truth."

"Whose truth? The truth changes with the story-teller."

"Stop all the shit and be honest. Fuck the games and the lies. I'm not James."

I took a seat on the couch and gave him his drink. I was tired. Tired of the deceptions and the secrets, tired of lies and games. It was a full-time job trying to hide the bruises and coming up with new lies to avoid the truth. It took more energy than I had left.

"You want honesty? That's what you'll get. I want you to know this is not easy for me to tell you. I vowed a long time ago to never tell anyone. I didn't want to deal with the looks of pity and disappointment."

"Bruh, don't worry about that." He leaned back against the sofa and waited patiently for my words to come. My eyes nervously danced back and forth to avoid his gaze, but I soon felt a calm overcome me. I'd make my stand right here, right now. I sat motion-less as my life played back in my head, and all of the pain that I thought I'd buried came back to me in hurtful flashes. I took a few gulps from my glass to loosen up my throat. I couldn't remember in detail all of the times that I had suffered when James lost control and snapped, nor could I recall all the humiliations he'd put me through over the last year. It was hard trying to find a place to start, and even more horrific to relive my darkest days. When I began to speak the words flowed from my tongue. A single tear paraded its way down my cheek like a slow-moving funeral procession.

I told Tony by the time I recognized the signs of abuse, it was too late, the cycle had already begun and I didn't know how to undo it. All the promises for change, the apologies, all the I-love-you's, the gifts; it all added up to a textbook case of abuse. I learned from searching the Net and reading a few articles that domestic violence transcended race, class, and even sexual orientation. The insidious thing called abuse is not a random phenomenon. It happens systematically, methodically, and with surprising frequency. I was afraid to tell Tony that I'd been hospitalized four times related to James' violence. He once pushed me through the glass patio door; I was cut in so many places that I didn't think there would be enough bandages. I told everyone that I'd slipped on the wet floor and fell through the glass. I didn't know if I had the strength to tell him about the sexual perversions and the things we did. Tony barely said anything during the time in which I unburdened my soul; words were unnecessary because his spirit grieved with mine.

"Kevin, I'm so sorry this is happening to you. You know that you don't deserve to be treated this way. How fucked-up is that? How have you been living?"

"This may sound crazy, but a part of me wanted the abuse. I felt like I had to be punished…for Keevan."

He moved closer to me and gave me a hug. "Stop trippin'. What happened to Keevan was not your fault, and Keevan wouldn't want you living like this. I don't want to sound cold, but it's time to put your life back together, and to move on. You are self-destructing. Let me—let us—help you find yourself again." It was strange, but the shame I thought I would feel upon revealing the truth wasn't there. Instead of shame and guilt, I was feeling more alive than ever. "The first thing we have to do is get you out of this house. Like I said earlier, you can stay with me."

"I don't know, Tony. I don't know if I'm strong enough to leave right now. I've left him two other times, but I managed to find my way back to him after a couple of days. I can't deal with the loneliness. With James, at least everything is familiar. Being alone is not something I can deal with."

"Kevin, there are times in all of our lives when we *have* to be alone, but right now, you are not alone.

You have Danea, Daryl, and me. We will stand by your side and get you through this."

"No," I said as I jumped up, "Promise me that they will never know. I don't want them to know. It's hard enough telling you."

"Kevin, you don't have to be alone. Let us help."

"There's no reason for them to know. You and me. We can handle this. Tony, promise me."

"Okay, I'll promise, but you've got to make me a promise. You've got to promise to leave his triflin' ass. You've got to get out, tonight. Let me ask you a question. Did you ever call the police? Did you try to get help?"

"James and LCS are big financial supporters of the policeman's fund, and the mayor. Who was gonna believe me? A couple of times the neighbors called the police, but when they got there, I never said anything. I didn't want help."

He looked at me and I could tell something about my story was not registering as the whole truth to him. He had doubt, or something, in his eyes.

"Kevin, what else is there?"

"What do you mean?"

"There is something else that you're not telling me. I'm not stupid. I've known you for years, and this is bullshit. There's something more that you're not telling me. What is it?"

"There's nothing else. Keevan's death changed me. I don't know how to grieve for him. I don't want to grieve. If I grieve, that means he's really dead."

"I'm gonna say this, and it might hurt, but stop using his death as an excuse. It's been your crutch for too long already. We all loved Keevan, but he's gone now, and he's not coming back. And that's not all that's bothering you. You are running from something, but you'll never be able to live until you move past it. I can see it in your eyes. It's time to be honest. Stop hiding from the truth."

Suddenly, I felt the force of his eyes barreling into me. It felt like a freight train. I heard the whistling warning me, but there was no time to move. I got a warm sensation all over my body and it felt as if I was being pulled into a brilliant light. In the gray areas of my mind, the images kept flashing like the brilliance of a camera flash. The pictures twirled around my head at a frantic pace.

"You're right, there's more to his death than you know. *I killed Keevan.*" The muscles in my throat tightened as if to block passage of my voice. "Keevan and I had the best relationship two brothers could ever hope to have. We were more than just brothers; we were twins, and best friends.

"You remember Darius? Keevan loved Darius so much. When Darius decided he was leaving for the

Marines, do you remember how hurt Keevan was?" Part of me wanted to choke the words before they left my mouth, but it was already too late. I had begun, and the tears in my eyes blurred my vision. "Before he left, Darius and I started…having an affair. It started out as simple flirtation. He'd wink at me when Keevan wasn't looking, and I'd wink back, and it eventually led to more. Much more. It was exciting. I didn't plan on taking it too far, but one night he came over to my house. It was nearly midnight. He came over, and we had sex. I felt horrible, but there was something about him that drew me to him. I understood the attraction Keevan had for him and I wanted to experience it myself. I don't know if I wanted him, or the excitement of what he represented. It happened more than once, but we finally decided that we were playing with fire and that we both loved Keevan too much to hurt him like that and we swore to never tell him." Tony's eyes widened.

"I guess Darius felt a need to confess before he left. I never told you, but on the day that we found Keevan's body, I found a note on his bed from Darius detailing our affair. Keevan must have read it and starting drinking 'cause there were a couple of empty bottles of vodka on the table. And you know Keevan never drank. You and I were in D.C. at the time, but I know that's what happened. I killed him. He was drinking because of what I did to him!"

"You didn't kill him. He had an asthma attack and stopped breathing. It's not your fault," Tony said with concern.

"Why do you think he was upset and drinking? He was upset 'cause I was fucking his man! It's my fault. I may as well have put a gun to his head and pulled the trigger. It's the same thing."

I broke down and my entire body trembled from the outpouring of emotions. If only I had a chance to apologize to him, to let him know that I was sorry. Why did I do that? How could I have done that to him? Everything that James did to me, I deserved, and more. I'm still alive. Keevan is not. "He asked me to pick up his asthma prescription and put it in his apartment before I left. When we got to D.C., I still had the medicine with me. I forgot to leave it! I was in such a hurry to get to D.C. to get my party on. Don't you understand what I'm saying? It's all my fault!"

"I understand that, but it happened in the past and you can't change it. You know your brother, and you know he would have forgiven you about Darius. I'm not saying it would have been easy. It would have taken some time, but he would have. He certainly would not have wanted you punishing yourself like this. He would have just given you the ass-whuppin' you deserved and gotten over it. If you want, I can kick your ass for him," he said.

Tony knew how to make me laugh; that's what I loved about him the most. He held his head down for a second as if he was undergoing some transformation. In his Sophia voice he began: *"You told Harpo to beat me…"* We finished that entire scene from the movie with him continuing as Sophia and I filled in for Whoopi as Celie. And then we laughed hysterically. It was just like the good old days.

After we calmed down, he spoke. "But seriously, you've paid the price for your sins from the day he died up until this very day. Now I understand why you're here living like this. It's time to let go of the guilt, and learn to live again."

"How do I let go? How do I do that?"

"For one, you've got to confront the pain. You can't run from it or lock it away. You've got good friends here to help," Tony said. "You can do this, and you have to talk to Keevan and ask him to forgive you," he added.

"What?"

"Have you asked him to forgive you? You know he can hear you." The simple truth and power of his words opened my heart in a way that I didn't expect. Not once did I ever think to talk to Keevan like that. "You need to talk with him." I was blown away by the simplicity of what I heard. I was frightened, but intrigued.

"You know, I've been too scared to go to the cemetery. I haven't been there since the day we buried him. I need to see him. I need to visit him, but I'm not ready for that right now. I want to go so badly, but I'm afraid. Of seeing him there. Of being there. Of losing control. I think if I start crying, I'll never stop."

"You know you have to go. You can't keep living with this. You've got to forgive yourself, ask him for forgiveness, and move on. This guilt is tearing you apart."

His words were as true as they come. Everything he'd said to me I'd heard in my head a thousand times already, but I wasn't sure where to start this whole process. I'd lived like this for so long that I didn't know if I could move beyond this existence.

"Let me ask you a question," Tony said. "What do you want, Kevin? What do you want right now for yourself?"

"I want to learn to live again."

CHAPTER 15

I closed the door to my office and looked at the four walls. They looked like ordinary walls. I looked at the desk, and I could detect nothing unusual about it at all. The carpet in the room seemed soft enough. This office wasn't spectacular, nor was it the biggest or the best office. It wasn't a corner office with some breathtaking view of downtown, yet something about it made me smile like I hadn't smiled in a long time. When I first walked toward the office, I could see my name mounted on the door outside. Once inside, I picked up the nameplate from the desk and rubbed my fingers across the letters just to make sure the letters on the wood were real. And it was as real as anything I've ever touched. I read my name out loud just to hear how it sounded. A half-hidden smile now lit up my face like fireworks on the Fourth of July. This job was just what I needed.

I plunged down into the chair and stretched out my arms as if I was about to take flight. I looked at the memos already on my desk. Some of the information regarding company policies and procedures were already familiar to me since I used to work for the company a few years back. There was a memo from the previous account manager that stressed adherence to the company dress code and another one that urged discretion at using company phones on company time for personal business.

"Mr. Davis," a small voice said with a knock on the door. When I looked up, I saw a cute white girl, probably no more than nineteen years old, standing in the doorway, looking as if she'd been called to the principal's office. Her head was slightly lowered, and she nervously twirled her fingers around the hem of her pink floral dress.

"Yes?"

"I'm Emily Gray, your secretary—I mean, administrative assistant." When she changed titles, her attitude changed slightly, and she stopped tugging at her dress.

"Nice to meet you, Emily Gray."

"I was just transferred to your department by Katherine—I mean Mrs. Delaney. I'm here to help you in any way that I can."

"I appreciate the support."

"We have a staff meeting at 11 o'clock with Mr. Hodges, and before that," she said while looking at her notes, "Mrs. Delaney has you scheduled for a meeting with her at 10. Is there anything you need me to do in the meantime?"

"While I'm gone, draft a memo and set up a meeting for my department for tomorrow morning. I want to take some time to get to know everyone here."

"Okay. I'll get right on it. Is there anything else?"

"No, that'll do it for now. Thank you, Emily." As she left the room, I looked at my watch. I began to prepare myself for the meetings. Katherine Delaney was my old manager and was one of the most sincere people I'd ever met. It was her guidance and nurturing that helped prepare me for corporate world and life. As far as Mr. Hodges, I'd only met him during my second interview. He was director of Financial Services, which meant he was my boss. He seemed relatively down to earth for a middle-aged, balding, overweight white man. Our interview went well, but I knew that had Katherine not given me such a glowing recommendation, he would have been much tougher. It felt like I had the position without having to say much.

When I walked into her office, she got up and gave me a big hug. "I knew one day we'd get you back," she said with a smile. "You didn't think I'd let you go, now did you? Come on in. I hope you're prepared for this. We have a lot of work to do," she said with a wink. This was classic Katherine, always about business. She was in charge of my training because she once held the job that was now mine. She told me that working for the company for the next couple of weeks would be a little bit crazy because a lot of potential clients would be in and out of the door. Some old clients were scheduled to come in to review the company's work on their accounts as well. The impression we made would either win or lose the company's business. I was told Mr. Hodges was all about the bottom line and bringing in new business, so the pressure was on.

As she talked, I tried not to be distracted by the pictures of her family that covered her walls. They looked like the perfect all-American family, with one exception: It was an interracial family. As a black woman married to a white man, I knew she took a lot of shit from people, black and white, but that never held her back. She proudly displayed her family without a second thought. I always admired her courage and confidence. I knew dating someone white was not for me, but to each his or her own. In the black gay world, black men who exclusively dated white men were considered snow queens —not a term I wanted to be saddled with.

"You know I wanted to get you back on board as soon as possible. I wanted to get you in here so we can go over some things because a lot has changed since you were here last, and we don't have a lot of time. We have several investors and clients coming in, and we'll all be poring over information, numbers, and business strategies." She gave me three packages of material, each containing information about clients that would be in the office next week. "Mr. Hodges will expect you to be prepared. You know I have all the faith in the world in you. We'll all have to help each other out, and it'll be rough for a little bit."

"I'm not worried. Just give me a few hours to prepare and I will charm the pants off them." *That depends on if they're cute or not*, I thought to myself with a smile.

"See, there's the Kevin I love. That raw confidence."

We continued talking strategies until 11, when we went into the conference room for the staff meeting. The room was packed, and after a general pep talk, Mr. Hodges wiped the sweat from his brow and introduced me as the new accounts manager. I was surprised at how many familiar faces there were in the crowd from when I used to intern. After a brief speech, I went into my office and had Emily bring me whatever additional information she could find on the three clients. The rest of the day, I reviewed business plans and financial data. I had forgotten how good it felt to work.

✖✖✖

James had been out of town so much that I'd

barely seen him. He had wanted me to come to Austin with him, but I found a way to avoid it. Even if I had gone with him, what would have been the point? He would have been so tense that we would have fought and probably torn up some hotel room. I was not going through another experience like the one we had when we went to Atlanta. His absence worked out for me since I hadn't really had time to prepare myself for the battle that was sure to come over my job.

After a couple of days, I was settled into my office and the job. Somehow having this job uplifted my spirits; it gave me a sense of purpose. I'd been thinking a lot about what Tony said: that I had to face Keevan at some point. I knew that I'd be haunted by my guilt as long as I ran from it—and I couldn't run from it even if I was Carl Lewis. I was trying to build up my courage and strength so that one day I could do it. I knew that day was imminent.

When I came home that Friday after work—my third day—I was surprised to see that James' car had been moved. That meant he was home. I slipped my key into the lock and quietly opened the door. I walked in slowly, hoping he wasn't downstairs. I removed my tie, put it in my briefcase, and put the briefcase in the coat closet. I then went into the kitchen and poured a tall glass of orange juice before going upstairs. James was sitting on the bed upstairs.

He had a drink in his hand and was obviously waiting for me to get home.

"Where have you been?"

"I wasn't expecting you until late tonight." I tried to appear calm and under control, but a part of me began to get nervous out of habit. There was no way that I could lie at this point, and there was not even a desire on my part to lie. It was time to come clean. "I'm glad you're home." I moved over to him and gave him a small kiss on his cheek as I sat down next to him. "There's something I want to talk to you about."

"Does it have anything to do with you lying about having a damned job?"

His words shocked me. "As a matter of fact it does. I wanted to tell you, but you've been out of town so much that we've hardly seen each other."

"Bullshit! The last time we talked about this I told you I didn't want you working. What part of that didn't you understand? I thought I was clear."

"It doesn't have to be like that. We can work this out."

"I know we can because you're quitting. I want you to call them right now and tell them you won't be back tomorrow." I got off the bed and took my shoes over to the closet. "Do you hear me?"

"Yeah, I hear you." I closed the closet door and walked toward the bathroom. When I came out, he was standing at the door holding the phone and waiting for me to take it from him. A phone in his hand was a dangerous weapon. Instinctively, I froze, but then managed to walk right past him and out of the room into the hallway near the staircase. He caught up with me and grabbed me by the arm just as I was about to walk down the stairs.

"What the fuck is your problem, you little bitch! This is my fucking house and you will respect me or I will kick yo' ass! And don't forget I still owe you an ass kickin' for the bullshit you pulled staying out all night with Tony that night." The veins in his forehead began pulsating, but I stood firm. I would not be intimidated. This surge of confidence had been growing in me for some time, and I felt nine feet tall.

"What are you gonna do? Huh? You've done just about everything that can be done. I'm so sick of this shit. I'm not quitting my job, for you or anyone else. You have two choices: Deal with it, or don't." He pushed me, and I smiled. "I don't have time for this shit. I have a lot of work that I need to do for my job." I looked at him with a smile and walked away as he stood there, confused about his next move.

Surprisingly enough, he didn't follow me. And I didn't look back.

The tension in the house was so thick you could cut it with a knife. Even though I felt confident, I was still cautious. James remained upstairs and barely made a sound. I knew it was only a matter of time before he would come down and explode. He was probably up there plotting his Texas Chainsaw revenge on me.

I didn't want to fight. I was so tired of always having to struggle. In an effort to avoid him, I decided to pay a long overdue visit to Danea. I yelled to James that I was leaving, but he didn't respond. I knew he heard me. I shrugged my shoulders, grabbed my keys and briefcase and closed the door behind me. As I drove off, I could see him standing in our upstairs bedroom window, looking.

CHAPTER 16

When Monday morning came, I felt confident and self-assured. I had spent all weekend at Danea's so that I wouldn't have to deal with James. I intentionally did not return to his house because I wanted him to get the message that he could no longer control me. I wanted him to know I no longer feared him and that his wishes would not always come true. He didn't own me. I knew staying away for the entire weekend was tearing him apart, but he needed a fresh dose of reality, and I needed peace and quiet so that I could get some work done.

We were meeting representatives from a nonprofit organization that was looking to invest about a million dollars recently bequeathed to the organization by a wealthy philanthropist. Mr. Hodges wanted to meet with all of his management staff prior to the clients' arrival. This was potentially a huge account. As far as I knew, they would be spending a large portion of the day with us, observing our operations, and making sure that we were prepared to handle their money.

"Good morning, Emily," I said as I walked past her desk. She handed me a couple of messages written down on a pink pad, and told me the meeting would be in the conference room at 9 a.m. I took a few moments to settle into my office, went over some figures, and drank a cup of café latte I'd picked up at Starbucks on the way to work. I wouldn't be a central player in the meeting today, but Mr. Hodges thought it would be prudent if I was familiar with the client and its history just in case.

When we assembled in the conference room, Mr. Hodges gave us a nice speech to rally our spirits. His robust face was lively and his voice was as energetic as a football coach preparing to send his team onto the field to face their cross-town rivals. It felt like I was at a pep rally back in high school. I remembered whenever my school played our cross-town rival, John Tyler High School, we had an evening pep rally to raise the morale of the team. Keevan was the high school quarterback, and I was a running back, so when we took center stage, the entire school rose in a thunderous round of applause. It felt like we were at the top of the world. Back then, we were.

Before I knew it, an hour had passed and the client's representatives had arrived. I was expecting a delegation, but only two people arrived: the organization's president, Mr. Cromwell, and their executive director, Cynthia Hughes. The executive director was a petite white woman with long black hair and a sagging face.

She sort of looks like that old cartoon dog Droopy, I thought to myself. She spoke with a soft but confident voice. The president was an older man, the former president of a small college in Baton Rouge, Louisiana. He walked slowly, but had a hearty voice that rose when he became excited.

We all had lunch together at Houston's restaurant downtown, and I tried to force myself to pay attention to the chatter about the organization, its future, and its fate. The president was proud to boast about his accomplishments and how he resurrected the struggling organization from the brink of bankruptcy. He said they'd come too far now to just trust the firm's money with any investment firm. That's when Mr. Hodges chimed in, pulling out news articles about the success of our company. It was quite a sales pitch. I think it worked, because lunch ended with a firm handshake and what appeared to be a renewal of faith and the contract.

When we got back to the office, Emily told me that my brother was in my office waiting. My heart stopped. My brother? As I slowly opened the door, I saw James sitting smugly in my chair, fiddling with my computer. "What are you doing here?" I asked as I shut the door.

"I just wanted to see what kind of place was strong enough to steal my baby from me. I just wanted to see where you worked."

"Fine, you've seen. Now leave. I'll see you tonight."

"So, you're coming back tonight? What makes you think you can just skip out on me, and then show back up as if nothing happened? Who the fuck do you think you are?" He stood up and placed his hands down on the desk as he leaned his huge body forward.

"This is not the time nor the place to have this conversation. We can talk about it tonight, or not. You make the choice."

"We'll talk about it now. Right now." He moved from the desk and approached me, just as Emily knocked on the door.

"Is everything okay in here, Mr. Davis?" she asked.

"Mr. Davis is fine. We're just catching up on old times," James said. Emily looked at me for confirmation.

"Everything is fine, Emily, but I think my dear brother here would like an escort out of the building. Would you see that he gets one?"

"Yes, sir." She closed the door and James looked at me in shock.

"So you're gonna throw me out of your office? You really think you're bad, don't you?" I guess my smirk was too much for him to take. With one fell swoop, he knocked everything on my desk to the floor.

"What the hell are you doing?" I stepped to him and pushed him away from my desk and into the wall.

In return, he pushed me into the door, and my back hit it with a loud thump. That's when the yelling got loud. His yells and my yells rose to intolerable levels. I couldn't hear myself think over his voice. Emily had come back into my office screaming for help. James' deep voice filled the air with all sorts of profanity. Our noise attracted the attention of Mr. Hodges, who was coming down the hall with the clients. If I could have turned red, I would have been the color of a vine-ripened tomato.

"What is going on in here?!" Mr. Hodges yelled.

"I don't know, sir. I called security and they're on their way!" Emily screamed.

"Davis, stop this at once!"

I was too busy arguing with James to even notice the security guards approaching. The next thing I remember is being pulled apart by a couple of guards, and the both of us being escorted out of the building. The last words from Mr. Hodges' mouth were, *"You're fired!"*

CHAPTER 17

"I guess you got what you wanted. I'm out of a job."

"Kevin, all I wanted was for you to be here for me and for us. I want to trust you, but this shit you have been pulling lately has been way out of line. I don't know what's wrong with you. It's like you're doing all of this on purpose just to piss me off. I don't have time to chase you. I have way too much going on with work and being in Austin to have to worry about what you're doing here."

"I have been telling you for months now that I need a job, so I don't know why you're acting as if this is some big surprise." By the time we had started this conversation, I wasn't sure exactly what I was feeling. I knew it was part rage, part embarrassment, and a lot of resentment. James was calm, like the sky after a storm. He sat on the bed, removing his shoes, proud of his latest accomplishment.

"Kevin, I'm going through some serious shit with LCS and I need you at my side. I need to come home and know that you'll be here for me. Is that too much to ask? Maybe one day, in a couple of months, we can talk about you getting a job, but now is not the right time."

"Who the fuck do you think you are? You can't control my life anymore. Don't you understand that? You can't tell me when I can work, and what I can do. Just because I lost this job doesn't mean that first thing in the morning I won't be out looking for another."

"Then we have a serious problem, don't we?"

"No, we don't have a problem. There is no *we*. You have a problem, but you'll have to deal with that on your own. I'm leaving…for good."

I moved over to the closet, grabbed a small bag and started stuffing whatever clothing I could fit in it. He sat on the bed and watched me for a few seconds, trying to figure out if I was serious or not. This time would be different. This time, there was no turning back. This time, I felt strong enough to leave.

"And where are you gonna go?"

"You don't have to worry about that. I'll be okay." I zipped up the bag and walked out of the room into the hallway. James followed.

"You are so full of shit! You think you can just walk away after all of the shit I've done for you? It doesn't work that way, baby!"

"Is that it? Is that all you have to say?" I turned to walk down the stairs when I realized I had left the picture of Keevan on the mantelpiece in the bedroom. I quickly turned, but felt my feet come from under me. It must have been a split second, but in that small measure of time, I saw so much of my life race by me just like the cliché. I teetered atop the stairs, attempting to regain my balance, reaching for the railing, for James, for anything to steady myself. It was too late. I was falling. And falling hard. I hit the next few stairs, and then I tumbled down the long staircase, feeling a few of the hard stairs pounding into my skull before losing consciousness.

✖✖✖

When I opened my eyes, my view was obscured by the glare of the hospital lights. I sat up in the bed, and looked around the pristine room. Something hung in the air. Some force loomed above, below and around me. It was as complete and ever present as the air I breathed. Somehow, I felt on edge, yet at ease. It felt familiar and terrifying; comforting and strange, all at the same time. I wasn't sure what was going on, why I was here, but I heard a noise near the door. I got up out of bed. I was floating on the cold air, somehow suspended above ground, not needing to move my feet to go forward, but being pulled gently by some power. The door opened to reveal the busy hallway. Nurses were at their stations tending their duties and talking to who I assumed were the families of the patients. They looked completely engrossed with their work, and they didn't notice me at all. People rushed by in an

*almost panicked state as they looked for answers to what-
ever tragedies had befallen their loved ones.*

*I turned my head to the right, and at the end of the
hallway I saw Keevan. He waved me forward and then
turned the corner. I wanted to follow, but the air in which
I rode carried me to the left. It took me down a long and
winding corridor. I looked down at my bare feet and tried
to move my toes. They wouldn't move. I could move my
hands, and my arms, my head, and every part of my body
except my feet. The force carried me into a room where a
woman lay in the bed, unconscious and badly beaten. Her
children sat in the room next to her, hoping that their
tears would possess some magic quality to bring the woman
back. I wanted to speak to them, to comfort them, but I
had no voice. I wanted to touch them, but my hands passed
right through their flesh. Suddenly, the machine flat-lined
and the long beep from the machine covered their sobs. I
panicked. I wanted to help. I had to help. The force that
held me released me. I ran over to the bed and shook the
woman. She didn't move. I ran out into the hallway and
tried to call for a doctor, but no one could be found at all.
In fact, the hallway was dark, except for the light that shone
from her room. When I went back in, she stood before me as
her children and family cried over her lifeless body.*

"It's too late for me. Save yourself," she said.

*"Lady, don't go. Your family needs you. Look at how they
cry." The voice that came out wasn't mine, but sounded
familiar.*

"*Save yourself. Live again.*" *The voice that was hers wasn't hers; it sounded like Keevan. Her face distorted and contracted into another being. I could see Keevan in her eyes, smiling at me. It was surreal. He seemed trapped by her eyes, but free. I reached out, but the force seized me again. I shook my head and closed my eyes. When I opened them, everything was gone. A light shone from the ceiling and I heard Keevan's voice say, "Live."*

woke up in a hospital bed, disoriented from the
dream. It took a few seconds for me to understand
and remember the events that brought me there.
But then it all came back to me. The first few minutes after I regained consciousness, I felt like a rat in
some university experiment. I was poked and prod-
ded incessantly. Every time I looked up, the door to
my room was opening and some unattractive nurse
with bad skin would come in to either bring me a pill
or make me turn over to give me a shot in the ass.
The white lights of the room, the various beeps and
the murmur of the machines in the room were giving me a serious headache. All I wanted to do was to
put on my clothes and leave. I hated hospitals. When
I tried to get up, a surge of pain rushed to my head
and my side. I was forced back to the bed. I felt the
bandages wrapped around my waist so I knew that I
must have a broken a rib or two. I was in pain.

I had been in and out of consciousness for two
days, or so I was told. Severe head trauma, according
to my doctor. When I came around for the first time,
my room was empty. Somewhere in the back of my

mind I remember James being in the room talking to someone about my condition. It must have been the doctor. Bits and pieces of the conversation stayed in my head, and then I remembered. I grabbed the call button and sent for the nurse who had just left my room.

"Yes, Mr. Davis?" the nurse asked as she moved about the room monitoring the equipment and charts.

"What is my condition?" I asked impatiently.

"You suffered some head trauma. The damage is not permanent, but you do have a pretty severe concussion, along with a couple of broken ribs on your right side. Other than that, you're okay, but the doctor will be here in a bit to talk to you more."

"Has anyone been here to see me? Where's James?"

"Would that be Mr. Lancaster? He's been here every evening, and he calls at least three times a day to check on you. He seems like a great friend."

"I need to use the phone."

She walked over to the table and brought the phone into my reach and then left the room so that I could have some privacy. I tried not to wince in pain as I dialed the number. I picked up the phone to call James at home. There was no answer, so I called his office phone and sure enough he picked up. I didn't know what to say, so I just hung up the phone. Why had I called? As I rolled over, I heard a knock at the door and when I looked up, there was Croix.

"The nurse told me you were awake," he said.

"Croix? What are you doing here?" His presence was a pleasant surprise.

"My wife is a nurse on this floor and I was here waiting on her when they brought you in." I wondered which nurse was his wife, and I hoped that it wasn't the one who'd been coming into my room on this day. He could do better than her. Then, one of the nurses came into the room and grabbed my chart. She looked at us, smiled, and walked out the door.

"I'm glad that's not your wife," I said, and we both laughed.

He took a seat on the bed right in front of me. His presence comforted me, but I could see the worry in his eyes. He wanted to say something, to ask questions, but he didn't. He just looked at me with sadness draped in hope. Finally he had to speak.

"What happened? My wife said you fell down some stairs?" He looked at me as if he expected me to say something earth-shattering. Instead, I smiled and took a deep breath.

"That about sums it up. I fell down the stairs."

"Kevin, where is your boy? I mean your lover. You're here, in this bed, and where is he?"

"He's at work. You know it's business above all else. But that's okay. I don't really feel like seeing him now, anyway."

"If you were my lover I swear to you that I would

never leave your side while you're in the hospital."

"That's so sweet, but I'm okay for the most part."

"Tell me the truth. Is he the reason you're here? Did he do this to you? You've told me about the fights you have with him. Did he push you?"

"Yes, he's the reason I'm here, but he didn't push me down the stairs. I fell on my way out the door. I was leaving him, but I turned around because I left my picture of Keevan, and I lost my footing at the top the stairs and fell down. I knew something like this would happen. I told you about this connection we have. Something didn't want me to leave. There I was, standing at the top of the staircase. We were arguing and I turned around too quickly and lost my balance. I don't really remember anything after that."

"That's bullshit. Don't leave your fate to some cosmic force that binds you to him. Don't let him keep you in that house 'cause you had a fall down the stairs, and don't you believe for one second that you fell because of some kind of divine intervention. You have to leave James. Surely you realize that now more than ever. Get out while you can."

"I know it's time that we go our separate ways, but..."

"No buts. If you need help, money or anything, just let me know. I'm there for you. You deserve better—someone like me," he said with a smile.

"I'm sure your wife would love it if I moved in with

you and the kids. I can see it now, *Happy Days* for the new millennium. She could cook, and I'll clean. We'd have to get one of those big king-sized beds so the three of us could cuddle up and watch reruns of *I Love Lucy* on Nickelodeon."

"You are silly," he said with a laugh. "Of course I was kidding. All jokes aside, if you need me, don't hesitate to call. I told my wife that you and I were old friends so it's okay to call me at the house. I'm gonna keep checking on you. Have you told your friends?"

"Actually, I haven't called them yet."

"Are you going to?"

"I haven't decided yet."

"There you go again. If they are your friends, they have a right to know. You need to learn to let people be there for you. You don't have to do it all on your own. You're a great guy, but stop being selfish."

I chewed on his words for a second and I knew that he was right. It was selfish of me not to open my life to the very ones who loved me the most. "You're right. I'll tell them. I need someone right now to make me laugh."

"Well, that's why I'm here. To make you laugh and smile." He grabbed my hand and held it tightly. It was a comforting feeling that I needed very much. He stayed with me for the next hour, making sure that I called my friends, and waited as long as he could for them to arrive. He didn't want me to be alone. I had left messages for Tony, Danea, and Daryl on their machines, so I knew they'd be calling or coming by as soon as they could.

While he was there we shared a lot of laughs and great conversation. His situation and feelings for his wife had not changed and his feelings for me, he confessed, were growing. He wasn't sure how he would contain them. He felt that he was fighting a battle that he couldn't win. He and his wife argued over little things that he admitted were his fault. Sometimes, he said, he'd just pick a fight. He was hoping that he could somehow make her leave without him having to ask for a divorce. He knew that his wife was confused and didn't know what was going on with him, but this was one secret he could never tell. Just as he listened to me, I listened to him. I listened and understood.

After an hour, he said, "Unfortunately, I have to be going now. But I'll be back tomorrow."

"I appreciate you stopping by and spending time with me."

"You know the pleasure is all mine. I want you to do me a big favor, though. Hurry up and get your ass out of this hospital."

"I will make every effort because you asked so nicely. I feel fine for the most part, just a little bit sore. Don't worry, I'm okay." I watched him walk toward the door. As he walked out, he stopped, turned, and smiled at me.

✖✖✖

As the evening wore on, my friends, one by one, matriculated into my room wearing looks of despair. This ain't no funeral, I had to tell each one when they entered. Tony was the first to rush in, bringing with him all of the drama that he was famous for. I spent more time trying to calm him down than he did making me feel better. I didn't have to explain to him that James was involved in this on some level, which was part of his hysteria. He was pissed off, and ready to kill James.

"You are not going back to him so don't even think about it," he said with fury.

"Don't worry. I know it's over. I think I know that now."

"I know some friends in the ward that could really fuck him up. I would just love to slit the tires on that nice Jag of his."

"I'm sure you would, but this time, it really wasn't his fault." I explained to him what happened and exactly how I fell, but that didn't make him calm down.

Before I knew it, the door to my room opened and the next thing I knew I was explaining to Danea and Daryl the same story. I gave Tony a look so that he would be careful not to add in his little two cents' worth. I simply told them the truth: that James and I were arguing and I fell down the stairs. They didn't need to know about the scene at my job. That was one thing I would keep to myself.

"I think I'm leaving James," I said slowly and deliberately.

"What?" Danea said in an astonished voice. "It's about time. I knew something wasn't right. You can stay with me, and I won't take no for an answer."

"I'll stay, but it's only temporary, until I get on my feet."

"Did James push you?" Daryl asked out of the blue.

"What? No. No, he didn't push me. It was an accident. I just lost my footing, that's all."

"You sure have a lot of accidents in that house," he continued. "Kevin, what's going on?"

"There's nothing going on. I just don't see a future with him."

Daryl knew there was more to the story, but he didn't press. They all knew. It was written all over my face.

"I want to find out when you're getting out of this place. I hate hospitals. They're full of sick people," Danea said as she went into the corridor. Danea was having a hard time seeing me in the hospital. While she was in law school her father died of cancer and she spent a lot of time holding vigil at his bedside. I knew those memories must've been flooding her right then. She'd never admit it, but I knew she wanted to break down.

"I'm staying with you tonight. I can sleep in that chair," Daryl said.

"That chair will mess up your back. I'll be okay by myself. Really, I just need some time right now. I just need some rest. I'll be fine. I want you all to go home and don't worry about me. Daryl, I'll be okay alone. Just go home, and call me later."

After a few more minutes of talk, I convinced them that I was tired and wanted to go to sleep, which was partially true. No sooner had they left the room did the nurse come in to give me some more medicine, and before I knew it, I was feeling drowsy. She gave me a couple of pills and quickly made her way out of the room without conversation.

They were right. It could be as simple as it sounded. I took a few moments to contemplate the course of my life. No money. No job. But my faith and spirit were returning to me. And faith can move mountains. It took me a few seconds for the sound of the phone to register in my mind. I reached over to pick it up. It was James.

"Hey, baby. I was just checking on you. How are you?"

"I'm fine, James."

"I just called the nurse's station and they told me you were awake. Why didn't you call me?" I wanted to say that I didn't call because I didn't want to talk to him, but I didn't. He sounded as if everything between us was okay.

"I'm tired, James. I need to get off the phone." The medicine was making my eyelids feel heavy.

"I wish I could see you today, but I have so much to do. I'll be lucky if I'm outta here by 10. Do you need anything?"

"No, James. I'm fine. I think I'm just going to go to sleep. My head hurts."

"Okay. I'll try to see you tomorrow, but it's going to be rough. I need to be in Austin tomorrow afternoon."

"Whatever." I hung up the phone and tried to roll over onto my side to get some sleep, but I couldn't. So much pain, but the medicine soon put me to sleep.

CHAPTER 19

I hadn't spoken to James in any detail since that brief call when he told me that he had to go back to Austin to take care of some business, but he would try to be back by the weekend.

In the meantime, my remaining stay in the hospital was divided between all of my friends. Danea and Tony called me throughout the day to see how I was doing. Daryl and Croix seemed particularly involved in my recovery. Daryl brought food to eat so that I would not have to be subjected to the barely edible hospital food. Croix brought magazines for me to read and kept me smiling. Daryl was there for me every day with laughter, and that helped ease my healing process. At least it made the time in the hospital more bearable.

"Have you wondered what it would have been like if we'd gotten together?" Daryl asked me.

"Sometimes."

"And what do you think about it?"

"I think that you and I would have been the perfect couple. This friendship we have would have laid an important foundation to building something between us. But we didn't."

"Do you think we made a mistake?" I was silent. My heart knew the answer and my head silenced it.

"I think we did what we thought was best."

"Don't evade the question."

"I'm not. I just don't see the point in talking about something that happened, or didn't happen. For whatever reasons, we didn't get together. Maybe we should have. I don't know, Daryl. All I'll say is that there has always been and always will be a part of me that is you."

"What if I told you that I still have feelings for you? I'm talking about strong feelings. What if I told you that I know you feel the same way?" He moved closer to me on the bed and rubbed my face with his hands. The moment was filled with such gentleness that I let myself go, and I allowed my feelings to rise to the surface. "What if I told you I was in love with you?"

After some thought I said, "I'd probably say the same thing to you." He leaned his body over me and kissed my lips with passion that I'd never known. His soft lips brushed gently against mine, and then our kiss became deeper and much more intense. I lost myself again. I didn't want to be found. This was a moment long overdue.

"That's how you kiss when you're in love with someone," he said. There was no fighting the fact that we loved each other, but where does love go when it can't be fulfilled?

"What are we going to do?"

"Well, I know this *thing* you have with James has to have time to pass, so I guess we'll take it one day at a time." He motioned to the arrangements of flowers that James had sent. I knew what I needed to do, but I still felt as if he had some kind of hold on me with a grip so strong that I couldn't free myself. Way back in the depths of my mind, I knew that if I left James I'd have to face Keevan. At least James kept me occupied. He was my diversion. In the last few days or so, I'd been thinking a lot about something Tony said. He told me to stop using Keevan as an excuse and that I had to face up to what happened. I knew that day was coming soon and I tried to prepare myself in small ways for it. It was not today, nor would it be tomorrow. But it would come.

"Honestly, I feel so confused right now. If I left James..."

"If? What do you mean *if*?"

"Let me finish. *When* I leave James, I know that I won't be ready for another relationship for a long time. Daryl, I'm telling you this 'cause I don't want to lead you on. I don't know when or if I'll ever be ready. I need time so that I can find myself. Somewhere over the course of the last year I lost the person that I was. I know you all can see it. I have some serious demons to face."

"We can face them together. I can wait for you. I've waited this long."

"You can't wait forever. Daryl, I can't offer you anything right now except friendship."

"Talking about a relationship between us is premature. Even if you and I never get together, you need to get away from James. Can we agree upon at least that?"

"There is no doubt about that. I just don't know..." I stopped my sentence because in walked James carrying a new bouquet of fresh flowers. He walked over to my bed. Daryl stood there, front and center, and waited. Finally James turned to him and spoke.

"Daryl."

"James."

"I appreciate you coming here and keeping Kevin company in my absence, but I'm here now. You may leave." James sat on the bed and waited for Daryl to leave.

"Kevin and I were in the middle of a conversation," he said defiantly. It was all Daryl could do to keep from losing his cool. I could see the anger building up in his eyes.

"Daryl, can we finish this conversation later? I'll think about what you said, though," I said, trying to keep the peace.

"I think we should finish it now."

"Later would be better for me, but I'll call you tomorrow, okay?" I needed some time alone with James so that I could end this misery.

"You'll be okay if I leave?"

"He'll be fine," James answered. "I've been taking care of him for years; I know what he needs."

"I was talking to Kevin."

"Daryl, I'll be okay. If you talk to Danea tonight, tell her to call me." Daryl nodded his head and unwillingly left the room.

"I won't ask what that was about. How is my sweet baby today?" James asked.

"Absolutely wonderful, couldn't be better. Let's see, I'm in the hospital, I've lost my job, and now you're here. What more could I ask for?"

"What does that mean?"

"It means that I don't think I want to see you right now."

"Why? What's wrong?"

"What do you mean, what's wrong? James, look at me. Now, you tell me what's right."

"I know that you're a little upset about how things are going between us."

"I'm not upset, and at this point, there is no us. There never was."

"I know that you're angry at me, but this attitude is unnecessary, don't you think? Falling down those stairs was an accident and you know it."

"It may have been an accident this time, but what happens the next time you get angry? Push me out of a second-story window?"

"That's not fair. I've gone to great lengths to improve my attitude and temperament over the last few months."

"You call this an improvement?" I said while motioning at my surroundings in the hospital room. "I'd hate to see what happens when you don't try."

"Look, Kevin. There won't be a next time. This won't happen again."

"Whatever."

"I'm serious, and I promise."

"How many promises have you made? How many times have you said those same exact words?" He looked at me with his sad brown eyes like a little puppy dog in the window of a pet store. His head hung low while he fiddled with his thumbs. This innocence he portrayed was a facade and I refused to fall for it.

"I don't know what to tell you. All I can say is I'm sorry, and ask for your forgiveness."

"It's over, James. I can't do this anymore. I won't live like this."

"You can't..."

"I can. And I will."

"Baby, let's talk about this. I'm sorry. I don't want you to leave. I need you. I know that I don't deserve you and you have every reason to leave, but I promise you I'll change. I am changing. I just need you to give me a little more time. I'll do whatever it takes. I'll see a counselor. I'll do whatever you need me to do. Please, just don't leave me."

"This really isn't open for discussion. This relationship is sick. We are both sick, and I've decided that I'm gonna get well."

"We can get well together."

"Your issues are separate from mine."

"We can work this thing out. We've been through too much to let it all end." A look of desperation formed on his face, as if he knew he was losing the battle. He held my hand as if his touch would make me change my mind.

"What are you talking about? Don't be stupid. James, I don't love you. I don't think I ever did. I'm miserable with you and I've allowed myself to live that way, but now I know I deserve better."

"I know you do, but if you give me just one more chance we can work this thing out. I know we can.

Baby, I love you and I would do anything to keep you at my side. Please, don't leave me. Don't give up on us."

"I don't know how many times I have to say it, but this *thing* is over. We both need to get on with the rest of our lives and be free of each other."

"What about Keevan?"

"What? What the hell are you talking about?"

"I knew about you and Keevan even before I knew you. I saw you that day, you remember? That day at the drug store? That day you wanted to kill yourself? Do you remember the day I saved your life?" Bits of that day raced before my eyes. The hotel room. The candles. The wine. The drive to the store. The sleeping pills. "Didn't I warn you that danger was near? I told you something didn't feel right. If you leave, who will protect you? With the connection that we have, you can't walk away and expect everything to be okay. Some things are just meant to be. *You and me*. Together."

"James..."

"Baby, I know you feel the power and connection between us as much as I do. You can't deny it. I think Keevan connects us because he knows that we should be together. Don't fight fate. Don't destroy our love."

CHAPTER 20

*L*ike a moth to a flame. Before I could stop it, or think about it, I was back with James. In that house. With his things, with only a picture of Keevan to call mine. Like clockwork, the cycle began again. First, it was the romance stage where James tried to right his wrongs. Then he kept talking about how much he would change for me. My friends couldn't believe that I went back. I couldn't believe it. They were disappointed with me. I was disappointed with me. But this was my life and I knew I couldn't leave him now. This connection that we have had to be broken in order for me to be free.

Once I was out of the hospital, James hired a nurse to be with me until I felt better, but after a few days, I told her that we no longer needed her services. The last thing I needed was another body hovering over me, pretending to care about me. I needed time and space to myself, and luckily, that's what James gave me. He kept himself in Austin so much that I thought he'd moved there. During one of the few conversations we had, I told him that things were gonna have to change, and I put a few conditions on this arrangement: I was getting a job and there was no compromise or negotiation on that issue. I felt as if I had some power and control over my future with him. My ultimate plan was to free myself of this bond and heal myself. I could feel myself getting stronger, but I still was not strong enough.

Within a few weeks, most of the soreness and pain had left my body. I felt brand-new. I spent a lot of time looking for a job and sending out resumes. RaChelle made herself and her resources available to me, and sent copies out as well. Through her good graces, I had an interview, and then another one, and finally a job at her company. This all happened within a week. I didn't really have too much time to think about whether or not I wanted to work that closely with her, but at this point, I needed a job. I was the associate director of operations for Inertia Mutual Funds. I didn't know exactly what I would be doing, but the title sounded impressive.

✖✖✖

At the end of my first day at work I stopped by RaChelle's office to say thanks. I had a nice bouquet of fresh flowers that I knew would put a smile on her face. Inertia Mutual Funds had recently started a program called Texas House to help mentor at-risk children. The idea of the project had come from RaChelle while she was in Dallas, and she wanted to tell me about it. As executive vice president of Human Resources, she had a lot of influence in the company.

"Kevin, I'm so glad you stopped by," RaChelle said as she hung up the phone and waved me in. RaChelle's office was decorated with the kind of elegant class I'd expect from her. The flowering plants and wonderful crystal gave it the feel of the lobby of some five-star hotel. Her huge desk was made of glass, and the legs looked like white elephant tusks. It was definitely a power desk.

"Have a seat. I hope you'll be as excited about the program as I am," she said after a few minutes of small talk and flirtation. "Texas House is a comprehensive program for at-risk children in the Houston area. Any number of sources refers the teenagers to us. Once they come into our care, we do our best to make sure that they get the best possible treatment to meet their needs. Our facility is state of the art. We provide everything from after-school tutoring programs to mentors to shelter if they need it. We are the center's major corporate supporter and we are looking to bring in other companies to help offset some of the costs. Right now, we desperately need black male mentors for the boys. It's hard getting good men to take the time to give back to their community."

I listened for the next half hour while she went into detail about the program and how her company felt the need to be civic-minded. She had already sold me on the program right from the start, but since she had this whole presentation planned out, I decided to let her have her glory. Her excitement and enthusiasm came through in her words and the glitter in her eyes.

"The program sounds really interesting, but I do have a lot going on right now. Can I think about it for a few days and get back with you?"

She leaned in over her desk. "I don't want you taking too much time. We really need you, Kevin. The kids need you."

"I understand. I promise I will think about it seriously. I just don't want to get involved in someone's life and then not be able to really commit to making a difference because of the other things going on in my life."

"I'll let you think about it, but I'll contact the director of the center and let him know to be expecting a wonderful and positive role model. I'm not letting you out of this one." She smiled coyly. I could see there was no use in trying to disarm her with logic when she had made up her mind. I had been officially drafted, but I wasn't sure when I'd be able to start my tour of duty. I wanted to make sure things in my life were settled first.

"I agree with the need to give back to our communities," I said.

"We have so much in common," she said as she looked at her watch. "I wish we could talk more, but it's about time to get out of here. I am so ready. The people in the office today have been getting on my nerves. My secretary is not the brightest girl in the world." She stood up and starting packing papers into her briefcase.

"I hope I haven't gotten on your nerves. I'd hate to be on your bad side," I said with a laugh.

"You've been the absolute highlight of my day, but if you don't start returning my phone calls, I'll put you on my hit list," she said jokingly, I think. "Listen, what are your plans right now?"

"Right now? Well…nothing, I guess. Why?"

"There's this new happy hour I wanted to try on Westheimer. I think it's a Mexican place called Café Raul, but a lot of brothers and sisters tend to go there, so I've heard."

I thought for a few seconds and then decided that I had nothing better to do. "I'd love to go."

✖✖✖

When we got to the cafe, it was already packed. Men and women of all races filled the room. The music pumping from the speakers generated a wave of excitement throughout the place and onto the dance floor. RaChelle and I watched for a few seconds as drunken people danced clumsily. We took a seat in a booth in the back, trying to shield ourselves from the noise of the crowd. The close seating fused us together like sardines in a can. As tough and assured as she tried to be, there were some insecurities slightly detectable on the surface.

When the waitress came to take our order, RaChelle ordered a glass of Chardonnay, and I got a Long Island Iced Tea.

"Are you hungry?" she asked. "Don't forget they have a free buffet in the back. Do you want me to get you something?"

"No, if you want something, go ahead. I'm not hungry." She got up and headed toward the back of the club. By the time she returned, I was halfway finished with my drink. She carried two plates full of fruit and crackers. She scrambled her way through the crowd and back to our small table. When she sat down, she let out a sigh of relief, took a napkin and patted the moisture that now gathered on her brow.

"I thought you got lost," I said jokingly.

"It's a madhouse back there. Have you ever seen a hundred drunken people in line for food? I thought I was gonna have to take off my pumps," she said with a laugh. Her smile suddenly vanished as she spoke. "And to top it off, this idiot spilled some cheese on my skirt!" We looked at each other, and my face exploded in laughter. At first, she looked slightly embarrassed, then she joined in the laughter with me. "It isn't funny. This skirt was $200," she said in a playful screech as she grabbed my leg under the table. I was starting to have a really good time with her. Her wild personality and amazing sexiness pulled me into her. She was the kind of woman that other women loved to hate. Physically perfect in every way, and she knew how to carry it to crush any other woman in her path. She said she didn't have female friends, and I understood why. We talked, laughed, and flirted with each other for the next two hours. At one point, she took my hand and placed it on her inner thigh. If that wasn't an invitation, then I didn't know what was.

"I'm so glad that you'll be working with us. I think you'll like it at Inertia. There are almost unlimited opportunities for growth. Who knows, when I become president one day I just might make you a vice president, if you act right," she said. I definitely appreciated and respected her ambition.

"Thanks for the vote of confidence, but I think I'll take it one step at a time."

"I'm serious. If you work hard and don't let anyone or anything stand in your way, then you can conquer the world. I mean, look at me: I'm already a vice president. I can only go up from here."

"You've done well for yourself. How did it happen so fast for you? I mean you haven't been out of school for more than three years and look at you now, *Vice President Roland.*"

"Believe me, I've paid my dues, in more ways than one. I learned a long time ago it's a dog-eat-dog world. My teeth are very sharp."

"Look at the time. It's getting late," I said. By the time we noticed our watches, it was a few drinks later and almost 8 p.m. I needed to be getting home because there were some things I wanted to review before work the following day.

"We could finish this at my place," she said coyly. For a brief second, I thought about taking her up on the offer, but, realizing that may cause more harm than good, I declined.

"I really need to be getting home."

"Girlfriend?"

"Uhh...not exactly," I responded evasively.

"Then, what is it?"

"I am involved with someone."

"Is it serious?"

I shrugged my shoulders and said, "We've been together for a while." A small sadness descended upon her face with those words. She forced a smile. She leaned across the table and pulled my face close to hers. She started nibbling my ear ever so gently, and my body was beginning to respond. She recovered well from her disappointment.

"Tell her I said she's a very lucky woman. I hope she appreciates you. Men like you are hard to find."

"Thank you. I'm sure I don't have to tell you that you are a wonderful and incredibly beautiful woman. Any man would be lucky to have you." She smiled, I think out of politeness. I wasn't saying anything that she hadn't heard a million times already.

"I have something I want to give you...about Texas House. Just stop by my place for a second, I'll give it to you, and you can be on your way." She smiled again. This time, there was something else there. I smiled back.

"Let's go."

✖✖✖

By the time we made it to her place, I felt something inside of me building up. I don't know what it was, but there was an expectation of something to come.

"Make yourself at home," she said as she stepped away from the door and let me into her luxurious town home. She took my hand and led me over to her couch. The lights in her apartment were dimly lit and the place demonstrated her impeccable taste. Decorated in light colors, the room felt warm and soft. The two African masks on the wall in the dining room added just the right touch of Afrocentrism. "Welcome to my home. Have a seat. I'll be right back." She disappeared behind me and the next thing I knew I heard Prince's "The Beautiful Ones" from her stereo.

When she returned from the bedroom, she was dressed in a green lace nightgown; she walked past me as I examined the artwork on her walls. She went into the kitchen and returned with two glasses of wine.

"You read my mind," I said as I took the drink and put my lips to the glass.

"Kevin, I won't pretend that I don't find you fascinating. Even back in college, I had this big crush on you, but you never seemed to notice me." She stopped in the middle of her thought and let out a little laugh as if there was some inside joke going on in her head.

"What's so funny?"

"Nothing really. Well, one of my friends thinks that any man who doesn't flirt with her must be gay."

"That's not always the case," I said a little too defensively.

She gave me a terse look and continued her conversation. "I tried telling her that, but you know how people can be once they've made up their mind about something." She took a few more sips from her glass.

"I know exactly what you need." She got up from the couch and headed toward her bedroom. This time when she came back, she had a couple of joints in her hand, and some incense. She put one in her mouth, pulled out a box of matches, and lit the joint and an incense stick all in one smooth stroke. "You want some of this?" She inhaled deeply and looked down between her legs. I took the joint out of her mouth, placed it to my lips and began to puff. I choked a little bit. *If you ain't chokin', then you ain't smokin'.* Soon, the room was filled with the thick smell of weed.

After we finished both joints, she took my hand and started nibbling, licking and then sucking my right index finger. Her tongue made fluid and rippling motions over my skin. She started with one finger, but before she finished she managed to taste them all. My fingers, as an erogenous zone, are highly underrated. She moved slowly at first, but then as her temperature rose, so did the speed of her tongue. She took my other hand and gently placed it between her legs and into her warmth. She climbed on top of me, her flesh pressing against mine. Powered by passion, ruled by emotions, she ripped apart the buttons on my shirt with her mouth, and soon I lay on the couch completely naked, and erect. Her clothes came off and the next thing I knew we were rolling around the floor.

CHAPTER 21

James had distanced himself from me for some reason. Whether or not he was consumed with work or other activities, I didn't know. Sometimes, he'd walk into the room and not say a word. I wasn't sure what was going on in Austin, but all of a sudden he stopped spending as much time there and was home more often. I wanted to ask him what was wrong, but I wasn't sure whether or not I really cared. He barely talked to me or even acknowledged my presence at times. Under normal circumstances, he'd stay awake long after I went to bed, but lately he was spending more time sleeping. His eyes were puffy and he looked worried. What was on his mind?

After a big meeting I had at work, I came home exhausted. My feet hurt, I was tired of being in a suit, and I was mentally fatigued. *Corporate America at its finest.* For most of my trip home I'd thought of nothing else but taking a nice hot bubble bath and soaking my aching feet. When I walked into the room I saw James sitting on the floor at the foot of the bed, his face in his hands. The only light in the room slipped in from under the bathroom door. I put down my briefcase, but he didn't move. I don't even think he realized that I had come in. I didn't want to disturb his silence, but I'd never seen him so withdrawn. I wasn't sure how to react. I wanted to walk away, but he looked like all of the world's troubles lay upon his shoulders. I walked over to him and took a seat next to him on the floor. He looked up with watery red eyes and embraced me. I don't know why I felt any compassion for this man, but I had never seen him like this. Even though his arms were around me, his mind was somewhere else.

"I don't know what to do. My life is so fucked up. All I do is destroy and hurt people."

"Your life isn't that bad. Look around, you're living your dreams."

"What I'm living is a nightmare. I keep everyone far away from me, and those who get close, get burned. I don't deserve any of this," he said, motioning to the room around him. "I know I don't deserve you. Why are you still here? I love you, but what do you get from me besides heartache and pain?"

"I have my reasons. But I don't want to talk about that now. What's bothering you?" He handed me an old torn picture of a very attractive woman who appeared to be in her mid-thirties. "Who is this?"

"I was cleaning out some things and I came across that picture of my mother, and then I remembered."

"What did you remember?"

"The nightmare."

"James, what are you talking about?"

"I had a horrible childhood. I have tried to forget most of it, but that picture brought it all back. When I was fifteen my father raped me and killed my mother before shooting himself in front of me." He spoke slowly and without expression. The words flowed out of his mouth, but he wasn't speaking to me. He was simply giving voice to the pain that had haunted him for years. "I came home from school one day and walked into hell. The living room was torn to pieces. I swear every piece of glass we had in that house was broken. The windows, dishes, picture frames had all been destroyed. The couch was over-turned and everything was wrecked. I thought we had been robbed. It looked as if a storm had blown through and destroyed everything. I was so scared. I smelled blood. Can you recognize the scent of warm blood in the air? I called out for my mother. There was no answer. I raced through the house like a maniac. When I got to the kitchen, I stopped because I could see a pair of legs sticking out from the door. I recognized the shoes. It was Mama. I moved closer. She had on her favorite blue dress. Her head was split open on the right side. Blood was everywhere. It stained her beautiful face. I bent over her, but she wasn't breathing. Her eyes were focused on the ceiling, but they were empty. Lifeless. I shook her. She didn't move. I shook her again. Still, nothing. I needed her to say something, anything, but she was silent. I didn't shed a tear. Instead, I placed my hands on her face and closed her eyes. I was angry. Who could have done this? I could feel my breathing accelerate. I didn't think my lungs could take in enough air. I crawled on the floor and sat against the cabinet and just looked at her. I remember thinking *no more pain, Mama, no more pain.*

"From upstairs, I heard a sound like someone was crashing into the wall. Then I heard my father's hacking cough. When I heard that sound, I leapt up from the floor and raced upstairs without thinking. He was in the bedroom, sitting on the bed with a half-empty bottle of vodka to his lips. He looked at me. To this day, I know he smiled. The sick bastard smiled and winked at me. I looked at the gun he had on the bed next to him. He drank the rest of the liquor in one gulp. As he put the bottle down, I walked over to him and grabbed the gun. I put it to his forehead. I asked him what happened to mama even though it was obvious. I just wanted to hear him admit what he had done so that I would be able to pull the trigger. He didn't say a word. I asked again. He refused to answer. Then he told me to pull the trigger. *'Pull the mutha-fuckin' trigger, you little bastard,'* he said. *'Be a man for once. Do it!'* As much as I wanted to, I couldn't. He called me a bitch and told me to use it or he'd make me wish I had. Then, he grabbed the gun from me. He hit me across the face with the butt of the gun and I fell to the floor. I managed to stumble my way back to my feet and I tackled him. My father was a big man, so it wasn't long before he'd taken control. All the while he kept laughing and telling me to fight like a man and not like a bitch. I tried to hurt him, to move him off me, but he was too strong. He kept hitting me in the face until blood poured out of me. I coughed up blood. As I lay on the floor, too much in pain to move, he pulled off my pants. I didn't really understand what was going on until I felt him penetrate me. I screamed. It was like nothing I've ever felt before. But he kept going. When he was done, he went over to the bed and blew his brains out in front of me."

I listened to James' words. That story, filled with so much pain, violence, and anger, contained so many parallels to my existence. For the first time, I understood him, at least a part of him. Even though his world had been destroyed so many years ago, I resisted the temptation to find pity for him. Like I told Tony, we couldn't continue to blame our childhood for the lives that we now led. At some point, we'd have to be grown enough to face the past head-on. I knew I wasn't the right person to preach this lesson to him, so I didn't speak. I held him, because in that moment that's what he needed.

CHAPTER 22

"You did what? Kevin, why?" The alarm sounded in Danea's voice as I told her the whole sordid story. "You know how women are. She probably thinks she has some sort of chance with you. You know she's looking for a relationship."

"I told her in the beginning that I was in a relationship, and that I had no intention of leaving, so she knows that we're not going to be together. She's the first girl I've been with in almost three years. I guess I just wanted to see if I could still do it."

"You know that ain't right. She could get her feelings hurt."

"The only feeling involved was lust, and I think we took care of that." I thought for a few seconds about the entire experience. It lacked the passion and anticipation I experienced in having sex with a man. With her, it was just something to do or something to prove to myself.

"I'm really worried about you. You've always been faithful to the man in your life, and now all of a sudden you meet this girl and have sex with her? What's going on between you and James? And remember, this is me you're talking to." I realized after I told her about RaChelle that it was a mistake; she'd always remind about this. Her attorney mind went to work searching for a motive for my actions, and I realized she would not let me off the hook without some explanation; only now, I knew I couldn't lie anymore. Something in my head just clicked; it was like a light coming on.

"Why don't I come over there so we can talk about this? But I don't know how you'll react after I tell you. I want you to promise me that nothing will change between us." I wanted to let Danea in on my secrets. I had rehearsed the lines many times. I hoped when I got to her place they would come out. I grabbed my keys and shot down the highway. As I drove, I rehearsed and practiced my lines over and over. I needed to get to her house and tell her every-thing before I changed my mind. When I got to her complex, I parked my car and hurriedly made my way to her door. I had to tell her this while I could. Even though I had told Tony, it still was not easy to find voice for the pain. I rehearsed my lines again, but wasn't sure what would come out of my mouth.

✖✖✖

"I want you to know this is not easy for me to tell

you. In fact, I vowed a long time ago to never tell anyone because I didn't want to deal with the looks of disappointment, and the judgments, but I value your advice and I need your support."

"Come on now, I'm your friend. You don't have to worry about that." She handed me a warm mug of tea with steam seeping slowly into the air. "Just take your time." She leaned back against the sofa and waited patiently for my words to come.

"Have you ever wanted something so badly, but you didn't know how to get it?"

"I think we've all been there."

"What did you do?"

"I had to evaluate and decide if the goal I set for myself was realistic. Once I decided that it was, I went after it, and never stopped moving toward it."

"That sounds good and all, but that's not really what I mean. It's kind of hard to explain."

"Well, keep trying."

"I'm in this situation and I want to move beyond it, but each time I try, I feel like I get sucked right back into that same hole. I'm at the point where I want to change, but a lot of things keep holding me down. I don't know what to do."

"What do you want to change?"

"My whole life," I said cynically.

"You want to narrow it down a bit?"

"I don't know, Danea. You remember how when we first went to college we had all of these big dreams and plans for the future? I had my entire life plotted out from beginning to end. None of the stuff I planned for happened."

"That's not true. You graduated from UT, and you have your master's in business. You are close to having it all."

"Everyone keeps telling me that, but it sure doesn't feel that way. I used to think I could conquer the world. Now, sometimes it's a struggle just to make it through the day and keep my sanity. What happened? I want to be that person I used to be."

"What is making you feel this way?"

"There's too much. Too much of everything." She leaned over and touched my hand. Her warmth was reassuring and put me at ease. "I want to leave James, Danea, but I can't. I just can't."

"It's a lot easier than you think it is. A lot of times in life when decisions need to be made we put them off because we get comfortable with the status quo. It's a lot easier to stay with the same than to change to something new."

"I'm not really afraid of changing; I just don't know how to break this bond that we share. There's so much about our relationship that you don't understand. No one does."

"Why don't you tell me?"

"I don't know if you want to hear this. I know I don't want to say it." Something told me she'd understand. "Danea, a few weeks after Keevan died, I tried to kill myself, but James saved my life." I looked at her wide eyes and I knew she wanted to speak, but she allowed me this time uninterrupted. "I had it all planned out. Everything was set in motion. I was in the store buying a few last-minute items for it, when this stranger came out of nowhere and saved my life. He walked up to me and told me that what I was about to do was wrong and wouldn't solve my problems. He told me basically that someone I loved didn't want me to do it. That stranger was James. He saved my life, and things have never been the same since. I think I'm afraid of breaking this bond with him. What if..."

"What if what? What if you try it again?"

"Exactly. I never thought I was capable of suicide, but Keevan's death changed so much about me. I'm afraid of what I might do."

"You have to deal with whatever issues that brought you to the brink of suicide."

"I want my brother back."

"One day, in a different place, on a different level, you'll be reunited. As for now, right now, the best thing that you can do is remember him, and love him."

"I do love him. I love him more than I love myself.

I just don't know if he loves me. I don't want to deal with the pain. I want it to go away. I don't want to feel hurt, or guilt anymore."

"Why do you doubt your brother's love for you? You forget that I knew and loved Keevan as well. I know he loved you just as much as you love him. Why should you feel guilty?"

"What?"

"You said you don't want to feel guilty anymore. Guilty about what?" The word had indeed slipped out of my mouth unintentionally.

"Nothing, I mean..."

"What are you feeling guilty about?"

I rubbed my hands over my face as if that would wipe away my shame. "Danea, you have no idea what I've been dealing with since his death. No matter where I go, no matter what I do, it keeps coming back to me. I want to be free more than anything, but I'm not sure what to do or say to make it go away. I can't change the past. I know this, but how do I live in the present?"

Slowly, I told about my affair with Darius. She tried to suppress her look of shock, but I could see it in her eyes. In so many weeks, I'd told two people the secrets I had locked away in the dark for so long. This was part of my liberation. Finally, I was opening the door of my prison.

"How do I let go? How do I learn to live again?"

"For one, you've got to confront the pain. You can't run from it, or lock it away. You've got good friends here to help. You can do this. Guilt is a terrible price to pay."

"I need to see him. I need to visit him."

The sound of the doorbell ringing brought us back to the present. Danea got up from where she sat and walked over to the door, while making sure that her blue silk robe was tightly closed. I wiped the tears from my eyes.

"Who is it?"

"It's me, Danea. It's Daryl."

"Daryl, I forgot you were coming over," she said while opening the door.

"What took you so long? You must have some man in here," he said jokingly.

"I wish I had a man in here."

"Hey, what am I then?" I asked Danea. "I guess I'm just chopped liver."

"You know you don't count. You're like my brother," she said with a little laugh.

"Kevin, I didn't know you'd be here. Danea should have told me." He looked at me as if he'd seen a ghost.

"Daryl, nice to see you." We moved toward each other and exchanged a brief hug. Daryl moved in and just as Danea was about to close the door, Daryl told her to wait. In walked a very attractive, dark-skinned brother with dazzling, deep-set eyes.

"Danea, Kevin, I want you to meet my friend, Aeryk."

"I'm sorry, I didn't know you were behind him," Danea said. Aeryk reached out and shook Danea's hand and then he walked over to me as Daryl introduced us nervously. This was a very awkward moment. Danea in her robe. Daryl with some man. And me, standing alone fighting off jealousy.

"I just dropped by because I need to get that information from you that I have on your computer, Danea."

"Right. I'm sorry. I completely forgot. I have to run upstairs and print it out. Come in guys, and have a seat. You want something to drink?" she asked, and they both declined.

I walked back into the den and took a seat. Aeryk came in and sat in the chair to my right while Daryl and Danea marched up the stairs. I picked up the remote control and started flipping through the channels.

"What's going on?" he asked, trying to be cordial. I really was not in a mood to entertain someone else's man, but I was getting curious.

"Nothing." I continued flipping channels. "How long have you known Daryl?" I didn't feel like being subtle or even pleasant.

"Just a couple of weeks. I just moved here from New York. "

"What brings you to Houston?"

"A change of pace."

"Are you running from something or someone?" I said with a little grin.

"Not at all. I just got tired of New York, and I got a job here. I'm a writer."

"What kind?"

"I write fiction. Primarily about the black experience."

"Where did you get a job?"

"Well, I will be teaching a few writing and English courses at the University of Houston. I used to teach in New York as well."

"You sound like a busy man. When did you meet Daryl?"

"We met on a plane to Houston. We found out that we share a lot of the same interests and became friends. He's one of the few people that I've met since I've been here."

I did remember Daryl telling me about a trip to New York, but I didn't get any details from him.

"Oh, I see."

"How do you know him?"

"Daryl and I have a *long* history together. We've been friends for a long time. I don't know if he told you about his friends, but we're really protective of each other."

"He did allude to that fact, but he said Danea was

the one that I had to worry about. I don't think he mentioned you...*at all.*"

He was trying to come for me, but I would not let his pompous ass get the best of me. "I guess he likes to save the best for last."

"That's one way of looking at it," he said smugly and with a chuckle. I couldn't believe that Daryl would be interested in someone like him. Who did he think he was? Danea and Daryl walked downstairs talking and laughing, and not a moment too soon.

"Thanks for the use of the computer." Daryl gave Danea a kiss on the cheek and motioned for Aeryk.

"It was nice to meet you, Kevin." He extended his hand for a shake, but I pretended as if I didn't see it and walked over to Daryl who gave me a quick hug and a frown as they bounced out the door.

"Who was that?" I asked Danea.

"Who was what? Oh, you mean Aeryk? I don't really know much about him."

"Is Daryl dating him?"

"You might want to talk to Daryl about that."

"Oh, no, Danea, you're not going to get off that easy. You're holding back."

"I really don't want to talk about this. I'm not getting in the middle."

"I'm not asking you to get in the middle. I just want you to level with me."

"Kevin, I know that you and Daryl have this *thing* going on, but I know you really don't expect him to sit around and wait on you, do you?"

"I didn't say I *wanted* Daryl; I just wanted to know if he was dating Aeryk. That's all."

"You can tell yourself what you want, Kevin, but don't try to feed me the same shit."

"I would love to finish this conversation with you, but in case you forgot, I'm in the middle of rebuilding my *life*," I said.

"I know you are, and Daryl can be a part of that."

"From the looks of things, Daryl has his own life to lead."

don't know what made this Saturday different than any other day. When I woke up, I arose with an overwhelming feeling of being tired. Tired of the same old shit. Tired of James. Tired of running. Sick of this house. Sick of the lies. *Sick and tired of being sick and tired.*

During the course of the day, I continued my usual activities, but I knew something was coming. Something about this day was remarkable. In my heart of hearts, I knew *this* was the day. As soon as my eyes opened and were greeted by the light of day, it was clear. It was clear in my dreams the previous night. It was my first waking thought. Earlier that morning, I sat up in bed and looked around the room and examined the space carefully. I scrutinized everything from the furniture to each small buckle in the wallpaper. The carpet, the dresser, the closet door, the paintings on the wall, the fireplace, the candlesticks—everything cried out to me that now was the right time. Right then. That day.

Later, after I planned it all, I called Danea, but her machine picked up, and I didn't leave a message. I called her cell phone, but got her voice mail. Then, I called Daryl.

"Hey, Kevin. What's going on?"

"I need you to come with me. I'm going to the cemetery to visit Keevan and I don't want to go alone. Will you go with me?" I didn't have time to beat around the bush.

There was a slight pause. "Of course I will. When do you want to go?"

"Right now. I've put it off far too long. I have to go now."

"How do you want to do this? Where should we meet?"

"I'll just meet you at your house and then we can ride together." It meant a lot to me that he would be there for me on this day of reckoning. "And Daryl, thank you for always being there." I hung up the phone and walked over to the mirror. I looked closely at myself and tried to remember what I used to look like before all of the pain and stress. I could see faint scars on my face from cuts and bruises I had received; permanent reminders of this life.

✖✖✖

We rode in utter silence all the way to the cemetery during the forty-five minute drive along a winding country road. He could tell that I was preoccupied and he allowed me this quiet time. The vivid brush along the edge of the road added springtime color to the otherwise dull ride. A few times I could tell that Daryl wanted to speak, but he held his tongue, not wanting to disturb me. For most of the ride, I stared blankly out of the window, void of thought and emotion, simply enjoying the quiet of the country. It was truly beautiful. As we neared the cemetery, I placed my hand on his leg and held on for support.

Dark clouds rolled in and began to pour rain down on us from the skies. I tried not to take this as some sort of omen, but it was beginning to affect my already nervous disposition. I looked at Daryl hoping to find comfort in his warm smile. I did. I was nervous, and he could tell. He turned on his wipers and I watched as the blades displaced the water from side to side. I closed my eyes and lay my head back in the seat and took slow breaths so that I could remain calm. Daryl placed one hand on my leg and rubbed it to comfort me.

As we pulled into the cemetery, I made Daryl drive around the property a few times to let the rain pass. Within minutes, the once torrential rain turned into a trickle. He parked the car and gave me a kiss on the lips for comfort. I looked at him, and somehow I knew that everything was going to be fine. I opened the car door and made my exit. The cemetery grounds were well kept with neatly trimmed hedges and sprawling green grass. The only noticeable detraction was the grass that had sprouted up through the few cracks in the concrete sidewalk. My steps leading to Keevan's grave were slow and calculated; each step brought me closer to my destiny, to fate. The more steps I took, the greater the distance seemed to become. I stopped suddenly, noticing that my breathing had become thick.

From where I stood, I could see the huge gray headstone now, and even from my distance I could see the letters of his name etched on the stone: *Keevan Lamar Davis, 1974-2000.* A strangely warm sensation pulsated in the air as I neared his resting place. A familiar scent descended from the trees until the entire area dripped with a noticeable fragrance. Instantly, I recognized his favorite cologne: Polo Sport. The scent was so strong that I looked around for anyone else that could have been around, but the place was empty. Where could it be coming from? Daryl stood some distance behind me, allowing me to make this journey alone.

When I got to the gravesite, I looked at the marble stone and realized this was the finality of life as we know it. Anything that lay beyond the grave was to remain a mystery. I knelt down, as if by instinct, and felt the wet grass soaking through my pants as I touched the cold stone with nervous and guilty fingers. I reached out my hand and let my fingers trace the letters on his headstone that spelled his name. I missed him terribly. I felt a vibration, as if he was touching me back. I could see my fingers moving, but it was as if some other force was controlling them. That part of me that belonged to him almost felt real again. I turned around to sit, placing my back against the cool stone block, and pulled my knees into my chest.

"Keevan, I don't know what to say." When I spoke his name I felt overcome by the warmth again. His presence was so real; I could feel him in the wind, and smell him in the air. The gentle way the wind blew the leaves on the trees told me that he was not far. "What do I say now? After all this time. It's been over a year and it still feels like yesterday. Where do I even begin? I miss and love you, man." Then, the tears started to flow. "When you died, most of me died, too. That's how I have lived for the last year. Living in the shadows of my guilt and pain...but I can't do it anymore. I don't want to die, but Keevan, I can't live without you. How do I do that?

"All of this is my fault!" I yelled out with such force that I thought the earth moved. I picked up a handful of mud and grass and threw it away from me out of sheer frustration. "I'm so sorry for what I did. God as my witness, I would take your place if I could. I never meant to hurt you, but I betrayed you in one of

the worst ways. I deserve to take your place, but I can't."
My salty tears streaked my face, but did not dissuade
my words or my confession. "What do I do? How long
do I punish myself? Keevan, I love you, and just to
have your forgiveness would mean all the difference
in the world." I lowered my head into my knees and
let the tears roll. I felt hot, as if I was sitting in the
sun in the middle of the day, yet I could feel the cool
air on my skin.

*"You have my forgiveness." I heard a voice whisper
through the darkness. "You've always had it. You didn't
have yours." I looked to my right and there he sat, looking
much different from the image that often visited my
dreams. He had a fresh haircut, and he was neat and well-
dressed, wearing his favorite shirt. I remember cleaning
out his apartment and looking for that shirt, and never
finding it. "I was wondering when you were gonna visit
me. Do you like my new home?" he said with his bright
smile. All I could do was stare at him, my mouth open.
This really couldn't be him, I thought to myself, but when
I reached out my hand to touch him, he didn't fade away
like some vision. His flesh felt real, as real as mine did. The
scent of the cologne was even sweeter now. Surely, this wasn't
him. It couldn't be. I reached over to him and gave him a
hug with all of the love I could. I hoped that my embrace
would last forever. "Okay, you can let me go," he said as
he pushed me away, pretending as if he couldn't breathe.*

"*You act like I'm dead or something,*" *he said with his usual poor sense of humor. I had no choice but to smile. This was classic Keevan. Even in death, his sense of humor was bad.*

"*Keevan, I can't believe it. You're real. You're not dead! I want you to come home with me. Let's go home!*"

"*I'm only real to you, only in this moment, only in this place. The funny thing about life is that it's for the living.*" *He clutched my hand and the warmth of his flesh was as real as any sensation that I had. The longer I held it, the firmer it felt. "Home for me is another place." The look in his eyes brought a certain sadness and made me realize this was a fleeting moment. I grabbed his hand with intensity, determined not to allow any force to tear us apart. "I know you didn't think that I knew about you and Darius, but I did. I was just waiting for you to tell me. Whatever happened between you two is irrelevant now. It happened so long ago. Yet, you keep clinging to that moment, allowing your mistakes of yesterday to determine your today. Kevin, you are my brother and I have always loved you. I never wanted you to suffer. I never wanted you to live in misery. My forgiveness of you is not based upon how much you have suffered for me. All you had to do was face your demons instead of running from them.*"

"*I was afraid to face them. I was so wrong. I caused your death.*"

"*You didn't cause my death. When it's your time to go, there is no power anywhere that can save you from that dreadful knock at the door. That's how it goes. It was my time."*

"When you came to me in my dreams, you blamed me for it. You said you came back for me."

"I didn't blame you. You blamed you. That wasn't me. That was your imagination. You let your guilt get the best of you. You know if I was going to haunt you, I would have been much more creative."

"Don't make me laugh. I don't want to laugh. I did have an affair with Darius. I can't change that. "

"No, you can't change it, but you must get beyond it. I moved past it a long time ago. Do you remember how we used to be? Fun and full of life? Over the last year since I've been gone, you've let James change you. Your spirit has been caged. Free yourself." He got up and knocked the dirt and grass from the back of his jeans. He reached out his hand and pulled me up. He looked around and listened to the sounds that were not there. *"It is time."*

"So soon?"

"It hasn't been soon. I've been waiting here a year for you to come to see me. I've had enough of this doom and gloom. I want the light." He took a few steps back and turned and began to casually walk away. He stopped and looked at me one last time. *"Never stop speaking to me and know that I can hear you. Always remember me. Remember that you have the power to control your life, and never give that to anyone. There are some dark days ahead, but*

look up for strength, and always look for love. Always look for me under your heart. You're free. You're free. You're free." He turned and walked away in the distance until his body vanished.

✖✖✖

"Kevin, Kevin, are you okay?" I looked up and Daryl stood over me with a concerned look on his face. "Did you hit your head?" he said while pulling me up. "Are you okay?"

"What? I'm fine. In fact, I've never been better." I let a big smile capture my face, and I pulled him closer to me. I had to be sure that he was real. I took his hand and held it. I was back from the brink. And I had survived.

CHAPTER 24

L ater that evening, James sat across from me at the table, carefully considering each bite of food before he put his fork in his mouth. I had taken time to prepare a nice meal for myself. I felt like having soul food, because finally I'd won back my soul. I whipped up a nice helping of fried chicken, greens, macaroni and a lot of cheese, smothered pork chops and sweet potatoes. It was like the meal you'd have after a funeral when all of the neighbors would drop off a favored dish. As a contradiction, I poured two glasses of Merlot to go with the meal, and when I took my first sip, the dryness of the wine caught me off guard.

We sat in silence. That was not unusual. I ate my food and he ate his, as if we were two strangers who had stopped for coffee in a café in a strange city. I had no words for him, and when he did speak, it was to ask me to pass the salt, which I did. His voice was restrained. I studied his face closely. I noticed a few wrinkles that weren't there only weeks ago. He watched me watching him, but did not speak. It's hard to describe the end. It's that feeling you get in the pit of your stomach when you know you have nothing left to give. The feeling was unmistakable. In that moment, it hung in the air like the smell of rotting flesh in a country field. He knew it. I knew it. Moreover, I knew that he knew this was it. He knew this was the last meal, the last glass of wine, and the last dinnertime conversation. We both knew there was no avoiding the inevitable. He watched me watching him and finally spoke.

"Why are you looking at me like that?"

With deliberate hesitation, I said, "No reason." I almost smiled. His breathing quickened.

I had always thought this moment, the final moment in this relationship, would be marked by more drama, more emotion, or something profound. The end didn't come to me in a brilliant flash of light; this epiphany was not born from some haunting nightmare. There were no sounds of rolling thunder or trumpets blaring. Even still, it was clear and I felt such calm. I looked in his eyes from across the table—they bore no shame or sorrow, nor did they show any love that I could recognize. This man that sat across from me was never my lover, but always my jailer. He was not my friend, but forever my foe. He was never my calm, but invariably my storm.

"Kevin, I'm expecting a very important phone call regarding LCS business tonight, so I don't want you answering the phone at all." I got up from the table, again with no words, and walked into the kitchen to put away my plate, and to pour another glass of wine. James followed me into the kitchen. He wanted some sort of reaction, some nod from me to let him know that he was still in control. I would give him nothing.

"Did you hear me?" he asked.

"Of course I heard you."

"I would appreciate a response from you when I'm talking to you."

"That's fine. If the phone rings, you'll have to answer it because I won't be here."

"What? Where are you going?"

"I'm not sure yet."

"What are you up to?"

"James, I'm not up to anything."

"Don't lie to me. You're a lousy liar just like you're a lousy lay."

"Whatever." I was so calm. I continued rinsing out my plate and putting things in order as if he wasn't there.

"What does that mean?"

"It means just what I said." I turned to face him. He took a long look at the glare in my eyes. We stood in the kitchen, facing each other, confronting the truths between us. He stared at me trying to figure out what

I was feeling. Part of him actually looked scared. "Is there something else you want to talk about?"

He didn't respond. "Don't do it," he finally said. "Don't even think about it."

"Don't do what?"

"Don't play games with me, Kevin!"

"*It's* already done, and if this was a game, I'd be saying *checkmate.*" At that moment, the phone rang. He looked at it, but didn't want to move. He was torn. Either take the call, or try to prevent the inevitable. He wanted to say more to me, but we both knew his business call would always take precedence.

He tried to sound intimidating, but his final words echoed without substance. "If you leave, I will *hunt* you." As he raced for the phone, I shook my head in triumph.

PART II

PART II

I felt like a caged bird suddenly given the power to fly high above the trees into the clouds. When I looked down, I had the ability to see the world and its beauty defined by sprawling fields full of green grass, rolling hills, and gently moving ocean waves. The simple joys of life, such as birds singing or the exploding colors of budding flowers, taught me the values of appreciating what you have at that moment when you have it. I could see and appreciate lovers walking hand in hand. There is something so profound about freedom and reclaiming your life. I had lingered in the pits, but now I felt high as the sky. It was euphoric.

Once I started taking control of my life and the mistakes I'd made, I took on a sense of power, a sense of control and well being. It took some time to learn to love myself again, and to forgive myself for my sins and indiscretions. With the help of my friends, and the help of my therapist, Dr. Kellie Manheim, I was getting through it. Dr. Manheim was the kind of person whose presence puts you at ease. Each time I walked into her homey office, I felt relaxed. Her soothing voice assisted in unburdening my soul, and she had a way of lifting the weight of the world off my shoulders. She usually sat in the corner in a big black chair with a high back, her auburn hair pinned up in a tight bun with a few strands dangling at the sides. She wrote fastidiously as I spoke with amazing clarity and insight about my life. She only spoke to ask probing questions, but she knew exactly what to ask to get me to open up. She was a thick woman who always wore a nice pantsuit and the same pair of black pumps. I don't recall ever seeing her in a dress.

Through discussions about my relationship with James, I discovered my greatest fear was losing control over my life again. I was terrified of becoming that shell of a person who surrendered it all. I was afraid that one day, under different circumstances, I could become that caricature again. I was terrified of retreating into darkness rather than facing my fears in the light. Luckily, she was helping me come to terms with James and the ordeal of being abused physically, mentally and sexually. My life was changing in so many ways. I was reclaiming me.

✖✖✖

Living with Danea was definitely a big change from life in the mansion with a demon. Before I knew it, two months had passed and we were doing fine. It was almost like having a college roommate. Living with a woman was different, but I was enjoying myself, and things could not have been better. Keevan used to say the best way to ruin a friendship is for two friends to move in together. Cohabitation with friends has caused some friendships to go under faster than the Titanic. I used to know these girls, Angie and Nicole, who moved in together, and their lives turned into a heavyweight championship fight after Nicole borrowed one of Angie's dresses and didn't want to return it. Danea definitely did not have to worry about that.

We were sitting downstairs on a Friday night, drinking Chardonnay and watching *Living Out Loud* with Queen Latifah, when the phone rang. We looked at each other trying to decide which one was going to get up to answer it. After the second ring she realized that I wasn't going to get up, so she maneuvered her body toward the phone while throwing me one of those sista looks.

"Hello? This is she," I heard Danea say. The expressions on her face began to change, metamorphosing from confusion to anger. I picked up the remote control and hit the pause button so that I could focus on her conversation.

"I don't even appreciate you calling my house like

this." The conversation was beginning to get heated when she started rolling her neck in that soulful way that black women perfected. "You need to get off my phone before I..." Danea pulled the phone from her ear and looked at it disgustedly. "She hung up on me! I know she didn't." Danea put the phone down just long enough to have a thought form in her head. She snatched it off the receiver and said she was about to *69 her back and get this shit straight.

"Danea, just let it go right now. Just let it go." She looked at me as if I had just cursed at her, and kept the phone to her ear. Apparently, the other woman was not about to pick up the phone and had turned the machine off. Danea slammed down the phone, put her hands on her hips, and said, "Ain't this some shit."

"What? What was all that about?" She picked up her glass of Chardonnay and poured it down her throat, before plopping back down on the couch with a thump.

"I can't believe this! I ought to go over to that nigga's house right now." She shook her head from side to side, in disbelief, hoping to shake this off like a bad dream.

"Danea, what are you talking about?"

With a deep inhale, she spoke. "The guy that I've been seeing, Lyle—that was his wife."

"The attorney you met in court last month? He's married?!"

"Yeah, that's the sorry bastard. I knew something wasn't right about him. I felt it in my gut, but I didn't listen. I know better. Always listen to your first instinct. *Always*. I had a bad feeling about him, but I didn't listen."

"What did she say on the phone?"

"What do you think she said? The bitch said she was gonna kick my ass if I didn't leave her man alone!" Her braids began to dangle and she grabbed them with her hands and pulled them back in a ponytail. "Wait, it ain't right for me to call her a bitch. I don't even know her. I'm the one that's been sleeping with her husband."

"It ain't your fault. You didn't know he was married."

"Kevin, I knew something was wrong, but I didn't listen. Why do I always do this?"

"You both should be mad at him, and not each other."

"I know, you're right. I guess when someone calls me and threatens to beat the hell out of me it sort of makes me snap, if you know what I mean."

"I know what you mean. Remember, I've seen you snap. You remember that fight you had with Charmaine back in college? That was one catfight that people are still talking about." Danea looked up at me with a small smile that exploded into a big laugh. This Delta back in college accused Danea of messing with her man. One night Danea and I went to one of their sorority parties on campus, and the girl confronted Danea again. Danea told the girl that she did not want nor had ever been with her man. All night long Charmaine and her sorors kept messing with Danea. They were doing silly shit like bumping into Danea as the Deltas paraded around the room in one of their endless party struts. At the end of the night, as usual, the entire party ended up at IHOP. Charmaine dashed Danea with a glass of water, hoping she had enough backup with her sorors in the room. She was wrong. Charmaine got the hell beat out of her in the middle of the restaurant, and caused a few of her other sorors to catch a stray fist or two. It was truly a mess.

"I had forgotten about that. You know I saw that girl a few months ago and she looked at me like I was gonna run up and slap her face. It was a trip."

"I wish I'd had a video camera that night."

"I bet you do." She poured herself another glass of wine. "I'm so tired of meeting men who conveniently forget to tell you that they have a wife or girlfriend." She took another sip of Chardonnay and leaned back in the chair. "I have an idea; let's go out tonight. I don't want to be in the house."

"Where do you want to go?"

"Let's go to one of your clubs."

"My clubs?"

"Yeah, we could go to Rascal's. Isn't that the name of it?"

"That's the right name, but why would you want to go there?"

"That will keep me out of trouble. There is no way that I would meet someone in there and want to get involved. Don't worry, I'm not turning into a fag hag," she said with a laugh. "Call Tony and Daryl and see if they want to meet us."

"Knowing them, I'm sure they will already be there."

CHAPTER 26

Before the club, we downed a few more glasses of wine. This would be the first time I'd been to a gay club in well over a year. I went upstairs to my room and did a quick wardrobe change. I put on a black Armani fitted shirt, black slacks, and my new pair of Kenneth Cole black shoes with the new shine. I walked over to my dresser and looked at the various watches, rings, and necklaces laid out on the top. I chose a gold, thin herringbone necklace and my gold watch. When I looked at myself in the mirror, everything looked in place. I went downstairs, grabbed a bag of half-eaten Ranch Doritos and took a seat on the barstool. I picked up Danea's latest issue of *Essence* magazine, and a gorgeous dark-skinned model with a chiseled body and powerful smile on the cover stole my attention.

It took Danea the next hour to finally emerge from her salon, and we were out the door. I called Daryl and Tony, but neither was home, and I hated to leave messages sometimes. I was somewhat excited about going out and seeing the children again, even though I didn't want to admit it. The club was a place that black gay people in Houston could go and meet other gay people and be totally at ease with themselves, and not be worried about being "gay." It was a safe haven for a lot of people who had to pretend the rest of the week. We all pretended. At work. At school. At home, in some cases. We did it for ourselves, for our families, and our friends as a way of coping. Those gay people brave and bold enough to be out in the black community often wore their battle scars on their sleeves. Although many of us could admire their courage, most knew we weren't ready to deal with the alienation that comes with being "out." Some people simply had too much to lose. For some, the club was a sanctuary. For some, it was a breath of fresh air. Once, I went to the club and ran into one of my college professors. He never looked at me the same after that.

We drove down the cramped and winding road on Westheimer and finally parked next to the Wendy's in front of the club. A group of young club kids, in their tight jeans and body shirts, stood next to the pay phone with wanting eyes, hoping to have their sexuality or allure validated by someone. Anyone.

"You sure about this?" I asked, not really sure if I was sure, but walking toward the club anyway. I took a moment to reflect on some of the good times we used to have in this club. Back then, Houston's gay life was something to talk about. Now, for a myriad of reasons including mass relocations to hipper cities, it just wasn't the same, from what I'd heard.

"What's to be sure about?" She grabbed my hand and led us through oncoming traffic to the other side of the street. Horns blew and people yelled, but she was in such a rush that it didn't faze her. After standing in line for a few minutes, we entered the club. Not much had changed since the last time I was there. The sunken dance floor in the middle of the room was packed with men and women dancing to pumping R&B beats. Slinky bodies moved with sexual overtures and seductive enticements. Sweat dripped off hard and soft bodies, male and female. Along the sides of the floor, a lot of people stood by, talking, looking, and giving that club pose and 'tude that gay men had perfected. It was your club presence that separated you from the rest. It was a look that said, "I am somebody that you want to be with," which was far from the truth in most cases. Those were the kinds of men I rarely talked to. *They were too many things—none of them good.*

When we walked through the club we looked up, down, around, side to side, over, under, and in between to get acclimated to our environment. I'd been there before, but it had been a long time. There was a bar immediately on the left side of the club when we entered, another one in the back by the patio, one upstairs near the pool room, and one in the VIP room. I went into the VIP room only once. That's where the club strippers performed special routines for a clientele that paid good money to have the honor of a private show. The club itself was actually pretty small, but that didn't stop people from pouring in like rain.

Danea stood in line at the patio bar because there was more room there, and I stood by and watched the gyrations on the floor. I was mesmerized. I watched this dark-skinned guy with baby-smooth skin—I think he used to be a stripper—contort his body so hypnotically that I fell in a trance. He commanded the attention of the entire room with his sensuality and the dancers all stepped back and let him do his thing. *And what a thing it was.* By his facial expressions, I could see that he was in another place, far from here, removed from the hoots, hollers, and catcalls. The music, its erotic beats and pounding rhythm, put him over the top. He was in his own place and time, undaunted by our heavy stares that dripped with desire. He danced for himself, and people began dropping dollar bills all around him as if this was one of his strip shows. I don't know about the rest of them, but I'd pay money to see him shake his *naked* groove thang.

"Here's your drink," Danea said as she handed me

a colorful glass filled to the brim with a milky liquid. I snapped out of my trance.

"What is this?"

"It's a Screaming Orgasm. I think we both could use one of those," she said laughing. "Only your chances of finding one in here are a lot greater than mine."

"I don't know. I saw some women checking you out when we walked in. I'm sure they'd be more than willing to help you out."

"I'm sure they would, but you know that's not my style."

"Don't knock it till you try it. I hear they can do wonders with their tongues." She gave me a push and we both laughed.

When I looked around the club again, I realized that it was a sea of new faces. The crowd seemed to be younger and wilder than the last time I was here, but what did I expect after a year hiatus? The fashion police would definitely cite some of the clothes these kids wore. Where the hell do you buy see-through lace shirts with white polka dots and shoes with a thick five-inch heel all around? Some things weren't meant for me to know, I guess.

"Are you having fun yet?" she asked me.

"I'm relaxing. So far so good." We let the music take control and before we knew it, we both were out on the dance floor shaking our asses, drink in one hand, and smiles on our faces. I saw Tony pushing his way through the crowd in a beeline toward us. When he got there, he said something, but the music was so loud that I didn't understand him. I just winked at him, continued my dancing, careful not to lose a beat. He joined us as the music played on and the beat moved up my spine. By the time we left the dance floor, my shirt was soaked with sweat, but I didn't care. It felt good to be able to enjoy the good times again. We moved to the back of the club and I saw Daryl leaned against the bar in a cool pose.

"Damn, it looks like y'all got your serious dance on," Daryl said while handing us a few napkins from the bar.

"You don't know the half of it," Danea said. "This is so cool 'cause I don't have to worry about impressing anyone. I can just be free and dance. You know at a regular club I never would have danced that hard. Look at me. I couldn't walk around like this at the Ritz."

"I wouldn't recommend walking around like that anywhere," Tony said jokingly.

"Oh, shut up. It's not like you look any better."

"That may be true, but I can still pull the boys."

"Y'all are crazy," Daryl said. "Kevin, I am surprised to see you out. It's been a while."

"Blame Danea, it's all her fault." I took one of the thin white napkins and began to dry my face, but the cheap paper crumbled into little pieces of white flakes. Daryl took his hand and wiped the paper fragments from my skin. His touch was gentle yet masculine. The pheromones in his cologne were magnetic, and I felt like I was being pulled into him. "How is that guy you're dating? Aeryk?" I asked as I took a few steps back.

"Who said I was dating him?" I gave him one of my *nigga-pleeze* looks and he cracked a smile. "He's okay, I guess. We don't talk very often anymore."

"Ahhh, so now it's strictly booty calls?" By this time, Tony and Danea were back on the dance floor wiggling everything they had that wasn't strapped down.

"You want a drink?" he asked.

"No, I'm fine, but if you want one I'll be right here." He nodded to me, turned and fought his way through the crowd. He went upstairs to the less-crowded bar.

Daryl was wonderful, and I knew I loved him, but I had too many issues. I wasn't at a place where I needed or wanted a long-term relationship. I had just gotten out of one, and I knew if we got together, it would be for the long haul. I wanted to tell him what I felt, but I wasn't ready to. I didn't want to lead him on, but I couldn't let him go nor could I be with him. During my sessions with Dr. Manheim, she noticed that he was usually a part of my conversation. He knew how I felt, but I didn't want to say it again. For now, like Jennifer (that's Ms. Holliday) said, he'll have to "Read It In My Eyes."

While he was gone, I decided to use the restroom.

The one across from the back bar had a line waiting, so I eased my way through the crowd, fought off inviting smiles, and finally made it out to the patio. I grabbed the metal railing and moved my way up the staircase. On the metal balcony, there were a couple of people hugged up in the corner, enjoying a private moment. Quickly, I opened the glass door and walked into the upstairs pool room. The restroom was on my left.

After I finished my business, I zipped my pants, and turned only to be startled by the image of someone. *James*. I looked at him, and he looked at me.

"I saw you downstairs and I wanted to say hello. I didn't come here to start anything; I just wanted to see you, and I wanted to talk with you for just a few moments." His shaky voice sounded as if it was about to collapse into a whisper. I turned my back to him, turned the water on, and pumped some soap out of the dingy metal container. Seeing him gave me a horrible flashback, but I didn't want him to think that he had made me nervous, so I inhaled in annoyance. Casually, I dried my hands and leaned with my back against the sink to face him. I crossed my legs at the ankles, and folded my arms.

"Say what you have to say."

"I just wanted you to know that I miss you, and that I love you, and that I'm sorry for the way things happened."

"Now you've said your piece, so move out of my way." Inside, I wasn't nearly that composed. I wasn't afraid of him, but he was a painful reminder of who I used to be. I hadn't seen him face to face since I left, even though he'd called several times.

"Wait, I'm not finished."

I looked at him, raised one eyebrow, sucked in some air, blew it out loudly, and sighed again. "What?"

"Is there any chance, I mean, do you think that one day—I don't mean tomorrow—but sometime soon, I could take you to dinner? I was thinking that we could start over again. You know, from the beginning, and fall in love again."

"When did you ever love me, James?" The agitation in my voice became increasingly apparent with each syllable that I spoke.

"I loved you from day one. I've always loved you. I still love you."

"I guess you loved me so much that you beat the shit out me just to make me feel special? Is that how it goes?" His eyes sank low into his skull. "No, James, you and I cannot have dinner, we cannot start over and try to be what we never were." As I moved toward him, he turned sideways in the door, partially blocking my exit. "And stop calling my fuckin' house, nigga."

As the door swung open and I stepped out into the pool room, I heard his faint voice say, "I'll never let you go."

CHAPTER 27

I woke up in the middle of the night and felt Keevan's presence in the room. It wasn't threatening, but offered comfort. I touched the lamp on my nightstand and the room glowed with a yellow light. The picture of my brother on my dresser faced me. I sat up in the bed and smiled. For some reason, I thought how during our pledging process he was kidnapped by a group of renegade fraternity brothers from Prairie View A&M University. I remembered looking for him all day. He wasn't in any of his classes, and when I called his job I was told that they hadn't heard from him. By the time the rest of the brothers called us that evening for a session, we still hadn't heard from him. That night, I took his wood. My ass was so sore that I could barely sit for a week. After all the trouble I'd gotten him into over the years, I guess it was my turn then. Sometimes, you have to pay the price.

I got out of bed, stretched and headed downstairs for a glass of water. As I slid my foot into my slipper, the phone rang and I answered it instinctively. It was 2:54 in the morning. "Hello?" I said. No response. I looked at the caller ID box, but the number registered as unavailable. I heard breathing on the phone and what I thought was the sound of someone's hand stroking flesh. "Hello?" The pace of the breathing quickened and became sexual. I don't know why I didn't hang up the phone. I continued to listen until I heard short moans and grunts. By this time, I had become so angry that I was yelling into the phone, but the more I yelled, the louder the moans became until I finally hung up. Some pervert jacking off on my phone in the middle of the night. This was not my idea of a hot date.

✖✖✖

Reinvention of myself was the primary key I hoped would allow me to redefine my life. Out with the old and in with the new. Throughout college, Keevan pushed me into getting involved with some community service project, but I always resisted. I was too busy running around, or just not interested enough to give back to the community. Having survived his death, and my life with James, I realized there are far more important things than just having a good time and gettin' my party on. *I am changing.*

When RaChelle presented me with the idea of mentoring, my first instinct was to brush her aside, but the more I thought about it, the more I began to like the idea. I kept going back and forth on deciding, but she was relentless. I read through the brochure about the program several times and became intrigued. I knew I had a lot to give, and if I could be a positive influence on someone, then that's what I should do.

I had put the brochure about Texas House down, picked up a glass of orange-pineapple juice, and started reading another report for work at the kitchen table when the phone rang. The familiar voice seemed a bit shaken, but in control. "What's wrong, Croix?" I asked.

"I did it. Man, I can't believe I did it."

"What did you do?"

"What do you think I did? What have I been talking about for months now?"

"You've been talking about a lot of things. Don't make me guess. What did you do?"

"I left her."

"You did what? Are you sure this is what you want? Where are you now?"

"I've never been more sure about anything, but Kevin, I'm scared."

"What happened? "

"Can we talk about this in person? Can I come over?"

"Of course."

"I'll be there in half an hour."

✖✖✖

I don't know why my heart skipped a beat when the doorbell rang. When I opened it, Croix stood there, breathing slightly accelerated, looking as if he'd just stepped out of an ad for *GQ*. I invited him in, or at least he stepped forward, and I offered him something to drink. He looked like he needed something strong so I stepped behind the bar and fixed a martini. His eyes, almost glowing, reflected the joy that I felt when I left James. This I could relate to. Freedom is breathtaking.

"So, start talking."

He took his drink from me and killed it in one quick gulp. Even though he looked calm, I could see his hands shaking.

"I got home from work early and when I walked in, the house was a wreck. I mean the cushions from the couch were on the floor, and the chair was turned on its side. Man, it was so bad I thought we'd been robbed."

"Is she okay? Nothing happened to her, did it?"

"No, her ass is okay. I went upstairs and she didn't hear me come in because she was on the phone with her ghetto-ass sister. She was in the closet going through her clothes, with her back to me. She was telling Gina that she couldn't find her wedding ring, *and get this, Kevin,* the last time she remembered taking it off was at Keith's house."

"Who is Keith?"

"That nigga she was *fucking* a while back. I thought it was over between them, but she's been seeing his ass all this time." He handed me his glass again and indicated that he'd like a refill. "You should have seen her face when she turned around and saw me. I thought she was gonna have a heart attack. She dropped the phone and started begging and crying, saying that nothing happened when she went over there." I gave him another drink, and this time he sipped instead of gulped. "You should have seen how cool I was. I looked at her and just turned around. She knows it's over."

"What are you going to do now?"

"I'm going to call my lawyer first thing in the morning and get this divorce thing started. I'm tired of putting my life on hold with her. She's not worth my time. And you know the best thing about it? We have a prenuptial agreement. She may walk away with the clothes on her back. I'd like to see that broke-ass nigga take care of her. She's in for a rude awakening."

"What about the kids?"

"I'm filing for joint custody. I don't want to take them away from her. She is a good mother, just a lousy wife."

I raised my drink for a toast. "Here's to new beginnings."

CHAPTER 28

Something *must be in the air tonight*, I thought to myself on that hot and muggy Thursday evening. Everything appeared to be fine, but Croix dropped some unexpected news into my lap. Croix is a good man and deserved respect and happiness, and he wasn't getting it from his wife. I can't imagine why a woman would cheat on a man as fine as Croix. I have learned that people will sometimes cheat regardless of how good they have it at home, or how fine their significant other is. People cheat… because they can,

For a second, my mind drifted to the thought of Croix finding happiness in the arms of a man. I could see his warm smile and sincere eyes loving a man who could offer him the love that he missed during the course of his marriage. I wasn't sure, however, if Croix was ready for that. But then again, after years of denying that burning desire, a man may be what he needed to quench that flame.

About an hour after Croix left, Tony arrived with his friend LaMont, followed by Daryl, and when Danea came through the door, the set was complete.

At some point within the past several weeks Tony and his eternal love LaMont had reconciled. We sat aroud and talked until Tony got up and returned with a deck of cards. The next thing I knew, we were engaged in a serious game of spades. We were laughing, arguing and having a good time doing something very simple. Just like we used to do.

I couldn't help but think about Keevan. Our circle seemed empty without him, but I knew he was somewhere looking over us. This was the kind of thing we used to do when he was alive: Get some people together, get some drinks, and a deck of cards. Those trash-talkin' games would sometimes last until the morning.

When I thought about my brother, I smiled. No longer did his memory haunt me or bring me to the verge of tears. I could sit around and think about him all day and remember the good times we had. I could sing, laugh, smile, dance, do cartwheels, play music, and watch movies while basking in the joy of his memory. They say death is that place where you exist only in the minds of others. If that is true, Keevan is very much at my side, now and forever more.

"Okay, this game is ovah!" Danea said as she reached over the table and gave me a high-five. This was the second game in a row that we'd beaten Tony and Daryl, and they were not happy. Tony was really competitive about this game, and if it were a sport in the Olympics, he'd surely be a contender. "You feel like another round?"

"If we play again, I need another partner. I can't win with this novice," Tony said snidely at Daryl.

"Novice my ass. I was carrying you!"

"Carrying me where? I don't know what game you were at, but if it hadn't been for me, you'd never even come close to winning," Tony shot back. "LaMont, I need you to play."

"Y-Y-You know I don't play cards." LaMont continued looking through the magazine on the table. This caramel-colored brotha with the sandy-brown dreadlocks looked as if he was having about as much fun as waiting for the grass to grow. He thumbed through the magazine without reading a single word, or even looking at the pictures. Tony looked at us and smiled, trying to be cordial.

"What do you wanna do, LaMont?"

"I-I-I don't wanna be sittin' up here watching no card game all night." It took him an extra few seconds to complete his sentence through his stutter, but we all pretended not to notice.

"Then you need to decide what you want to do."

"I have an idea," Danea interrupted. Then she blurted out, "Let's go to New Orleans."

"New Orleans? Get serious. We can't go to New Orleans tonight," Daryl said.

"And why not?" she shot back. "Live a little, Daryl.

Where is your sense of adventure? What's keeping us here?"

"For one thing," Daryl said, "work. I can't just up and roll to New Orleans on a whim. I have this big project that I'm working on. I don't know if I can afford to take time off."

"You know how busy I've been with work, too, Danea. I don't know if I can afford to take time off either," I added.

"You'd only be missing one day. Let's listen to the girl. She just may have a point," Tony said.

"My friend Curtis is the manager at the Versailles Hotel in the French Quarter. He's one of my…well, let's just say that he's an old friend. He said if I was ever in New Orleans, to give him a call and he'd hook me up with a room." Without blinking or changing expressions, Tony handed Danea the cordless phone. "His number is upstairs. Give me five minutes."

"You've got four," Tony said. Danea left the phone on the table and darted upstairs.

I thought a bit: Maybe a vacation was just what I needed. "Hmmm, New Orleans is sounding pretty good right now," I said to Daryl. "Shit, if she can get these rooms on this short notice, I'm in."

"What about work?" Daryl asked.

"I'll call right now and leave my boss a message. It's been a long time since I've been on Bourbon Street, and I feel like a road trip. Tony?" I asked as I turned and looked his direction. He took a sip of water, rolled his head, and responded.

"You know you ain't said nothing but a word." Tony then turned to LaMont and gave him a quick look.

"Oh, y-y-y-y…y-you know I'm down." Daryl gently nudged me in the side trying not to be obvious. LaMont was a round-the-way kind of guy, but his stuttering problem took some getting used to. And when he pronounced words like "street" or "straight," he did it ebonics-style, saying "screet" or "scraight."

When she raced down the stairs, the glow on her face spoke far louder than the words that escaped her mouth. "Okay, Bourbon Street, here we come!"

"We're going?" Tony asked. When Danea replied in the affirmative, they grabbed each other and started dancing around the room like they'd never been to New Orleans before.

"We need time to pack," Daryl asserted. He looked down at his watch and thought for a second before continuing. He was always very calm and collected. "Okay, if we all meet back here at 10 tonight, no later than 10:30, we can be on the road by 11 and in New Orleans by 4 or 5. We can sleep when we get there and get out into the city in the afternoon. How does that sound?"

"It sounds like a plan to me," I answered, and soon

everyone was in agreement. "Go home and get packed," I said. "We've got some partying to do." Danea smiled, clapped her hands in excitement, and moved upstairs. I walked them over to the door, and when I opened it, RaChelle was standing there, just about to ring the bell.

"Perfect timing," she said with a glowing smile. " I was in the neighborhood, so I thought I'd drop by and return your CDs. Hello, everyone," she said with a big wave. On their way out, they exchanged simple pleasantries and spoke briefly, more out of courtesy, and not due to a particular fondness for her. The few times she'd been in their presence for more than ten minutes, she managed to say something to rub one of them the wrong way. I knew what her next question would be.

"Where is everyone going in such a hurry?"

"We're going to…New Orleans," I answered. I didn't want to give her too many details and I didn't want her hanging around here. I just wanted her to give me back my CDs and hit the road so she wouldn't overstay her welcome, like she usually did.

"Really? What's going on in New Orleans this weekend?"

"Nothing, just us. We all need a vacation."

"Spontaneity is a good trait," she said with a wink. "It has so many possibilities. Me and some sorors back in college were quick to jump on a plane and end up in New York or somewhere." *I bet a plane ain't the only thing she was quick to jump on,* I thought.

"I just wanted to say thanks for letting me borrow these CDs." Danea's voice called out my name from upstairs.

"You're welcome," I said to her. Danea called out again. "Just a minute, Danea," I yelled back.

"And don't think for one second that I've forgotten about Texas House. We need you, Kevin. If you want, you can come over when you get back into town and we can discuss the project again." She winked at me. I know she wanted me to come over and hit it again, but that was going to be just a one-time experience.

After I walked RaChelle out to her car, and after she surprised me with a kiss, I went into my room and grabbed a duffel bag from the closet—the same bag I used to pack my clothes when I left James. I found my garment bag and put some of my finer clothes in it, and stuffed some socks and underwear in the duffel. I went into my bathroom and pondered which three bottles of cologne to take. I never traveled with less than three. I liked options, and I didn't necessarily like wearing the same scent two days in a row. I chose my favorites, Jean-Paul Gaultier, Dolce & Gabbana and a bottle of Escape by Calvin Klein. Thirty-five minutes later, I was good and ready.

✖✖✖

We were on the road by midnight, and in New Orleans by 6:30 a.m. We ran into some heavy traffic right outside of Baton Rouge, because of an accident involving an eighteen-wheeler and a tree. From what we could tell, the driver was okay. I couldn't say the same about the truck or the tree.

While stuck in traffic, and for most of the way, we sang just about every song known to man, with Danea and Daryl playing lead vocals most of the time. They were the only two that could sing with any sense of hitting the right notes. Sitting in the back, I felt like a Pip, and we had our Gladys. Danea sang the hell out of that old Shirley Murdock song, "As We Lay," when Tony put the Kelly Price CD in the player. I liked listening to Danea's voice perform vocal wonders and improvisations. She added a few extra runs and some alternative notes that gave that song a fresh new appeal. She and Daryl gave a great performance of "Fire and Desire" by Rick and Teena.

We found the hotel and checked into adjoining suites. We were all feeling tired because we were too busy singing and acting silly on the way there to get any rest; plus it was still very early.

"Y-y-yo b-b-boy h-h-h-h-h-ooked us up! Dis joint is off da hook," LaMont said as he dropped Tony's bag in the middle of the room, then rushed to the balcony. The sun, rising slowly and confidently in the morning sky, ignited the city with the sparkle of day. "Yo, ch-ch-check out dis view! We overlookin' Bourbon Screet."

I tried not to laugh, but Danea couldn't help it. I can't remember the last time I'd seen anyone so excited about New Orleans. It was his first time here, and the sun had barely risen, but he was about to have a fit. *Just wait until this evening when the streets are packed*, I thought to myself. We all moved closer to look over the balcony. Danea went over to the bed and plopped down like she had just finished working in the fields.

"Okay, who's sleeping where?" Daryl, the eternal organizer, asked. Danea sat up in bed, and looked around the room.

"Since there are two double beds in here, and one king in the other suite, I guess Tony and LaMont should have the other room, 'cause I'm not trying to listen to any slurping sounds tonight," she said with a laugh.

"Don't hate on me 'cause Tony's Got A Man," he shot back in the melody of Chante's song.

"That leaves the other bed for me and Kevin," Daryl surmised.

"And like I said, I'm not trying to listen to any

slurping or any other sounds for that matter." She directed that comment toward us.

"Yeah, Kevin, and don't be trying to feel on my booty," he said with a wiggle of his firm ass.

CHAPTER 29

After we did some light resting, we changed clothes and decided to have a late lunch. We were going to eat in the hotel, but Daryl insisted on finding some authentic New Orleans flavor, which meant we ended up driving around for about an hour looking for a suitable restaurant that offered that special Creole taste. We ended up stopping at this small place called Dauphine's in the French Quarter, which was three blocks from the hotel. I had the best crawfish étoufée! It was so spicy that I lost feeling on my tongue for a few minutes, but that didn't slow my appetite.

We then did some sightseeing, shopping and took a nice long riverboat ride on the Mississippi. While on the ship, I rested my arms on the railing and stared into the murky water below us. This river had so many stories to tell, stories about a people from a faraway land forced into servitude, stories that were washed away with each wave. The city of New Orleans is indeed a unique place. As I leaned over the railing, Daryl came and stood beside me. He looked at me with his sweet face and didn't say a word. His eyes said all that he was feeling. I smiled at him, and he smiled at me,

By the time we returned to the hotel it was about seven in the evening. We didn't know this weekend there would be a jazz festival on Bourbon Street, but that made it all better. That city just looked for reasons to have a celebration. I could hear trumpets blaring and the saxophones singing in anticipation of the evening crowds. The music beckoned people from their homes, their hotels, their cars and lured them with the promise of good times and laughter. When I looked out of the window down onto the street below, a parade full of color and sound was slowly making its way down the narrow street. People filled the sidewalks and held up their drinks in celebration. The boisterous noises of revelers filled the warm evening air with merriment as the parade crept by.

"We need to hurry. The streets are getting packed."

"I hope there are some fine men down there," Danea said with laughter.

"Can I get a witness?" Tony said. LaMont gave Tony a don't-get-hit-in-the-back-of-the-head look. Tony just smiled and gave him a little peck on the cheek. "We'll be right back," he continued as he led LaMont by the hand through the doors that led into their suite.

"I need to take a shower," Daryl stated.

"You know, guys, it would save time if you showered

together," Danea said to us with a huge grin. Daryl looked at me and winked. It wasn't a bad idea. "Oh, don't act like you don't want to," she said to us.

"Thanks for the suggestion," I started, "but I think I can shower alone. I'll go first. It shouldn't take long."

Danea raced over to the phone when it rang and picked it up with an excited "Hello?" Two minutes into the conversation it was obvious that she had plans of her own that night.

"Let me guess, you and Curtis are going out?"

"Yeah, we are. We haven't spent any real time together in about two years, and he is still so fine." I hadn't seen her this excited about the prospects of a date in quite some time. It was a pleasant change to see her face glow. "I've got to find something to wear."

"Don't spend too much time trying to decide," Daryl said. "I'm sure your clothes won't be on long anyway."

"If I'm lucky," she retorted.

✖✖✖

By the time we hit Bourbon Street—without Danea—it was jam-packed. People in New Orleans definitely knew how to have a good time. The air was thick with the smell of alcohol. A multitude of people lined the streets like festive decorations. Music filled the air as if it were an outdoor concert. A huge jazz band commanded center attention as they parted the sea of people with their trombones, trumpets, tubas and saxophones. Another band followed shortly thereafter, and then another one. As each band passed, from the hotel balconies above us, a few women started a trend. Each time a band passed, they'd raise their shirts and let their breasts dangle in the evening breeze. It was contagious. Before I knew it, breasts were all around me. It was the craziest scene I'd ever seen. The only thing missing was a cheap pair of Mardi Gras beads. *Damn, I love New Orleans.* No other city could party like this one.

We made our way through the thick crowd toward the Daiquiri Factory for one of those huge yardstick-sized drinks. I ordered a Hurricane, which started to make my head spin after only a few gulps.

"L-l-l-et's check out d-d-dat joint," LaMont said while pointing to a sign that read "Live On-Stage Orgy." "Dat shit looks tight."

"I'll pass on that one. The last thing I need to see is a bunch of naked white people on stage having sex," Daryl said. LaMont looked at Daryl, and grabbed Tony by the hand. Before Tony knew it, he was being dragged through the crowd. He looked back at us and shrugged his shoulders.

"Don't be in there too long," I added. "You know

you wanna go in there. Don't act all innocent," I said to Daryl.

"Trust, they are the last people I'm trying to see naked." Daryl waved at Tony, grabbed my hand and led me down the street through the crowd. The funny thing is that we continued to hold hands until we reached the end of Bourbon Street, near the gay clubs, and chose one to enter. Daryl looked around the small, smoky bar for a stool, or a corner, or just a little bit of space that we could occupy, but people were crammed in there like sardines. I knew he was hoping for a little peace and quiet, but this was Bourbon Street. Peace and quiet departed a long time ago. This was not the time or place for a meaningful conversation.

After about five minutes, we were ready to leave. Some old white man approached us about a three-some. Like Whitney said, "It isn't, it wasn't, it ain't neva gonna be." Or was that Aretha? Those white boys were looking at us like we were the main course at a family dinner. Oh yeah, it was time to go.

Thrust back into the madness of the crowd, through the alcohol, through the noise, through the organized chaos, we ran into Tony and LaMont again.

"Was that orgy everything you hoped it would be?" I asked.

"M-m-m-man, dat shit was so whack! These f-f-f-fat

white ch-ch-ch-chicks up there. M-m-man, I want my money back."

"I tried to warn you," Tony said. While we were standing there, I felt something. I don't know if it was because of the alcohol, or the whole frenzied street, but something no longer felt right. The hairs on the back of my neck began to literally stand on end. I turned my head and surveyed the crowd around me. I focused my eyes across the cramped street. Through the narrow opening the passing band provided, my eyes met a familiar pair of eyes intensely focused my direction. In the distance, standing on the curb, in front of an old pink building with fading paint, I saw James. He looked at me—no, not at me, but through me. Our eyes locked in a stare. *What the hell was he doing here?* The scowl on my face caught Daryl's attention. He spoke to me, but his words did not register. He spoke again and broke me out of my trance. I looked down for just a second to collect myself. I knew this was not my imagination. I frantically scanned the crowd, but I was unable to locate James again. I could feel beads of sweat forming on my forehead in little puddles.

"Kevin," Daryl said with concern, "What's wrong?"

"What?" I looked back toward the building and the image of the man who once terrorized me had vanished. I looked into the crowd, but he was gone.

"You look a little dazed. You okay?"

"I'm fine." LaMont and Tony wanted to go inside one of the gay clubs at the end of the street, but I was not going back down there. I'd already finished my second daiquiri, and was ready to go back to the hotel. Daryl decided to go back with me.

"You can't go back. It's still early," Tony said. Daryl and I looked at each other, looked back at Tony, and promptly turned away, leaving him standing there with his mouth open.

"Oh, just gonna leave us hangin'?" I heard Tony say, but we kept moving.

CHAPTER 30

I questioned my sanity. Had I seen James, or was it just a figment of my imagination? Was I being paranoid? What would James be doing in New Orleans? How would he know that I was here? I convinced myself that it was the drinks. *It had to be.* Once I got back to the hotel with Daryl, I felt secure. I breathed a light sigh as I heard the electronic key trigger the door to unlock. The quiet of the room provided a sense of relief. My shoes were killing my feet, and I immediately kicked them off, and collapsed onto the soft bed like it had been days since I last slept. I felt suddenly drained.

"When are you going to tell me what's up?" Daryl asked while taking off his shoes. He took off his white socks, put one in each shoe, and stacked the pair of Jordans neatly in the corner. He walked over to his suitcase and pulled out a white T-shirt with the Nike check mark on it. He slowly unbuttoned his shirt, revealing the curly black hair on his thick, defined chest. He had a smooth line of hair that ran seductively from his navel into his pants, and my eyes curiously traced the line, wondering what treasure it would reveal. When he looked in my direction, I quickly turned my head. He smiled. I had been caught in the middle of a peep. I picked up the remote for the TV and fumbled for the small, red button marked "Power."

"Well?" he said. "What's going on? I know how much you like New Orleans. The last time we were here, we had to drag your ass off Bourbon Street. What happened tonight?"

"I think the drinks made me sick," I lied. Daryl reached into his bag and pulled out a couple of Advil to avert a possible hangover. I wasn't drunk, but I took them anyway. He crawled into bed next to me as if we were two old friends about to watch their favorite movie. I was a little nervous. I could already feel my temperature rising, among other things, and I had a serious longing for his touch.

"At least we get to spend a little quiet time together," he said. I flipped through a few channels on the tube, not really expecting to find anything worth watching. "Are you nervous?"

"Nervous? About what?" I said, trying to be cool. He turned in the bed and looked me directly in the eyes.

"I can see it. You are nervous," he said slowly, and with a smile. "You can admit it." He was eating this up.

"Well, you do make me a little nervous sometimes. In a good way."

He took the remote from my hands, pointed it at

the set, and I watched as the coffee commercial disappeared into itself.

"Let's just talk."

"About what?"

"About whatever is on your mind. Or in your heart."

"I don't have anything on my mind."

"What about in your heart?"

"Daryl..."

"No, wait. Let me talk. I want to know something. I need you to tell me where we are." I didn't know where we were, but I knew exactly where he was. Right there in the center of my heart where he'd always been. But I wasn't ready to deal with those feelings, or even have this conversation. We hadn't really talked about our feelings since I was in the hospital. Maybe it was fear. Maybe it was something else. I looked down at my hands, and all around the room. "I can read a lot into your silence."

"We both know what's up, but honestly, I don't know what to do. I think you are sexy, fine, smart, beautiful, strong, passionate, and a whole bunch of other things, but now is just not a good time for me."

"You keep saying that. If you love me, now is the perfect time. Love doesn't wait and it doesn't care about timing. We get a small window of opportunity to deal with love, and then it fades or becomes something else. We need to deal with this while we can."

He spoke with some annoyance. The look of frustration across his face was almost enough for me to grab him and hold on for dear life. I didn't want to frustrate him.

"I've just been through so much this last year and a half. It's taken a lot out of me. I don't want to rush anything."

"James really hurt you, didn't he?" Nothing I could say would make him understand the hell I'd been through, the hell I'd put myself through. Part of me wanted to open up and share that experience with him, but this wasn't the time or the place.

"You have no idea."

"Tell me about it. I want to know so I don't make the same mistakes."

"There's no way you ever could. I'll tell you about it one day, I promise." He shook his head in agreement. "As far as we are concerned, I don't want to rush into anything."

"Rush? If this thing gets any slower, we'll be 90 years old in a nursing home. We've been dealing with this for years now, and you know it."

"I know you're right, but..."

"Ain't no mo' buts," he said with slang. "In case you can't tell, you're pissing me off." He rolled onto his back and looked up at the ceiling as he let out a big sigh. "If you don't love me or ever want to be with me, then just be a man about it and tell me. I don't wanna hear nothing about you not being ready. That's bull-shit. You know it. I know it."

"I just don't want to hurt you."

"Let me worry about that. If I'm willing to risk it, that's on me. I just don't want to look back in a couple of years and think about what we could have been. If we get together and it doesn't work, then fine. But at least we would have tried."

"You really want to be with me that badly?"

"I love you and always have. I've tried to move on, but I can't get beyond the anticipation of being with you." *Relationships are so much work*, I thought. "Damn it, say something!"

"I have so many things in my head right now."

"Don't make me guess. Tell me one thing on your mind right now."

"Just one?"

"All I'm asking for is one."

Without hesitation, "I love you." He flipped his head in my direction and smiled like he'd waited forever to hear those words. We'd said them to each other before, but now they seemed much stronger. I knew this was the truest feeling I'd ever experienced. He laid his head in my lap and I lowered my face onto his and our lips met with love and passion. This kiss could last forever. I felt electric currents race up and down every inch of my skin. He tasted of pure honey, sweet and sticky. His flesh upon my flesh overpowered my senses and I dug deeper into his mouth with my tongue. We were insatiable.

"I can get used to this," he said, pulling away.

"What do we do now?"

With a devilish grin, he said, "I can think of a few things."

"That's not what I mean. Get your hormones in control." I smiled.

"I'm trying to, but you make it hard, pun intended."

"You are so bad," I said, kissing him again.

"I'm much better when I'm bad."

"I asked what we do now, because I think we should sort of ease into this."

"You saying you want to take it slow?"

"Yeah, I am."

"That's fine. I ain't asking for your hand in marriage right now. I just think whatever we have or will be, we should start nurturing it."

"That sounds cool to me. Why don't we go downstairs to the hotel bar and have a little nightcap?"

"I thought the alcohol was making you sick."

"Let's just say I'm much better now." I didn't want to leave the room, but if we stayed I knew what would happen. I knew he was feeling what I felt, and it was hot.

✖✖✖

When we got within earshot of the bar, I heard a powerful voice singing, "I'm every woman, it's all in me." With singing like that, it could only be Danea. We walked into the dark and smoky bar, and there she was, center stage, microphone in hand, singing with all of her soul. Her voice was luring hotel patrons into the bar from the lobby. The girl had skills. Curtis was sitting at the table immediately to her right. He sat back in his chair, cigarette in one hand, drink in front of him on the table. We moved over to him and he extended his table to us with a wave of his hand.

Just as the song ended and she returned the mic to the stand, the crowd begged in a unanimous voice for one more song. They were like drug addicts needing one quick fix to help them through the turmoil that was their lives. It was unreal. When she performed, happiness took over her body and mind. The already dim lights in the bar got lower except for the bright spotlight that highlighted her on stage. *A diva at her best.* Then the words came, slowly, confidently, and seductively.

"I Am Love." A powerful song by a phenomenal voice. I thought only Jennifer Holliday could do that song justice, but Danea proved she could hold her own. She seized control of the song like it was written for

LEE HAYES

her and sang it like it was the last song. When it was over, a thunderous round of applause brought the crowd to its feet. Karaoke night had turned into a one-woman show. Then she made her exit. She was fierce.

"What were you doing up on stage singing like this was your concert?" I asked.

"You can't tell me my baby wasn't great," Curtis said in her defense.

"I was entertaining my fans. That was a lot of fun." She called the waitress over and ordered a drink.

"I guess you think you're Diana Ross now?" Daryl said playfully.

And Danea returned a playful answer. "You know I'm a diva-in-training."

"Pardon the interruption. I just had to say that your performance was wonderful—no, it was fabulous—no, it was *amazing*. You have remarkable stage presence. You could be a star." Standing before us was a thin-faced white man, with little, brown spots sprinkled over his face. He spoke with a slight European accent, German, I think. He looked at Danea with great interest and affection.

"Thank you," she said. I noticed he was wearing an expensive Armani suit and a thousand-dollar pair of Gucci shoes.

"I'm Helmut Rich of Amazon Records," he said, while pulling out his card and writing something on the back of it. "I'm working on this new project that I think would be perfect for you." Danea took the card with some skepticism and placed it onto the table without really looking at it. "Why don't you give me a call next week when I get back to L.A.? I wrote my direct office number on the back of the card."

"What project are you talking about?" Curtis inquired.

"The soundtrack for a new Disney movie. I have this song that was made for your voice." Curtis and Danea eyed each other, not sure exactly what to think. Was this guy for real?

"Helmut Rich," Daryl began. "Didn't you just have a big birthday party in L.A.?"

"As a matter of fact, I did."

"I remember seeing something on the E! Network about it. I knew you looked familiar."

Neither of us, with the exception of Daryl had heard of Helmut Rich, but the fact that one of us knew of him lent some validity to his words.

"If things work out right, the next party I have will be for you," he said to Danea. "Make sure you give me a call."

With a quick smile and turn, he was gone.

Danea picked up the card. "Can you believe that?" she asked. I knew her well enough to see that she was intrigued by the idea of it.

"I think this guy is legit," I began. "Big record executives don't approach people unless they're serious. And did you notice his shoes? That was a couple of mortgages for some people." Living with James had taught me how to spot expensive clothing and accurately price them within a few dollars.

"You need to share your voice with the rest of the world." Curtis leaned over and gave her a kiss on the cheek. *This brotha was sprung*.

"If I remember, I'll give him a call. You never know, right?" A hint of interest danced in her eyes. She tried to hide it, but I could tell she was excited.

CHAPTER 31

That was one of the best trips I'd ever been on. The trip was good not only because New Orleans is an extraordinary city, but also because of the events that happened. Tony and LaMont opened a new page in their relationship, and Danea and Curtis rekindled an old flame. As for Daryl and me, our life together was filled with potential and promise.

I was happy for Danea. She and Curtis wrapped themselves in each other and had a wonderful time. When Danea described him as an old friend, she left out a lot of details. An old friend doesn't make your eyes glow. It was refreshing to see that spark of enthusiasm about something other than work. The only thing that compared to it was her singing, but that was a different kind of glow entirely. In the past, she hadn't had the most successful relationships but neither had the rest of us. She'd had some rough times with men. This negro named Anthony she once dated, who professed to being part owner of a chain of local restaurants, stole her credit card and ran up her bill at the same restaurant he claimed to own. He was probably dining some other woman.

Then there was Larenz, the man who raised lying to an art form. For a while, he had her going, but she was eventually able to see through his shit. It took some time for her to find out the whole story: that he had a wife and three children. They were not estranged. They were not separated. They were definitely not divorced. They lived together as husband and wife, yet he spent quite a few nights at Danea's. I can't imagine what he told his wife. I shuddered to think what other unsuspecting women Larenz might have had.

Daryl. What is there to say about Daryl? He made me feel so many of the wonderful feelings that love should bring. There were so many things that I'd forgotten I was capable of feeling. I was amazed at his patience with me. A lesser man would have headed for the hills a long time ago, but not him. He'd always been there, in the background, holding on to more faith in us than I knew. I was finally able to take a deep breath, put fear aside, and just let my feelings be. He was everything. Soft and gentle. Masculine and strong. Charismatic, yet shy. I'd never felt this way about anyone.

When I walked into the apartment after my evening workout, the first thing that I did was drop my keys on the desk, and my gym bag in the middle of the floor. I walked over to the answering machine and hit the play button. The first message was for Danea, so I skipped it. The next message was from Daryl. He wanted me to meet him downtown at the Crescent View, a very upscale high-rise apartment complex in downtown Houston. He told me when I got there, it would be made clear. What was going on? I wondered. I still had a couple of hours, but there was already a smile on my face. It was wonderful being excited about seeing someone and having that feeling where your pulse starts to race at the mere thought of being in someone's presence. I turned to go upstairs just as the phone rang.

"Hello?"

"How are you, Kevin?"

"What are you doing calling me?"

"I just wanted to see how you were doing, and to hear your voice."

"I'm fine, and you've heard it. Goodbye."

"Wait, please. I need to ask you something."

"What is it, James?" I said sounding annoyed.

"I wanted to invite you to dinner so that I could apologize."

"We've had this conversation before, and you know I'm not about to meet you for dinner. If you feel the need to apologize, that's fine, but you'll have to do it over the phone."

"Don't make me do it over the phone. After all we've been through, I think you should at least let me do it in person. Give me that much, please."

"This conversation really is a waste of time. I'm not meeting you anywhere, I'm not accepting anything you have delivered to me. In fact, I don't want to speak to you again." I hung up the phone and pulled out the directions on how to use Call Block. I entered his home phone numbers, his office numbers, as well as his cell phone. I knew that wouldn't stop him from calling, but maybe he'd get the message.

✖✖✖

When I got to the Crescent View, I found a place to park my car right outside of the huge, silver skyscraper. It gleamed seductively in the moonlight, like a tower of dreams. Each step I took brought on a new set of excitement and chills, and by the time I got to the lobby I was floating. When I opened the door, a bell sounded, alerting the young, uniformed security guard to my arrival. He looked up slowly from the book on his desk as I approached him. I told him my name, and he directed me to follow him to the elevator. When the elevator doors opened, he jumped in, pulled out a key from his pocket, inserted it into its proper hole in the elevator, and hit the button marked "Penthouse Level." Before I could mutter a word, he stepped out and the doors closed.

When the doors to the elevator opened on the

50th floor, I saw a trail of red rose petals, and a blue envelope with my name propped up on the glass table against the wall facing the elevator. I took the envelope, opened it, and read the note. I was instructed to follow the trail of rose petals. I examined the note; it was written in black ink in an artistic style of calligraphy. A border of soft, pastel colors and flowers surrounded the paper. When I put the note up to my nose, an erotic fragrance overwhelmed my sense of smell. I recognized that enticing scent. It was Daryl.

Hurriedly, I moved down the long hallway until I came to the end of the trail of petals. I could not quell the smile on my face. The trail stopped at a brown door marked "Penthouse 50C." Slowly, I placed my hand on the knob and turned. It was unlocked. I stepped into the interior of the apartment. This was one of the most luxurious rooms I'd ever seen! The dark color of the room provided a certain intensity that added to my excitement. A shiny black baby-grand piano was cornered in the back of the room next to the open balcony. The smooth marble floors reflected a soft light that hung in the air like a smooth October sunset. Beautiful floral arrangements and expensive crystal were scattered about the room. I followed the trail of roses out onto the balcony. The commanding view of downtown Houston and the night sky took my breath away. A round table covered with a red tablecloth adorned the center of the balcony. I watched as the ends of the cloth swayed back and forth with the night breezes. Two black chairs sat across each other, and the flame from a lone white candle inside a wineglass flickered slightly. A bottle of wine in the center of the table chilled in a bucket. Little beads of perspiration ran down the sides of the bottle and disappeared into the ice.

Everything was in place, except for Daryl. I didn't know where he could be. A dozen peach roses were laid across the table. I moved closer to the table, looking around for him. When I picked up the roses to smell them, a slow and melodious harmony filled the night air with the sound of music. Out of the darkness of the night, a voice began to sing. I turned around, and from the shadows near the door I saw him standing erect like the perfect man, dressed in an all-black tuxedo with a white bow tie and white gloves. The night partially shadowed his face; he took one step forward, and then stopped. With the beauty of downtown Houston below us, and the glimmering of a million stars above us, his voice echoed out with passion and soul. The song he sang was a familiar song; in fact, it was my favorite: "I Feel Good All Over" by Stephanie Mills. He stood there, without moving so much as a muscle, and bellowed out that song from the depths of his heart. His voice provided new dimension to the song. My knees felt ready to give way under the heavy weight of his love. Chills ran through my body like an erotic electric current, and the hair on my forearms stood at attention. He then moved closer, never missing a note in the song. I sat down in the chair and he took a few steps toward me. He dropped to one knee, handed me a single rose, and sang the last notes of the song. His timing was perfect. The shine in his eyes rivaled the sparkle of the stars above. His lips moved so seductively. I was touched beyond tears. Never had I imagined a night like this. He got up and kissed me gently on the lips. He opened the bottle of wine, filled each glass only about halfway, and handed me a drink.

"Daryl, how..." He put his forefinger to my lips and said, "Shhh." He sat down in the chair across from me and sipped his wine. I sipped mine, but wine was not the sweetness I longed for. For seconds, minutes, for hours in time, we looked at each other without saying a word. Our eyes carried the feelings words were incapable of conveying. Finally, he spoke one word: "Surprise." A smile parted his face, and finally he let out a laugh. I wanted to speak, but words seemed so inappropriate now. I wanted this time with him to last forever. I wanted this night's beauty to be as eternal as the glow that shone down on us.

"I wanted to make this a special evening," he said. I just looked at him, at a loss for words, desperately searching my soul for voice. "Aren't you gonna say anything?"

Finally, I could speak. "I have no idea what to say, but I'll start with thank you for this magic evening. I've never felt more special in my life."

"You're the only one I could ever share something like this with."

"I'm glad to know that. How did you do all of this?"

He shook his head with a smile. "The *how* isn't important. I want you to be concerned with the *why*. I just wanted to find a way to show you how much I love you." He got up from the table and grabbed my hand, and led me to the edge of the building. When we looked down below, and above, and around, the troubles in my life seemed trivial. Against the backdrop of time and eternity, nothing but love mattered. He stood behind me, with his arms wrapped around my waist, and began humming the melody to that amazing song again. He was so close to my ear that I could feel the vibrations from his lips in my ear. It gave me chills again.

"What do you see when you look out?" he asked.

"I see buildings, and I see stars."

"No, you're looking with your eyes. Look from your heart. Now, what do you see?" His hand move gently across my eyes, forcing them closed with a gentle sweep. "Look from your heart." With my eyes closed, I *saw* love for the first time. I saw vivid colors rolled together in playful balls of light. I saw stars dancing in the night sky with the universe as the stage, and a rainbow inside the heart of the night. Whatever web he had spun, whatever spell he'd cast, and whatever chant he moaned, set my heart ablaze. "Do you see it? Can you see forever?" He spun me around and kissed my lips with the passion I thought only heaven could provide. Every sense I had was amplified. His touch felt electric, his scent was overwhelming, and his taste was ambrosia, the food of the gods. Nothing I had ever experienced compared to this night. No other love could measure.

That night, we talked about many things. We shared our hopes, our fears, our dreams. We laughed, we wanted to cry, we played. That night, we loved. With our minds and souls. There were so many things that the two years we'd known each other hadn't revealed. We crossed great distances: through the valleys, above the mountains, and across the seas. His first male sexual experience happened when he was 17. His brother brought a guy home with him from school for spring break. Daryl said the moment they met, a spark ignited. After sending covert signals with their eyes, and engaging in a seductive battle of body language over the course of three days, they were finally left in the house alone, and from then on, he knew he needed the love of a man.

"My first experience?" I began. "I haven't thought about that in such a long time. I was 21. This was when I was in Austin. I'd confessed to a frat brother that I thought I might be gay, but I told him that I had never done anything with a man, and didn't know if I ever would. He, of course, was gay, too. This was around September of 1994. On December 9—and I remember the date like it was yesterday—we were having a fraternity party at somebody's house, and someone suggested we go to this Kappa party on campus. I didn't want to go, but finally they convinced me. We got to campus, and found out the party had been moved to a club downtown. We get downtown, find the club, and go in. It was an okay club, but after dancing I got tired and sat down in this chair next to some guy. A friend came over and asked for the time, which I didn't have, so I turned and asked the guy next to me what time he had. My friend went back to the dance floor, and this guy and I just started talking to each other over the music. We talked about general stuff like what school we went to, each other's major, etc. A few moments later, this girl came over and asked him to dance, and I got agitated. He went to the dance floor, but when he got there, we just started staring at each other. I don't know who started looking first, but we didn't break eye contact. Then, this Salt-N-Pepa song came through the speakers, and they started singing, 'If I wanna take a guy home with me tonight, it's none of your business.' From across the room, we smiled at each other and mouthed the words. He left the dance floor, and went to the patio outside. I wasn't sure if I should follow. This was a new experience for me. After some confusion about what was going on, I finally decided to go back to the patio with him. When I got there, he was all the way in the back, facing the wooden fence. I stood in the doorway, confused, and finally moved back inside the club just a bit. It was getting late and the crowd was moving toward the front of the door. Somehow he got in front of me, and then suddenly turned to look at me, staring me directly in the eyes. I was scared because I didn't know what was going on. I looked down and saw a white piece of paper between his fingers. Quickly, I grabbed it and stuck it in my pocket. He turned around and we all left the club.

"I was really excited. When I got back to my dorm, I called him, and we talked for a while, and decided I would pick him up tomorrow night after my fraternity/sorority Christmas party. This was December 10. When I picked him up, it was late, and we drove around until he suggested we go up to the mall parking lot. From there, we could see the whole city, including downtown Austin. That night, I had my first kiss from a man, and it was powerful. I felt as if the sky had opened. All my life I have lived for that kiss. I had lived with this nagging sensation that something was missing, but as his lips met mine, the mystery was solved. I'd never felt like that before. I thought that evening was perfect, until now," I said with a smile as I leaned over and kissed his lips again.

"It sounds like magic."

"For me, it was. We dated for the next six months, and finally broke up for good that summer. We were both young, and confused. We grew apart, but remained friends. Part of me will always love him because he taught me that loving a man could be a mystical experience. It's too bad he wasn't mature enough to handle my love."

"He didn't know what a good thing he had."

"I know. A couple of years later, he came back to me and wanted to date again, but that wasn't a good idea. I mean, why tamper with the love and memories we had already shared? I know I'll always have a special fondness for him in my heart."

"If you let me love you, I promise it will be an experience of a lifetime. Books will be written about it. Our love will be legendary, even in fairy tales." He knew exactly how to weave a spell strong enough to break the hardest of hearts.

"I want you to love me. I need you to love me, but I'm so scared of messing that up."

"Don't be afraid, baby. I won't hurt you."

"I'm not afraid of you hurting me; I'm afraid of you getting hurt."

He moved closer to me, and put his lips on mine. The brilliance of the night stars intensified his kiss by a thousand-fold. Slowly, he began unbuttoning my shirt and gently caressed my nipple with his tongue. Chills of ecstasy overtook my body as he continued kissing me softly from head to toe. I basked in the power of his touch, and tried not to stumble. I took him by the hand and led him into the bedroom of the penthouse suite. Once in the room, our bodies pressed against each other as we rolled around, each one struggling for dominance. At times, I'd let him control, and he would do the same. The equality of the relationship only intensified the passion. That night, we made love over and over again, and we did it to perfection. I wanted to shout from the rooftops to all the lovers in the world that paradise had been achieved.

CHAPTER 32

I had fallen asleep on the couch trying to read a report for work that was excruciatingly dull. The ringing of the phone ejected me from the comfort of my nap. I reached over and grabbed the phone off the receiver, managing to get out a muffled "Hello?" only to be greeted by the sound of heavy breathing. The breathing, deep and concentrated, inhaled me, body and mind. I felt violated. The caller had reached across vast distances of space to molest me. I slammed the phone down and rolled over onto my side, but the phone rang again. It rang with force and power and endeavored to violate me again. I stared at the wall until I could no longer bear the fierceness of the ringing. I snatched up the phone. I put the receiver to my ear without saying a word.

"You are mine," a maniacal voice said. Then, I heard the dial tone. I yanked the phone cord out of the wall and stared at the walls. There was no way that I'd be able to go back to sleep, so I got up and went to the refrigerator, but then the kitchen phone rang. I looked at it. Then, it stopped. And started again. Then, the doorbell rang. I stopped for a moment and looked at the clock on the microwave. It was 11:30. Who was at my door at this time of night? I moved toward the living room and peered out of the peephole. It was Tony. I was relieved to see his familiar face.

"Hey, man. What's up?" he asked as he walked past me. "I really had to talk to someone tonight," he said with a huge smile.

"Well, come on in, why don't you?" I said while closing the door. He gave me a hug and we walked back into the kitchen. "Where have you been lately? I've called you a few times, but you have not returned the calls. What's up with that?" My voice sounded raspy and aggravated.

He moved in front of me and spoke. "Before I answer that question, why don't you tell me what's wrong with you?"

"I'm fine. I was trying to get some work done, but I fell asleep on the couch. Then, some prank-ass phone call woke me up a minute ago."

"First, why are you working on a Friday night? Second, what happened?"

"To answer your questions, I was working because I have a lot to do. And secondly, the phone call is really not important. Now, what's going on with you? You've been a ghost lately. Danea and I thought you found the new love of your life and moved. What's the deal?"

"Can a brotha get some food before getting the

third degree?" He pushed passed me and made his way toward the refrigerator. "By the way, where's Ms. Thang?"

"She had a deposition to take in Dallas, so she won't be back until tomorrow."

He opened the refrigerator door and pulled out a leftover box of Kentucky Fried Chicken, some macaroni and cheese Danea had made, and the apple pie I'd picked up from the store. He had a pep in his step and was humming a song that I couldn't quite make out. He looked extraordinarily happy as he bounced about the kitchen. I could see it all over him. *That thing called Love.*

"Why are you looking at me like that?" he finally asked.

"I'm waiting for you to talk to me." He put his plate in the microwave, set it for three minutes, and leaned his back against the countertop so that he could face me. Now he wore a stern look, his head tilted toward the floor. He was trying to play tough, but he couldn't hold it in.

"I'm getting...married!" he exclaimed with a deep bravado that raced up the scale until it turned into a high-pitched yelp.

"What?"

"Stop looking at me like that," he retorted. "I'm serious. I'm getting married."

"Getting married? To whom? Or better yet, to what?" I sat down and he pulled up a chair in front of me and looked me in the eyes. He didn't smile, or flinch, or even blink. His sincerity did not dissipate. In fact, it stood between us, a force of reckoning, commanding all due attention and respect.

"I guess I shouldn't say married, but I'm—we're, me and LaMont—are having a wedding. He's gonna be my permanent LPF."

"LPF?"

"Lover-partner-friend. You know I hate the term *lover*. So, we're having a commitment ceremony."

"A what?"

"A commitment ceremony. The gay equivalent of a marriage ceremony." Again, he looked at me and waited for my response. I didn't know what to think or say or do.

"I know what it is; I just don't know why *you're* having one."

"What does that mean?" His defensive tone ricocheted off the kitchen walls. I wasn't trying to offend him, but I had obviously struck a nerve.

"When did this engagement happen?" I asked, trying to take the edge out of the conversation.

He looked at me, cracked a smile and cleared his throat. "Well," he began with a change of inflection, "he asked me in New Orleans, so I've been keeping it a secret since then."

"How did you manage to keep that a secret? I'm sure you're ready to burst."

"Ohhhhhh, it was so hard. But we decided not to tell anyone until the last minute, but you know me, I couldn't hold it any longer."

"I'm surprised you haven't popped an ovary by now," I said with laughter. He gave me one of those you-ain't-funny looks and continued his story.

"You know LaMont and I love each other in spite of our ups and downs. We've known each other for years and we've had this on-again, off-again and on-again relationship. We realized in New Orleans that we were in love and it wasn't going to change no matter who else was in our lives. Through the years, I've had other men..."

"A lot of men," I added in jest. He ignored my comment.

"But there has always been LaMont. No matter who I've been with, he's always been there. He's always had my heart. I was running away from it until he made me face it. Kevin, what I feel for him is real and I know he loves me. I know we have our issues, but hell, so does everyone else."

"This means a lot to you, huh? And you're really serious about LaMont?"

"He means more to me than I could ever describe." I looked into his eyes and the depth of his honesty and emotion appeared endless. It was a bottomless well of emotion and love, deep as the sea and as wide as all outdoors. My friend was in love.

"If this is what you really want and need, then you know I'll support you and whatever this ceremony is for you."

"Why you gotta say it like that?" His defenses went up again.

"I'm sorry. I just have never thought about any one of us having a ceremony like that. I've never really given any serious thought to the whole issue of gay marriages. That's all I meant."

"*Uh-huh,*" he said in his Sandra-Clark-from-*227* voice.

"When is the ceremony?"

"In three weeks."

"Three weeks?"

"That's why I've been so busy lately. I've been planning my wedding. We're having it in a church, and it will be fabulous!"

"In three weeks," I said again, trying to get it to sink in.

"You hard of hearing or something? Read my lips—*three weeks.*" He exaggerated the movement of his lips just to stress his point.

"What do you need me to do?"

"I wanted to plan this all by myself, but it's getting hard keeping shit straight. I need you to be my backup."

"Not a problem. What kind of ceremony have you planned?"

"It's a surprise."

"I know how your surprises can be. Are you going to have Cookie LaCook and the Rascal's Untouchables do a drag number?" The thought of Cookie and her girls doing a show at his wedding made me laugh. It would definitely be entertaining.

"No, but that's an idea," he said with a wink.

"I was kidding." He didn't say a word. "You know you can count on me for whatever you need." He went to the microwave for his plate, which had cooled. He put it back in for another minute.

"I do need one thing. I want Danea to sing at the wedding. Could you help me with that?"

"I'm sure she won't have a problem with it."

"Yeah, but you know how she hates to be kept in the dark."

"Don't worry about her. I'll take care of it."

✖✖✖

Tony ended up staying the rest of the night, and we got up early the next morning to go to the gym. As we were heading out the door, the phone rang. Luckily, it was Daryl calling to say good morning and to confirm our plans for the afternoon. I hung up the phone, grabbed my keys and we headed out the door for the gym. We were hoping to get a good workout so that I could spend the rest of the day with Daryl. I think we had planned on going to Six Flags. I liked the excitement of amusement parks, even though I hate heights. I didn't like the idea of riding through the air at sixty miles an hour on two thin pieces of metal, all while buckled into a flimsy plastic seat.

As we walked toward my car in the lot, my eyes grew wide. I dropped my gym bag and rushed over to the pile of twisted metal and broken glass that used to be my red Accord. The tires looked as if they had fallen victim to some knife-wielding serial killer who sliced away until they were nothing more than strands of black rubber. The windows were mostly broken and shattered, and a mountain of glass covered the inside seats and the parking lot. Spray-painted in bright rainbow letters on the mangled hood of the car were the words "FAG," "DICK-SUCKER," and "BITCH." The leather seats were cut beyond repair, and it looked as if a small fire had been started on the passenger side. All of the CDs that I had in the car were either cracked or completely torn to pieces.

"What the fuck?!" I screamed.

"I know that muthafucka James did this! That's it. You ain't taking his shit anymore." Tony grabbed his cell phone and started dialing a number.

"Who are you calling?"

"The police, of course."

We went back into the apartment and I called Daryl. After I told him what happened, he was on his way. I paced the living room in random patterns. I hadn't had the car very long. With a loan from Danea, I had bought it immediately after I moved away from James. Now, there it was, nothing more than a pile of scrap metal. I tried to remain calm, but Tony's hysterics weren't helping to ease my anger.

When the officers arrived, they took pictures of the car and began to question us in a lazy Saturday-morning sort of way. I tried not to be upset by their lack of urgency. Daryl snapped at them a couple of times, and it was all I could do to keep him calm. He was more upset by this tragedy than me. The police wanted to know who I thought did this, but I wasn't sure what to tell them. If I told the truth, they would want details on motive, and I didn't want my sexual orientation a part of some police department's permanent official record. One day, it could come back to haunt me. So I simply responded by saying I didn't know, and I could feel Daryl's and Tony's collective stare.

They asked questions alluding to my sexual orientation because of the words written on the car. If I was gay, they said, this crime might fall under the Hate Crimes Provision, and if the person were caught, they'd be charged with a more serious crime. My answer, again, was no. They informed me that a cold crime like this, with no witnesses, no motive, and no suspects, had very little chance of being solved. They advised me the best thing to do was to call my insurance company, and try to put it behind me. With that succinct advice, they took a final statement and left. It just keeps getting better and better, I thought to myself.

I could barely speak for the tremble in my voice. I knew James was behind this, and he was going to get away with it. *He always got away with it.* I also knew that it was unlikely that they could've proved it was James anyway. I didn't need fingerprints or DNA samples to know he did it. I didn't need an eyewitness account or photographic evidence to place him at the scene. I knew it was he, and he knew that I knew. Somewhere, he lay in wait, gloating at his early victory. James had raised the stakes.

❌❌❌

I reported the vandalism to my insurance company and they set me up with a rental car until the damage could be fully assessed. Meanwhile, work had taken off with a serious vengeance. This job was taking more of my energies than I expected, plus there was the added stress of being new at the company and trying to figure out the office politics. I checked my voice-mail and the first voice I heard was Croix, asking me to call him because we hadn't really chatted or seen each other for a couple of weeks now. He mentioned something about everything with his divorce working out right.

The next message was from James. His voice sounded excited, like he'd found the secret of joy. He started saying that he really would like to see me, but as soon as I realized where he was going with his next few words, I deleted the message. I had no time for him. He called me as if nothing had happened, as if we were old friends. We definitely shared a history, and a present, but we were never friends. Even though I would never be able to prove that he destroyed my car, my gut feeling told me that it was him. Dr. Manheim urged me to let go of the anger. After all, it was only a material possession, and not even an expensive one at that. It could be replaced.

I didn't know what I needed to do to be clearer to him that we were over. Maybe I should've rented a plane and had someone write it in the sky for him to see. The notes in the mail, the flowers sent to my office, and the phone calls had to stop. I continued listening to the remaining messages while browsing through the mail on my desk. I stopped at an un-marked brown envelope. I looked at the back, but there was no information listed. I put the phone down, picked up the letter opener, and slit open the parcel. In my hands I held pictures. Pictures of us on Bourbon Street, pictures of Danea singing at the hotel bar, pictures of LaMont and Tony holding hands on the riverboat, pictures of me and Daryl walking back to the hotel. The scariest picture showed me and Daryl lying in the hotel bed after we fell asleep holding each other. What the fuck is going on? I raced out into the receptionist's area and asked did anyone know where this package had come from. They were taken off guard by the rage on my face. When I walked back into my office, I slammed the door. This nigga was still fucking with me. How did he have access to us in the hotel room? Is he having me followed? I knew I'd seen him in New Orleans. Now, he was just playing games with my head, trying to show me that he was still in control and that he could get to me at any time. In a rage, I tore the pictures into a million pieces and scattered them across my office. I looked down at the torn fragments, and vowed not to allow him to dictate the course of my life. I called Dr. Manheim's office and set up an appointment.

✖✖✖

The next day, I picked up my cappuccino and headed

for RaChelle's office. I didn't know if she'd be in this early. It wasn't quite 8:00, but I figured it was close enough. When I got to her office, her secretary—*administrative assistant*—told me she had just stepped away and offered me RaChelle's office.

"Make yourself comfortable. She should be back at any moment." I looked into her office and found a seat on the couch in the corner by the window. I grabbed the first magazine on the table and thumbed unenthusiastically through it. There was something about skinny white women in bathing suits that wasn't working for me. I looked at the cover, and the picture of the anorexic-looking model, and promptly put it down.

As she walked into her office, she didn't even notice me in the corner. She wore a scowl on her pretty face and had her left hand on her stomach.

"Good morning," I said, trying not to startle her.

She jumped back and replied, "Kevin. I didn't see you there. You trying to give a girl a heart attack or something?"

"I was hoping my presence would be an early morning surprise."

"It's always a delight seeing you; I just don't need you creeping up on me. You're lucky you didn't get maced," she said, trying to find some humor.

"What's wrong? You don't look so good."

"You know better than to tell a woman that she doesn't look good."

"You know what I mean."

"Since you asked, my stomach is doing flips. It must have been that breakfast I had."

"Well, if you cooked it, that explains it."

"How you gonna talk about my cooking when you don't know anything about that? Every time I invite you over for dinner you conveniently have something to do," she fired back with the same flair I had come to appreciate in her.

"From what I can tell, I made the right decision," I shot back.

"You sure know how to kick a girl when she's down. Just like a man."

"We are not turning this into a male-bashing session." I watched her move unsteadily over to her desk. Her legs looked shaky, almost as if they couldn't support her. I rushed over.

"You okay?"

"No, I gotta go to the restroom." She hurried out of her office, one hand on her stomach and the other covering her mouth.

CHAPTER 33

On my way home I got the urge to stop by and check on RaChelle. It had been three days since she'd been to work and she had not returned any of my calls. I didn't want to worry too much, because I knew how she could be. Some-times, she just needed to be left alone, and I believe in giving people their space.

Traffic on I-610 was surprisingly light. Since I'd decided to stay late at work, I had missed rush hour by a few minutes. This merger was really turning up the heat on a lot of us. It was a trial by fire. *Just throw me out there and hope for the best.* I had complete confidence that I could do the job and do the job well. I had the feeling there would be a lot of late nights in my future. The powers that be wanted each department head to give a full and complete status report, right down to how many paper clips were on each desk.

At RaChelle's condo, I rang the bell a few times before I could hear anything that remotely indicated life beyond the door. I rang the bell again, and called out her name. I waited. I rang the bell again, and tried to get a quick look through the window when the door opened. She scowled at me, turned, and walked away. I watched her back move down the corridor and disappear into the interior, without words. Who the hell was this? RaChelle? I had never seen this woman with even one hair out of place, yet right now, she looked like she had been dragged by a truck for a few blocks. This woman, with frenzied hair, dressed in a raggedy, old, sky-blue terrycloth robe with dingy, loose-fitting tube socks around her ankles, could not be the RaChelle I knew. When I called her name, half-scared to enter the room, she did not respond.

Her place was a wreck! I stepped inside and was slapped in the face by the dirty scent of cigarette smoke, whose thickness clung to the room, making the already dark space darker. Empty bottles of Chardonnay—I counted at least six—were scattered across the room. Her ashtrays were so dirty and filled with soot that I couldn't even see the bottom.

She stood in the center of the room, hand on her hip, and waited for me to enter before she plopped down on the couch. She grabbed a maroon blanket and pulled it over her head as if she was shielding herself from the light. When I pulled down the covers, just enough to see her face, she shot me an evil look. She sat up on the couch and brushed the hair out of her face. She then grabbed a cigarette, lit it, inhaled, and blew the smoke out through her mouth. I watched as it slowly drifted my direction in a crooked spiral pattern.

"I came by because I was worried about you," I began. "You haven't been to work in a few days and I wanted to check on you. From the looks of things, I'd say I came by just in time. How are you feeling?"

After a pause, she said, "I'm as happy as pigs in shit. Can't you tell?" *Now there's an old saying you don't hear every day*, I thought to myself. I was trying to read her face and eyes for some hint as to what might be wrong, but they gave up nothing. She inhaled again, and repeated the same exhalation of the smoke. I tried not to cough.

"Okay, then. Do you need anything? Have you eaten?"

"I'm not hungry, Kevin."

"Why don't I help you straighten out this place?"

"I told you I'm fine. Stop trying to be so damn helpful. You've helped enough."

"What does that mean?"

"Never mind. Is there something else you wanted, Kevin?" She put out the cigarette in the ashtray, and reached to light another one.

"You know you really shouldn't be smoking. It's bad for your health," I said half-jokingly.

"Are you the fucking Surgeon General?"

"Okay, RaChelle, what is your problem? Talk to me."

My patience had run out. It had already been a long day. For the next fifteen minutes we sat in dead silence, with the exception of her inhaling and exhaling.

"When are you gonna talk to me?" I asked.

She rolled her eyes and then began to speak. "I am the executive vice president of Human Resources, and the youngest vice president in the history of the company. Plus, I'm black and female. Aren't those accomplishments I should be proud of?"

"Of course you should. You worked hard to get where you are. You deserve your successes."

She let out a chuckle. "Do I?"

"Why wouldn't you?"

"I bet you think I got where I am by being smart and talented, right?" I nodded yes, but her question needed no response. "Wrong! I'm where I am because of these." She grabbed a handful of her breasts and held them there, like they were on display. *I've seen them before*, I thought.

"What are you talking about?"

"Most of those bitches at work are so fucking jealous of me. I know they talk about me behind my back. I know they do. They're just bitter because their asses got fat. I mean really fat. Like Janet in payroll. That's a big bitch. Some of them used to be fine; I can still see it a little, but they fucked up when they started spitting kids out of their coochies like they're some baby-making factory."

"What does all of this have to do with anything?"

"I give 'em glamour every day so that they'll know that I'm the top bitch. And those white bitches can't stand me 'cause they know that if they're not careful I just might fuck their men, too. Nowadays, you have to strategically fuck. You don't lie down with anyone without a reason." I wanted to ask her what was her reason for fucking me, but I let her continue. "It's those white men who are in positions to help you. Those bitches keep saying that's how I got my job. On my back."

"Why do you care about what they say?"

"Because…they're right." I tried not to look surprised, but I could feel my eyes widening. "Yeah, I fucked the boss, so that I could advance my career. I wanted this job in Houston so bad that I would have done anything. What's the big deal? I mean, I ain't one of these tricks that will fuck anybody for free. He kept coming on to me, so one day, I took him up on his advances. After a couple of hours with me, he was whooped. I put it on him. I know my pussy is all that." She got up and paced back and forth across the floor, practically rubbing her carpet thin. "This position came open in Houston, and I wanted it. It offered more clout, more pay, and a move. What was not to want? I had to put it on him real good, too. I think I did it too good 'cause he didn't want me to move to Houston. He wanted to keep me near him in Dallas so we could fuck all the time, but I wasn't having that at all. I had to convince him that I wasn't above telling his wife about our little affair. When I said those words he changed his mind with a quickness. He wanted me outta Dallas. I ain't no ho, I'm a business-woman. I get paid."

"I believe that we choose our lives and our destinies, for better or worse. If these are the choices you've made, and this is who you are, then why is this bothering you now?"

"'Cause I don't want the whole office saying shit like that, even if it's the truth! I can't figure out how they found out, 'cause I know he didn't tell. He's got a wife. And I know I am more than qualified for the job." She was smoking those cigarettes like they were going out of style. She didn't even notice the ashes falling all over the room until I handed her an ashtray to catch the falling remnants. "I've always had problems with women. I know they're just jealous. And you're right, why am I letting those heffas get to me?" She became quiet for a few moments. There was something else on her mind. Her words were carefully contrived as if to skate by the real issue. I could sense it and I could see the apprehension in her eyes. I wasn't gonna press her about it, though. It would come out when she wanted it to. "All my life I've used my looks to get me what I wanted. Any man, any job. In college, it helped me get grades. I'm used to thinking that all I have to do is work a man a little, and he'll give me what I need. I've never had a man tell me no. Don't you understand what I'm trying to say?"

"You're going in so many circles it's hard to tell."

"I can't be a mother right now. I'm not a role model. Do I sound or act like I want to be a mom again? Not now, not like this."

"Huh?"

"Don't be so dense. Kevin, *look at me*. I'm pregnant. Can't you tell?"

"Pregnant?" My mouth dropped open.

"Oh, it gets better." She took a huge drag off the cigarette and exhaled in an exaggerated motion. "You're the father. I'm pregnant with your child."

I looked at her without emotion. She spoke coolly and casually as if she had told me that she was about to go shopping.

She continued to speak, her lips moving rapidly, but I was unable to hear. I was lost somewhere in her words. *"I'm pregnant with your child."* Was she kidding, playing some sick joke? Or were the words she spoke the truth? I searched her face for the veracity of her statement. She leaned back on the couch and stared at me, waiting for my reaction.

I wanted to laugh, but nothing was funny. I wanted

to cry, but I wasn't sad. I felt happiness, and fear, and confusion all at once. All of a sudden my life flashed before my eyes in the very sense people on the verge of death describe. Only for me, it wasn't that I felt as if I was dying; a part of me suddenly came to life in a flood of light. I didn't know why exactly I was so happy, but I knew this baby could be a good thing, at least for me. This wasn't the most convenient time and it definitely wasn't planned, but this might've been my only opportunity to have a child. I immediately took the cigarette out of her mouth. She would not smoke up my child.

"I had an appointment yesterday at the clinic to take care of this problem, but I couldn't go through with it. I guess I needed to think about it more. I'm not a mother. I don't have one maternal instinct. I don't even like children!"

"You're wonderful with kids. I've seen you work miracles in Texas House."

"That's all bullshit. That's all for show. My company wanted to get more involved in the community and I wanted a chance to impress the upper brass. It worked."

I was stunned by her words, but I didn't let it show. "I'm glad you told me about your appointment before you went through with it. Think about it for a second. This baby could be a wonderful thing. We can handle this." I tried to contain my joy because I could see that it wasn't mutual.

"We? Kevin, I'm still certain that I don't want to have this baby. Just 'cause I didn't go through with it yet doesn't mean I've changed my mind completely. I shouldn't have told you. This is my problem."

"The baby you're carrying is our child. This is our problem. What if I wanted you to have the baby? What if I asked you to have our baby?"

"You don't want me to have this baby."

"Just humor me for a moment. How do you know? What would you do if I asked you to keep it?"

"I don't know. All I know is I don't want to raise a child by myself. I don't want to be a single mother. Men leave all the time, and you and I aren't in a relationship and we aren't even dating. Men leave and the women are left holding the child and trying to raise a kid by themselves. My mamma was a single parent. I don't even know my father. I watched my mother struggle working two and sometimes three jobs just to take care of us. I have two sisters with kids and neither one of them is married. When my sister Jeanetta was being rushed to the hospital in labor, she called her boyfriend and told him she was having the baby. He said he'd see her in the hospital, but to this day, he's never seen his daughter, and that was two years ago. I told myself I'd never be in a situation like that."

"I'm not those men. I'm not your father and I don't even know your sisters. We have a lot to talk about.

Promise me one thing, please? Promise me you won't do anything without my knowledge. Not my *permission*, but my knowledge. I have a lot to think about, too." She looked at me and nodded her head yes. "But in the meantime, you've got to stop smoking and drinking," I said as I took the drink out of her hand. The rest of the night we sat in silence, occasionally looking at each other and wanting to speak, just not knowing what words to say. So many thoughts filled my head. I had to tell Daryl.

CHAPTER 34

I tumbled through the sky on some marvelous ride, and when I came down I was rolling through fields of fresh daisies. I was overwhelmed with fantastic feelings of fancy and fatherhood. This pregnancy was not in the least bit expected or planned, but Keevan's sudden death taught me to appreciate and cherish the magic of life. RaChelle carried my seed, a seed that I wanted to nurture, water with love and watch grow and sprout into something divine.

That evening Daryl and I took a shower together and were preparing to get settled for the rest of the evening. Thoughts of little children with my eyes danced through my head, and I needed to contain my enthusiasm until just the right moment.

We decided on a quiet night at his place instead of going out. We needed some quiet time for us. No friends, no work, nothing planned. We rented a couple of movies and figured we'd just order some Chinese food. One of the things that I loved doing for him was feeding him. He'd lie back, relax and submit unto me. He was perfectly at ease being controlled, allowing me to dominate. His masculinity was strong enough for him to be at ease. So many men could learn things from him. But there were days when I'd come to his apartment and he'd wait on me hand and foot. Our relationship was reciprocal.

I took the towel from his hand, turned him around so that his backside was facing me, and rubbed the towel across his moistened shoulders. His skin was so smooth and soft that I had to plant a kiss in the middle of his back. He turned and smiled sweetly. Something about being in his presence put me at ease. I didn't have to worry about what anyone else thought.

"Which one do you want to watch first?" he asked.

"I don't really care. Just pop one of them in." I pulled the T-shirt on over my head and slipped into a pair of white BVD boxer briefs as he slid into a pair of black silk boxers and a black muscle shirt.

I sat in bed, my back against the headboard with Daryl lying between my legs, his back resting on my chest. I placed my hands so that I could feel his heartbeat.

"I love you," I said.

He squeezed my hands. "I love you, too. Someone is in a good mood tonight."

"I should tell you every day, because it's true."

"I know it is. Not that I'm complaining, but where is all of this coming from?"

"It's just weird that we've known each other for years and it has taken all this time for us to get to this point, the point where we needed to be. I just don't want it to end."

"Why would it? You leaving me already?"

"Of course not. How much time do you think we have? How long do you think we'll last?"

"What?"

"It just seems so many people are by themselves nowadays. RaChelle is single and who knows what'll happen with Danea and Curtis. Croix is getting divorced. Does anyone stay together anymore?"

"I don't know what the future holds for us, but let's hold on to the moments we have and enjoy each other. You can't compare us to anyone else. All I know is that if loving you lasts two weeks, two months, or twenty years, we can only take it one day at a time."

"I have something to tell you. Now may not be a good time, but it will become an issue." I took a deep breath and searched for the words. Any words I chose wouldn't lessen the sting I was about to deal him, so I decided to be direct. "I found out this evening that RaChelle is pregnant—with my child."

He sat up and turned to face me. He looked at me in confusion, but remained silent for the next few minutes. He wasn't sure whether I was joking or not, so I explained the details of our brief encounter—the how, the when and the why. He was waiting on the punch line, but this wasn't a joke. I wasn't sure what his reaction would be, but the suspense was almost too much. I wanted him to say something—anything. I tried to be patient, but those seconds seemed to span a lifetime. What was he thinking? I wanted to hear him say something, even if it was just a simple acknowledgment that he heard my words.

Finally, he spoke. "How do you feel about that?"

"I think it's a good thing. It's weird that this has happened. I gave up the idea a long time ago that I'd ever be a father. Of course, I know that gay people are finding ways of having children, but I'm not into that high-tech stuff like artificial insemination and finding a surrogate mother. This may be my only chance at fatherhood."

"That may be true, but are you ready to be a father? That's the most important job you'll ever have. Your life will change."

Somewhere in between being blown away by the news and preparing myself to tell Daryl, I'd forgotten to ask myself those questions. *Was I ready to be a father? And what kind of father would I be?*

"I don't know. I guess I haven't had time to really think about it."

"Who'll raise the child? Will she keep it? Somehow, she doesn't strike me as the motherly type."

"You got that one right. If she has it, I'm sure I'll be the one raising it, but we didn't talk about that."

"If that's the case, and she doesn't want to raise the child, you'd be the primary caretaker and that will take a lot of your time and your best effort. It seems you have a lot to talk and think about."

"I know. I did just find out, though."

"I don't want you to glamorize parenting. It's a tough job. It won't be all fun and games. *Our* lives will change." I liked the way he thrust himself into the equation. It showed that he planned on staying around.

"Since this is a decision that will affect us, what do you think?"

"You know that I like children and I know one day I'll have my own biological child, so I can't fault you for wanting yours. If she keeps the baby, I'll deal with it just fine. And, if I'm gonna be a parent, I might as well start learning now. I ain't getting any younger."

"You are *so* wonderful," I said with a kiss.

"I guess now we just have to wait and see what she decides."

"I hate not really having a say in the matter."

"Isn't that strange?"

"What?"

"The fact that if a man doesn't want a woman to have his child, and she decides to have it anyway, then he's responsible for caring and taking care of the child even though he didn't want her to have it. Yet, if she decides to abort it, he has no choice in that either. It's like the man's wishes don't even count."

"I never really thought about it 'cause I didn't think it was an issue I thought I'd have to deal with. But it is a little one-sided, I guess. Then again, we're not the ones carrying the baby, either."

"True. I'm going downstairs for something to drink. You want something?" he asked.

"No, I'm fine." He moved out of bed and headed out of the room just as the phone rang.

"Grab that for me, will ya?" I heard his feet move down the stairs as I reached over and picked up the phone.

"Hello? Hello?"

"Kevin?"

"Who is this?"

"You don't recognize my voice? It hasn't been that long, has it?"

"What are you doing calling me here? How the hell—what do you want, James?"

"I need to see you. I need you to meet me tomorrow."

"Don't you ever call me here again with some bull-shit like this."

"I just need to see you so that I can apologize. My therapist says it's all part of the process. Please, help me. Will you meet me tomorrow at Andre's at 9 p.m.?"

I heard Daryl downstairs and didn't want him to be privy to this conversation, so in haste I agreed.

"Fine, but I'm warning you, no bullshit. And this will be the last time."

I hung up the phone just as Daryl called out to me. I reached down and erased the number off the Caller ID box. I did have a few choice words that needed to be said to Mr. Lancaster, so this meeting was a necessity.

"Who was on the phone?"

"No one. I mean, just Danea. She wants me to pick up some milk."

"I hope you told her you were staying here tonight."

"Believe me, I did."

CHAPTER 35

As I drove down the dark Houston freeway the knot in my stomach tightened into a ball. The traffic slowed with each passing second, and the fiery sea of red lights before me indicated this snail's pace would continue for some time. Interstate 10 had been under serious construction for years now, and the road crews had turned it into a virtual labyrinth, complete with tight lanes and blind curves, making it a very dangerous road to navigate. Crimson flashes lit up the crowded roadway while I took in a few deep breaths in an attempt to relax. Traffic was the last thing I wanted to deal with on this night. I looked at the clock on the dashboard and realized this traffic would make me late if it didn't dissipate soon. I wanted to do this and get it over with. For some reason, I started thinking—more like reliving—some of the moments we'd shared together.

The disjointed sound of car horns blaring into the darkness of the night broke the stillness of my thoughts. The traffic had begun to clear up and move on. Moments later, I saw the restaurant in the distance—the first restaurant where James and I had dined together. I allowed him to talk me into meeting here, and I suspected he was trying to play in the past.

When I entered the restaurant, it all came back to me. The deep scent of Mexican food hung in the air like flowers in a field of living colors. The bright decor mixed with the intoxicating environment and brought back memories. I could barely hear the faint music over the hustle and bustle of the noisy establishment. The wait staff rushed by, carefully weaving their way around whatever and whomever stood in their way. The thing I remembered most about this place were the purple margaritas, the strongest margarita in Houston. For a brief second, a smile tried to force its way onto my face. I loved this place. The smile was chased away by James' voice, beckoning me from the back corner.

"Kevin," he called out in his deep, baritone voice. His voice added to the strength of his image. He still spoke with a confidence that emanated from the core of his soul. "I'm glad you could make it. I wasn't sure if you were going to show."

"Well, I'm here," I said without emotion. I positioned myself in the booth directly across from him, avoiding his eye contact. "What is this?"

"Long Island Iced Tea, what did you expect?" I looked at the drink and pushed it to the side. "You don't want the drink?"

"I'm not drinking anything you ordered for me. That shit might be poisoned. What did you want to talk about? Say what's on your mind."

"Slow down, baby. Let's eat first. We have all night to talk."

"I didn't come here to be social, and I have no intention of being here with you all night. I suggest you start talking, or I'm out of here. And I'm not your baby."

"Okay, calm down a bit. I was hoping we'd have some time to get to know each other all over again."

"James..."

"First, I wanted to apologize to you for all that I've done to you. Looking back, I know I've been horrible to you, and you didn't deserve it. Kevin, I love you..."

"No, you loved to control me. There's a difference."

"You know I've changed. I'm seeing a therapist now. I know I have some issues that I have to work out. I need your help."

"You can't *imagine* how happy I am now that you've changed—all of a sudden—but you'll have to solve your problems without me. They have nothing to do with me now." My sarcasm rang in his ears.

"Baby—*Kevin*—these last few weeks have been really rough for me. There are things going on that you wouldn't understand. There are reasons why I was so distant and spent so much time out of town. Work has really taken a lot out of me." I gave him one

of my I-don't-give-a-shit looks. "I know you still are
a little bitter about how things ended up between us.
I can't feel any worse about the past. All I can say is
I'm so sorry. I offer you my apologies from the bottom
of my heart. Please, forgive me. I can't live without
your forgiveness." He reached across the table, tears
accumulating in his sad eyes, and grabbed my hand.
The warmth of his grip did little to comfort me, and
I snatched my hand away from the table like I'd just
touched a hot stove.

"Maybe I've been too nice, so I'll say this one more
time. I won't forgive you, not now, not ever. When I
think about all of the things you did to me and put
me through, I could..." I noticed James looking around
the room. My voice had begun to carry over the bustle
of the restaurant, and people were beginning to stare.
Out of the corners of my eyes, I could see heads
turning in sync. "And don't think for one second that
I don't know that it was you who fucked up my car,
and it was you who sent me those photographs. I
don't know what kind of game you're playing, but
this shit will stop! I don't want you coming by the
apartment, or calling me, or trying to contact me in
any way. When I decide I want to talk to you—if I
decide I want to talk to you—I'll let you know. But if
I were you, I wouldn't count on it. And if you keep
fucking with me, I will call the police. Let's see how

popular you'll be in this city if everyone found out that The Great James Lancaster likes beating up his gay lover."

"Don't threaten me, Kevin. You're out of your league. Besides, I don't know what you're talking about. Pictures? Your car? In spite of what you think, I'm still worried about you, and very much in love with you. I always want the best for you. In fact, I have something for you."

He reached into the inside pocket of his blazer and pulled out a brown envelope. I took the envelope with some hesitation and opened it cautiously. He'd transferred the title of the Mercedes into my name, giving me ownership. I put the title back into the envelope and handed it back to him.

"When will you learn you can buy everything except happiness and love? I'm not for sale."

"I wasn't trying to buy you, it's just that…it's your car. I never drive it. I don't need or want it. And besides, you need a car after that incident." The image of James vandalizing my car raced through my head and I fought back a wave of anger.

"I don't want or need anything you have to offer."

"Kevin, please take the car. I want you to have it."

"I said no."

"I'm trying to make things right between us. Just take the goddamn car."

"I knew you'd never change. Thanks for the evening," I said sarcastically as I stood up. He grabbed my hand again, and tried to force me to have a seat. I forcefully yanked my hand away.

"Kevin, sit down. I'm not through talking to you. I can't live without you." His voice sounded frantic as he lost his composure. His face looked flushed and drained. "I'll die if you leave me. I'll kill myself." A knife on the table provided me with perfect opportunity. His words made me angry instead of building up the sympathy he'd hoped. I snatched it up, looked over it for a split second and tossed it on the table right in front of him. I wasn't trying to injure him, but I wanted ~~him to know that taki~~ng his life was his decision, if he so chose.

"If you're serious about it, go ahead. Slit your wrists and bleed over your fine suit. This conversation is over. I don't know why I even bothered to come here. Fuck you." I turned and exited the room. He was still calling out to me when I heard the door behind me close. I didn't look back, but I could feel his eyes watching my every step until I disappeared into the restaurant parking lot.

I drove slowly down the same dark and winding road, paying particular attention to any fast approaching headlights. At this point, I wasn't sure what he'd do next. The only thing I was sure about was this wouldn't be the last time I'd see him. James was a master manipulator, this much I knew. He could win over the hardest heart with a few well-chosen words and a few canny looks. He could give more drama than Erica Kane, and he definitely would have won that Emmy more than once. The pathetic image that he presented that night was not the real James. It was an act. In fact, there was very little that was familiar about him that night. He didn't sit upright and proper, his shoulders dipped slightly, like a child begging for attention but knowing he didn't deserve it. He wasn't dressed as neatly as he usually was, and his eyes lacked that special sparkle. Either this was a master performance, or there was something really wrong with him.

When I reached the empty apartment I went into the kitchen, poured a glass of orange juice, and lit some incense to help me relax. Its sweet smell lifted the stench of James out of my clothing, right out of my mind.

I looked at the blinking light on the answering machine and decided to play the messages. A tiny smile spread across my face in anticipation, hoping Daryl had called from work, and he had. The next two messages were from James, at first threatening me and demanding I pick up the phone. His last message was an attempt to apologize again: *"Kevin, I am so sorry. I mean that. Baby, I just want you to come home.*

The reason I acted so crazy tonight is because I love you so much and I can't bear living without you. Please, pick up the phone. I need you. I miss you. You are my life. Baby, please…" I deleted each message.

CHAPTER 36

It was 1:12 a.m. when I heard the phone. I picked it up—against my better judgment. "Hello?"

"I'm trying to reach Kevin Davis."

"This is he. Who's calling?"

"Mr. Davis, I'm Sharon Strong, a nurse at Southwest Houston Hospital. I'm sorry to have to call you so late with news like this..."

"What news?"

"A friend of yours has been admitted with some severe cuts and he's asking to see you."

"Who?" I sat up in the bed, heart pounding like fists.

"Daryl Allen." Before she could utter another syllable, I had put on clothes, shoes and was in Danea's room. In exactly three minutes, we had called Tony and were out of the door and into the car, moving like the wind down Interstate 59. I wiped the tears from my eyes. I had talked to Daryl at 11:30 and he was fine. What could have happened? I hadn't felt pain like this since Keevan's death. I felt a tight rope around my neck slowly cutting off my supply of oxygen. As much as I tried to loosen it, it became even tighter until I felt light-headed. I was scared beyond words, and too frightened to blink.

"Danea, what if..."

"Don't do that, Kevin. There are no ifs. Daryl will be fine." She looked over at me and squeezed my hand. She exuded such certainty that I began to believe that my Daryl would be fine. I needed her confidence to carry me through this. I felt a tremendous ache in my heart.

✖✖✖

"Where is he?!" I yelled at the nurse across the desk.

"Where is who?" she responded evenly.

"I'm Kevin Davis. I received a phone call from someone at this hospital about half an hour ago. I was told that Daryl Allen had been admitted as a patient and was asking to see me. Now, where is he? Is he okay?"

Danea stood behind me and rubbed my shoulders in an attempt to calm me down. The only thing that would've calmed me was Daryl's face.

"Yes, sir. Everything has stabilized and he's gonna be fine."

"What happened?" Danea asked.

"He was admitted for lacerations on both wrists— self-inflicted lacerations," she said with some hesitation.

"What are you saying? He tried to kill himself?"

The nurse stepped from behind the desk and led us down a long white corridor. The pale hospital lights and the lifeless walls were almost unbearable. When we reached the end of the hallway, the nurse paused and indicated that only one of us would be allowed to see Daryl. Danea said she'd go back to the front and wait for Tony to arrive.

When I opened the door to the room, I took a few seconds to notice all the gadgets and machines. Green and red lights dotted the computerized equipment and several mechanical sounds blended to harmonize into an electronic symphony. I looked at the body in the center of the bed. I wanted to run over, grab and hold him, protect and never let him go. Instead, I moved slowly toward him. He was lying on his right side facing the window. When I moved around to that side of the room, the body shifted a bit. The closer I got to him, the more I could see that the shape of the body didn't match my Daryl. Then it all became clear. As I rounded the bed, his arm reached out and grabbed me as he used my body as a crutch to pull himself up. When he sat up in the bed and looked me in the face, it wasn't Daryl. It was James.

"What the fuck is going on here?" I screeched as I jerked my arm away from him and took a few steps backward.

"Kevin, I need you." He reached out to me, but I

let his arms dangle in open space. He rotated his arms to show me the thick bandages covering each wrist. "I had to do it. I couldn't stand the thought of living without you. When you told me to slit my wrists in the restaurant, something just snapped in my head. I love you, Kevin. I have to have you."

"You sick bastard! Did you think this would make me feel sorry for you?"

Danea and Tony burst through the doors.

"Kevin, what the hell is going on here?" Danea asked. Tony looked at James with a look of complete disgust. His face twisted into hate.

"What is this asshole doing here? And where is Daryl?"

"I'm sure Daryl is at home in bed where he should be."

"I don't understand," Tony continued.

"James was pretending to be Daryl so that I would come here and see him in the hospital."

"You sorry muthafucka," Tony said as he moved toward James. I held Tony back.

"That's it, James. I don't know who you think you are, but we are taking legal actions against you. This harassment will stop now," Danea said with the authority of the law.

The nurse opened the door to the room and looked at the three of us. "Only one visitor at a time," she said.

"You'll have to leave." She motioned for Danea and Tony to leave the room.

"We're all leaving," I said with contempt. We all followed the nurse back to the main room. Tony and Danea were almost out of the door and into the parking lot when I turned back.

"Excuse me," I said to the nurse. "How serious are his wounds?"

"He was never in a life-threatening situation. Luckily, the wounds are shallow."

I straightened out the confusion they had with his name. I gave them his real name, address, work number and home phone number just so they would know this was not my Daryl.

As I caught up with Danea and Tony, I thought about Keevan. This whole episode brought forth the specter of death again in my life. The thought of being responsible for another person's demise was overwhelming. I knew James was manipulating this situation for his benefit—for sympathy, to wear me down, to make me feel guilty—and I knew I'd be strong, but I did not want another death on my conscience.

After leaving the hospital we paid a surprise visit to Daryl, who was not expecting our late-night call. I used my key to clandestinely enter his apartment. I made the others wait downstairs while I climbed the stairs leading to his room. I watched my feet move slowly up the staircase, one above the other. I didn't want to wake him just yet. My desire was to catch just a glimpse of him sleeping peacefully. I moved down the hallway until I entered the interior of his room. It was dark, but I knew the whereabouts of all of the furniture. I glided over to his side of the bed, knelt down before him, and watched. The rhythmic pattern of his breathing and the rise and fall of his chest put my heart at ease. I wondered what he dreamt about, and if I was a central part of this nocturnal thoughts. The thought of losing him hit me suddenly like a fireball. I reached out to him and kissed him on the lips, gently, yet forceful enough to wake him. He smiled.

"This is a pleasant surprise," he said. "Baby, what are you doing here?" Instead of answering him right off, I just looked at him and stroked his head. He loved for me to scratch his head, so I dug my short fingernails into his scalp and applied a bit of pressure. "Is everything okay?"

"As long as you're okay, everything is fine."

"Why wouldn't I be okay?"

"It's a long story." By this time, Tony and Danea had climbed the stairs and made their way into the room. Tony clicked the switch on the halogen lamp. They raced over to Daryl, and dropped hugs and kisses upon his head and body.

"Whoa...what is going on? What's with all the love?" Daryl asked. Before I could begin telling the story,

Tony blurted out every detail in his usual dramatic fashion, which inflamed the situation. Daryl was mortified. His anger was evident through his tight eyes and clenched fists.

"Baby, calm down, okay? Everything is fine. Nothing happened. I don't want you flying off the handle and doing something we'll both regret." He smiled at me, and held my hand.

Since we were all gathered, we went downstairs and turned on the television. As the pictures moved across the screen, we talked. Tony surprised us by taking center stage and commanding our attention.

"I have an announcement to make," he said. I knew what he was about to do. This was a good time to shift the tone of the evening with an infusion of happiness. He fidgeted like a little child in front of a room full of classmates.

"Okay, Tony, if you have something to say, then say it, and get your ass out of the way. You're blocking the TV," Daryl said playfully.

"There is a lot more to life than TV."

"You're right about that," Danea chimed. "But could you get on with it already?"

"Okay. There's no easy way to say this…"

"Oh, Lord, what have you done this time?" Daryl asked.

"Nothing. Well, nothing yet. Believe me, this is good news, oh ye of little faith. Anyway, I just wanted you guys to know that I love LaMont very much and in New Orleans, he and I decided to get married. I mean have a commitment ceremony."

Daryl and Danea looked at each other, looked at me, and looked at Tony as he spoke. They were searching for some sign that would allow them to believe this was true.

Daryl turned around. "Am I on *Candid Camera*?"

Danea sat for a moment to chew on his words for flavor. After she was convinced, she rushed over to Tony and gave him a big hug. "Congratulations! I told Kevin a long time ago that you two would be together. Didn't I, Kevin?"

I nodded my head in agreement. She had this ability to successfully predict relationships. I used to tell her that if she ever wanted to stop practicing law and the singing thing didn't work out, she could always go work for Dionne. Of course, I told her this before she and her friends went out of business. Daryl joined in the hug circle as we all congratulated him.

"Kevin has been helping me with some details, but I know everything will work out. This will be the biggest wedding—Texas-style."

"You knew about this, Kevin?" Daryl asked. I nodded my head again and he immediately pinned me to the couch and tickled me without mercy. "How could you keep something like that from me?" I wanted to answer, but I couldn't speak for laughing.

CHAPTER 37

Daryl walked into the living room just as I put down the phone. I had just tried contacting RaChelle for what seemed like the hundredth time. Again, when I called her, no answer. This whole situation was pissing me off, even though I tried to be patient and understanding.

"Who was on the phone?" he asked casually.

"No one. I mean, RaChelle. Actually, it was her machine."

"You called her again?"

"Yeah, I really need to talk to her."

"Baby, listen to me. I know having this child is important for you and I know you two have a lot to talk about, but if you keep calling her she's gonna feel pressured, and you don't want that."

"This is driving me crazy. To think she's out there somewhere, alone, about to make a decision that will affect a lot of people."

"I know it has to be hard, but you have got to be patient with her. Let her come to you."

As much as I could, I took his advice. At work, I tried to refrain from walking by her office during the day just to see if she had come. I knew how much she loved her work and wouldn't want to be away too long. Her administrative assistant told me she'd taken a few vacation days and would be back next week sometime. That didn't sound like RaChelle, but then again this wasn't an ordinary circumstance. I would pay money to be able to speak with her.

A couple of nights later, I received a brief message from her saying she decided she needed some time to herself to think about her life. She indicated that she was okay, and wasn't quite sure when she'd return, but it wouldn't be too long. She didn't make any mention of whether or not she'd decided to keep the baby or to have an abortion. I was anxious to know, and to be a part of the decision-making process, but she didn't leave any contact phone numbers, nor did she mention where she was. Her last words were, "Don't worry, I'm okay. See ya soon."

Somewhere between being preoccupied with thoughts of being a father, being in love with Daryl, being pulled in a hundred directions at work, and helping Tony and LaMont plan their ceremony, I had to plan a small surprise party for Danea. Just like I knew it would, her trip to Los Angeles had been a success. She knocked them completely off their feet and they were interested in her as an artist. They had already committed to producing at least one single.

Stuff like this was not what normally happened to people I know. It's the sort of thing that you read about in magazines. Some celebrity being interviewed would say one day they were just singing on the bus and got discovered by some big-time agent, or some guy who was playing basketball in a park became a supermodel. I knew it could happen; I just didn't think it *would* happen. I looked forward to the day when I could drive down the road listening to the radio and instead of hearing Mariah, I heard Danea. When she becamethe next diva, I could read about how she got discovered while singing karaoke in some smoky hotel bar in New Orleans.

The song that she sang for the Los Angeles group was a song she had written years ago called "Victory." She told me that she had planned on singing something that might be more familiar like an Aretha song, but when she opened her mouth, her song poured out, much to her surprise. They liked the song so much they wanted to buy it from her and maybe have her sing it on the soundtrack to an upcoming movie. This story just kept getting better. To think, one of my best friends—a star.

I'd only invited our immediate friends over to the house for a few snacks and a glass of wine or two. Of course, when Tony arrived he was on the arms of his soon-to-be partner for life, LaMont. The thought of

LaMont becoming a part of our family of friends through marriage made me smile. It was an interesting thought. I wondered if one day Daryl and I would have a ceremony.

A friend of Tony's had managed to get us last-minute tickets to see Rachelle Ferrell perform live at a small venue called Dante's off Richmond Avenue. Danea would flip out at the thought of seeing one of her favorite artists.

I invited Croix, who was becoming an extension of our family. He wasn't a brother yet, but he hovered somewhere around "cousin" status. Since he had filed for divorce and his wife had moved out, he seemed much happier. He surprised me when he told me that a couple of days earlier he had met someone, *a guy*, and he was going to bring him to the show. I couldn't wait to meet the guy. I hoped Croix was ready for this step. In the back of my head I hoped that he wasn't about to lose control. He had a lot of wild oats to sow, but these were not the safest times to spread your seed around. When I talked to him, he said he'd meet us at Dante's.

✖✖✖

We listened as we heard Danea fumble with her keys trying to insert the right one into the lock. The door opened, and we heard it close behind her. With the lights off and the house quiet, we jumped from our hiding places and yelled, "Surprise!" She dropped her briefcase and almost started swinging at us.

"What are y'all doing? Trying to give me a heart attack!"

"Surprise!" we yelled again as we showered her with hugs and kisses.

"This is to say congratulations. Just don't forget us when you're a star," I said.

"Yeah, girl, don't forget where you came from," Tony added. I could see a tear forming in her eyes as she returned the hugs.

"We have a big surprise," Daryl said. "We have tickets to see Rachelle Ferrell tonight!"

Danea screamed. "You're lying!"

"No, I'm not, and you have about forty-five minutes to get ready."

"Don't start crying. I don't wanna see no mascara running down your face," Tony said.

"G-g-g-g-g-ood luck, lady," LaMont said. "I-I-I don't really know who Rasheal Ferill, is, but you'd betta hurry."

Tony looked at him, then me, and back at LaMont. Tony grabbed his hand and led him to the back while mumbling something about being embarrassed. I couldn't wait for their ceremony.

"You'd better hurry up. Rachelle's waiting."

By the time we reached the club, the line was out the door. Luckily, we had VIP tickets and were able to walk right up to the door and into the club. *Talk about getting the hookup.* We sat at a table almost center stage, just off to the right a bit. We'd be so close that we'd be able to hear her breathing.

As Danea recounted the story about her experiences in Los Angeles, I slowly sipped on a glass of wine and held onto Daryl's leg under the table. When I looked up, I saw Croix moving our direction with a grin on his face.

"Wassup, black people?" he said.

"Nothing, man. What's up with you?"

"I thought I'd come out and celebrate Danea's big night. Congratulations." He gave her a kiss on the cheek and presented her with a yellow rose.

"Thank you, Croix. Have a seat."

"I will in a minute. My date is parking the car."

"Date?" Danea said probingly. "This is new, isn't it?" In the excitement of the evening, I had forgot to mention to Danea that Croix would be joining us with a date.

"You can say that again. I'm nervous as hell. Can you tell?"

The lights dimmed and the club started to get quiet.

"You're doing fine, Croix," Daryl added. "You're a

great guy. Just be yourself, relax and enjoy the show."

"Thanks, man. Oh, here he comes now," Croix said. When I looked up and saw the man coming our direction, I knew it had to be a mistake. *Walk past us, keep moving,* I prayed to myself. *This was not about to happen.*

"Everyone, I want you to meet my friend, Alex."

He was using his middle name, but the man who was introduced to us was James Lancaster. We all gasped.

"What's wrong?" Croix asked.

"What the fuck is going on?" I asked, looking directly at James. "What kind of shit are you trying to pull?"

"I'm not pulling any shit. I didn't know he knew you, and your *friends.*"

"Wait. You know them?" Croix asked James.

"Shhh, you need to sit down," Danea said, trying to prevent a scene. "Kevin, take this outside or somewhere."

"This man is my ex that I told you about. James."

"What? What is this shit?" Croix asked with disgust.

"You need to get your sorry ass out of here," Daryl demanded. He stood up and was about to approach James. This situation was about to get heated.

"And what are you going to do if I don't?"

"I'm gonna put my fist through your fuckin' face," Daryl said loudly. "We are sick of your shit, you bastard." Daryl lunged forward across the table and had it not been for Danea who stood in between them, he would have been all over James.

"*Do not cause a scene in here*," Danea pleaded. "Take it somewhere else."

"Come here, James," I said as I headed toward the restroom. Daryl and Croix started to follow.

"Let me handle this, guys. Stay with Danea." I said.

"I am not leaving you alone with this sorry piece of shit," Daryl said. He was not about to let me be alone with James, but I begged him to stay with Danea, who grabbed his arm and forced him to sit. If he followed, I knew there'd be a fight. Croix whispered something to Daryl and they reluctantly sat down. "If you're not back in three minutes, I'm coming after you," I heard Daryl say. I didn't want a fight to break out, so I had to keep Daryl away from James. James was right on my heels when I threw the restroom door open.

"You have a lot of fucking nerve."

"Kevin, I didn't know you'd be here, although I must say it is a nice surprise."

"For who? This ain't no pleasant surprise."

"You can't tell me that you're not at least a little bit interested in seeing me."

"Yes, I can. And you show up with one of my good friends. What kind of bullshit is that?" Just then, a stall door opened and a brotha looked at us with a look of surprise. *"This gay-ass shit,"* he said as he rushed out the door. We paid little attention to him or his comment.

"How did I know he knew you?"

"Don't play that innocent shit with me. I know you. This wasn't no fuckin' coincidence, and you know it."

"Kevin..."

"Shut up. I'm about to go back out there and enjoy the rest of the evening with my friends. Trust me, Croix doesn't want to be anywhere around you."

"Where am I supposed to go now?"

"For all I care, you can go straight to hell."

"I am sick of this hard-nigga attitude that you've been giving me. I have always gone out my way to make you happy. Everything I do, I do for you. I'm entitled to just a little bit of respect from you. I'm a patient man, but my patience with you is running low. It's time that you brought your ass back home with me where you belong and leave the rest of those fools alone."

"Nigga, you trippin'. You and I are over. What part of that don't you get?"

"I don't get the part where you think you can just walk away like everything's okay. That's the part I don't get."

"I suggest you get some help."

"You don't seem to get the fact that you and I will never be over. I will never let you go. You are mine, and I am yours, and there is nothing either one of us can do about it."

"You are sick. Did you forget to take your medication this evening?" I asked smugly. "I'd rather be dead than spend one more night with you."

"Is that what you really want?" He spoke in a strong whisper between clenched teeth.

"You threatening me?"

With a smile, he said, "Of course not. I don't make threats. I think you should know that there are a lot of things worse than death."

"What is that supposed to mean?"

"It means just that. I'd hate for something to happen to you, or even worse, one of your friends. It would be awfully tragic."

I stepped into his face. "Get this straight. If you lay one hand on any one of my friends, God as my witness, I will kill you."

"Are you threatening me?"

"You goddamned right I am!"

"After having lived with me I thought you had more insight. I thought you knew me better than this. You have no idea who you're dealing with, do you? I would do anything to make you mine. There is no price too great, or no cross too heavy. I will do anything and everything for you—for our love."

He was detestable. Still, I had to stand my ground and be strong.

"You've been fucking with me the whole time since I left. I may not be able to prove it yet, but I will. Why don't you stop playing these little games? If you want me, nigga, you know where I am. I'm not running from you or your threats."

"When I decide to get you, you won't hear me coming. Now, if you'll excuse me, I need to find a table." He walked out just as coolly as he had approached our table. The simplicity of his words reverberated off the white-tiled walls in the restroom. I knew this man. I knew he was not one to give up easily when he'd set his mind to something. I had hoped that he'd soon forget about me and move on, but I was wrong. Right now, I couldn't worry about it. All I could do was keep my guard up.

At the end of that rather eventful night, we all went back for some wine at Danea's place. We walked into the empty house, trying to forget the episode with James. I was worried about Croix. He hadn't said much, so I didn't know where his head was.

"Croix, come here for a second, please." I said. We walked upstairs to my bedroom and he took a seat.

"Wassup?"

"I wanted to see how you're doing. I know this night has been a little uncomfortable for the both of us with James there all night."

"What is his problem?"

"Crazy."

"Damn, I can't believe this is happening. My first date with a man in years and this is how it turns out. Maybe I'm not as ready for this as I thought."

"Don't let James take from you what you've been wanting to give yourself for years. He's a master at taking things. Don't give him that power over you. There are a lot of good men out there. Sometimes, they're hard to find, but I know it'll work out for you, if that's what you want."

"I know it will, too. I'm not looking for a relationship right now. I just wanted to see what I've been missing, and right now, I don't think I can get involved with all this."

"What do you mean?"

"This is no offense to you, Kevin, 'cause you know I think you are wonderful. If you weren't so perfect with Daryl, I'd be trying hard to get at you, but I'm gonna have to re-evaluate some things."

"Like what?"

"I'm in the middle of a divorce and the issue of custody of my kids will come up. If they were to find out about me, I could lose my kids. I'm gonna have to pull back from our friendship for a while."

"As much as I hate to say it, I think you're right. Your kids should be your primary focus and I have way too much shit going on right now. I don't want you to jeopardize your case."

Our conversation was abruptly interrupted by the sounds of breaking glass and Danea screaming. I heard the front door open and LaMont's voice yelling obscenities. We ran downstairs and saw Danea standing there, using her dress to wipe blood off her face. Glass from the bay window littered the room like sand on a beach.

I rushed over to her. "Danea, you okay?"

She felt her face with her hands for any cuts, but wasn't able to find any. "I don't think it's my blood. It's not my blood," she stated with some certainty and then rushed into the bathroom.

"Tony, what the fuck happened?" Croix asked.

"I was standing over there pouring a glass of wine when this thing comes crashing through the window."

"What came through the window?" I asked.

"I think it was a brick," Daryl said.

"Where is it?" I asked. Daryl walked over to the corner and I followed. Then I saw it. A red brick, but something was attached to it. Something wrapped in silver duct tape. As I got closer, I saw the source of blood. Barely moving, but alive, was a precious black kitten with glass covering its fur. It was so badly hurt that it couldn't even make a sound. Before my eyes, I could see its life slip away. It was dead.

"I-I-I didn't see nothing b-b-b-ut the back of a black t-t-t-ruck. It didn't even have n-n-no lights on," LaMont reported back to us. I knew of only one fiend capable of such an act of cruelty.

✖✖✖

"I'm not sure what to do, Daryl. The nigga is crazy. He's been calling at all hours of the night and hanging up. It's not just one night, but it's every night. He even calls at work and on my cell phone, and does the same thing. I know it's him."

"Why didn't you tell me this before? I could have handled it a long time ago."

"That's precisely why I didn't tell you. I didn't want this situation getting any worse than it has to be."

"Kevin, you have dead cats and bricks flying through the damn window. How much worse could it be?"

"I didn't think it would get to that point. I guess I was hoping he would fade away."

"You know better than anyone that James is not the kind of person to fade quietly into the background. You need to start thinking about protecting yourself." Daryl looked at me and got up and moved over to the closet. He reached up and grabbed a shoebox off the top shelf and brought it back over to me. He placed it down beside me. "Open it." I looked at him, not sure what to expect, and took the lid off the box.

"When did you get this?" I asked.

"I've had it for a while. It's for protection. Luckily, I've never had to use it." The gun in the box made me nervous. I had never been this close to a real gun.

"Is it loaded?"

"No." He took the gun out of the box, looked at it, and aimed it at the wall as if he was about to fire. He handed it to me. I grabbed it and it felt heavier than it looked. Its silver metal frame was cold to the touch, but something about holding that weapon provided a sense of security. "I'll teach you how to use it. I don't like the thought of you out there without some sort of protection."

"I don't know about this, Daryl."

"What's to know? You have some maniac stalking you. You have to protect yourself. I'm not gonna let him do anything to you without you having an opportunity to defend yourself. I don't want to argue about this, Kevin, but you are going to learn to use the gun."

I could see there was no use in arguing with him. He was right; I had to do something to ensure my safety, and the safety of my friends. Texas law allows an individual to carry a concealed weapon. All I had to do was pass a background test and take a short class to get certified.

"When is my first lesson?"

✖✖✖

After I ran a few errands for Tony's ceremony, I decided to stop by the store so that I could surprise Daryl with a nice meal. He had been such a supporter and lover in these dark times that I felt like I owed him a debt that I could never repay, but I'd have fun trying. His favorite was soul food; just like a Southern man. Fried chicken, sweet potatoes, collard greens, macaroni and cheese with cheese so thick it would weld your mouth shut. His favorite dessert was peach cobbler, but that's way out of my league. For food like that, you'd have to wait until Sunday and hit up one of the church ladies for a meal. That night, I wanted something more sensual and less fattening. Baked chicken with some angel hair pasta, a salad, and some nice wine sounded great.

When I walked into the store, I grabbed a cart and pushed it over to the fresh fruits and vegetables. Just my luck to grab a cart that didn't want to roll. I stopped in the aisle and looked down at the four wheels. One of them was on backwards. When I looked up, darting down the end of the aisle, I saw someone who I thought was James. I left the basket in the middle of the floor, and walked hurriedly toward him. At the end of the aisle, I looked both ways and saw him turn onto another aisle. *He's fucking with me.* I turned the corner and almost ran over an old lady, who looked at me as if I was gonna dart by and grab her purse and continue my sprint out of the store. Just then, I stopped. What the hell was I doing? Had he taken so much control of me that he had me acting like a lunatic in the middle of the store?

As much as I hated to admit it, he did have me on edge. I'd been watching my back when I walked down the street. Strange voices in the crowd sounded like him, sudden movements took me by surprise, and there seemed to be shadows everywhere. It was at that moment that I resolved to regain control. I would not let him do this to me. This is exactly what he wanted me to do. I turned and walked back toward my cart, still in the middle of the store. When I reached the vegetables, I saw the guy I'd been chasing through the store, and he was not James. I felt like an idiot. I took another moment to regain my senses and regain control. I would not live like this. Not again.

CHAPTER 38

'd taken extra time getting ready for work that morning. I made sure that my shirt and tie complemented each other. My Liz Claiborne slacks had a nice crease, my haircut was fresh, my mustache was neatly trimmed, and I wore a nice pair of glasses with clear lenses that made me look professional. I took a quick glance in the mirror downstairs, smiled at my reflection, and strutted confidently out the door. There was a major luncheon downtown at the Hyatt Regency regarding the merger. The new officers would be announced officially, even though we knew who they were, and all of the department heads would be introduced. The report and presentation for my department was perfect. All of the I's were dotted and all of the T's were crossed. I remembered how I used to love giving presentations, and I'd have to call upon that past experience to guide me. I wasn't nervous because I had skills.

Much of the luncheon presentation was just for show. It would give everyone the opportunity to meet and greet the new upper-level executives, and to place names with the new faces. There would be bad jokes, fake smiles and ass-kissing. In general, it would be what I expected. As an associate director I had to go along with the song and dance.

When I walked into the crowded room, people were huddled in small groups, eating little squares of cheese and nibbling on crackers as they made small talk. All of these people worked in my building, but most of the faces were unfamiliar to me. There was only one person I was really interested in seeing right now. I scanned the room for RaChelle, but I didn't see her. When I talked with her two nights earlier, she said she'd be there with bells on, and I couldn't imagine her missing this occasion to be in the spotlight. There was even a nameplate at the dais for her, but the seat was empty.

I found the table reserved for my department and took a seat next to my assistant. She looked dazzling. We talked a little bit, mainly about nothing, but she was unusually quiet. On the table in front of each seat was a thick copy of the company report. I thumbed through it, barely taking note of the sales figures and growth reports. RaChelle had me distracted. Just then, I saw her out of the corner of my eye. She was coming in my direction, and I excused myself from the table to meet her half-way. She smiled an awkward smile, and we moved to a corner near the back.

"I'm glad to see you. You look great." I pulled her into me for a quick hug.

"Well, thank you. I feel good." She looked at me, but her stare carried a hidden message. "I know you and I have a lot to talk about. I want to thank you for giving me some space and not pressuring me."

"Have you…?" The suspense was killing me.

"Yes, I have made a decision about my situation, but I don't think we should talk about it here."

"RaChelle, I've been waiting a long time now. Please, just let me know what you've decided." She contemplated my words for a few minutes as her eyes danced around the room. As the lights in the room dimmed, she motioned for me to come closer. The speaker took to the stage and asked everyone to take their seats because the video presentation was about to start.

She whispered into my ear, "I've got to get on stage, but I hope you're prepared to be a father." She smiled and I smiled and we smiled together. My heart breathed a sigh of relief. I really wanted to be a father, and I was happy with her decision. Immediately, I started planning for this child, this little person, this little me. I was on cloud nine, and no power on this earth could bring me down. Me, a father! It sounded great. I had visions of spending summer afternoons in the park teaching the son I hoped to have how to play football and baseball. It was hard not to smile as I watched RaChelle, the woman who carried my child, walk away and take her place among the other executives at the head table. I didn't have all of the answers, but at least I knew a part of it. I was going to be a father!

I made my way back to my seat and found a large manila envelope in my chair.

"What is this?" I asked my assistant.

"Some guy delivered it a second ago. I don't know what it is."

As I thumbed through the packet, I was surprised to find a very graphic photograph. My breathing increased and I could feel my eyes widening. No matter how wide they got, I could not seem to focus completely on the image I held. I looked at it, and it stared back without blinking, without flinching. It was a picture from Keevan's autopsy. His decomposed body lay on some gray metal table, his chest cut open to reveal his internal organs.

When the video started to play, my head was held down still looking at the photograph. I then heard heavy breathing and a familiar voice saying, *"Shit, that feels good. Don't stop. Yeah, oh shit!"* At that moment, my worst nightmares exploded into reality. My face cracked into a million pieces. It was stomped on, ground into the floor, and scattered across the room by images from the past that found their way into the present and on wide-screen! I wanted to disappear under a rock. The video James recorded of me having sex with his horrible friend Carl was now playing in full view of every one of my colleagues. Heads almost twisted off their necks as they turned to look at me. Sighs, gasps, oh-my-gods, laughter, and shock filled the air like the cackling of a coven of witches over a bubbling cauldron.

"Turn that off!" I screamed. I raced across the room toward the technical booth at the back. I wanted to die. Again. And again. And again. When I reached the booth, the door was locked, and there was no one inside. I yelled, screamed, cussed, and really lost control. I banged on the door, tried to kick it in, and finally grabbed a chair and threw it through the window, sending glass all over the electronic equipment. I found the recorder, and hit eject, and when the tape was thrown out of the black machine, I took a steel microphone that was to my left and started banging the tape without mercy until it lay in pieces. I yanked on the black film from inside the tape and ripped it to shreds, but my destruction couldn't erase what they had already seen. My face felt like it was about to explode. All of this happened in the course of a couple of minutes, but it seemed like a lifetime. I heard an indignant voice call out my name, but I raced out of the room before it could be identified.

Like a madman, I raced out of the building, across the parking lot, and into the rental car I still drove. I drove downtown toward the high-rise that housed LCS. Never once did I stop to think about what I was going to say or do when I got there. I just knew that I had to find him. I threw my car into park, jumped out, ran inside the building, and hit the "up" button for the elevator. I waited for the elevator as the security guard eyed me suspiciously. I caught a glimpse of my reflection in the silver doors and realized that I looked like a wild-eyed psychopath ready to kill. I took in a few deep breaths and tried to regain some semblance of control. Luckily, the elevator doors parted and I stepped in. The elevator stopped at almost every floor between the first and the twenty-seventh, and I had to remain composed as a group of ladies entered on the fifteenth floor and filled the elevator with the sound of laughter and happiness. What the hell did they have to be happy about?

Once on the right floor, I went into his office and made my way to the back, walking right past his secretary, Deborah, who tried to stop me. I heard her say something like "Kevin, wait. You can't go in there. Mr. Lancaster is..." I threw open the big mahogany doors and walked in. James sat comfortably behind his oversized marble desk, with the phone in his hand. He looked up at me for a second and then looked back down. He said, "Let me call you back," and hung up the phone. Deborah raced in, her red hair scattered about her thick head.

"I'm sorry, Mr. Lancaster. I tried to stop him. Do you want me to call security?" Her tight brown skirt looked like it was cutting off her circulation and the run-over shoes she wore begged for relief from the pain of her stout frame.

"No, Deborah. I can handle this."

He waved her away, and when she closed the door, I leapt forward closer to his desk.

"You sorry muthafucka!" I said. "Who the fuck do you think you are?"

"Is there a problem, Kevin? You're a bit worked up."

"Don't patronize me! You know exactly what the problem is! The problem is you. Don't sit there and act innocent, you bastard!" James casually got up and strolled from behind his desk over to a pitcher of orange juice on the other side of the room on the bar. I would not allow him to ignore me. He would not reduce me to nothing by feigning ignorance. I lost control and reason abandoned me. I picked up the blunt marble penholder that matched his desk and threw it with all my force across the room toward him. Just in the nick of time, he turned, saw it coming and, ducked down low, barely avoiding a painful surprise. It hit the wall with a thunderous blow, and then crashed into the pitcher of juice, coloring his white shirt orange.

"What the fuck is your problem?" he screamed. "You could've killed me!" Deborah ran back into the room and let out a ghastly sigh.

"Mr. Lancaster, are you okay?"

"I can handle this, Deborah! Go back to your desk!" he commanded. The door slammed shut again.

"Stop fucking with my life!" I yelled.

"You're always looking for someone else to blame your goddamn problems on. For once, be a man! I really don't give a shit about your life right now. I have too much shit to deal with on my own."

"That little stunt you pulled today was way out of line, but I guess I should've expected some tacky shit like that from you. With all of your money, you still have no class!"

"Fuck you! I don't even know why I bothered with you. You're so pitiful. Look at you. Your life is falling apart without me. Do you really think you can survive without me? I'd like to see you try. When you fail, when all you *think* you've achieved is gone, you'll come running back to me like the little bitch you are! I made you, and I can just as easily break you!"

"You really think you bad, don't you?"

"Don't fuck with me. I can help you through all of this. Just come home. I'm begging you."

"I'd rather die than go back to living with you." I looked him right in his cold dark eyes, and all that greeted me was bitterness.

"Just like your brother. He couldn't take living in the world, so he killed himself. Why don't you do the same and save us both the trouble?" His words felt like sharp fingernails digging into my chest and pulling up patches of skin. The utter harshness of his voice knocked the wind out of me. He didn't know anything about my brother. "See what I mean? What are you gonna do now? Cry like a baby?"

Crying was the farthest thing from my mind. I wanted him dead. I looked at his desk and something caught my eyes: a sharp pair of scissors. I looked at the tool, and the smirk on his face compelled me to grab it. I lunged at him. Before I knew it—before he knew it—I was on top of him, with the scissors dug in his throat. A small puddle of blood began to form at the entry point, and the next thing I knew the doors to his office swung open and two big guys in gray uniforms pushed me off James. The scissors flew out of my hand and were lost behind the bar. I struggled to get free as the two guards held me back. Deborah stood in the doorway, her skin a bright red, clutching her neck as if she'd been the one with the scissors pressed against her fleshy neck. They pinned me against the wall, and when I attempted to free myself, one of them hit me in the ribs with his black stick, and the pain forced me down. Deborah saw the blood oozing out of James' neck and rushed to her desk, coming back with a first-aid kit. James rubbed his right hand over his neck and looked at the blood on his fingers. The wound I inflicted wasn't deep or life-threatening; just a small flesh wound. Just something to let him know.

"You really shouldn't have done that," James said. "Get him out of here!"

The guard with huge forearms and a tattoo of a heart on his left bicep asked if he should call the police, but James told him no. Instead, he told them to get me out of the building and to never let me in again.

CHAPTER 39

Out of control. My life was out of control, again. Ever since I'd met James, my life had changed in so many ways. It had taken a few unexpected turns over the course of the last months, catching me off guard. I veered so far off course that I thought I might be lost in the forest forever. Things were spinning frantically out of control. All this because I refused to love a man who refused to be loved. My life, buried in the ashes of vengeance and rage, lost its luster. Its once-promising shine dimmed into a small flicker that was about to fade off screen.

When I looked down at my watch it was almost 8 p.m. I couldn't remember where I had been for the last few hours, but I knew that a lot of that time was spent driving—driving my thoughts away. Trying to run away from life. But wherever I ended up, my problems were only a few steps behind. When I was able to clearly focus my thoughts, I was at the cemetery. I needed to speak with my brother. I needed Keevan. He always knew what to say and what kind of advice to give whenever I ran into trouble. I didn't see why that should change.

I sat in the car and took a few quick breaths to help clear my mind. I listened intently to the sounds of nature, from the rustling of leaves on the trees to the crickets singing their familiar evening song. I needed this anger to pass so that I could assess my life with precise clarity. The longer I sat, the more subdued my heartbeat became, and my thoughts grew calmer.

I got out of the car and walked toward the gravesite. It was hard to imagine that it was so easy for me to come and visit my brother when for months I had avoided this place as a reminder of my guilt. Dr. Manheim had been encouraging me to visit often, and I did. I'd been there several times in the last few weeks, bringing flowers, enjoying the laughter we used to share, and just spending some time with my brother. The process was usually very therapeutic. This time was different. No laughter. No smiles. No flowers.

As I rounded the corner toward the gravesite, I noticed two uniformed police officers standing there talking with Mr. Grimes, the grounds-keeper. I moved toward them. Something was wrong. Keevan's grave had been disturbed, to put it mildly. As I made my approach, their eyes fixed upon me as if I was an interloper in forbidden territory. Immediately, one of the officers put up his hands as if to say "stop." Mr. Grimes told him who I was and the officer invited me closer.

"What the fuck is going on here?" I asked. All my tendencies for reason and logic failed me. I could see a broken headstone, piles of freshly dug-up dirt, and a casket half out of the ground. "Did you hear me? What the hell happened? Somebody answer me!"

"Mr. Davis, I'm Officer Childs. We tried contacting you earlier, but we got no answer at your home. I'm sorry you had to see this."

"I'll ask once more: What the fuck happened?"

"There's been some vandalism in the cemetery."

His knack of pointing out the blatantly obvious struck a chord with me. "No shit. Who did this? When did it happen?"

"Sometime last night. When I got here, this is what I found. I ain't touch nothin'." Mr. Grimes' raspy voice bore a painful line in my head. His unkempt gray beard and dirty overalls blended well with this macabre death scene.

"And where were you last night? Aren't you supposed to be watching out for shit like this?"

"I hafta sleep, too, Mr. Davis."

I took a deep breath. "I'm sorry, Mr. Grimes. I don't mean to take it out on you, but this has already been a rough day, and then I come here and find this."

The officer spoke. "We've had a rash of cemetery vandalism in this area over the last couple of months, but we don't have any suspects at this time. And this really doesn't fit the M.O. of the others. This is the only grave in the whole place that was wrecked."

Before his words had time to completely leave his mouth I knew what he was going to say, and I knew who was responsible. The sound of my teeth grinding together didn't amplify my anger nearly enough.

❊❊❊

By the time I reached Daryl's place, I was completely exhausted. Not just physically, but mentally. I had suffered so much and there was no end in sight. This was the ultimate act of cruelty, *the unkindest cut of all*. When I walked into his place, I kicked my black shoes off and left them in the middle of his living room as I collapsed on the sofa. I was frustrated, tired of the struggle, and fully drained. I lay there, stiff and sullen, and wondered what it would take to get James to leave me alone. He'd told me more than once that I was his forever and that he owned me. Was death our only solution? Whose death?

My face was buried in the cushion on his sofa when I heard a noise coming from upstairs. Instantly, I rose up and faced the staircase, breathing so lightly that it would not interfere with the sounds. I heard another noise. I wanted to rush upstairs and confront whoever was there, but the sensible thing to do was to get the hell out of there. The thought of running away didn't sit well in the pit of my stomach. I'd spent much of the last year running from the truth, hiding from my friends, and living life in fear. I was tired of running. I wanted to take a stand, but I thought about all those horror movies in which people chased mysterious sounds only to meet the end of some maniac's machete.

I tiptoed over to the hall closet and pulled out Daryl's gun. I had placed it in the closet the previous day after my evening target practice. I moved up the stairs, barely breathing, until I reached the top of the dark staircase. I crept down the hallway until I reached the partially opened door to the bedroom. I peered inside for anything that could be a human form, but it was too dark. I kicked open the door with a sudden thrust. If there was anyone behind the door, I wanted to make sure he felt the blow. When the door slammed into the wall, I flicked on the lights and slowly entered the room. I needed to check everywhere, but when I moved over to the closet, I heard someone run down the staircase. They must have been hiding in the bathroom. I raced out of the room just in time to see a darkly clad figure escape down the stairs. I followed suit, but I stumbled on my way down the staircase and by the time I got into the living room the figure had raced out of the apartment and disappeared. I closed the door and then called the police, and then Daryl.

"Kevin, I'm five minutes away from the house. I want you to get out of the house in case there is more than one intruder. Get out of the house, Kevin. I don't want you in there."

"I'm okay, Daryl. I have your gun."

"I don't care. Don't fight me on this. Get out of the damn house." His stern words offered no latitude for argument or debate. I knew he was right, but I didn't want to be chased out of his house.

"Kevin?"

"Okay, I'll meet you outside."

About five minutes later he sped into the parking lot, and hugged me with strength and love. He checked me over, kissed me on the lips, and squeezed my hand.

"You sure you're okay?"

"I'm fine, really."

We moved toward his apartment and opened the door slowly. From where we stood, the living room area was clearly visible. It seemed secure. We moved further into the interior of the house, being mindful that we might be entering a "hostile environment." We stood still for a moment, just long enough to listen for any strange sounds that might echo in the house. He took the gun from me and gripped it firmly.

We checked out the kitchen area and as we made our way up the stairs we heard the sirens. We stopped and looked at each other and decided to go outside for the police. We decided with no conversation or words spoken. It would be our luck for the police to come into this suburban neighborhood, see two black men and open fire before opening their mouths to ask questions.

After the police secured the premises we were allowed to re-enter the place. They took their report, suggested we get a dog or some sort of security system, and were on their way.

"I know this was James, but what was he doing here?" I asked Daryl.

"This man is really sick, but I've got the cure for him," he said as he held the gun.

CHAPTER 40

After having one of the worst days of my life, early the next morning I was served with a restraining order forbidding me from coming within one hundred feet of James, LCS, or his home. *Ain't that a bitch*. I was the one being tormented, yet the courts had identified me as the menace. I should have acted earlier. Now, if I wanted to get an order, it would just seem to be in retaliation for the order against me. What kind of society are we living in when the victims of crime are falsely identified as the perpetrators?

I tried calling Danea at the house several times, but the phone just rang. The answering machine didn't even pick up, which was strange. I tried not to worry, but I couldn't help it. I didn't want to take her safety for granted, especially when I didn't know when James would strike, or who he would move against. I waited until Daryl got out of the shower and told him what I was feeling.

Before I knew it, we were dressed, in the car, on the road, and at my house. The door was locked, and all was quiet on the inside. On the way in, I didn't see her car in the lot and I knew she liked to work out at the gym early on Saturdays. Hopefully, that's where she was. We slowly checked out the house and everything was in place until we got to my room. On my bed was a red gift box and a note that read, "I'm everywhere you are."

"Let me check it out, baby," Daryl said, holding me back with his arms as he moved forward. He took his shoe and gave the box a nudge, turning it over on its side. The box obviously wasn't heavy, and we could detect no sounds from within, so he picked it up carefully and untied the white silk bow.

"Baby, be careful," I said while moving closer to him. He finished opening the box and dug through the mounds of tissue paper.

"Daryl, what is it?"

"Just a pile of dirt," he said in confusion.

When I looked at the dirt I understood. "This is dirt from Keevan's grave. That bastard dug up my brother's grave!" Upon closer examination of the soil in the box, I found the ring that we buried with Keevan. It was a silver ring with black grooves that reminded me of a maze. I remembered buying that ring at the mall on the San Antonio Riverwalk. We had matching rings, but I had lost mine a long time ago. From behind, Daryl hugged me tightly.

✖✖✖

"So what are we supposed to do?" I asked the officers when they came to take a report. "Just wait around here for him to do something? Wait until someone gets killed? This man is obviously very sick. He is capable of anything."

"I'm not sure what is going on here," the stocky red-headed cop said. He looked like a thick Opie from Mayberry. He looked at me, and then Daryl and I saw a smirk in the corner of his mouth. "According to my report, this James Lancaster you are talking about has a restraining order against you. I have to advise you that filing a false police report is a crime."

"Look, this man is dangerous. I may not have pictures of him doing these things, but believe me, he is the one. If my roommate had been home, there is no telling what he could have done to her."

"There are no signs of forced entry anywhere," the other cop quickly pointed out. His lips barely moved when he spoke. His face was cold and unconcerned. I watched his rough hands grip the pencil and scribble a short note on his black pad.

"Are you saying we're making this up?" Daryl interjected. I could hear the anger swelling in his voice. "You think he dug up his own brother's grave, and brought dirt from the grave into his own house to frame James?"

"Hey, I don't know anything about you people, and what you do."

"What the hell do you mean, you people? You mean black people? Or did you mean gay people?" The scowl on Daryl's face wrinkled his forehead and his eyes became tight.

The other cop said, "No, he didn't mean either one." He looked at the other cop quickly, as if in disapproval.

"Why don't you let him speak for himself?" I questioned.

"Listen, fellas, there's not much we can do here." Opie closed his little black book and put the cap back on his pen before stuffing it in his shirt pocket.

"So that's it? Now what?" I said.

"We'll file a report, but beyond that, without proof, there's not much we can do."

"Before you leave, officers, I need the correct spelling of your names and your badge numbers. I'm filing a complaint," I said.

After the cops left, we drove to the firing range so that I could have more practice on using a gun. I applied for a permit to carry a concealed handgun and had received the license in the mail a few days earlier, but I wanted to make sure that I was wholly comfortable with a gun. I had been to the range several times with Daryl in the last week or so. Daryl was serious about my training and paid attention to every detail so that I would get the most out of the training. He taught me how to hold the gun, how to load it and how to take aim. We tried unsuccessfully to convince Tony and Danea to take lessons, but they wouldn't even consider it. Each day, I prayed for their safety.

CHAPTER 41

E ven in the midst of this raging storm, and as much as I tried not to think about it, thoughts of becoming a father found their way into my consciousness. With all of the other drama in my life, it was hard not to consider everything, including being a father and how my life would affect and shape the child's. Each waking moment, it seemed like there was something there to make me think of how wonderful it would be to be a father. In spite of what was going on with James, fatherhood still brought me much joy. I would not allow him to take that away from me, too.

I was at home flipping aimlessly through an old Labor Day issue of *Clikque* magazine when I came across an ad with a picture of an adorable baby boy. His hands were clasped behind his head, his big dark eyes were open wide, and his tiny lips were pursed together as he gave attitude. The caption above his curly, black hair read, "I am fearfully and wonderfully made." I wondered what my child would look like. I chuckled to myself as I heard my mama's voice in my head saying ugly folks sure can make some pretty babies. What hope did that leave my child? RaChelle is a gorgeous woman, and I look good, too. I hoped the opposite of that old saying didn't hold up.

I was supposed to be searching the paper for a job, but I didn't really see anything worth applying for. With James running rampant, what would be the point? I'd already lost two great jobs because of James, and I knew that unless the situation rectified itself soon, there would be no use in me getting another job because he'd just find a way to make me lose it. I hated him for the control he *still* had over my life. I hated him for the time I spent living in misery. I hated his smugness and arrogance. I hated *him*.

When I heard the low ring of the phone, I raced across the room and picked up the receiver on the third ring. "Hello?"

"What are you doing?" the inquisitive voice on the other end of the phone questioned.

"Hey, Danea. Not a damn thang."

"I was thinking about you. I just wanted to call and check on you."

"Thanks, but I'm fine."

"By the way, how is RaChelle?"

"I haven't spoken with her since that fiasco at the luncheon. I know she must be freaking out. She already had doubts about being a mother, and now she finds out the father of her child is gay. She's called a couple of times, and I've called her, but we keep playing phone tag. Honestly, I don't know if I have the strength to speak with her. I don't know what to say."

"You definitely need to speak with her soon. If she feels like you've already abandoned her, she might be more inclined to have an abortion. Plus, this is some pretty serious stuff to find out about the father of your unborn child. You need to find out what's going on in her head. You know she's not the most level-headed person around."

"I know I should call her."

"Should? Kevin, call her."

"You're right. I can't avoid her forever."

"Okay, now that that's out of the way, what are you doing this evening?"

"I don't know yet. Daryl mentioned something about seeing a movie. You wanna come?"

"And be a third wheel? You know that's not my style. Besides, I have to do some more rehearsing. I have to go back out to L.A. this weekend to meet with some other people, but I don't feel comfortable about leaving you here in this drama."

"Don't worry about me. I'll be fine. You know Daryl will be at my side. Go to L.A. and make us all proud. You have more talent than any of those wannabes on the radio."

"They've suggested a few changes to my song and

at first I was reluctant about changing anything, but the alterations don't change the song significantly. I just have to practice singing it differently."

The record company wanted her song, "Victory," for a movie soundtrack. "Victory" was about the triumphant human spirit. It was that spirit that could not be beaten, destroyed, or wished away. It was the strength of that spirit that allows us to press on and to stand firm. It was that spirit that was allowing me to stand.

Before she hung up, she mentioned that she'd called an attorney friend of hers who dealt with police misconduct and had some experience in dealing with stalking laws. She said he should be giving me a call later on.

I picked up the remote control to the television and flipped through the array of daytime talk shows, games shows, and soap operas. *The Young and the Restless* was on, but I didn't have time for Nikki Newman's problems that day. I had my own issues. I had finally turned off the set and walked toward the kitchen when the doorbell rang. I wasn't expecting anyone so I casually walked over to the door and opened it without checking through the peephole. When the door opened, there stood RaChelle, hand propped on her hip, cigarette dangling out of her mouth. She looked me up and down and walked into the house. I took a deep breath and closed the door behind her.

The first words out of her mouth were, "Where the hell have you been? I've been calling you for two fuckin' days!" She took aim with her fiery words, but I managed to deflect the thrust of her blows. She took the cigarette out of her mouth, took a defensive stance, shifted her weight to one leg, and searched with her eyes for an ashtray.

"I thought we had agreed that you would stop smoking?" I took the cigarette from her hands and discarded it.

"And I thought I told you to call me back? What is going on with you?"

There wasn't much I could say. Her anger and confusion was completely justified and I had no words that would make anything easy. This was about to be a very difficult moment in my life, but the time had come. I'd been through so much and I knew that this too would pass. After the luncheon fiasco, I didn't know what to say to her or how to say it.

"Are we alone?" she asked.

"Yes. Would you like some juice?" I had hoped that a beverage would take some of the edge off the situation.

"No, but I would like some answers." She took her left hand and moved her long hair out of her face. I shook my head and directed us both into the living room.

"Okay, RaChelle, let's talk." She took a seat on the couch and placed her purse at her side. She leaned back with a deep inhale as if she was awaiting news about some terminal illness from a doctor. "Where do I begin?" I asked rhetorically.

"How about you start with the video? What was going on with that? I mean, I know what was going on. How did that video get up there? Was that Keevan? I didn't know he was gay. When was that video made?"

My mind raced over a myriad of images and subjects, all in an attempt to process the information she had just provided. I first thought that Keevan would never have been in a situation like that. He would have died first. I was almost insulted by her comments about my brother, until I realized what had just happened. Inadvertently, she'd given me a way out. She had provided me with a way of explaining the video without indicting myself. This could be the answer I was looking for. If she knew I was gay, knowing her, I would be willing to bet my life that she'd want to have an immediate abortion. I cringed at the thought.

While looking at her bewildered face, I got a nagging sensation in the pit of my stomach. It was that feeling you get when you are on the verge of breaching some universal truth. It was my conscience calling out to me. It was that feeling that made the difference between right and wrong, that instinct that could decipher between truth and fiction. When I cringed, I don't know whether I cringed at the thought of an abortion, or at the thought of dishonoring the memory of the most honorable man I've ever known.

"Kevin, are you listening to me?"

"Of course, I'm listening."

"I know it must be difficult to have a gay brother, particularly since you're twins. It's not your fault. I bet everyone thinks you're gay 'cause he is. I remember hearing rumors in school, but I never paid any attention. You two were too fine to be gay," she said with a chuckle.

"Too fine to be gay? What the hell is that? RaChelle, we do have to talk. There are some things about me that you don't know. I don't really know how to tell you, so I'm just gonna say it."

"Did you always know he was gay? How did you deal with it?" She moved in closer to me as if I was the town gossip.

"You're right. Keevan is—*was*—gay."

"I knew it. When I saw that video, I knew that wasn't you..."

"And so am I. I am gay, RaChelle." Her eyes shifted uneasily. She shook her head in disbelief. Then, she jumped to her feet. "And that was me in the video. It was made a while back, and should have been destroyed."

"You're *not* gay. You were one of the best lovers I've ever had. No fag could make me feel like that."

"Fag? RaChelle, it's true. I am gay. I have always been, and I will always be. When you and I first started becoming friends, you asked about my relationship. That relationship was with a man."

"I don't understand. We had sex. *You and me*. You can't be gay!" Tears rolled down her face, leaving a black trail of mascara and makeup.

"I am."

In that moment of truth, everything shifted. "You lied to me. You son of a bitch! You fuckin' faggot! How dare you! I hate you!" She yanked her purse up from the couch and stumbled back. She regained her balance as she wiped the tears from her eyes and smeared makeup across her face. She headed for the door. "If you think I'll ever have a child with you, you're dead wrong. Go to hell!"

"RaChelle..."

She pointed her figure at me. "Don't you ever speak my name again. You have made me feel so dirty. I can't believe I had sex with you."

"RaChelle," I said as I grabbed her arm to prevent her from leaving. I wasn't trying to force her to stay, but I wanted her to listen to me before she sped off.

She jerked away violently and slapped me across the face. The sting of her blow was minimal, but the force of her words took their toll. Then, she moved unsteadily backwards until she reached the door. She stormed out of the place and into the parking lot. I wanted to go after her, to convince her, to apologize, to make things right, to save this child, but it was best that she leave—for both our sakes. Down came another wall from my house of cards.

✖✖✖

The slamming of the door caused my head to spin. I marched directly into the kitchen and took a small glass out of the cabinet. I opened the freezer, took exactly two ice cubes from the bucket, and listened to the clank as they fell into the whiskey-sized glass. I moved over to the bar and grabbed a bottle of Hennessy. The ice cubes made a crackling sound as the dark liquor filled the glass around them.

What about the child? My thoughts were directed toward my unborn child who would never see the light of day. In my head, I could see a small figure, that of a formless child, twirling around in an encompassing darkness. The child tries to call out, it struggles to make a sound, but its underdeveloped mouth could not yet make sounds. Suddenly, its heart starts to race.

It is not alone in the darkness. Something, some-where is lurking. Then, without warning, an instru-ment slices away at my child.

I shook my head as if I could shake away those thoughts. I picked up the glass of liquor and just stared at it. It called out to me. This madness I had come to know had a name. It, too, had a face. It was a face and a name that would forever be a part of the fabric of my life. As much as I wanted to reinvent myself and to start over, *this* name and face kept resurfacing. James thwarted my plans to remake myself. He stole my joy, and now he had stolen the child I was destined to have.

Later that evening, before I knew it, I was standing on the lawn of his house. I remembered getting into the car and driving over, but it was almost as if I was in a trance. I looked up at the building and remem-bered all of the times I spent inside. I remembered all the energy and blood that was expended. I walked up to the door and stuck my key into the lock. It turned. I chuckled. He never even bothered to change the locks because I'm sure he knew I'd return to him. He was partially right. I had returned, just not in the way he'd hoped.

Because of the darkness of the house, I assumed he was away, so I didn't bother to call out to him. His car wasn't in the driveway, but it could have been in the garage. I stepped in and closed and locked the door behind me. The house looked exactly the same. Every picture, every fixture, and every piece of furniture was the same. Nothing had changed. I visually scanned the dimly lit foyer and crept deeper into the interior of the house. It felt cold. The house felt familiar and it sent chills down my spine. So many memories. I stepped quietly through the house, looking for my antagonist, and I found myself nearing his office. I had a hunch he'd be there bent over a mound of paperwork. As I neared, I heard voices. I wasn't sure if someone was in his office, or if he was on the phone. I inched close enough to decipher the ending conversation.

"We don't know what's going to happen at this point. We should just sit tight and be ready to react to whatever decision is returned," the voice pumping through the speaker phone said.

"We need to do whatever we have to do. I don't pay you to sit tight. I have worked too hard to let this stop me."

"James, I have never let you down in the past. Let me handle this. I promise, I will make this right. Trust me, the best thing we can do right now is wait. Whatever happens, we'll take care of it just like we always do."

"I hope you're right. I'll talk to you in the morning."

James disconnected the call and sat back in his chair, his hands locked behind his head. He looked tense. I emerged from the corner. His face lit up like I was his long-lost child returning to the nest for protection from the father. He rose to his feet, eyes wide, and called out to me. I stood there, facing him, not knowing what to say, or even why I was really there.

"I knew you'd come back to me," he said. "I have missed you so much. I need you in my life. I love you, Kevin." As he confessed his needs, I stood still, staring at him, at this man who had ruined my life and scarred me emotionally. "Say something, baby. Say you love me."

He moved from behind the comfort of his desk and approached me. It amazed me that his one-track mind could really believe that I'd come back to love him. After all he'd put me through, all the misery he'd hurled at me, he had the audacity to think I could love him. His bubble was about to burst. Methodically, I reached into my jacket pocket and pulled out the gun Daryl had given me. I'd taken enough of his shit, and this insanity was about to come to a screeching halt. The gun was fully loaded, and I'd become quite a marksman. When he saw the gun, James immediately stopped, shocked by this revelation.

I didn't know what I wanted to say to him. What

could I say as I held a gun to him? Was he afraid? Did he even care? Did I care about his life and mine? I squeezed the trigger and let a bullet fly out of the gun. I aimed it at his computer and the machine sparked and made a low explosive sound. Smoke bellowed upward, and James' already big eyes grew bigger in shock. I wanted him to know I meant business.

"What the hell is your problem? Are you crazy?"

"I just might be crazy enough to kill you. You wanna take that chance?"

"What is this about?"

"Now is not the time for you to play innocent. I'm not in the fucking mood."

"Is this about the video thing? That was just a joke."

"Very funny, muthafucka."

"Kevin, you know I have a restraining order against you. If the cops were to find out you were here with a gun, you'd go straight to jail."

"That's assuming you'd be alive and could call them." I spoke slowly and coldly.

"What do you want from me? You want me to drop the restraining order? You want me to let you go? You know you don't want to kill me."

"Don't tell me what I want."

"Kevin..."

"Stop saying my name! You have no idea how much I hate you, do you?"

"You don't mean that."

"Leave me the fuck alone or I will kill you. And I'll go to jail for it, but I would find comfort in your death."

My words and hollow eyes must have convinced him, because for the first time, I read fear on his face. He had to know that I was serious about what I said. I would kill him and find solace in my actions. I stared at him and did not blink. I lowered the gun without changing eye contact and exited the room. He did not pursue.

CHAPTER 42

Tony and I sat on the floor in the living room as we continued to hammer out some of the last-minute details of his impending ceremony. Since I was no longer working, and wasn't sure when I'd be able to get a job, I used his wedding as a distraction. RaChelle had all but disappeared and my phone calls to her went unanswered. I didn't know what to do. I wanted—needed—to find her so that we could bridge this distance, but I feared it was a lost cause. I prayed about it and released it to a higher power.

As the big day drew nearer, Tony became increasingly excited. He walked with a newfound pep in his step and there was always a smile on his face. The way he felt about LaMont was the way I felt about Daryl. Daryl made me complete and filled me.

"Okay, now it's your turn. I've been talking so much about me. What's been going on in your life? How's Daryl?" He removed the plate from the microwave, grabbed a fork from the drawer and began plowing food into his mouth.

"He is his usual wonderful self. And we are doing great. You know how much I love him."

"I've always known. Hell, we were just waiting on you to figure it out," he said with a wink of his left eye. "Now, what's going on with that thang you used to live with? You know, James Lancaster, your ex?"

I didn't want to tell him anything about my visit with James the other night, so I just told Tony I didn't know or care how James was doing.

We moved into the living room and continued to chat for the next hour. I filled him in on all of the details of my life, including Danea's singing career. He reached for the remote control and turned the television on to watch *All My Children*, but it was on break. After the commercials, we both were startled to see James' face on the news. We both leaned closer to the television even though the volume was up loud enough. The cute Asian newscaster, Cindy Liu, began to speak.

"Local businessman James Lancaster, of Lancaster Computer Systems, has been indicted by a federal grand jury in Austin on charges ranging from tax fraud to bribery. The seven-count indictment was handed down about two hours ago, and has sent a shock wave through the Houston business community. According to the information released from the grand jury, LCS has been under investigation for over a year and is said to have cheated the government out of millions of dollars. If convicted at trial, Mr. Lancaster

*could be facing federal jail time and could be ordered
to pay millions of dollars in fines and restitution."*

Cindy Liu showed footage of her doing a kamikaze-
style ambush on James as he headed for his car in the
parking garage of LCS. She shoved her black microphone in his tense face hoping for some feedback.
His only comment was "no comment," but she pressed
him and stayed close on the heels of his thousand-
dollar pair of shoes as they clicked and clacked on the
cold cement foundation of the garage. "Mr. Lancaster,
the people of Houston would like to know what a
man once voted Entrepreneur of the Year has to say
in his own defense." Even though James' legs
stretched out farther than hers, she did not give. Her
fast walk turned into a slow jog trying to play catch-
up. His expression changed from tension to utter
indignation. It was a look that I was all too familiar
with, and it usually preceded a slap to the face. I
wanted to tell her to bob and weave, but I think she
had it under control. James turned off the alarm on
his convertible Jaguar, got in, and slammed the door
shut. As he sped away, she continued to question
him, even though she was now talking to the back of
his car. She ended her report by saying, "More on
this story and the latest national news to-night at 6.
I'm Cindy Liu, and this has been an Action News
Brief."

We both sat on the couch with our mouths gaped open in shock. I leaned all the way back on the couch and we both let out a sigh. *This is what you call poetic justice.* Now, it all was becoming so clear. I understood why he was under so much pressure and why he spent so much time in Austin. He was trying to save his ass. The late night calls from his attorney that couldn't wait until morning, the clandestine meetings on the weekend and the inexplicable mood swings. Now, it was clear—it was crystal clear.

Tony looked at me, his eyes wide, and spoke. "It looks like your problems have been solved."

"Or maybe my problems have just begun." The greatest enemy is the man who has nothing to lose.

I called Daryl at work to tell him what I had just heard on the television, but his voicemail picked up. I left a message and told him to give me a call at home when he got the chance. In the meantime, I wasn't sure what to do. I couldn't believe James had been caught up in some mess like that. Another promising black business ruined by greed. One thing we all should know is you don't fuck with the IRS. Someone said the only two certain things in life were death and taxes. You have to pay your bills.

When I thought about all of the shit that he put me through and was still putting me through, that indictment might be his just desserts. If he were stripped down to his bare essentials and his naked ass was hitching a ride on I-59 South, I don't think that would be enough to make up for the horror that he'd caused me and many others, I'm sure. Keevan said it a thousand times if I'd said it once. *Karma*. What you put out there comes back times three, because by the time the shit comes back to you, it has gained momentum and created one giant ball of shit. That's what he was in now. Up to his eyelids in shit. I knew it wasn't right to laugh at someone's misfortune, so I just smiled.

❌❌❌

We all gathered to celebrate not only Tony's big day, but also Danea's big debut. She got the final word that her song would be turned into a single and released. I had no doubt that she would take the world by storm and ascend into divadom. She deserved it, and she certainly had paid her dues by performing any and everywhere she was allowed.

As much as I loved my friends and as proud as I was to share in their joy, I couldn't help but feel a little jealous insofar as my happiness was concerned. I tried to take the bull by the horns, to control my life, but it all back-fired. Right then, I was mired down in mud, not able to move forward, and certainly not about to move backward. I was there, treading water, buying time until that day came that I'd be free. I should have known James would not give me up easily. I should have been prepared for it, but he caught me off guard. And so there I was, unemployed, and not fully able to enjoy the only love I'd really known because of the shit I was dealing with.

From across the room, Daryl winked at me. That man was so righteous. The simple thought of him set my heart to racing, and a touch of the hand was sometimes overwhelming. I looked at him, and he blew me a kiss, which I caught in my hand and placed in my pocket for safekeeping. I blew him a kiss, which he devoured. I moved over to pick up the phone when it rang.

"Hello?"

"I guess you heard about me by now." I didn't respond for a few seconds. I wanted to hang up, but part of me wanted to hold on for just a second. I wanted the pain in his voice to somehow alleviate my own grief. Knowing he was suffering brought me a callous comfort.

"The whole city knows about it now."

"That is so fucked-up. I've done more for this city and Austin than most people and they are ready to turn on me on a dime. I can't get into my damn house because there are at least three television crews camped out in front of my house. Damn."

I held the phone to my ear and listened to the silence for a few seconds. I wasn't sure what he wanted to say or even while he was calling. I knew he didn't want me to offer him a place to sleep.

"I don't feel sorry for you. You're getting exactly what you deserve."

"Don't be cruel, Kevin. It doesn't suit you."

"And putting up with your shit does?"

"Wait. Please wait just a second. I don't have anyone else to talk to. Please, just listen for a second."

"You need to say what you have to say."

"I love you and need you more now than ever. I'm in trouble."

"Don't start talking that bullshit again. Listen, I have to go. We have people over here."

"I know."

"What do you mean you know? Where are you?"

"Outside in your parking lot." I slammed the phone down and rushed over to the window and saw him sitting in his Jaguar, top down, cell phone pressed against his face. Daryl noticed me at the window and came over. He saw James and immediately raced out the door, across the small yard toward the parking lot. James sped off, disappearing around the twisted curves of the parking lot.

"What the fuck was he doing here?" Daryl asked. The phone rang again and Daryl snatched it off the receiver.

"Who is this?" he demanded. When he started apologizing, it was clear that it wasn't James on the other end of the phone. He handed Danea the phone, and told her it was Curtis.

"What the hell was that about?" Daryl asked angrily.

"I think he just wanted someone to talk to."

"Why the hell is he calling you?"

"I have no idea."

"If he ever comes over here again, or near you, I'll shoot first and ask questions later."

CHAPTER 43

Time has a unique way of sometimes passing without mention, of sneaking out through the back door. The moment you're not looking or expecting it, time has slipped away and the minutes we lose are gone forever, never to be recaptured or replaced. The last few days before the wedding ceremony breezed by with such ease and harmony that it was hard to believe all of the other things going on in my life. James, preoccupied with his present troubles, was remarkably quiet. I suspected that he was in Austin trying to find a way of beating or lessening his imminent downfall. I knew somehow—some way—he would find a way to survive this: That was his style, winning at all costs. Like a cat, he'd land on his feet.

In the meantime, we were preparing for the big day: Tony and LaMont's wedding. The closer the day got, the surer they seemed. Never—not once—was there any doubt expressed by either one of them that this may not be the right time. Never did they express any fear that this was a mistake. The idea of cold feet was not a thought that either of them entertained. Their unwavering faith in their love and future put all of us at ease. We supported them in any and every way that we could.

Finally, their day arrived.

I ran a few errands before the wedding, then went home for a few minutes to change. I wanted to get to the church early so that I could do some trouble-shooting. When I got home, I checked the machine and there was a message from RaChelle. I hadn't heard from her in a while, despite my repeated attempts. She sounded calm. I immediately picked up the phone and dialed her number. The phone rang and rang. I disconnected the call and dialed the number to her cell phone. No answer. I really wanted to talk to her, so I called back and left a message giving her directions to the church. I hoped she'd show, if only for a minute or two.

By the time I made it to the church for the after-noon ceremony, I had been up and in the streets for hours. I found myself preoccupied with thoughts of RaChelle, wondering why she had called. Had she had an abortion, or was she still carrying my child? I needed to know.

LaMont and Tony were busy getting dressed in different rooms of the church because Tony said it was bad luck for them to see each other before the wedding. He wasn't usually superstitious, but this time he didn't want to take any chances. I spent a lot time working with the minister to make sure that things would go smoothly. The minister was a slim Jamaican fellow with long salt and pepper dreadlocks dangling down to his shoulders. He had a bright smile with pearly white teeth. He covered his suit with a long, white flowing gown that was part of the ceremony.

After about an hour and a half of taking care of little things, I sat down for a moment. I tried calling RaChelle again, and followed up by calling Daryl and Danea, but I guessed they were on their way. I checked on Tony and LaMont a few more times and things were cool with them. I made my way to Tony's room and found him putting the last-minute details together. He looked sharp in his black tuxedo with coattails and white gloves. His shoes were polished so much that you could see your reflection in them. Everything was in place.

The wedding they planned was nontraditional, but that went without saying. The only people at the altar would be both grooms and their minister. No wedding parties, no one to give them away, no one to bear rings. The happy couple had been pretty tight-lipped about the ceremony, so most of the events were shrouded in secrecy. Even though I helped them with some of the details, there was a "surprise" they were planning. I'm sure it would be quite a show.

As the guests started arriving, I met some of them at the door, and directed them to the book where they were to sign their names. Daryl and Danea walked into the church, fashionably late of course, and they were astonished at the dozens of flowers that lined the walls around the church. Roses of every imaginable hue and hybrid filled the room with an enchanting aroma. I met them at the door, and I gave Daryl a hug and a kiss. They picked up a copy of the program and signed their names in the guest book and moved toward our seats.

"Okay, guys, this is it. The big day," Daryl said.

I looked at my watch and the three o'clock hour was swiftly approaching. "It should start in about thirty minutes."

"Is that thirty minutes in C.P. time, or real time?" he asked.

I laughed. "In real time."

"Somehow, I always thought I'd be the first to get married," Danea said with a smile. "I just hope I'm ready for this song."

"Me, too," Daryl said.

At the last minute, Tony and LaMont had requested a duet. They wanted Danea and Daryl to sing that song from the movie *An Officer and a Gentleman* titled "Up Where We Belong."

"I still can't believe this," Daryl said.

I looked through the purple and white program I'd grabbed at the door. On the cover, highlighted in a lavender box, were two white candles whose fire joined and became one magnificent flame. The caption read, "Now, two lives burn as one."

I thumbed through the program and read about the rituals in which they were to partake. Libation was an African tradition that invokes the ancestors to bless and protect. There was the Lighting of the Candles, the Tying of the Knot and the Jumping of the Broom. All of the ceremonies were based, at least in part, on African tradition.

"What does Tony know about African wedding traditions?" I asked.

"You know he took some sociology class on African tribal societies, but that was a few years ago. I'm surprised he remembered any of it." Danea looked at the program in bewilderment.

"He only took that class," I looked at my watch and the three o'clock hour was swiftly approaching, "'cause he had a crush on Professor Watkins," Daryl said.

"He did have a nice butt," I added. Daryl gave me a push on the shoulder and went back to reading the program. "I'm going downstairs to check on Tony one last time."

"Show me where LaMont is and I'll check on him," Daryl said.

We walked down the long hallway and I pointed Daryl in the direction of LaMont's room. As I approached Tony's room, I heard some shuffling around; I slowly opened the door as I called out his name. Tony was standing directly in front of the door, his back facing the window, and he was fully dressed in his black tuxedo. He had several candles burning in the room as a calming factor.

"Tony, the guests are arriving, and it's getting kind of late so I wanted to make sure that you didn't need anything. I must say, you look very good. If I wasn't with Daryl, I'd marry you myself," I said playfully.

Tony just stood there, not uttering a word, and barely breathing. It was as if a deep breath would upset the balance of the room. His position was firm and defensive. "What's wrong? You're not having second thoughts, are you?" I moved closer to him. The door behind me closed and when I turned around, there was James. He was dressed in a dirty black warm-up set with dirty Nikes. He looked as if he hadn't slept in days, and from the smell of things in the room, I'd say he hadn't bathed in days either.

"I was waiting on you to join us," James said dryly.

"We don't have time for this today, James." I grabbed Tony's hand and moved toward the door. James pulled a gun from his pocket and we stopped dead in our tracks. He pointed the gun directly at Tony, his aim high, as if it would shoot him in the head. Tony squeezed my hand so tightly I could feel my circulation being cut off.

"What is this about, James?"

"Fuck you! You know exactly what this is about! You think you can pull a gun on me and not expect me to come get you? What, you didn't think I'd return the favor? You fucking with the wrong nigga!" I could smell alcohol on his breath with each word that flew out of his mouth.

"This is about you and me. It has nothing to do with Tony or anyone else here. Let him go and I'll do whatever you want."

"You'd like that, wouldn't you? I have a better idea. How about I shoot him in his head and then fuck him in the ass while you watch? How about that?" From the crazed look in his eyes, I wouldn't put it past him at that point. I didn't show it, but my life started to flash before my eyes in little bursts of concentrated light. I knew this was it: the final showdown. He'd come here to kill me, and he wouldn't be satisfied until that happened.

"You are going to suffer just like I have. All of this is your fault. I have lost everything because of you! They've taken it all! I've lost my fucking business trying to keep your ass happy, and then what do you do? You leave me! I invested so much time, money and effort into making you happy. It was always about you! These bitches you call friends helped destroy us, so I think it's only fair that I destroy them!"

He marched forward with such an approach that the next thing I knew the gun was pressing against Tony's forehead. Tears formed in Tony's eyes.

"James!" I yelled.

"You so much as breathe and this little faggot will get his brains blown out." He looked at me as I stepped back. My heart was beating about as fast as hummingbird wings. "Get on your fucking knees," he commanded. I began to kneel when James yelled again. "Not you," he said to me. "I'm talking to this little bitch." Tony lowered himself onto his knees in front of James. "You like that position, don't you? You wanna suck my dick, don't you?"

"James, you are not mad at him. This is between you and me. Please, I'll do anything. I'll go anywhere you want; just let him go."

He looked at me and snarled his lip in disgust. While still looking at me, he took the gun and struck Tony across the face and Tony tumbled over backward. He screamed. I moved toward him, but James forced me to stop by pointing the gun my direction. I didn't know what to do. He was drunk, enraged and out for revenge. His whole world had collapsed and he was definitely looking for someone to absorb his anger. There would be no reasoning with him. His wild eyes offered little room for anything but violence. As I stood there, my fear was not for myself, but for Tony, and anyone else who should happen to wander unknowingly into this hell.

"You need to ask my permission to speak or look at him."

I took a deep breath. "May I please go over to him?" James reluctantly indicated I could approach Tony.

"Tony, are you okay?" I asked.

Tony hesitated and looked at James for permission to speak.

"I think so," he said, holding his face. "People are going to come looking for us in a few minutes. If you leave now, we won't tell anyone," he said to James.

"Shut the fuck up! This is why I told your ass to shut up, stupid bitch. Don't say another word! If someone comes in here, they'll wish they hadn't."

"Now, Kevin. Do you love me?" I looked at him in disbelief. "I know you still love me. Say it. Say it now."

"James..."

"What?"

"Is this really necessary? You know how I feel about you." I tried to give him what he was looking for without giving him much. Forcing myself to say those words to him felt like a betrayal to me, to Daryl, and to Keevan. Tony's expression begged me to give James what he needed: my pledge of undying love.

"I want you to say it, and mean it." He looked at me as if he really expected my next words to be sincere and heartfelt. I mustered up the strength to form the words, and hoped they wouldn't get stuck in my throat.

"James…I …love you." Saying those words hurt more than I realized.

"I knew you did!" In that instant, his demeanor changed and he planted a warm kiss on the cheek. He was like a kid who had just found a lost puppy. The stress of losing everything had apparently pushed him to insanity. "That's all I wanted to hear. Was that so hard?"

"James, you have to let Tony go."

"What?"

"You have to let him go."

"Why are you so concerned about him? You need to worry less about him and more about me. See, that's your problem, always worrying about them. I mean, what has he ever done for you? He's nothing."

"Like I said, this is between you and me."

The next second my heart skipped a beat as I heard Daryl's voice calling out for me in the hallway. It sounded as if he was speaking with someone but the other voice was not audible. He called out to me again. When James heard Daryl's voice, he raised the gun again.

"I will kill that muthafucka! Let him in."

"James, no..."

"You left me so that you could be with that bastard, and now you expect me to have mercy on him? You were probably fuckin' while we were together. I bet he used to come over to the house while I was out of town on business. You were never there for me. I bet you thought it would be easy to get back into my good graces. Did you think a simple 'I love you' would do the trick?" His scattered thoughts and emotional highs and lows showed that he was now capable of anything. If Daryl walked through that door, James just might shoot him.

Daryl called out again, this time with a knock at the door. I held my breath. James raced over to the door and snatched it open.

"James!" I screamed, but it was too late. He pressed the gun against Daryl's head and led him into the room. Behind Daryl was RaChelle, whose look of horror said all that could be spoken. Once inside the room, James gathered us all on the same side of the room and pointed the gun at each of us, one by one.

"Who the fuck is this bitch?" he snarled, referring to RaChelle.

"She has nothing to do with this either, James," I said.

"Was I talkin' to you? Shut the fuck up."

"Who are you?" he asked her.

"I'm-I'm-RaChelle. I'm a friend of Kevin's."

"RaChelle, let me ask you a question. How well do you know my lover?"

"Kevin?" she responded.

"Who the fuck else would I be talkin' about, dumb bitch?"

"James, if you want me, why don't you put that gun down and let's handle this like men."

Daryl stepped forward as if to confront James. When he moved closer, he wore no fear and no hesitation. James moved forward and pistol-whipped him across the face. Daryl went down.

"Daryl!" I moved over to him and helped him back to his feet. "Are you okay?" He rubbed his face and nodded his head. "Let me handle this, Daryl. Please don't say anything else to him." I turned to James. "This is out of hand. It's not too late. You can stop this now, and I'll go home with you. I'll do whatever you want."

"It's not that simple. You think you can leave me and then just come home when you realize you need me? Fuck you!" He took a few steps back and looked at one of the candles burning in the room. He stared at the flame as if it was the first time he'd seen fire. Methodically, he took the candle and placed it underneath the curtain hanging across the window.

"What are you doing?!" RaChelle screamed.

"James, you don't have to do this. You have me now. I'm yours."

"Shut up."

"Where is LaMont?" Tony whispered to Daryl.

"He said he had to go and get something out of his car. He said he'd be right back," Daryl whispered back. "Does that gun make you feel like a man?" Daryl asked James.

"Daryl..." I tried to get him to be quiet, but he continued talking. James paid little attention. Instead he watched the flames devour the cloth curtain.

"You are pitiful," Daryl said. "Look at you." Without another word, James pulled the trigger. The bullet hit Daryl in his right shoulder and blood splashed on RaChelle's face. We all screamed. Daryl fell against the door and hit the ground. I moved over to him and held him in my arms. RaChelle attempted to wipe the blood from her face, but she only wound up smearing it.

"Get up!" James yelled. I helped Daryl to his feet and the four of us stood there, side by side, as if this was a firing squad. By now, the flames had shot up to the ceiling, and smoke had filled the room. We tried not to choke.

"James, let them go. *Please.*"

"If you say another word I will blow his fucking head off," he said to me while pointing the gun at Daryl.

He turned to RaChelle. "I'm sorry you got involved in this, but you know every war has its casualties." She tried to be strong, but the tears had already starting running down her face. "Open the door." She moved over and slowly opened the door. He motioned for us to leave.

We walked in a single file line down the long hallway that led to the sanctuary. James held the gun above his head so that when we all walked into the room his presence was known. The church collectively gasped. There were about seventy-five people in the room who watched in disbelief as James marched us up to the pulpit. The preacher rose and tried to speak, but was silenced when James hit him with the gun in the face. The old man hit the floor and did not move. James fired two shots straight into the ceiling.

"If anyone moves, I will fuckin' shoot you." He pushed Daryl forward to show the crowd the injuries he had already sustained. "If you don't think I'll shoot you, just ask him. Now, are there any questions?"

There was silence in the room. In the back row of the pews, I detected some movement—and so did James. He darted from the pulpit and raced to the back of the church. Without a word, he fired. I couldn't see who was hit, but I heard screaming, and I could see James kicking a body on the floor. Tony let out a cry.

"Oh my God!" Tony screamed. He tried to run down to LaMont, but I held him back. If he moved, James would surely kill him.

James raced back to the pulpit. "Don't fuck with me! He didn't have to die, but he left me no choice. I am a man of my word!"

"James, for heaven's sake," I began, "let these people go." As I spoke, I could see flames in the back of the hallway moving our direction. The room was filling with smoke, and people were beginning to choke.

"Now, you people came here today to see a wedding. You will have one. Kevin and I are getting married, and you know marriage is forever." He grabbed my hand and pulled me forward. We stood looking out into the audience.

"James, if we don't all get out of here, we're gonna burn to death," I said.

"No one is leaving until we have our ceremony. Where is that bitch Danea? I want her to sing for us. Danea, where are you?" Danea slowly rose to her feet and started coughing. The smoke was thick and black and I could hear the sound of the flames approaching.

"Sing, bitch," James demanded. She hesitated. "Sing!"

"What do you want me to sing?"

"Baby," he turned to me, "what's our song?"

"We don't have a song," I shot back.

"You don't remember our song?" I could tell he was getting annoyed.

"Why don't you choose the song?" I said to him to keep him from getting more upset.

"Fine then, I will. I want you to sing that Patti LaBelle song from that damn movie."

"What movie?" Danea asked.

"Bitch, don't get smart. You know exactly what I'm talking about." He pointed the gun at her and I could see him squeezing the trigger.

"Sing it, Danea," I said. I knew he wanted to hear the song from the *Waiting to Exhale* soundtrack, but I couldn't think of the name of the song. Luckily, she knew it. She opened her mouth and tried to sing, but she started coughing from the smoke.

"Cunt, you better sing that song!" he ordered. She took a few seconds to compose herself and then she let the words flow. In the midst of this storm of fire and bullets, she managed to sing the song without missing a beat. The preacher finally pulled himself to his feet. As the flames raged and made their way into the sanctuary, the sounds of people choking filled the room. The back row provided a new pathway for the fire to spread. I knew we didn't have much time, because the ceiling, too, was on fire and it was only a matter of time before it collapsed.

James snatched up the preacher and propped him up on the podium.

"We need you to marry us." He put the gun directly to the preacher's forehead. The preacher was at a loss for words until James pointed the gun at RaChelle. She let out a scream. In order to protect RaChelle, the preacher began to speak.

"Dearly beloved, we are gathered here today..." The preacher's words were lost on me. I had to find a way out of this situation. James stood in front of me with a smile on his face. Everyone was petrified; a madman with a gun in the front, a raging fire in the back. I had to take action. "I now pronounce you... husband and husband. You may kiss..." I stood still. James leaned in for a kiss and when he did, I lunged for him. A shot rang out. The preacher was hit. Everyone in the audience screamed and scattered for safety. Pieces of the wooden ceiling were falling all around the room. Daryl raced over to us, but James was able to fire again. Daryl went down.

"Get out of here!" I screamed to Tony. "Get him out of here!" James and I hit the floor, rolling and struggling for dominance. I was able to free myself. He had lost control of the gun and it flew across the pulpit. I got up and raced down the aisle toward the exit, but I was hit in the back of the leg with a bullet. Somehow, he managed to grab the gun and fire at me. I went down suddenly in a haze of pain. As I lay on the floor clutching my leg, James raced toward me. The fire in the ceiling forced a piece of wood to fall just as he approached me. The falling wood hit his arm and knocked the gun out of his hand. He dove on top of me.

"I'll always love you. *Even in death,*" James managed to say between breaths. James pounded me in the head with his fists. He was on top of me, and I tried to force him off. I turned my head to the side and just for a second, through the smoke, I saw a small glimmering light. I tried to see more clearly as we continued to fight, but the image was blurred. In a flash, I saw Keevan's face, and then it vanished.

The flames raged out of control. I continued to wrestle with James. He hit me. I hit him in return. We could not breathe, yet we fought. He held onto me. I was able to bring his arm close enough to my mouth to bite him and draw blood. He let go. Just as I forced him off me, a piece of the ceiling collapsed and fell on top of him. I rolled further away, narrowly escaping a wall of flames. As I crawled out of the smoke-darkened room, I heard a loud crash and saw flaming wooden boards falling from the ceiling. I didn't see them hit James, but I heard him scream.

I made it outside. Barely. Faces aghast in the size-able crowd and gasps of shock greeted me. Tony rushed over to my aid. Sirens could be heard in the distance.

"Where's Daryl?" I asked.

"He's over there. Danea's with him and LaMont. He's okay, so don't worry."

"What do you mean he's okay? He's been shot twice."

"Luckily, neither bullet hit a major organ. You've been shot, too," he said.

"Don't worry about me. I'm okay."

"Danea's okay? What about LaMont?"

"Danea's fine, LaMont was shot in the arm, but RaChelle..."

"What about RaChelle?"

"She's unconscious. She was hit by a falling piece of wood from the ceiling. The ambulance is on its way."

As I watched the flames consume the church and glorify James' last testament, I wondered, did it have to end this way? I wondered why all of the suffering he had caused and endured wasn't enough to quench his dark desires. Violence begets violence, and they say those who live by the sword, die by the sword. He was a remarkably brilliant man, and his creative vision led to the creation of a rising firm, yet his character failed him, as it sometimes does with some great men. His lasting legacy would not be of LCS, but of that macabre scene of flames and bullets, of madness and death, and of love and rage.

✖✖✖

The preacher, LaMont, Daryl, and I were taken to the hospital where we underwent surgery to remove the bullets lodged in our bodies. RaChelle's injuries caused her to have a miscarriage. My child was dead.

Danea came to my room after I woke up from surgery. We sat in silence—except for the murmur of the radio—holding hands, and let the moment and its fullness surround us. We bathed in it, and it glorified our lives in victory, in love and friendship and in death. At that moment, a gleam of light shone across Danea's face. She reached down and turned up the volume on the radio. A familiar voice singing a familiar song came through the speakers.

"Victory." This was the first time we'd heard her song on the radio. There had not been a more appropriate time than now for that song, full of love and the hope of inspiration. We had achieved victory. Still, we didn't speak. Instead, we closed our eyes and listened to her profound words champion the human spirit's ability to conquer obstacles.

The End

EPILOGUE

After all was said and done, a few days later, I received a phone call from James' attorney, who wanted to set up a meeting. I couldn't imagine what he had to say to me. I wasn't exactly thrilled about seeing anyone even remotely associated with James and my past. After he insisted, I finally agreed to meet.

I walked into the large office in downtown Houston and was pleasantly greeted by the receptionist.

"I have an appointment with Mr. Hill." She smiled and announced my arrival. I was directed to an office down a long corridor and nestled in a corner. The door was open.

"Thank you for coming. I know this is short notice." Mr. Hill was a forty-something black man with short hair. He had a stocky but muscular frame. I tried to detect any hidden message in his face that would give me some clue as to why I was there. "Would you like something to drink?"

"No, thanks. I'm on a pretty tight schedule today. If we could just get down to business?"

"Okay." He motioned for me to have a seat in the chair in front of his desk. He took a file off a stack of other manila files and flipped through them with some interest. "I'm not sure whether or not you are completely aware of Mr. Lancaster's estate."

"I know his business was seized by the IRS for unpaid taxes."

"Yes, that much is true, but there is more to the story. Some time ago Mr. Lancaster transferred a large amount of money into an account in your name."

"What?" I wasn't sure exactly what he was talking about, but I suspected his next words were going to inform me that I was now in debt to the IRS.

"That account contains $250,000."

"Wait a minute, I don't know anything about that. If the IRS wants that money, they can have it."

"No, I don't think you understand. This has nothing to do with the IRS. The $250,000 is money that is yours. He created an account for you so you'd be taken care of in case something ever happened to him. Additionally, Mr. Lancaster has two life insurance policies in which you are the sole benefactor. One policy is $350,000, and the other is for a half-million dollars." My heart began to palpitate. I wasn't sure if I was hearing him correctly. What was he talking about. Bank accounts in my name? Life insurance policies? "After the IRS seized LCS and his personal bank accounts, that settled his debt with the government. His house, valued at a quarter of a million dollars, was bequeathed to you, as well. The way I see it, Mr. Davis, you've just inherited a pretty large estate."

Never in my wildest dreams did I imagine or suspect this. Instantly, my life had changed. I didn't know how to respond, but I was sure of one thing: I didn't want anything that would remind me of the past.

"So, you're saying the house is mine?"

"Completely."

"I want to sell it."

"That's your prerogative. I just need you to sign a few documents."

Afterward, I went into the restroom and grabbed a paper towel to wash my face. I then walked out of the office in downtown Houston, got in my car and drove. Finally, I smiled at the irony of it all: The one lesson I tried to teach James that he never learned: Money never buys true happiness.

ABOUT THE AUTHOR

Lee Hayes is a native Texan who graduated
from the University of North Texas with a
degree in sociology. He currently lives in
Washington, D.C. This is his first novel.
He is also the author of *A Deeper Blue:
Passion Marks II*. His next novel, *The Messiah*,
will be released in July 2007.
You can email him at lhayesbooks@aol.com or
visit at http://www.passionmarks.com.

BE SURE TO LOOK FOR

A DEEPER BLUE: PASSION MARKS 2

BY LEE HAYES

AVAILABLE FROM STREBOR BOOKS

Simmering with passion, betrayal, and a woman's contempt, Lee Hayes delivers a fiery sequel to *Passion Marks* in *A Deeper Blue*.

Intense from the beginning, *A Deeper Blue* hypnotizes readers into a story of lust and love. Kevin Davis finds his tumultuous relationship with his lover Daryl Harris in serious jeopardy. Pulled in different directions, Daryl must choose between the lover he's dreamed about or a new temptation.

Meanwhile, Cerina Ford is a woman desperately and whole-heartedly in love with Temple Moore. They share a passionate physical relationship, yet Cerina really desires an emotional connection with Temple—a connection that he is not willing to give.

Eventually Cerina discovers that Temple has fallen in love with Daryl and Temple and Kevin learn that they can run, but there is nowhere to hide from a lover scorned. Even years later, they each find themselves the target of a vengeful plot from a forgotten love, who will stop at nothing to ensure total destruction of their lives.

With gripping detail, *A Deeper Blue* intertwines love, hate, jealousy, infidelity, revenge, and ultimately, murder. Author Lee Hayes shows that the line between love and hate is a thin one—and that sins from the past can evolve into nightmares of the present.

SNEAK PREVIEW! EXCERPT FROM

THE MESSIAH

BY LEE HAYES

COMING FROM STREBOR BOOKS JULY 2007

CHAPTER 1

The buzzing sound of flies will resonate in his ears *forever*. That annoying, dissonant sound caused by the rapid vibrations of tiny wings that had stolen the peace from a hundred languid summer evenings was the only thing that he could focus on as he lay battered and bloodied in a field of orange, yellow and blue. Stunning summer hues dotted the landscape on the grassy knoll as his world morphed from living colors to a gray and mangled mesh of madness. Jazz McKinney struggled to keep his eyes open, but he knew the uncontrolled swelling would soon blot out his vision and his view of the world would darken. *Maybe forever*.

Yet, given that grim reality, that buzzing sound had his full attention.

Even now, he can still hear the sound.

That ceaseless buzzing numbed the pain of a million ant bites which stung his limp body.

That buzzing sound rang louder than his own listless voice, which stalled in his inflamed throat. Each time he opened his mouth to scream for help, the sound rang hollow, not even a decibel and barely a whisper. So, he sent his silent prayers to the heavens and hoped that God was listening.

He can still hear that never-ending murmur. It drowned the sound of screeching tires and jarring horns. That buzz had power. It had control. In retrospect, it probably saved his life.

He remembered trying to scream, but there was no sound. He remembered trying to move, but the only movement was the involuntary shooting pains that kept him immobile.

It is true what they say about your life flashing before your eyes before you take your final breaths. Sadly, all he could see was the disembodied faces from a thousand midnight encounters. Their ethereal faces haunted him in the killing fields.

Even as he struggled to breathe, he could smell the bewitching masculine mix of cologne, sweat and sex. *It still intoxicated him.* Even as his inflamed eyes blocked the fierce sunlight, he could see their bright faces hovering above him as painful reminders of a meaningless existence and emotions disconnected from the real world. He existed in a world of make-believe, created by fantasies and fearless notions of actions free from consequences. This night, his actions produced gruesome results. He lived in a carefully crafted world of folly, of jest, of reckless-ness, without care and without remorse. Back then—only moments ago by some accounts—when his body free and easy like the breeze, he easily dis-missed their faces at the conclusion of their lustful rendezvous, sometimes not even concerned about knowing their names. It's funny that those strangers, who had been the one constant in his life, were poised to be the one constant in his death. Their faces assaulted his senses.

He didn't imagine his body would survive very long in its present condition—broken and battered. *And isolated.* In this moment of ultimate desperation, when all seemed lost, something more meaningful should have filled his head. He should have been focused on life after death and his final resting place in perpetuity, yet he could not free his mind of their faces. *And that buzzing.* That damned buzzing tormented him.

As he lay there, blood oozing from his busted body, the details of his sordid deeds haunted him.

The cacophonous chainsaw song of the flies who

feasted on his open wounds and drying blood distracted him from the hollow faces and dark eyes that swirled about his head like a ghastly merry-go-round. Their faces circled and spiraled around in a choreographed ritual of torture. *Go away*, he thought, but the past reflections of his misdeeds were permanent fixtures in his mind. The images were so real to him in those fevered moments that he wanted to reach out and touch their textured flesh, but he didn't have the strength; yet, he could almost feel their lips on his.

He wanted the insects to abandon him and discontinue their endless torment; he wanted them to leave him to his fate, but he could not force them to leave. They had the upper hand because he had lost all control and power over his medium-sized frame. He was too feeble to fan them away. *Why did they stay?* he asked himself over and over. After all, he had grown accustomed to being left alone.

The buzzing was persistent. The nasty flies were drawn to his rotting flesh, which sizzled in the intense summer heat. Jazz feared they would devour him and there would be no remains left for his family to claim. All that would endure after he faded would be naked bones. The moonlit violence he experienced only hours ago at the hands of a stranger now gave way to a dazzling daylight despair. His fears of dying in an abandoned field and the intensity of his pain did not fade as the sun rose majestically.

The South is notorious for its blistering temperatures that stretch far beyond the summer months and linger well into the autumn, but the Georgia heat had always been his friend. *Until today.* summer was his favorite season and the heat had never bothered him before—until today—when he lay naked and bleeding in a glorious field underneath an unforgiving summer sun. *How quickly things change.*

As he lay prostrate in the field, he recalled the evening's events. He remembered *his* face; he remembered every scar, every visible tattoo, *his* gapped tooth and crooked smile. He vividly remembered what *he* did to him. He could still feel every thrust, every fist and every kick. He remembered *his* wild laughter which echoed in the night like a victorious hyena.

He remembered crying out *why*, only to be answered by a kick to the face.

He can still see and feel the boot that caused blood to gush from his nose. *It was a Timberland.*

Jazz remembered begging *him* to stop and apologizing profusely for his actions—which clearly had offended him—but that only caused *his* laughter to swell and overflow from his cruel mouth.

Naked, dizzied and pleading for his life, he remembered staring up into *his* wicked face right before he felt the release of warm urine on him.

He can still hear the splatter.

He can still taste it.

Even as he lay in the field, he remembered.

Broken, bloodied, naked and now humiliated with *his* piss spread across his frame, he tried to imagine being somewhere else. He tried to imagine this was someone else's nightmare.

He tried to shift his body. He wanted to sit up, to stand up, to cry out, and to move, to giggle, to raise his fist in protest— anything to let the world know that he survived, but his body would not yield to his desire. The only thing it yielded was pain when he attempted to move.

The details of that treacherous night raced through his fleeting consciousness like the currents of some out-of-control river. He fought desperately to force the images out of his head, but they did not bend to his wishes. The horror committed underneath a starry and still midnight sky resonated deep within his soul. The evening started with promise and purpose and ended in pain and despair. He felt a pain in his chest as he took rapid breaths; it felt like his last breaths. He could feel his heart racing and then everything went black.

Jazz was three days into the new school year and he was excited about starting his senior year in college. He missed his friends—his roommate in particular—who went home to California during the summer and left him in Atlanta to fend for himself. He felt partially betrayed because the duo had discussed subletting an apartment for the summer and working at Lenox Mall to pay the bills. Jazz had envisioned a carefree summer full of life-affirming activities. When Carlos told him that he had to go home for the summer to help take care of his ailing mother, Jazz was disappointed, but he understood. He survived all summer only to meet this fate early in the new school year.

He was thrilled at the thought of graduating in a few months and moving to New York City to jump-start his stagnant modeling career. After years of local modeling, he told himself he'd give the Big Apple two years and if it didn't work out, he'd get a job using the degree in mechanical engineering that he'd earn in May. Quite an accomplishment for a disowned preacher's son.

Dark memories crept in as he remembered arriving at the designated location. He stepped out of his car, locked the door and kept his keys splayed between his fingers in case he needed to defend himself from some fiend lurking in the shadows. An unusual and slight chill, which lingered in the summer air that night, unnerved him, but he dismissed his intuition as paranoia and pressed on. He took a moment to scan the area and when he was satisfied that no one was around, he moved with speed toward the structure. Trepidation was his traveling partner as he moved briskly forward. During these midnight meetings, a sense of fear stimulated his desire. As he walked with due speed, he continued to look around for other people, including the campus police. He couldn't imagine having to explain to the police why he was lurking near the football stadium at such a late hour.

The warning in his heart grew with each step he took, but he would not yield to that feeling. An ominous presence rode the stiff night air, as if some unseen force lurked from all sides. Partially excited and partially terrified, Jazz pressed deeper into the darkness. The fear of being caught and the fear of meeting this stranger to do whatever deeds men who met in the dark of night did is what Jazz was counting on to multiply the force of his orgasm threefold.

As he scurried across the vacant parking lot, he heard a slight rumbling behind him which sent a cold shiver up his spine, in spite of the heat of the night. He stopped, spun on his heels and exhaled in relief as he saw an old soda can rolling across the lot in the breeze. He resumed his march toward ecstasy. Once he reached the structure, he prayed that one of the doors of the football stadium would be unlocked so that he could walk through it instead of going around it, but when he yanked on the door, it barely moved. *Damn*. With his hands in his pockets, he turned and quickly walked around the behemoth structure, anxious to meet *him*.

When he got around the corner, he found that the gate was locked and chained, but he remained undeterred. Quickly, he looked around the perimeter and with surprising prowess, he had scaled the fence like it was nothing—it would not stand between him and what *he* had to offer. He landed flatly on his feet and immediately looked around the area before moving toward the field house. The closer he got to the small white structure in the back, the quicker his heart raced. These mysterious encounters he had grown accustomed to made sex wildly exciting. He had grown out of missionary sex when he was seventeen and moved quickly into things that were more…titillating.

For Jazz, sex was freedom and power. Thoughts of that next encounter and taking it to the next level occupied much of his daily thoughts. Pushing the envelope and stretching sexual boundaries was his drug—his driving force. He wasn't a sex addict, but he loved sex. He loved doing the unspeakable and having it done to him. He loved gobbling and rubbing and pulling and yanking and plowing and breathing and using fingers and tongues and holes and toys and ropes and candles and wax and anything to intensify the experience. He loved meeting people who, like him, weren't afraid to explore the universe and to be used as a willing vessel to that ultimate orgasm. That's what he wanted that night. That's *all* he wanted that night, but he got so much more.

He leaned against the field house for only a few minutes, blowing nicotine smoke-circles into the air to calm his nerves, but out in the darkness, with no signs of life, it felt like hours. He listened for any sound of movement, for the slightest disturbance, for anything that would announce *his* arrival. Jazz took a long drag from the Benson & Hedges which dangled from his lips. He rolled an empty beer bottle underneath his foot to take the edge off the night. Then, he heard a sound. He looked to his right and he saw a figure cloaked in darkness. *He* didn't move. Neither did Jazz, but through the darkness, Jazz smelled the lust that oozed from this stranger's body. *He* took a step and stopped. Jazz took one last puff and let the cigarette fall to the ground. Jazz then took a deep breath and moved a step in *his* direction and then he suddenly stopped. He loved the cat and mouse game. The moonlight that reflected off *his* skin revealed only a portion of his face. Even from this distance, Jazz could see his structured face and masculine features. The curls that adorned the top his head spiraled like miniature halos. *He* stood there like stone, unable or unwilling to move, with legs shoulders-width apart. Then, he started rubbing himself through the sweat pants he wore. Jazz felt a rise in his jeans and he had to move closer. Soon, they were face-to-face, but they did not speak. Jazz admired *his* perfectly shaped goatee; *his* full lips made Jazz want to kiss him, but kisses during these detached encounters were not something accepted. Jazz knew what he could do.

Instead, Jazz kneeled.

He smiled.

He pulled his dick out of his pants and Jazz took it into his hand and started stroking it. It was heavier than it appeared. *He* moved Jazz's head closer to his member and then the sound of *his* moans was carried by the light breeze that crept slowly into the night. Jazz looked up into *his* twisted face—a face contorted by the power of pleasure—as *he* pushed in and out of Jazz's mouth. *He* grabbed Jazz's ears and forced his head to move to the rhythm of his pelvic palpitations; it was a rhythm Jazz knew too well. Jazz placed his hands on *his* ass and forced him to push harder into his mouth. *His* ass felt strong like stone, but the power of Jazz's mouth caused his muscles to tremble. In a few seconds, he'd be singing a new song and when he released, *his* hardened exterior would fall, giving way to Jazz's power. Jazz knew the routine well.

Often, kneeling before a man is viewed as weakness; but to the contrary, it is ultimate power. Taking a man's most prized possession into your mouth and having him yield to your dictates could only be described as power. Jazz controlled *his* pleasure and *his* pain. Only Jazz stood between him and orgasmic intensity. It was his lips and tongue and mouth and throat that *he* worshipped.

Faster and faster *he* thrust *his* hips while moans rose and shifted from a deep baritone murmur to a more melodious crescendo that signified the nearing climax. Jazz pulled *him* out of his mouth, worked him over with his hand until *his* magic moment arrived in star-spangled delight.

He looked down at Jazz as he adjusted himself in the sweat pants. The look shot right through Jazz who suddenly wished he was back in his apartment playing on the Internet. *He* turned his back to Jazz and fell to his knees with a thud.

"Uhhhh, are you okay?" Jazz asked out of curiosity. This wasn't the typical reaction most men had after an act of fellatio. Besides, Jazz hadn't gotten off yet and he wanted his turn. He stood up and adjusted himself. Jazz stood behind him, not sure if he should approach him. "Do you need some help?"

Still, *he* remained quiet on *his* knees.

Jazz took a few steps backward deciding it was best to move away slowly. He wasn't sure what had just happened, but he knew he didn't need to stick around to find out. He turned to move toward his car when he heard a voice emanating from *him* that sounded as if night itself was speaking words which were not meant for him to decipher. His raspy voice rose to just above a whisper as he spoke with rapid speed. It almost sounded as if he were speaking in tongues.

"Hey, do you need some help?"

"THE LORD is my shepherd; I shall not want. He maketh me to lie down in green pastures: he leadeth me beside still waters. He restoreth my soul: he leadeth me in paths of righteousness for his name's sake."

Jazz moved closer as *his* words became clearer,

but the stranger did not stop his chanting. Jazz put his hand gently on his shoulder.

"Yea, though I walk through the valley of the shadow of death, I will fear no evil; for thou art with me; thy rod and thy staff they comfort me. Thou preparest a table before me in the presence of mine enemies: thou anointest my head with oil; my cup runneth over. Surely goodness and mercy shall follow me all the days of my life: and I will dwell in the house of the Lord forever."

The stranger sprang to *his* feet like a panther. Suddenly, panic gripped Jazz like an immovable force around his neck. The stranger whipped around to face Jazz, and as *he* did, *his* fist landed on Jazz's jaw with what felt like the power of a hundred men. Jazz hit the ground with a boom. Dazed and confused, he looked up into the face of this stranger as he struggled to make sense of what had just happened. *His* face twisted into something unrecognizable. The hairs of *his* moustache seemed to come to life and reach toward Jazz like hissing serpents poised to strike. Only moments ago *he* had looked at Jazz with pleasure-filled eyes. Now, his face resembled flesh that was seared by hatred and disgust. *His* eyes changed into black holes that showed nothing but contempt. Even *his* full lips that Jazz admired moments ago no longer appeared the same; they had morphed into small and dangerous slivers of tightly drawn flesh. *He* turned *his* back to Jazz and recanted the prayer again. Jazz, trying to seize upon this opportunity, forced his legs to stand. He tried to run, but he heard the breaking of the bottle before he actually felt the impact on the back of his skull. In the flicker of the second that it took for him to realize what had happened, he felt the presence of evil looming on the edge of night, dancing a wicked jig in the dark and laughing at his misery.

Jazz fell to the ground on his back and looked up to see the menacing figure above him. *He* looked down on him in his helpless state and kicked him in the ribs with his boot.

"You see what you've brought upon yourself? You and your kind are an abomination," he said in a voice that wasn't quite human. It was a throaty whisper that felt like fingers on a chalkboard; yet, his gruff voice carried enough force for Jazz to feel it in his chest like a punch. Jazz tried not to show panic or fear, because he knew the stranger could smell fear like an attack dog.

As he lay on the ground, trying to come to terms with the pain in his head, he could feel *his* greasy hands yanking at his body and then his clothes. Jazz tried to kick him away but to no avail. Jazz's feeble attempt at resistance angered *him* and *he* kicked him in the side so hard that Jazz heard his ribs crack. *He* repeated the prayer, this time in a more coherent voice while *he* continued to disrobe him until Jazz lay naked—his brown flesh exposed to the world.

"Wait, stop," Jazz managed to utter, but his broken words landed on uncaring ears.

Jazz's vision became blurry as the impact of the bottle to the head became to take effect.

"You will lay naked before the throne of God and repent your sins. You will renounce your wicked ways," *he* said. *He* seemed to be in some kind of trance, walking back and forth and uttering the prayer. *He'd* walk away from Jazz only to return with a kick or a punch. *He* ordered Jazz on his knees and Jazz tried to comply, but he was dizzy from the pain. When he was able to kneel, *he* back-handed Jazz across the face and sent his body reeling back to the ground.

Jazz will never forget *his* laughter.

In *his* depraved mind, *he* found humor in torment.

His stranger, the one he had willingly given pleasure to, shocked him by punching him in the eye so hard Jazz thought it exploded in his head. Jazz had never known pain so intimately. That fist to the eye unleashed his fury. Other fists pummeled his face and body from every angle and every direction. Jazz didn't have enough hands to cover his face or protect his exposed genitals. Heinous words dripped from *his* heated mouth as the beating continued. Jazz cried out from the pain, which only added to *his* satisfaction.

When *he* was satisfied that Jazz was weak enough, *he* dragged his limp body across the course grass to the tattered fence that separated the school from the woods. Jazz grabbed at mounds of earth to anchor his body, but it did not make the slightest difference. When *he* got to the end of the field, *he* loosed his grip on Jazz and let him go. *He* walked through the hole in the fence and opened the door to a black van that was parked on a dirt trail. Jazz lifted his head to ascertain what was going on, but dizziness forced him back to the ground.

Then, *he* stepped from the van with a metal rod that glowed bright orange. It was a brand. *He* moved quickly to Jazz and forced his left hand open. When *he* stuck the fiery metal to his palm, Jazz screamed as much as his pain would allow him, but it wasn't much. The smell of burning flesh permeated his nostrils and Jazz almost choked at the thought that the flesh that burned was his own. Then *he* took the brand and stuck it to Jazz's right palm. The unbearable pain raced rapidly through every cell in

Jazz's body. A hurt like no other hurt he had ever felt suddenly consumed him. He then found his voice. The sound that escaped from Jazz's mouth was previously unknown to the human ear; it reached the heavens and came back down again with a soul-shattering thump. He spoke a language of pain he never knew was even possible. The sound of his jagged voice startled *him* who stepped back and watched his masterpiece. Jazz shook violently, contorted his face and tried to force himself to pass out. He didn't want to know what came next. He wanted to die, but that was not *his* goal.

He stood above Jazz and released his urine on him. Jazz could not find the strength to protest or the strength to turn his head.

The he spoke is a hell-inspired voice.

"The reason you are alive is because I will it. You have a job to do. You will be my messenger. You will tell the world what happened here. You will tell your kind to repent. You will tell them I am watching. I am always watching. You will do this or I will visit you again. You will be my sacrifice to righteousness. Do you understand that task I have given you?"

Excruciating pain sealed Jazz's lips, but his will to survive broke through and he mustered just enough strength to look up and mumble the word *yes*. Jazz wanted to see the face of this maniac when he spoke that word, but his ragged body could not be moved.

"You will tell them The Messiah has returned. And he is angry."

"THE LORD is my shepherd; I shall not want. He maketh me to lie down in green pastures: he leadeth me beside still waters. He restoreth my soul: he leadeth me in paths of righteousness for his name's sake." Then, The Messiah walked toward the van and rode off into the darkness.